TYRANT

A ᴎILLETTI CHRONICLES NOVEL

SARAH BAILEY

Published by Twisted Tree Publications
www.twistedtreepublications.com
info@twistedtreepublications.com

Paperback ISBN: 978-1-913217-38-9

This one is for Ashley and her love of mean daddies

ONE

Zayn

The woman contorted her body around the pole like she was a snake wrapped around its prey. It was meant to be alluring, seductive even, but for me, it held no interest. Nothing seemed to pique it these days. I'd seen it all. Seen too fucking much if you asked me. Everything was mundane when it should have been arousing. The display in front of me should make my dick hard, but it lay flaccid like it had done for weeks… perhaps even months.

Life had become monotonous, and I was done experiencing it.

I was only out on the club floor of Desecration tonight because the king has to make an appearance. The image I'd laid out for myself needed to be upheld. Here I was, surrounded by women who did nothing for me, on one of the special nights the club ran for members.

You had to be someone to know of Desecration's existence. It was a well-kept secret for a reason. The men and women of this city did not want their private business being aired to the public. Especially not business involving sex. And extreme versions of it at that. I provided them with a safe space to act out their most depraved fantasies. They paid me for the privilege. Win-win all around.

Except… I grew tired and weary of it all. The same faces and same bullshit day in, day out. This might be my club. My fucking house, but I was bored. So fucking bored, I was even considering getting further involved in the family business. However, it would only come with another set of responsibilities I had no interest in.

Gennaro Villetti understood, to an extent, I had my own aspirations. We'd been at odds since I was a child. I railed against his restrictions, but I never did it publicly. Never allowed anyone outside of the family to see the fractures between us. When he realised I wasn't going to be the easily mouldable son he'd wanted, Gil quickly became his favourite. My younger brother, Gilberto, would be the better choice for our father to bequeath his crown to. Shit didn't work like that in our world. I was the eldest. I would become the kingpin and that was fucking that.

The family didn't deal in drugs and weapons here, but money laundering and property. London. The epicentre of the financial industry. A place where you had to know someone to be someone. You didn't go around pissing in each other's shoes unless you wanted to cut your face off to spite yourself.

It's exactly what that cunt Frank Russo did and look where it got him. Dead. And rumoured to be by the girl he raised as his daughter. His death had rippled across the fucking city like a live wire. Now, there was trouble everywhere. I kept out of it unless my father summoned me. These days, it was rare for him to interfere with my business. I had made my own name for myself, even if everyone still referred to me as the kingpin's prodigal son.

At least I wasn't Enzo, who was the youngest and the fuck-up. He kept my father busy enough to stay the fuck out of my business. I had washed my hands of the situation a long time ago. If he wanted to cause our father trouble, on his own head be it.

Movement in my periphery tore me from my brooding thoughts. My men were walking through the club in a group, dragging along a figure behind them. I watched them as they approached before throwing the person down in front of me, startling the women around me. My patrons knew to turn a blind eye to my affairs, so no one else batted an eyelid, continuing to watch tonight's show.

My eyes flicked down to the hooded figure they'd brought in. They had their head bowed and their fists dug into the pockets of their zip-up hoodie.

"Said he has business with you, boss," Arlo, my right-hand man, said when I didn't speak, waving at the "boy" on the floor.

I knew it wasn't a fucking boy. Despite their baggy clothes, it was clear to me "he" was actually a "she". The way her full hips and thighs clung to the tracksuit bottoms she wore gave her away.

I leant forward as I slid a blade from my pocket and pressed it under the chin of the girl who had somehow fooled my men into thinking she was a boy. Drawing her chin up, I stared down into a heart-shaped face with full bow lips, tawny brown skin and chestnut eyes holding a defiant look within them. I almost smiled but kept my expression neutral. Giving away what I suspected to my men wouldn't be a good idea when it came to this girl.

Arianna Michaelson, the twenty-two-year-old daughter of Bennett Jerome Michaelson. A man I'd known since I was a teen. He ran a gang in Hackney. I'd met most of the big hitters in this city because of my father, not to mention I had dealings with Bennett. He used my land to run his underground fighting ring and other things. It suited me just fine. The site was derelict and had been since the accident that had happened during development. I'd bought it and the surrounding buildings after the developers went bankrupt. Property was often the best way to get rid of dirty money. It's why my family owned so much of it. It wasn't public knowledge. In this city, flying under the radar was the best way to go about your business. Didn't need the police sniffing around.

This girl turning up in my club was something I hadn't expected. I wasn't the type of man one came running to when they were in trouble. Judging by the bruise forming on her jaw, Ari had got herself into some.

What did you do, Tink?

I leant back against the red velvet cushioned seat, placing my knife back in my pocket and waved a dismissive hand at her.

"Take the boy to my office. Make sure no one else enters other than me. I'll deal with it later."

I wasn't going to talk to her out here where anyone could see us. There were questions I had for Ari. Ones I needed to ask in private.

4

"Are you sure, boss?" Arlo asked in a low voice.

I gave him a look. He scrambled to obey, pulling Ari up off the floor. She stared at me with no small amount of fear in her eyes, as if being alone with me was the last thing she wanted. Well, too fucking bad. She'd turned up in my club with a bruised face, pretending to be a boy. I wasn't stupid enough to let on who she really was. It was clear she wanted to keep her identity a secret. It meant she was here without her father's knowledge.

I may not owe Ari or her father any allegiances, but curiosity burnt in my chest like a fucking bomb had gone off. This was the most interesting thing to happen in weeks. I kept a lid on it. No one need know how fucking bored I was with my life.

I watched my men take Ari down to the back corridor leading to the private rooms and the back offices. Her eyes remained on me the whole way, leading me to believe this was a huge gamble on her part.

It took all my self-control to stay where I was and not question her immediately. When the fuck did I become so eager to deal with a problem? Never. In my world, you weren't reactive. You were always twelve steps ahead. So this? This was something I needed to address as soon as possible. I didn't like surprises. And Arianna Michaelson? She was a surprise I didn't need.

My fingers drummed on my thigh as I tried to focus on the show. My men came back through a minute later, minus Arlo. He would watch my office for me. As long as no one found out about Ari, it would be okay. Until I knew what she was doing here, the fewer people who knew she'd turned up at my club, the better.

The moment the current girl finished dancing, I stood up, straightening my sleeves. I gave the pole dancer, Theia, a nod. Striding across the floor towards the back, I felt for my cigar case and extracted it from my pocket. I took out a cigarillo before slipping my case back into my inside pocket. I didn't light it, merely holding it between my fingers as I strolled towards my office.

When I reached it, I found Arlo standing sentry outside. I rubbed my face with my free hand, eyeing him warily. His dark hair was swept back in a pompadour and faded at the sides, his dark brown eyes told me nothing of his feelings about the situation and his tanned skin was a similar shade to mine.

"Zayn," he said, nodding at me.

"Did anyone see her face?"

"No. Only me."

Arlo wasn't stupid. He'd played dumb in front of everyone else, but he knew exactly who Ari was. He'd seen her enough times. I rarely went anywhere without him. He was practically my shadow. Had been since I was a child, although he was a few years younger than me. My aunt, Martina, was very good friends with Arlo's father, Marco Turro. When I'd opened Desecration, Arlo had become my second. The man who would take a bullet for me if necessary.

"No one else finds out about this, we clear?"

"Yes."

"Good. You can go. I'll take care of our little problem."

He gave me another nod. Arlo knew better than to ask too many questions when I was eager to get business done. I watched him walk back down the hallway until he disappeared. Then my eyes went to my office door. I took a breath and put my hand on the handle.

It was time I found out what the fuck Arianna had done. And why, of all people, she'd come to me.

TWO

Arianna

I heard the office door open behind me and flinched. *Fuck.* I was in so much shit right now and coming here was probably a mistake. I had no one else to turn to and nowhere else to go.

Most people would call me insane for turning up on the doorstep of a sex club I shouldn't know existed, owned by a man who I should be scared shitless of. Most people weren't the daughter of a man embroiled in the beginnings of a gang war and had found herself caught in the damn crossfire. They didn't know violence the way I did. They didn't live with a target on their backs.

I heard his footsteps after the door clicked shut but kept my head down. My eyes spied his expensive leather shoes the moment they came into my peripheral vision. I swallowed hard, hating how nervous I felt in his presence.

Why did you come here? You know he won't help you, right?

I heard him settle against his desk, the wood creaking with his weight.

"You and I are going to have a little conversation, Arianna, and if you fuck with me or lie, I'll know. You better have your shit straight, or this won't end prettily for you."

I looked up then, startled by his harsh words, and stared into black soulless pits. At least, that's what looking into Zayn Villetti's eyes felt like. The man was not only twelve years my senior but intimidating as fuck. He wore a suit that fit his body like a glove, black with a dark red pattern over the jacket. No tie meant his shirt buttons were open. I could see the tattoos winding down his tanned neck. He crossed his legs at the ankle, his heavily tattooed right hand tapping against his thigh. The other rested on the desk with an unlit cigarillo between his fingers.

Zayn leant forward a little, his eyes narrowing on my face. I almost reached up to touch my sore jaw, where I'd been smacked around the face.

"What are you doing here, Tink?"

You could say I'd known Zayn most of my life. We'd met for the very first time when I was four and he was sixteen. I remembered it vividly because he'd called me Tinkerbell on account of the fairy wings attached to my back. I'd pestered Dad for weeks to get me some. The day he met with Gennaro Villetti, I demanded he let me wear them. Ever since then, Zayn had insisted on calling me Tinkerbell whenever I saw him, even though everyone else referred to me as Ari.

"Well?"

My response got stuck in my throat.

What are you doing here, Ari?

It would be better to show him. Words didn't quite cut it when it came to explaining why I'd run for my damn life to Desecration to find the only man I knew who could possibly help me. If he felt like it, that is. Zayn Villetti didn't do favours. Why would he when he was the eldest son of the mafia kingpin himself, Gennaro Villetti. People did things for him, not the other way around.

They'd have you think the mafia wasn't deeply embedded within society in this country, but they were either blind or lying to themselves. No one fucked with the Villetti family unless they wanted to end up dead.

With a very shaky hand, I reached up and pulled down the zipper of my hoodie, all the while staring up at the man I was about to throw myself at and hope he had some shred of humanity locked within his hard exterior. Zayn's eyes followed the movement of my fingers, but his expression remained the same. Stoic and deadly.

"This is why," I whispered, almost choking on the words when I pulled back the two sides of my hoodie, exposing my blood-soaked t-shirt to his gaze.

For a moment, he didn't say a single word. He barely even moved except for the slow rise and fall of his chest. His eyes flicked up to mine, the darkness of them making me aware I was trapped with a predator.

You were fucking stupid to come here.

"Who did you kill?"

It was obvious by the amount of blood what happened to me had been brutal and violent. I struggled not to replay the scene over in my mind.

"Uncle Justin."

"And why did you do it?"

"He tried to… hurt me."

I almost said rape. Almost. I could feel his hot breath on my neck, his branding touch on my skin as he tried to undress me. I could feel his skin give way as I stabbed a knife into his flesh over and over.

I bit down on my lip. The blood. There was so much blood. I was covered in it. It clung to me like a second skin. I wanted it off me. Wanted to wash it all away and forget the past two hours had ever happened. My life had turned into such a fucking mess, and I was about to make it even worse by appealing to the merciful side of this man.

Zayn cocked his head to the side. By the look in his eye, I knew he had figured out exactly what I didn't want to voice out loud. My uncle had tried to force himself on me without a second thought. He was a dick. I wasn't sorry for killing him. I was just sorry I was stupid enough to go with him and not listen to my gut feeling that something was very wrong.

"Why didn't you go to your father?"

I flinched. My father had enough problems without me being one of them. I'd murdered his right-hand man. It didn't matter if my uncle was double-crossing him. I couldn't prove it. I couldn't do a single damn thing. He wouldn't believe me if I told him Justin had been feeding his enemy information, and he'd taken me with the intention of blaming it on Derek McGovern's gang. My father trusted Justin with his life. Sometimes I wondered if he trusted me that way. It's partly why I came here. My doubts about my father and whether or not he would save me had driven me to it.

"I panicked… I killed his brother, for fuck's sake."

Zayn straightened and stepped closer. He drew a lighter out of his pocket and lit his cigarillo. I watched him place it between his lips, sucking down on it for a moment before puffing out the smoke. It made him even more imposing.

"So, you killed your uncle after he assaulted you, then you ran here… to me." He waved the cigarillo at me. "I can't help but wonder what you expect me to do about this situation."

I tried not to bite my lip again. Now came the hard part. Convincing this man to shelter me from my own stupidity.

"Help me."

The slow smile spreading across his face made me wary.

"With what, Tink? Be specific."

He stepped closer, almost right up into my personal space. Jesus, did this man have a degree in intimidation or something? I was practically shaking in my damn shoes and trying my best not to show it. This was the very first time I'd ever been alone in a room with Zayn. I couldn't say I wasn't terrified of what he might do to me.

"Cover up what I did… and… and keep me away from my father… and McGovern."

"What could Derek McGovern possibly want with you?"

I almost scoffed.

"He takes me, he gains the upper hand against my father. That's what Justin planned to do after he… he…" I couldn't say the words. "He was going to give me to McGovern."

Zayn stared down at me, puffing on his cigarillo again.

"Quite the pickle you've got yourself into, Tink."

I nodded, even though it wasn't a question. If anything, Zayn sounded amused. This was anything but funny to me.

He reached out, stroking a finger along the bruise on my jaw. I winced despite his gentleness. And tried to ignore how warm his skin was on mine.

"I don't do things for free. Not for anyone."

I daren't get my hopes up at his words. Zayn was bound to ask something from me in return. I'd been counting on it, not that I had anything of substance a man like him might want.

"What do I have to give you in exchange for your help?"

The way he smiled sent a chill down my spine.

"You."

THREE

Zayn

Ari blinked at my single word as if she couldn't believe it had left my mouth. What she was asking me for was beyond anything I'd ever done for anyone who wasn't family. Why I even felt the need to help her was a question I wasn't going to look too hard at right now.

The moment I saw her blood-covered t-shirt, I made up my mind. I wanted to see where this would lead. It was like a sickness in my blood, calling out to relieve me of the monotony of my life, wanting to have something forbidden. If I took Arianna Michaelson and hid her away from her father, away from everyone she knew, I could bring trouble to my doorstep. And what I didn't need was trouble.

You want it. You crave the challenge.

As I wasn't what anyone would call a good man, more like twisted, I was going to take her regardless of the warning bells going off in my head.

"Me?" she spluttered. "What about me could you possibly want?"

I almost laughed as she stared up at me with those rather defiant chestnut eyes of hers. My fingers left her chin, flipping down the hood hiding her hair from sight. Her ash-brown curls had been tied back into a ponytail.

"You don't have anything else to offer me in exchange for what you're asking for… do you?"

We both knew she didn't. I respected her for not looking away, even if it made me want to wrap my hand around her neck. Defiance was like a drug, calling out the darkest side of me I rarely let come to the surface. And right now, Ari was exuding it in spades.

"No, but I'm not going to…"

I gripped her chin.

"Not going to what?"

"Sleep with you."

I almost smiled, but instead, I dropped her chin and paced away, puffing on my cigarillo. That was far from what I had in mind. I ran my free fingers along my desk, wondering what to say to make it clear this wasn't about sex. If I wanted to fuck, I had plenty of women I could call upon. I just hadn't wanted to in a long time. It didn't interest me. But Arianna? She interested me for reasons I wasn't entirely sure of myself. I had the urge to keep her. A little pet who would do my bidding. Not sexually, but whatever else took my fancy. After all, she would owe me if I made her uncle's body disappear.

"I have no interest in fucking you, Tink. You're not my type." *You tell yourself that.* "If I make your problems go away, you'd be indebted to me. You will do as I wish, and I will keep you safe."

The very fact I kept calling her by the nickname I'd bestowed upon her when she was four years old told me this was a terrible fucking idea. I was letting recklessness take the lead. If I had Bennett's daughter, I could use it to my advantage. Gang wars were bad for business. Ever since Frank Russo's death, the underworld had gone to absolute shit. The power struggle was making everyone sloppy. Judging by the fact Ari had been assaulted by her own fucking uncle, a man I would have killed myself for the act if he wasn't already dead, things were escalating. Taking her off the board would be doing them a favour. That was the reason. There was no other. There could be *no* other reason for me to want Arianna Michaelson.

"Do as you wish? What exactly does that mean?"

"When I say jump, you ask how high."

"That's not an answer, Zayn."

The way she said my name made me tense. She was more well-spoken than her father had ever been, given he was from South London. He had shipped her off to a private school funded by his drug money. She'd lost some of her native accent since the last time I saw her.

"I didn't give you permission to use my given name."

"I don't remember asking for it and besides, it's a little late for formalities. Let's not act like you haven't known me since I was a kid."

Without me immediately realising, my hand clenched into a fist. If she was *mine*, I'd make her get on her damn knees and kiss my shoe for her insolent tone. I'd make her apologise to her... *don't you fucking dare think about it.*

I flattened my palm on the desk and sucked in a breath. Calm and control were needed. She wasn't mine... yet.

"If you want my help, you will call me what I tell you to and nothing else."

"Okaaay, so what are we going with?"

Ari couldn't keep the amusement out of her voice. She wouldn't be laughing if she knew what would happen when she disobeyed me. That would come after she agreed to my terms.

"You will address me as either 'sir' or 'Mr Villetti.' I don't do informalities, Arianna."

I turned around and met her eyes. She didn't look afraid, more pensive.

"Okay... sir."

Fuck.

If she was going to insist on saying it when her voice dripped with sarcasm, she was going to find herself in deep shit. I wasn't the type to grant mercy, not when it came to my pets.

"Do we have an agreement?"

"I don't really have any other choice."

"Life is full of choices. You can still go home to your father, and I will forget this little interlude ever happened. Or you can stay. It's up to you. I'm not forcing you."

She chewed on her bottom lip.

I would never forget the sight of her covered in blood in my office, but she didn't need to know that. Better she thought she could walk away now without any repercussions from me. I might not be a good man, but I wasn't a monster either.

"If I stay, I become what? Your…"

"You become *mine*."

"And what if I want to leave when everything between my father and McGovern is over? Can I do that?"

My lips curved up.

"If I feel your debt to me is paid, yes."

I couldn't always be called fair, but I was a man of my word. It's why I was careful with them.

"If… you say that like it will never happen."

"Please me and do as I say, Arianna, and I will set you free when you wish to leave."

The unspoken words hung in the air between us.

Displease me and you will face the consequences of your actions.

"Okay. Fine. I agree. Now, will you help me?"

I dug my phone out of my pocket.

"Where is your uncle's body?"

She rattled off an address as I put the phone to my ear.

"All right, Z?" came Penn's voice as he answered.

"I need you to get rid of a problem."

I wasn't in the mood for his shit tonight. Penn could be in one of two moods. Either he was flirting with anything with a pulse, or he was in full-blown psychotic 'I will kill anything that moves' mode. I preferred the former. That Penn was less problematic.

"What kind of problem we talking this time?"

Penn was the only Fixer I used in London because the psycho was good at what he did. The best. If it wasn't for that, I would have nipped his little stalking of one of my employees in the bud. Remi hadn't come to me, and I was inclined to let her deal with it on her own. I had a soft spot for her, but not in some weird fucked up sexual way. She was more like a little sister I wanted to keep safe. If she needed me to handle Penn, I would, but she didn't.

"A dead problem."

"Text me the address and I'll see to it."

"It will be messy."

"No worries. I like the messy ones."

I rolled my eyes and hung up before firing off the address to him. Then I looked at Ari. She fidgeted in her chair.

"Come, let's get you cleaned up."

She rose slowly, wariness crossing her features. She'd just sold her fucking soul to the devil. And she knew it, even if she was trying to be brave.

I placed my cigarillo in the ashtray on my desk before walking over to a door behind it. Opening it up, I stepped in and flipped on the light. When I looked around, Ari had followed me. I smiled before walking into the next room. She peered around the first room before coming into my private bathroom after me. I went over to the shower and turned it on. She twisted her hands in front of her, looking between me and the shower.

"Those need to come off." I pointed at her clothes. "I hope you're not too attached to them."

She crossed her arms over her chest.

"Okay."

"Now, Arianna."

I didn't like to say things twice.

She shot me a look of bewilderment.

"What? In… in front of you?"

"Did I not make myself clear enough?" I took a step towards her. "When I tell you to do something, I expect it done. No questions. No complaints. Defiance won't be tolerated, and trust me, I'm not above forcing you. I would prefer it if you did it yourself, but either way, you will take your clothes off and get in the shower."

We stared at each other for a moment. I could see the battle waging on in her mind before she dropped her arms from her body. Ari slid the hoodie off her shoulders, the fabric dropping to the tiled floor. Her eyes remained fixed on mine as she curled her fingers around her bloody t-shirt and pulled it up her body.

I didn't outwardly react to the sight of her curves. She was far too fucking young for me to be looking at her with anything but clinical detachment. And yet, I was far from detached. Especially when she unhooked her bra and allowed it to fall to the floor. The way her dark nipples pebbled in the cool air had my fingers twitching.

Her chestnut brown eyes dared me to say something as she kicked off her trainers and tugged at her socks. Then she was sliding down her tracksuit bottoms, leaving her almost bare. Her fingers hooked into the waistband of her underwear, pulling them off her body.

Fuck.

Her tawny brown skin glowed under the lights. Her body was all curves. The spark of interest I should have had earlier watching the fucking pole dancers flared inside me.

Before I had a chance to say a word, she flounced by me and got in the shower. My fucking shower. Where she'd use my products to wash herself. She'd smell of me. It made the deviant smile, even as I tried to keep my face neutral.

I knew then I was going to have a fight on my hands, both internally and with Arianna herself. Apparently, I didn't care because no part of me regretted this course of action. But perhaps she would come to regret her decision to seek me out and become indebted to a man like me. One who had few morals and even less patience.

You are mine now, Tinkerbell. Mine.

I wouldn't touch her, but she was still my possession. She would learn very soon why she should obey me. If I knew anything about Ari, it was that she had little regard for authority. And it would be her downfall.

FOUR

Arianna

aving Zayn watch me undress in front of him made me wonder what on earth he planned to do with me. He told me I had a choice, but seeing as I'd killed my own uncle, my options were rather slim. It was this or face my father. The latter was something I dreaded. At least this way I would be safe. Or as safe as anyone could be at the mercy of a man like Zayn Villetti.

I kept my hair out of the spray. Not having any of my products made me wary of getting it wet. I could feel Zayn's eyes on my back, burning into my skin like fucking brands. Not like I'd got naked for many men, and especially not one who told me he had no interest in sleeping with me. My hands fumbled with the shower gel in the rack when I reached out for it. The blood still stuck to my skin in places. It was a relief to wash it off, even if my every move was being watched.

When I was done, I turned off the shower and stepped out onto the mat. Zayn leant against the sink counter with a blank expression on his annoyingly handsome face. It was annoying because he had no right being attractive when he was downright terrifying.

A clean towel sat next to him. I didn't know whether to reach for it or await further instructions. I curled my arms around myself when his gaze drew lower, taking in every inch of my naked, dripping skin. Maybe I wasn't what he was used to. The girls in his club, especially the pole dancer, looked like they barely ate. I'd always carried extra inches, especially around my thighs. I wasn't ashamed of the way I looked, but then again, I'd never had anyone openly stare at me the way Zayn was.

When his eyes dragged down to the thatch of curls between my legs, my face grew hot. Especially when his teeth grazed across his bottom lip for the briefest of seconds. I almost missed the subtle movement. He straightened and picked up the towel. I nearly backed away into the shower when he stepped up into my personal space.

"If you run, I will drag you back by your hair and punish you," he murmured as if he sensed my flight-or-fight response flaring.

"Punish me?"

He wrapped the towel around my body, forcing me to move my arms.

"Yes, punishments are for possessions who misbehave."

I yelped when he picked me up like I was a fucking baby in his arms and carried me out of the bathroom.

"What are you doing?"

"Keep your mouth shut and let me dry and dress you."

24

I wanted to retort that I could do it myself, but he did just warn me about punishments. And I wasn't even going to start analysing the whole calling me a possession business. I didn't think I should antagonise him after he'd agreed to help me, even if every part of me bristled against being owned.

You did just agree to be his. Whatever the fuck that even means.

Zayn said he didn't want sex, so what did he want?

He set me down in a chair in the next room. I did not expect him to kneel and proceed to dry me from my feet, up my legs and torso, along with my arms. There was a strange sort of detachment in his expression as he did it. Like he was thinking about something else, and this was merely muscle memory. It made me wonder what went on in his head.

He stood when he was done, taking the towel back into the bathroom before returning. I watched him open a cupboard, select a grey shirt from it and bring it over. Zayn made me slide my arms into it before he buttoned it up.

I was in his arms again before I could take a breath. My eyes fixed on his jaw as he walked through his office and into the corridor outside. The stubble covering it was dark. I was tempted to touch the thick hair but decided against it. He wouldn't appreciate it. I needed to learn to control my impulses. My father had always said I was prone to giving in to my reckless nature. He claimed I got it from my mother. She wasn't in the picture. She never had been. Sometimes I wondered about her, but Dad didn't speak of the woman who'd given birth to me very often.

Zayn took me out the back door into the cool night air. I shivered, burrowing into him against the chill without a second thought. My face pressed against his shoulder, eyes fixed on the alley behind us as he walked down it.

"Where are we going?"

"Home."

I had no clue where Zayn lived. Guess I was going to find out.

At the end of the alley, a car sat idling. Zayn placed me down in the back of it, slamming the door shut. A man was sitting in the driver's seat. I didn't recognise him. Zayn opened the door on the other side and slid in next to me. He reached over and forcibly put my seatbelt on. Then the car moved off. He took out his phone and had a low conversation with someone. I couldn't make out a lot of the words because he wasn't speaking English. I hadn't realised he was bilingual, but I should have known, given his family's Italian heritage.

I pulled the shirt lower on my thighs. I had nothing with me. When I'd run from the scene of the crime, I'd left everything behind.

"Shit," I muttered.

Zayn looked at me before placing his hand over the phone.

"What's wrong?"

"My bag… it's with Uncle Justin."

"I'll have it brought to me."

And with that, he went back to talking to whoever was on the other end of the phone.

I stared out of the window. If he wasn't concerned about it, then maybe I shouldn't be either. I was trusting him to dispose of my uncle. The fact he was covering up a murder I committed didn't sit well with me. However, I had no other choice. Who would believe me if I told them what my uncle had tried to do? Girls rarely went around killing their would-be rapists. It wasn't self-defence. I could admit I wanted him to die for hurting me and betraying my father.

I had grown up around career criminals. Getting sent to a private school did little to shield me from my father's lifestyle. From his drug trafficking. From the gang wars. It was all I knew. A dog-eat-dog world. You lived and died by your actions. And Uncle Justin's had led to his untimely demise.

"Arianna."

I jerked out of my thoughts, whipping my head around to look at Zayn. The car had stopped.

"Are we here?"

"Mmm."

Zayn eyed me with suspicion before he got out. I didn't have to wait long. He wrenched my door open, undid my seatbelt, and picked me up. I wrapped my arms around his neck after he nudged the car door closed with his hip. He carried me up to a house with a black door and the number twenty in brass on it. Zayn adjusted his hold on me to unlock the door. He set me down inside a minute later.

My eyes darted around the lobby. It wasn't large but had a side table and a cupboard for coats. He took me by the arm, directing me towards the stairs. I swallowed hard when he herded me up them, reminding myself he said he had no interest in my body. Why the fuck was I nervous about where he was taking me?

He opened the second door when we got up onto the landing and shoved me inside. The light came on, making me blink.

"Go to bed."

I turned to him. He leant up against the doorframe, his hands dug into his pockets as if expecting me to say something.

"Where's the bathroom?"

He pointed to a door in the corner.

I twisted my hands in front of me. His dark eyes fixed on mine. I felt the undercurrent of tension between us. It made the air thick and foreboding.

Why had he taken care of me himself?

Did he often keep possessions like me?

Don't think of yourself as one of his possessions. You're a person, not a thing.

"If you have something to ask me, I suggest you do so now."

The harsh note to his tone made me flinch.

"I…" My feet had a mind of their own, stepping closer to him without my say so. "I want to understand what you want from me. I know what I get out of this, but…"

"I don't think you're ready for that conversation."

My back went ramrod straight at the condescending nature of his words.

"What do you mean?"

"Get some sleep, Arianna."

My hand curled into a fist.

"No. Answer my question first."

I knew it was a mistake the moment his eyes flashed. He shoved off the door and stalked towards me. I had no chance to back away. His tattooed hand came up and wrapped around my throat. He pushed me towards the bed, those dark eyes intense and unyielding. Zayn shoved me down on top of the covers, pinning me there. My legs unconsciously spread as he stepped closer and leant over me. I could feel the heat of his body. It was unnerving after the way I'd been assaulted this evening by my uncle.

"Listen closely, Tink. This is the last time you will talk back to me without consequences. I do not tolerate disobedience. There are no exceptions to my rule. You are here of your own volition. You made your choice. Obey or I will make you wish you never came to me for help."

My body trembled at his harsh words. There was no way he hadn't noticed. His thumb stroked over my pulse. It jumped as if he commanded my heart to beat faster with his touch.

He was practically pressed against me now. I felt exposed, as the shirt he'd given me had ridden up. If he looked down, he would see me again. See everything. And a really fucked up part of me wanted him to.

"Obey you."

"Always."

"I'm not good at doing what I'm told."

He smirked.

"I know."

He was counting on me screwing up. I could see it in his eyes. He would take pleasure in causing me pain to prove a point. To show me I wasn't in control. It was he who had the power. I'd given it to him when I accepted the terms of our deal.

"You want me to fail."

He dragged his teeth over his bottom lip.

"People tell you failing is a bad thing, but they're wrong. Failure teaches you how to succeed, but only if you're willing to learn."

He pressed a knee on the bed between my spread legs. My breath hitched at the direct contact. He brought his face closer. I fought against the urge to wrap my hands around his arms and hold onto him. To use him as an anchor because his mere presence was drowning me in urges I didn't want to acknowledge.

"I hope you're ready for your lessons."

His unspoken words hung in the air. I would push his buttons. It was inevitable.

"Yes... sir."

A chuckle escaped his lips.

"Such a troublesome little thing you are."

He released me and straightened. I couldn't catch my damn breath when his eyes flicked down to where my shirt had ridden up. The longer his gaze was fixed on me, the harder my hands fisted around the covers below me. He rubbed his hand across his jaw. My cheeks were burning so hot, I thought my body might overheat from embarrassment.

"Goodnight, Tink."

He left without waiting for a response, closing the door behind him. I listened for the click of the lock, but it didn't come. He wasn't caging me in.

I scrambled off the bed to turn out the light before returning to it, burying myself beneath the covers. Tears sprung to my eyes. I'd killed a man tonight and indebted myself to an infinitely worse one. My uncle had been family, but Zayn? He owed me nothing. It made him dangerous, even if I wasn't scared of him.

The thing I was scared of happened to be my reaction to his proximity. To his nearness. To his touch on my skin. I refused to voice it out loud. Refused to give it any weight. Instead, I pressed my legs together and tried to think of anything else but the way it felt to have his hand wrapped around my throat. The heat of his gaze. And how much I wanted him to stay, so I didn't have to be alone on the night I killed my uncle in cold blood.

FIVE

Zayn

I tipped my head back, staring up at the ceiling with my fists clenched at my sides. This whole thing was fucked. However, I'd made my bed. I may as well lay in it. Suffer through my self-inflicted torture. Having a half-naked Arianna Michaelson pinned underneath me was my penance for deciding to keep her.

I gritted my teeth and almost shoved my fist through the wall, trying to erase the image from my brain. It was stuck on repeat. The way her legs parted without hesitation. How her breathing came faster as I stroked my thumb down her pulse. The way her nipples had hardened and poked through my fucking shirt. And how my only thought had been to make her call me... *no, don't voice that out loud.*

One of my hands uncurled and rubbed across my neck, fingers brushing over the tattoo of the graffiti text I had there. My lips curved up, knowing no one could read the damn thing unless I told them what it said. And I wanted her to know, when I shouldn't want that at all.

My feet carried me downstairs. I needed to be as far away from the girl as physically possible in my own damn house. Had to, or I'd go back into the room and do things I shouldn't. She'd just killed someone. The girl didn't need me pushing her too far. Not yet anyway.

I went into my study, poured a glass of whisky from my drinks cabinet and sat in the wingback chair by the fireplace. My fingers went to the remote on the side table, turning on the faux fire and watching the fake flames glow. I sipped my whisky before setting it on a coaster and pulling out my cigar case, extracting another cigarillo. I lit it and took a drag, exhaling a moment later. Then I adjusted myself, internally cursing my dick for reacting to her when it had been uninterested in anyone for months.

This evening had gone awry. I wasn't going to allow some physical response to fuck things up further. It meant nothing. I could admit she was a beautiful girl. Emphasis on the word girl. Fuck, I'd known Ari since she was four and not even that well. Our level of interaction was always the bare minimum. I had nothing in common with the daughter of a gang leader. Her world and mine weren't exactly the same.

And yet you still managed to give her a fucking nickname.

It wasn't often I had a moral compass to speak of. I knew better than to get intimately involved with women twelve years younger than me. Especially ones whose fathers were gang leaders I did business with. Ones who were getting themselves embroiled in a fucking war I did not need to be a part of. My father would not be impressed, not that I cared what he

34

thought, but the family interests came first. It had been drilled into me from a young age.

Family first. Business second. Everyone else last.

Ari wasn't family or business. She should come last. Yet I'd gone out of my way to save her. It might have been for a price, but I didn't save people. Unless it was Remi. I would always save her. So other than my sick impulses, why the fuck had I rescued this damn girl from her own stupid decisions? And why had I reacted to her closeness? I'd never looked twice at her before. Now was not the time to start.

I knocked back my entire glass of whisky. Then I puffed on my cigarillo, trying to get my fucking head on straight.

Ari was not someone I could fuck. Toy with, yes, but that was it. No further.

My phone buzzed in my pocket. I fished it out, checking the message. Rising from my seat, I walked out into the hallway towards my front door. I took a drag as I opened it to reveal my Fixer standing on my doorstep with a wry smile on his face.

"All right, Z?"

I waved him inside. He strolled in like he owned the fucking place, making a beeline for my study. I shut the door, following him into the room. The fuck immediately helped himself to a drink. I didn't bother telling him to make himself at home. He did it anyway, just like he always did.

"You didn't tell me I'd be dumping Justin Michaelson's body."

"Wasn't relevant," I replied, taking a seat in my chair again.

My eyes fixed on the fake flames. Penn dropped a small handbag on my side table.

"She stabbed him in the neck. Bloody way to die, especially at the hands of your own niece."

I'd told Arlo to ask Penn to find her bag for me. I rarely spoke to my second in Italian but having Ari in the car made it necessary. She didn't need to know any more details about the cover-up, nor my future plans for her.

No fucking surprise Penn had snooped around the scene. He rarely cared who I told him to get rid of, but the brother of a prominent gang leader wasn't just anyone. He was a somebody whose death was bad for fucking business. Not that I believed the cunt deserved to live after what he'd tried to do to Arianna.

"Your point?"

"Not like you to do favours for anyone, Z. Just curious why now."

"I don't pay you to ask questions."

"Fair enough."

I looked at him then. His grey eyes glinted with amusement as he twirled the amber liquid around in the tumbler gripped between his heavily tattooed fingers. He had them everywhere, including on his scalp. They disappeared underneath his hairline but were visible on the sides of his head due to his haircut. Short back and sides, neat on top, not a single hair out of place.

"This stays between you, me and Arlo. No one else can know what she did."

"Goes without saying." He tapped his fingers on his skull, drawing my attention to the black nail polish on them. "Locked vault."

Penn wasn't the type to spill the beans. In his line of business, secrecy was paramount.

I reached out, picked up the handbag, and looked inside. It contained usual things women kept in them, like a purse and makeup. Fishing out her phone, I set the bag down again.

"Can you get into this for me?"

Penn rolled his eyes but took the phone. A few minutes later, he hacked into the passcode and handed it back to me.

"Her father probably tracks her with it, you know."

"Can you do something about that?"

"Of course."

I tapped through her most recent messages. Nothing out of the ordinary. Conversations between her and a Kaylee Grant. I assumed this was her best friend, given the frequency of their text messages. There were no missed calls or anything else I should be concerned about.

I gave the phone to Penn again.

"Erase any history of where she's been today. I need it to look like she disappeared."

He quirked an eyebrow.

"She here?"

"None of your fucking business."

"Never met Bennett's daughter. Heard she's a looker."

And I heard you're obsessed with Remi.

I had to keep my damn temper in check. I'd made a promise to myself I would not interfere in Remi's life unless it was strictly necessary.

"Is that what you care about? Whether a woman is attractive enough to fuck?"

He smirked.

"I have no intention of touching your property, Z."

The fact he'd worked it out without me saying a damn word about my deal with her pissed me the fuck off.

"Better stay that way."

I wasn't just talking about Ari. If Penn fucked with Remi, I would kill him myself. I didn't care how useful he was. She deserved better than what life had thrown at her.

That smile of Penn's grew wider.

"I see how it is. You planning on keeping her forever?"

I rose from my chair and gave him a dark look.

"Deal with the fucking phone and have it back to me before morning."

"A woman got under your skin, Z?"

I had him shoved back against the wall with my hand around his throat seconds after the words left his lips. He put his hands up, the tumbler of whisky he'd poured still between his fingers.

"She's not up for fucking discussion. I'm not above slitting your throat and leaving you in a shallow fucking grave. Keep your opinions to yourself and your damn mouth shut."

The psychotic fuck had the audacity to laugh in my face. I released him, paced away and wondered when the fuck I had become possessive over that girl.

Since she offered herself up to you on a silver fucking platter.

The images of her on the bed, legs spread and chestnut fucking eyes telling me she'd let me do anything crossed my mind. I ran my hand along my jaw, shoving them away.

"Just tell me one thing."

"What?" I all but barked.

"Why'd she do it?"

I didn't turn around to look at him.

"Sick fuck tried to rape her. Can't blame a girl for defending herself."

Penn didn't need to know about Justin's plans to give her to McGovern. I was keeping that piece of information to myself for now. And I had respect for the girl. She wasn't a wallflower. No, Ari had grit and determination. She wasn't blind to the life her father was involved in. Probably why she made me want things I shouldn't.

"Glad the cunt got what he deserved."

I nodded. Rapist scum deserved to be put in the ground. Forcing women held no interest for me. I had Ari's agreement. She was mine to do what I wanted with. While I admitted she was at a disadvantage and had little choice but to agree, didn't change facts. A deal was a deal.

"I'll drop this through the letterbox."

He didn't bother saying goodbye. Out of the corner of my eye, I saw him drop the tumbler on the side table before he walked away. I listened to the front door slam a minute later. Taking another drag, I sat down and let out a long sigh.

Knowing she was upstairs had me rubbing my thumb over my bottom lip. Tomorrow I'd have a conversation with her about my expectations. She wasn't going to like them. I'd remind her of why she'd agreed to be mine. And if she protested, well, the lesson she received wouldn't be pretty.

This would only end one way no matter what she did.

My way.

SIX

Arianna

M y return to consciousness was slow. The sheets I
lay beneath were so warm and soft, I barely
wanted to open my eyes. Cocooned in the duvet
meant I didn't have to think about where I was and what I'd
done last night.

Sold yourself to the devil. Real smart.

I rubbed my face and opened my eyes. The room came into
focus. Everything was a mixture of soft blues and whites. The
delicacy of it was so at odds with what I knew of Zayn. The
likelihood of him decorating his own house was zero to none.
This was his spare room, so maybe whoever had decided on
the décor had chosen a neutral, soft palette.

I sat up, my eyes darting to the end of the bed where a small
pile of clothes with a folded piece of paper on top sat. He'd
been in here and seen me sleeping. A shiver ran down my spine
at the thought of it. I'd been so deep in dreamland, he hadn't
disturbed me.

He'd warned me about obeying him last night. I didn't think I should test his patience the first day I was here. Reaching out, I grabbed the paper and unfolded it. His handwriting was all loops and swirls, not like my incredibly messy scrawl. The note had instructions to get dressed and meet him in his study after I'd woken up. I didn't think a man like him would have time to deal with me today, but I was mistaken.

Hauling myself up out of bed, I went into the bathroom and found he'd left me with a new toothbrush and toothpaste. I went about my business, then got dressed in the things he'd left me. The hoodie swamped me and smelt of him. I couldn't imagine Zayn wearing this, but what the fuck did I even know about him? Nothing of substance.

My feet carried me downstairs when I was ready. I took in the house. It had clearly been modernised over the years. It was white walls with exposed, dark wooden floorboards. The stair runner was black and white and soft on my bare feet. I made my way down the hallway and into the second door on the right, finding a rather cosy room with a faux fireplace, two wingback chairs in front of it. There was a large desk in the corner. Zayn was sitting behind it, his head bowed, drawing my eyes to his dark hair as he stared at a computer on his desk.

The very first thing that struck me was the man had glasses on. I unconsciously rubbed my fingers along my thigh, trying not to squirm. There was no way in hell I could deny the sight of Zayn in those was something unexpected and ridiculously attractive.

He's not attractive. He is NOT attractive to me.

"Good morning, Arianna."

His voice made me stumble as I approached his desk. He hadn't looked up from his laptop. I didn't realise he knew I was there blatantly staring at him. I tucked my hands into the pocket of the hoodie and felt my cheeks heat.

"Morning... sir."

The twitch of his mouth told me he was happy I'd called him that.

"Come here and kneel next to me."

Kneel? The man wants me to fucking kneel.

I took a breath, trying not to give in to the urge to tell him there was no way in hell I was getting on my knees for him. Forcing my fingers to straighten and not curl into fists, I moved around his desk and lowered myself to my knees by his chair. I was not expecting him to reach out and stroke my hair like I was an obedient little pet.

"Did you sleep okay?"

"Yes."

He sat back in his chair, his hand still on my head as he stared down at me. Those dark eyes of his were emotionless. It unnerved me not being able to get a read on him. His hand travelled down my face before he brushed his thumb over my lip. I tried not to react to his touch even as my thighs pressed together. I reminded myself he wasn't interested in me physically. He'd said so. And I wasn't interested in him.

Liar.

"This is how I want you at all times unless I say otherwise... on your knees by my side."

I swallowed back a retort at how fucked up the demand was. I could only be thankful he released me and set his hand on the arm of the chair, tapping his fingers on the leather. His touch made it harder for me to think straight.

"I'll reiterate what I told you last night. You are to obey me without hesitation. Any deviations from the rules will result in punishment."

"What are the rules? Other than obeying, kneeling at your feet and calling you sir."

He smiled at my question. Then he leant forward, making sure I met his eyes.

"They're very simple. You don't talk to anyone else without my expressed permission. You don't leave the house unless it is with me or Arlo, who you will meet properly soon. You don't ask questions about my work, nor do you repeat anything you hear. If you want or need something, you ask, and I will provide it for you." I didn't think his eyes could get any darker, but they did. "You're mine, Arianna. I'm the one who takes care of you now. No one else."

My fingers did curl into fists this time, my nails digging into my palms. The intensity of this man had me trembling. This was the only way I could stem it, and even that wasn't working. The absolute certainty and confidence in his voice was mesmerising.

He could tell his words affected me on a deep visceral level as he reached out and stroked my cheek. I'd never had anyone tell me they'd take care of me before. Not even my father. And I didn't know I wanted it… until right now.

"I want you to be a good girl for me, but don't think that means I won't punish you when you fail. I have many ways to make you wish you behaved. You won't enjoy them… but I will."

"You know I'm going to fail," I whispered.

He leant closer.

"I do, my sweet little fairy."

For a moment, he did nothing but watch me attempt to compose myself. I bit down hard on my bottom lip, trying not to voice all the words rattling around in my brain. The thoughts telling me to rebel. To earn a punishment to see how bad they'd be. To see if I could endure them rather than obey this man I'd signed myself over to.

"Are those all the rules?"

He nodded slowly, releasing me again before he stood, cracking his neck in the process. His gaze fell on me again.

"Now, I want to know about your diet. What do you eat for breakfast?"

The sudden change in conversation had me frowning.

"What?"

"Breakfast, Arianna. You need to eat."

I licked my lips before responding.

"Tea and toast. Don't usually have time for anything else."

I could tell it displeased him by the tiny furrow that appeared on his brow.

"Stay here."

He left the room. I stared after him, wondering where he was going and what he was doing. Then I looked down at my lap, trying to convince myself this would be okay. His rules weren't that bad… were they? I didn't like the whole "getting his permission to talk to people" thing. It grated on my nerves, but I could do as he'd told me. It wouldn't be difficult. At least, I hoped not.

Zayn appeared back in the office ten minutes later. His smile indicated he was pleased I'd stayed, but it dropped almost immediately.

"Come."

I rose to my feet and followed after him. The kitchen at the back of the house was huge with light granite worktops and white wood doors on the cupboards. To the left was a dining area with a light wooden table. A place was set with a plate of eggs and toast, along with a pot of tea. Zayn walked right over to it, pulled out the chair, and sat down. He patted his leg a second later.

I hesitated in the doorway.

He wants me to sit in his lap? What the...

"Arianna."

The stern note of his voice had me shivering and my feet moving towards him. I gingerly sat on his leg, allowing him to adjust me into the position he wanted.

"I expect you to eat everything I give you. You may start."

He wrapped one hand around my waist, holding his phone in the other. I choked back a squeak when his palm flattened over my stomach. His touch was so casual as if it meant nothing to him, but this was new for me. To have *him* be the one laying his hands on my body in any capacity was blurring the lines between what we were before last night and now.

Zayn had kept me at a distance. Always polite whenever I was in his company. He was an intimidating person, but he never truly scared me. Maybe because he hadn't given me the impression he might hurt me. Now he had me in his grasp, I didn't know how to react. Especially not when he nudged my shoulder with his free hand, telling me to eat what he'd given me without words.

I leant forward, grabbed the teapot and smiled to myself as I poured it into the mug. After dumping in two sugars, I stirred the liquid and added milk. Then I took a sip, letting out a sigh of pleasure. Zayn's hand around my stomach tightened at the sound. I ignored it as I set the mug down and started on the food. It didn't take me long to demolish the plate, having not realised how hungry I'd been.

With the mug in my hands, I sat back against his chest and sipped. What I didn't expect was for him to lean his cheek against my hair as he continued fiddling with his phone.

"Good girl," he murmured.

I shivered at the praise, not knowing what to make of the butterflies swirling in my stomach.

"I'm not going to turn down food out of spite," I muttered, trying to avoid the feelings his words and presence lured out of me.

"I should fucking hope not, Tink. You will look after yourself under my care or we are going to have a problem."

I stiffened and sat up, wanting to escape the mind-fuck this morning had already been. I set the mug down on the table, contemplating running. His hand rose from my stomach to cup my throat. I swallowed against his palm. His grasp wasn't tight, merely a reminder of who was in charge.

"Are we going to have a problem?"

"No, sir."

"I wouldn't want to handcuff you to my desk chair for the rest of the day, so you won't bolt."

"I'll be good."

"That's what I thought."

He let go of my neck. My hand went to it, rubbing the skin as if his touch burnt me.

"Now, I want you to write down everything you need so Arlo can get it for you."

I turned my head to look at him. Zayn's attention was back on his phone already.

"Everything I need?"

"Yes, I'm sure you use certain hair care products and other such things. What part of 'I will take care of you and your needs' did you not understand?"

"None, I do understand."

"Then write."

He waved his hand at the paper and pen I hadn't noticed before, sitting on the table next to my breakfast things. I pulled them closer, not wanting to incur his wrath, and did as he asked.

I placed the pen down when I was done, hoping I'd remembered everything.

The doorbell echoed through the house a moment later.

"Up, Arianna."

I scrambled out of his lap, fidgeting on the spot as he stood. He wrapped a hand around the back of my neck and directed me in front of him. We walked through the house to the front door. He didn't remove his hand from me as he pulled it open.

On the step stood Zayn's right-hand man, Arlo. I knew who he was, as my father had told me, but we'd never been introduced. He had a lot of bags in his hands.

"Come in, take those upstairs and put them away in the blue bedroom."

48

Arlo nodded, not looking at me as he walked in. Zayn shut the door. He then pushed me into his living room. It was a light and airy space with a large fireplace, a flat-screen TV mounted above it and comfortable looking dark sofas. He took a seat in one of them and pointed at the floor. Reluctantly, I knelt at his feet and dared to look up at him.

Zayn leant forward and stroked my face with his knuckles. This constant touching thing was making me wary.

"Did you finish your list?"

"Yes, sir."

"Good. I'm working at home today, but tomorrow you'll attend the club with me."

"I don't have anything to wear."

He smirked.

"Arlo has brought you new clothes. The blue bedroom will be yours for the duration of your stay here unless I decide otherwise."

I didn't know if I liked the fact he'd made his man buy me clothes but protesting might get me in trouble.

"Where else would you put me?"

The way his eyes darkened had my hands shaking in my lap.

"Don't ask questions you don't want the answers to."

What the hell does that mean?

"I'm not… sir."

He sat back, assessing me for a long moment.

"If you misbehave, I will take away your bedroom and make you sleep naked on the floor of mine until you've learnt your lesson. Then I can keep an eye on you."

I bit my lip to stop myself from reacting to his statement. The idea of being in his bedroom naked had my mind racing at a million miles an hour. Before I could shut those images out, Arlo appeared in the room. I felt my cheeks burn as Zayn turned his attention to his man.

What the fuck, brain? He said he's not interested in me like that.

My mind didn't want to listen, pressing erotic images of tangled bodies into my vision. Two bodies specifically... mine... and his.

Fuck!

SEVEN

Zayn

rlo gave me a significant look as he walked in. I was well aware of his disapproval over me taking Arianna in. Probably even more so when I'd made him go out first thing this morning to buy her clothes after he'd disposed of her bloody ones last night. He didn't have to tell me he thought this was a bad idea. I already knew.

His eyes darted down to Arianna, who was kneeling at my feet with a rather startled look on her face. I'd put it there after telling her I'd make her sleep naked on my floor. She was thinking about it, the idea of it. Little did she know it plagued me too. I'd already seen her bare. The image of it branded into my retinas. It was fucking torture at its finest. Apparently, I needed to be reminded of why the fuck I didn't go looking for trouble. Served me right for complaining about my boredom. I certainly wasn't bored now. Not when I had a little pet to play with. A very tempting pet who was giving my self-restraint a run for its money.

"Arlo, this is Arianna." My attention went back to her. "Be a good girl and say hello, Tink."

Her brown eyes widened a fraction, but she turned to Arlo, giving him a nod.

"Hello, it's nice to meet you."

"Likewise," he replied with a grunt.

I watched Arianna lean closer to me, almost as if she was wary of what he thought about this and was seeking my reassurance. Without thinking, I reached out, pulling her closer between my legs. She blinked, staring up at me with confusion.

"Relax, Tinkerbell," I told her, my voice quiet, so it didn't carry. "You're safe."

I wouldn't allow any harm to come to her. Not while she was under my roof. Arlo wouldn't lay a fucking hand on her unless it was to keep her out of danger. He knew better than to touch my possessions. And that's what she was now. Mine. All fucking mine.

Ari didn't say a word, just continued to look at me with those beautifully expressive eyes of hers. They told me exactly what she was thinking. She didn't know how to feel about the situation she'd put herself in with me. She didn't understand why I was taking care of her. The only person who was allowed to do a single thing to her was me.

Her teeth enclosed around her bottom lip, drawing my attention to them. A part of me wanted to bite down hard on it, make her cry out from the pain. I wanted to know if her moans, pants, and gasps sounded as heavenly as I was imagining they could be.

"Boss."

My eyes went to Arlo, who gave me a look that spoke volumes. The tension between me and my new pet was palpable. It was probably making him uncomfortable as fuck. I had to get my shit straight.

"Yes?"

He indicated the door with his head. He wanted to talk to me alone. Unsurprising really. I stood. Ari, as if on instinct, wrapped her hand around my leg. Her eyes took on a pleading look. She didn't want me to leave, but she would have to deal with it.

"Stay here."

I stepped out of her hold, ignoring the way her face fell, and followed Arlo from the room. The moment we were out of earshot, he stopped in his tracks.

"She's going to bring down trouble on us, Zayn."

"I know."

"Then why are you doing this?"

I didn't respond, continuing on into my office. I took off my glasses and threw them down on my desk before rubbing my temples.

"Allowing her to go back to her father would only put her in danger. Derek will try to take her again and use her in his war against Bennett."

"Still doesn't explain why you're getting involved. Why do you care about her safety?"

Yeah… why do you care, Zayn?

I cared because there was more at stake here than just Arianna. The criminal underworld was in fucking turmoil. Shit was going to hit the fan sooner rather than later. She was caught in the middle and, for some reason, I couldn't abide it.

I didn't like innocents being in the crossfire of war, not when I could do something about it.

"She has blood on her hands. It shouldn't be there, but it is. I've known the girl most of my life. I can't let her be fed to the fucking wolves."

I turned in time to see Arlo's eyebrows raise.

"So she's another Remi, is she?"

I scowled. Yes, I'd made a deal with Remi's mother, but it wasn't the same situation. I wasn't interested in Remi. She was like my sister. And, of course, she'd attracted all the wrong attention from people she should stay the fuck away from. I swear her sense of self-preservation was entirely lacking. It's why I protected her. Her mother was dead. She was estranged from her father. She needed someone to watch out for her.

"It's not the same. Ari knows she's indebted to me."

"One day Remi's going to find out what Roberta did and you're going to have to deal with the consequences."

"Don't fucking remind me."

If anyone else started calling me out on my shit, I would slit their throat. Arlo was the keeper of my secrets. He knew everything. Well, he didn't know how much I wanted to pin Arianna down and show her who her daddy was.

Jesus, you know you can't do that!

It didn't stop me from wanting to. From craving it. Now I'd seen her in all her glory, it was difficult to view her as the girl I'd known her as for all these years.

"If you want your father to continue leaving you alone, this isn't the way to go about it."

"Fuck Gennaro. This has nothing to do with him."

Arlo shook his head.

"What about Bennett? He won't be happy either."

"He doesn't need to know."

"She killed her own uncle, Zayn. Do you think this will—"

"Enough."

His lips thinned as he closed his mouth. Everything he'd said was true, but he didn't get to continue questioning my decisions. I wasn't stupid. I knew getting involved with her would bring hell raining down on me. The bored part of me didn't care. He wanted chaos. He needed it to feel alive. And the twisted part of me demanded she be the one I sacrificed to end the monotony.

"She stays and no one else finds out I have her. That's the end of it."

I turned away. Her phone sat on my desk. Penn had posted it early this morning. I wasn't going to give it back to her quite yet. She needed to earn my trust first. Not to mention her contacting anyone outside of these four walls would put all of us at risk.

"Okay. Just wanted to make sure you've thought this through."

As if I had. My common sense told me I should have sent her away the moment I saw all the blood, but it was the fire in her eyes that kept me from doing so. She'd killed a man. I didn't know if Ari felt any remorse for it or how it had affected her. I hadn't asked. Maybe I should. Her well-being was my priority now.

"Is there anything else I need to know?"

"Not right now. I did everything you asked me to last night."

"I have a list of things I need you to acquire for her. Make sure you pick it up from the kitchen table before you leave."

"Okay, *boss.*"

I heard his footsteps as he walked away. Arlo knew his way around my house. He could see himself out. I stood there staring at my desk until the front door slammed shut. Then I returned to Ari, who I found had tear tracks running down her face. The sight of it made me pause in the doorway. She wasn't making any noise. Her little fists were balled up in her lap and she was still kneeling where I left her.

Is this too much for you, Tink?

"Why are you crying, my little fairy?"

My voice was soft so as not to startle her. It's not like I didn't know how to be gentle. I just had no need to be when I was surrounded by the worst of society. I could be gentle towards her… if she behaved for me.

"I killed my uncle."

He deserved it.

"Do you regret it?"

She shook her head. I took a step closer.

"Are your tears for him?"

Another head shake.

"For yourself?"

She wiped her eyes and nodded before looking away.

I need to pry what actually happened out of her, but not now. She's not ready.

"I see."

"Do you?" she whispered. "Have you killed someone?"

More like someones. I had blood all over my hands. Hard not to with the life I'd been born into. I preferred dealing with

56

things in a civilised fashion where I could rather than resorting to violence to get the job done. That's what I had Penn for. He did my dirty work if necessary. Before him was a time I didn't wish to think about.

"Yes."

She said nothing. I drew closer until the tips of my toes were touching her knees. Reaching over to the coffee table, I picked up the box of tissues. Then I squatted down on my haunches and took a hold of her chin, turning her face towards me. She watched as I pulled out a few tissues and wiped her face down, careful not to aggravate her bruised jaw.

"You don't have to do that," she blurted out a moment later.

"I do."

"Why?"

"I take good care of the things I own, especially when they're feeling fragile or broken."

She swallowed at my statement. Silly little thing had no idea of the lengths I'd go to. She didn't realise how serious I was about looking after her. Yes, it would involve discipline and punishments, but right now, she needed me to make sure she wasn't going to break into tiny pieces after killing her uncle. I didn't like broken toys. They weren't fun to play with.

"Sir?"

I set the used tissues and box back on the table.

"Mmm?"

"If I asked you to hold me, would you?"

"Say please."

"Please, sir."

The way her voice shook on her words was disconcerting. I straightened, which made her eyes turn sad as if she thought I was going to deny her request. Taking a seat on the sofa, I indicated my lap with my hand. It took her a few moments of hesitation before she crawled into it. I pressed her head against my shoulder and curled my arms around her. She was stiff for a few seconds, then her breath whooshed out of her. Her hand wrapped around my neck and her body went slack in my hold.

I had things to do, but I could take half an hour of my day to make sure Ari got through hers. There were aspects of me people would call cruel and strict, but they didn't get to see who I really was. You had to be cruel and unforgiving in my world. It was the only way to survive.

If she was going to be with me for the foreseeable future, Ari might as well get used to all sides of me. She would be meeting them sooner rather than later. And I was absolutely certain she wouldn't appreciate some of the parts that made up the mafia kingpin's prodigal son.

You don't become feared and revered by being nice. You do it with threats and bloodshed. I bowed to no one… not even my father. Ari would learn and I would enjoy teaching her in whatever way I saw fit. Even if it made her hate me in the end.

EIGHT

Arianna

iddling with my new coat, I stared out of the car window. Outside it was drizzling, which wasn't helping with my nerves at all. We were on the way to Desecration. Zayn was quiet. It suited me just fine after yesterday. I was embarrassed about crying in front of him, but he'd been nice to me. In fact, I'd all but melted into him when he let me sit in his lap and held me.

You have got to get a grip.

Apparently, one comforting moment from him had me swooning and forgetting I was, for all intents and purposes, his possession. It was stupid. I was stupid for showing him my vulnerable side, even if I couldn't help it. My soul burnt with the knowledge I'd taken a life, even if it was in self-defence. Even if my uncle had deserved it. It didn't stop it from hurting.

It took me the rest of the day to regain my composure. Zayn left me to watch TV with an icepack for my bruised jaw so he could work in his office. We'd shared a quiet lunch and dinner together before he'd sent me to bed. I didn't ask him for anything else. I might be thankful he'd comforted me, but I couldn't afford to let my guard down. If I did, I'd be fucked.

The car pulled up by the curb to let both of us out. Zayn opened my door and helped me out, then tucked my hand under his arm as he led me down to the back door of the club. I didn't pull away. It wouldn't do me any good.

When we were inside the club, he took us down to his office, making me strip off my coat so he could hang it up with his on the stand. I fidgeted by the door as he sat down behind his desk.

"Arianna."

"Yes, sir?"

"Come here."

I moved around to his side. He hadn't told me why he wanted me here. I could have stayed alone at the house. Not like I would have gone snooping.

Zayn looked up at me, his brow furrowed.

"Are you forgetting the rules already?"

He pointed at the floor.

Rules? Wait, he doesn't expect me to kneel all day while he works, does he?

My hand curled at my side. Kneeling on his office floor somehow felt far more degrading than doing it in the privacy of his house. It was bad enough I'd done it in front of Arlo.

"The kneeling applies here?"

His lip curled up and his eyes darkened.

"Are you questioning me?"

My heart pounded in my ears, knowing I fucked up. Instead of rectifying the situation, I stood there staring at him. The dryness of my mouth prevented a response from forming on my lips.

Zayn rose from his chair, looking down at me with a stern expression on his face.

"I thought you would last a little longer, Tink, but perhaps I overestimated your ability to behave."

His hand slid behind my neck, cupping the back of it.

"Zayn."

The word came out hushed, almost pleading. I had no idea what he was going to do to me. My body trembled under his gaze and touch.

"If you think that will make me lenient, you're mistaken. You have no idea what I'm capable of."

He reached up with his free hand, tucking a curl behind my ear in a gesture so fucking tender, it made me shiver. It was at odds with his stern expression.

Zayn forced me to the floor, making me kneel at his feet. His fingers curled under my chin, tipping my head back. Those dark eyes of his were emotionless, making him ten times scarier.

"Hands behind your back."

I did as he said, noting my trembling fingers as I clasped them behind me. He stepped away, pulling open a drawer. My eyes followed his hand as he extracted what looked like a leather collar with a black chain attached to it. I swallowed at the sight of it.

"Disobedient little pets need to learn their place."

My body went rigid as he snapped the collar around my neck, buckling it at the side. He fisted the chain, tugging on it and almost forcing me off balance.

"Do I need to teach you to sit and stay, hmm?"

"No, sir," I whimpered.

The sound was fucking pathetic, but I couldn't help it. It was as if all of my power had been stripped from me. I was at his mercy. And mercy wasn't a word in Zayn Villetti's vocabulary.

"Good."

He held onto the chain as he sat back in his seat. It stayed wrapped up in his fist even as he turned his computer on. There was no slack. I was trying to stay balanced with my hands behind my back. The leather dug into the back of my neck, making the whole thing incredibly uncomfortable.

I watched as he wrapped the chain around the arm of his chair, securing me in place.

"Don't move or I will make you stay that way for longer."

I bit my lip, wanting to retort, but knowing it wouldn't do me any good. When I wanted to know what type of punishments he would inflict on me, I was not banking on wearing a collar like an actual pet. It was degrading. Then again, wasn't that the whole point? My place had been dictated to me. On my knees by his side.

Was this really better than going to my father and telling him I'd killed his brother?

His chestnut brown eyes full of disappointment flashed before my eyes. As did the way his hand would have cupped my face, a darker shade than my own, and how he'd have told me he would have to make an example of me. I didn't want that. Hurting my father was the very last thing I wished to do. I couldn't have faced it, but the situation with Zayn? I could face this. I could endure it to keep myself safe. No one could use me as leverage or bait if I was with the man who'd collared me. I'd rather this humiliation than facing my father and owning up to what I'd done.

I don't know how much time passed as I knelt there watching Zayn work. My thoughts were chaotic, but my body remained still. Obeying him was my only goal. Living through my punishment and getting out the other side unscathed.

A knock at the door startled me. I fought hard to stay in place even as Zayn called for them to enter.

Oh god, someone else is about to see me like this.

I didn't move from my spot. I was obscured behind Zayn's desk, so I couldn't see who had come in, but I heard their footsteps.

"Hey, Z," came a feminine voice.

"Remi, what can I do for you?"

He had a soft note to his voice like this was someone he cared about. Everything urged me to look at them, but my gaze remained on Zayn, waiting for him to tell me this punishment was over.

"Am I interrupting something here?"

Great, she's seen me.

"No."

"Are you sure? I can come back."

Zayn looked over at me. The way his dark eyes flickered had my mouth going dry.

"I'm sure, but you will not say a word to anyone about what you saw in here."

I heard the girl he'd called Remi scoff.

"The entire staff already thinks I must give you sexual favours because you're nice to me. They'd hardly bat an eyelid at you having a chained-up girl."

Zayn scowled, and his attention snapped back to Remi.

"They think what?"

"Chill out, it was a joke."

"Jokes are meant to be funny."

The woman he was talking to came around and leant against the desk on Zayn's other side. She had dark hair, green eyes, and golden skin. The way she smiled at Zayn made my stomach churn.

"Yeah okay, Mr Serious."

And just like that, Zayn smiled back at her. I'd never seen him smile that way before. Not with such affection and care.

What the hell? Who is this girl?

"What do you want?"

"For you to tell me who that is."

Remi indicated me with her head.

"None of your business."

She pouted.

"Fine, I'll ask her myself, shall I? Is she even allowed to talk?"

Zayn sighed and shook his head.

"This is Arianna. She's staying with me for the time being."

Remi leant across Zayn to look me in the eye and gave me a smile.

"Nice to meet you, Arianna. Watch out for this one, he's mean."

"Remi."

She straightened and put her hands up.

"Okay, I see when I'm not wanted. I only came in to say hello. Also, you remember the client who asked for the foursome scene on the club night?"

Foursome?

I knew Zayn's club catered for all sorts, but I hadn't been expecting that.

"What about him?"

"I recognise him from somewhere, but I can't put my finger on it."

Zayn gave her a look.

"He owns an investment company. You've probably seen his pretty-boy face in ads for it. And I'd remind you of our confidentiality clause if I didn't know you any better."

"Who would I even tell? I have no friends."

Zayn nudged her arm.

"You have me."

"You're more like my overprotective older brother than a friend, Zayn." Her eyes lit up. "Oh shit, yes, I remember now. He's one of those guys everyone calls the Four Horsemen. Well, what a kinky dude."

She gave Zayn a wink before walking away.

Older brother figure? Does that mean nothing else is going on between them? Why the fuck do I care?

"Remi."

Her footsteps paused.

"Yeah?"

"Stay out of trouble."

Her only response was a snort before she retreated from the room. The sound of the door closing made Zayn's attention snap to me. His eyes narrowed. I licked my bottom lip, a movement he watched with rapt attention.

"Sir."

"Yes, Arianna?"

"I'm sorry for misbehaving."

He unwound the chain from his chair.

"Are you now?"

I was... sort of.

"Yes, sir."

He spun around to face me, holding the chain loosely between his fingers and finally giving me some slack.

"Show me."

"How?"

He leant forward in his seat, eyes travelling down the length of me before landing on the floor below him. No, not on the floor, but his feet clad in expensive leather shoes.

"Good pets beg for forgiveness and show deference by bowing down at their master's feet."

He tugged on the chain slightly, jerking me forward.

"They show they are worthy."

I shuffled towards him before moving my hands from behind my back and pressing them to the floor as I bent down. My eyes landed on his shoes, my face inches from them.

"I'm sorry, sir. Please forgive me."

The fact I did it with such willingness was not something I wanted to think too hard on.

"You can do better than that. Show me you deserve it."

It took me more than a few seconds to register his meaning. He'd looked at his feet for a reason. Everything inside me screamed against the unspoken demand he'd made.

"I should have obeyed you. I deserved my punishment."

My face lowered until I was a hair's breadth from the leather.

"Please forgive me for my disobedience."

The moment my lips pressed against his shoe, I heard the rumble of approval from above me. It made my heart race, the noise sinking into my bones and rendering me helpless. My hands shook with the effort of holding myself up.

What the fuck is this man doing to me?

"Come here."

With shaky arms, I pushed myself back up onto my knees. He held a hand out to me. I placed my own in it, allowing him to pull me up from the floor and into his lap. My legs straddled his, bringing us face to face. The way his eyes searched mine froze me in place. He ran his finger along the collar on my neck.

"Who was that girl?" I blurted out, wanting to distract him from the way I trembled in his lap. The feelings thrumming under my skin weren't logical or normal. They built with every passing second, urging me to do something I might regret.

"Remi works here."

"Who is she to you?"

The question made his lip twitch.

"Her mother worked for my father before she did for me. Remi's a friend. That's all."

"A friend."

"Mmm."

I almost cursed my stupid mouth for asking those questions. I wasn't jealous, was I?

He'd reassured me without giving me a hard time over it. Did he realise he was making me feel things I shouldn't? Did he notice the tension between us permeating the air? It grew as his fist wrapped around the chain, pulling me closer.

"But we're not friends, Tink. You're mine, and I expect you to behave for me." His other hand gripped my waist. "Don't disappoint me."

I wasn't going to promise him I would behave. We both knew I would fail again. It was in my nature to push.

He twisted my face to the side and ran his nose up my cheek. I let out a quiet gasp.

"I like punishing my pets," he whispered. "It's the sweetest part, especially when they give in."

His warm breath fanned across my face. My hands went to his chest to steady myself. The way my fingers splayed out over his shirt had me letting out a harsh pant. His body was warm and solid. His heartbeat was steady against my palm.

"I'll tame you, Tinkerbell. It's only a matter of time."

"Zayn."

"It's sir to you."

It was the second time his actual name had fallen out of my mouth without me consciously making the decision to say it.

Before I could respond, another knock at the door rang through the room. He eased me back away from him.

"On the floor," he murmured.

I obeyed, slipping off him and kneeling at the side of his chair with my head bowed.

"Come in."

The door opened.

"I hate to disturb you, boss, but Gennaro is here."

I could feel the annoyance radiating off Zayn the moment his father's name fell from the person's lips.

"Okay, Liza, send him in… but give me a few minutes."

"Sure thing."

The door closed again.

"I need you to stay in the other room while I talk to him."

I looked up at Zayn, catching his irritated expression. It wasn't directed at me, though.

"Now, Arianna."

He pointed to the room he'd taken me in on the day I'd turned up here, covered in blood. I scrambled to my feet, eager not to earn myself another punishment.

I opened the door to the side room, slipping inside and shutting it behind me. My fingers went to the collar around my neck as I sat down on the sofa, curling my feet up underneath me.

A part of me questioned why Zayn was pissed off with his father turning up and what Gennaro wanted. It was none of my business, but curiosity burnt in my chest.

It made me wonder why Zayn had let Remi see me. He clearly trusted her more than he did his own father. Gennaro would likely tell my father I was here. Zayn was only protecting me by sending me in here out of the way.

I fingered the chain. It was black metal with a little leather handle at the end. Zayn had done more than merely collared me. This was a leash. One he would use to bring me to heel. And I couldn't deny I liked the idea of it more than I would ever willingly admit to him.

NINE

Zayn

My fist clenched on the arm of my chair. I willed myself to remain calm, but the burning sensation beneath my skin made my head throb and other places I didn't want to think about.

Why do I want her?

It was a simple question. One I had no answer to.

Ari was beautiful. No one could deny that. Her curvaceous body was something I admired, sure. Attractive women were nothing new to me. I had too many falling at my feet, something I generally found abhorrent these days. When a woman kneeled, it was because I wanted her there. I demanded it. Craved the sight of it.

Her looks mattered not to me. It was the fire in her chestnut brown eyes. The passion simmering below the surface. It pulled at me, making me want to give her all the things she deserved. Ari needed someone to take care of her.

And for some fucked up reason, I wanted to be the one seeing to her every need.

Every. Single. Need.

Uncurling my fingers, I ran them along my throat. Some might say it was a fucked up joke to have the word "padre" tattooed there in graffiti script no one but me could decipher. Well, myself and Penn, that was. He'd designed and inked the word on my skin.

Dropping my right hand, I flexed it. The inked skull on the back of my palm rippled with the movement. I had to admit to myself how fucked up it was. The desire to have her call me that. I was almost old enough to be her father. Bennett was only four and a half years older than me. He'd been sixteen going on seventeen when Arianna was born. It was only one of the reasons why I couldn't have her in any other way.

It was my pet or nothing.

I couldn't for the life of me understand why the thought of nothing made me nauseous. Until she'd come to me covered in blood, I hadn't much cared about Arianna Michaelson. And now… all I thought about was her.

The door to my office opened. My attention snapped to it. In walked Fiore and Stefano, my father's bodyguards without whom he never went anywhere, followed by the man himself. After him came my two brothers. Gil's face was stoic, while Enzo had a sullen expression on his. Arlo strolled in behind them and shut my office door.

"Zayn," my father said as he approached my desk and sat in one of the chairs in front of it. My mind went back to when Ari had sat in it covered in blood. Internally cursing myself, I schooled my features.

"Father."

Enzo and Gil called him *papà*. Not me. He wasn't a man I felt much affection for. Not when I knew what kind of person he really was.

Gennaro steepled his fingers. His two bodyguards remained close to him. They knew I wasn't a risk, but my father was a careful man. He didn't like to be left unprotected.

Arlo stood next to the door, fading into the background. Enzo threw himself down on the sofa in the corner, crossing his arms over his chest, and glared at my father. He'd recently returned from travelling. No doubt he'd been causing our father trouble since he'd been back. He had a habit of breaking the rules and being a nuisance.

Gil came around and stood close to me. My brother was the silent type who never put a foot wrong. He looked up to me. Fuck knows why. Not like I was the role model of the century. I'd disappointed our father countless times, but I'd got away with it being the eldest and the heir.

"What can I do for you?" I asked my father when he didn't say another word.

Gennaro regarded me with eyes matching my own deep brown ones. His hair was greying at the temples, but he was attractive for a man in his late fifties. Unsurprisingly, women threw themselves at him as they did me. His inability to remain faithful had driven our mother to abandon us when Enzo was fifteen. I hadn't forgiven him for what he'd done in response. I never would.

"A family meeting."

I raised an eyebrow.

"Right now?"

73

"Yes."

He nodded to his bodyguards. They walked towards the door and stepped out, glaring at Arlo as if he shouldn't be included in these discussions either. I wasn't going to send him out of my office, no matter what my father said. We had nothing to hide from him.

When the door closed behind Fiore and Stefano, my father leant forward in his chair.

"You haven't been answering my calls."

"I've been busy."

It wasn't strictly true. I didn't want to speak to him unless it was necessary. Besides, I wanted to get this over with. Leaving Ari alone for too long didn't sit well with me. Not after she'd cried over killing her uncle yesterday. I might be strict with her, but it didn't mean I wasn't going to look after her if she needed it. If she fell apart over what she'd done.

"You make time for family, Zayn. That is non-negotiable."

I almost rolled my eyes and caught Enzo's scowl deepening. He'd obviously been lectured before they came here, judging by his dark mood. Giving my father a nod, I sat back and traced the tattoos on my fingers with my other hand.

"Your brother has been causing trouble since he returned home."

I almost scoffed. When was Enzo not being a pain in the arse?

"Nothing I do gets through to him. I want you to deal with him. Put him to work here if you have to. I don't care, just make him understand his behaviour isn't acceptable within this family."

Did my father actually think I could get through to my brother? He had to be joking. Enzo didn't listen to anyone. I didn't need his shit when I had my own to deal with.

"I don't need a babysitter, *Papà*," Enzo grumbled. "Especially not him." He waved at me.

"*Silenzio*, Enzo. You will do as your brother says."

My father's hand curled around the arm of the chair, showing his displeasure with my brother. Honestly, I wished Enzo would stop pushing his buttons. It would make our lives a whole lot easier.

"You want me to give him a job?" I asked, waving at my brother. "He'll have to pull his weight, something he's incapable of doing."

I wasn't going to tell my father no, even though I had no interest in babysitting my brother and his wild ways. There would be no point. He'd tell me family took care of family. You couldn't argue with him about it. His idea of family was as fucked up as they came.

"He will if he knows what's good for him," Gennaro replied, sparing Enzo a glance. "He has no other choice if he wants to keep his allowance."

My father threatening to take away Enzo's funds was probably the only way to keep the damn boy in line.

I stood up and walked over to my brother. Enzo rolled his eyes at me. I leant closer and flicked his ear. He rubbed it and slapped my hand away.

"*Va' a farti fottere.*"

"Fuck myself, huh? Not very charitable of you when I'm doing you a favour."

"Shut up, Zayn, you're as bad as him."

I wanted to tell him I was a better man than our father would ever be despite the fucked up shit I'd done, but I refrained. We could have words when our father wasn't around. Enzo needed to sort his shit out. He was a twenty-four-year-old grown fucking man. It was time he acted like a Villetti instead of being a waste of space. I might not like being beholden to this damn family, but I wasn't out here giving us a bad name.

"Go see Liza. Tell her you'll be working on the door. I'm not having you on the club floor if I can help it. I don't trust you to leave the girls alone."

Enzo gave me a smile

"Me? I'll be good as gold."

"Don't make me flick your ear again."

I straightened. He shot me a dirty look before getting up and stalking from the room. I turned to our father, who was watching me with a blank expression.

"Anything else?"

He rose from his chair.

"Yes. It's time for you to become a real part of this family, Zayn. You are my heir, whether you like it or not."

My fist clenched at my side. This day was always going to come around. The one when my father wouldn't tolerate me being out here doing my own thing any longer.

"What would you have me do?"

He gave me a smile. It chilled me to my damn bones.

"I want you to find a wife."

I uncurled my fist and flexed my tattooed hand, wanting to wrap it around his throat and strangle the fucking life out of the man.

"A wife? Why the fuck would I do that?"

"Respectable men have good women by their sides. That is our way, Zayn. You are thirty-four years old. It is past time."

Oh, because you're such a fucking respectable man after what you did to our mother.

My father was a piece of shit, but he was family. A fact I hated. There were some days I wished I hadn't been born to take over his empire. I had no interest in being the next Don Villetti or whatever the fuck he liked to call himself.

My eyes went to Gil, who was watching us with a frown. He clearly hadn't been told about this beforehand.

"That's all you want? For me to get married?"

"No, that is not all."

"Next you're going to tell me you've chosen a woman for me," I muttered under my breath as I strode back towards my desk and threw myself into my chair.

"I have some women I wish for you to meet."

Here we go.

"I don't need help in choosing a wife, Father. I'm perfectly capable of finding a suitable woman if I was so inclined. I don't wish to get married."

And certainly not on his fucking timeline. I didn't have time for a girlfriend, let alone a wife. Not when I had Ari to look after. Whatever woman my father wanted to set me up with would not approve of my arrangement with my little pet.

"This is not up for debate."

"Oh, really now? You're putting your foot down?"

"*Un ragazzo così insolente.*"

My father calling me an insolent boy was nothing new.

"What else do you want?"

"For you to take your role seriously."

I waved at Gil.

"You have him."

Gennaro's eyes narrowed.

"Gil is not the eldest."

Fuck tradition. Being the eldest meant shit. I wasn't interested in running the fucking mafia. My club and my other business interests kept me busy and satisfied. This place was my baby. Somewhere my father couldn't stick his bloody oar into.

"That's the only reason you're pushing it onto me."

"It's the way of things."

I'd heard that fucking phrase far too many times in my life. Sighing, I glanced up at my brother. He didn't look perturbed by our discussion. He knew my feelings on the matter already. It wasn't a secret.

"If I promise to find a suitable woman and answer your phone calls, will you get off my case?"

My father inclined his head.

"Of course."

"Then consider it done."

Gennaro smiled and flicked his head at Gil, indicating it was time for them to leave. My brother gave me a nod and retreated towards the door. I'd speak to him in private at some point, but not now. I had Enzo to deal with.

"Don't disappoint me, Zayn," my father said before he left with my brother.

I rubbed my chin and scowled. Typical. Comes here to give me orders and leaves without a fucking care in the world once

I'd agreed to them. As if I was actually going to look for a woman to marry to satisfy his fucking backwards worldview.

"Fuck," I growled as Arlo met my eyes. "Go make sure Enzo isn't trying to flirt his way into Liza's knickers, will you? I don't trust the little shit."

Arlo gave me a dark look, but he nodded and left. I couldn't blame him. He had his reasons for disliking my youngest brother. Liza was my general manager for the club. She did a damn fine job and wouldn't take my brother seriously, but I didn't want her to have to put up with him. Enzo would flirt with anyone for shits and giggles, even a woman twice her age. The fucker was notorious for it.

I stood. Thinking about what my father said could wait. I needed to go see my pet. My feet carried me over to the door to my private rooms. Ripping it open, I stepped inside to find Ari curled up on the sofa, staring into the distance. She jolted when she heard me come in. Her chestnut eyes met mine, widening slightly.

Before I could say a word, she slid off the sofa and came over to me. I watched her drop to her knees at my feet. Her fingers brushed over the collar before she picked up the leash and held it out for me to take.

I had expected her to ask me why I'd taken so long or give me attitude, but this?

This was everything, and so much more.

TEN

Zayn

My hand reached out, taking the black metal chain from her small fingers. I slid my own into the handle, gripping it as I watched her pupils dilate. Did she like the collar? I'd put it on her as a punishment, but something about her demeanour told me she wasn't averse to wearing it. I could imagine a delicate little chain around her neck, one she'd never take off.

You're mine now, Tink. I don't think I can let you go free.

"Sir?"

"Mmm?"

"Are you okay?"

Her words startled me. Why would she care about me? She should be more worried about herself.

"Yes."

The light in her eyes dimmed at my lie. I wasn't okay after my father's visit. Seeing him always angered me, but Ari didn't need to know about my internal conflict. How I wanted to bury my father in an unmarked grave after throttling the life out of the man for what he'd done to my mother. It was more than he deserved.

"Can I do anything to make you feel better?"

My hand clenched around the leash. She hadn't bought my lie.

"*You* want to make *me* feel better?"

She nodded.

"Why, little fairy?"

Ari looked up at me with something akin to understanding.

"Families can be… taxing."

My eyes narrowed.

"What did you hear?"

"Nothing, I swear. You just became agitated when Gennaro's name was mentioned, and I thought…" She dropped her gaze to the floor. "I thought maybe his appearance bothered you in some way." Her hands fidgeted in her lap. "I'm sorry, I spoke out of turn."

Leaning down, I tucked my fingers under her chin and forced her to meet my eyes.

"You're a perceptive little thing, aren't you?"

Her cheeks flushed.

"I like to observe people… and things."

I cocked my head to the side.

"And make assumptions."

She waved her hands, looking stricken all of a sudden.

"No, not at all. I'm a photographer. At least, it's what I want to be."

I released her face and straightened. She liked to take pictures. I had no idea. Then again, I'd never asked the girl what she was into. It hadn't occurred to me until now.

"You like to document things."

"I guess so. You can learn a lot from a photograph, a snapshot or a moment in time immortalised in print. That's what one of my lecturers at uni taught me." She shrugged. "I only graduated a few months ago."

University. The mention of her graduating reminded me she was only twenty-two. Still so fucking young. Completely unsuitable for me in every way, shape and form, yet perfect all the same.

"You've had trouble finding work."

"Yeah, not exactly the easiest industry to get into. I'll work it out at some point... when this is all over."

Her eyes went to her lap again, fingers curling around her clothes.

This would never be over. I was keeping her, but I wouldn't let her know that. Dashing her hopes of escaping me one day would be counterproductive. I don't know when I decided to throw my best intentions out of the window, but I couldn't bring myself to care. Not when my father had pissed me off beyond belief with his marriage bullshit. Fuck him. I didn't even believe in marriage at this point. He saw to that. Him and my fucked up family.

Gennaro would go ape-shit if he knew about my deal with Arianna. My father would tell me to give her back to Bennett.

Not fucking happening. She's mine.

I internally shook myself. It was something to think about later.

"Indeed." I tugged on her leash. "Stand up."

She scrambled to obey, forcing me to hide a smile. Someone didn't want to be punished again today. I caught her face between my fingers. Her cheeks coloured slightly as if my proximity affected her. Fuck, she affected me. I wanted her close. Needed it like air. I didn't know how she'd dug her way under my skin in such a short amount of time.

"How are you feeling after yesterday?"

She frowned.

"Yesterday?"

"About your uncle."

"Oh." Her face clouded over. "I'm trying not to think about it." She rubbed her chest. "How do you reconcile the fact you're a killer now? Like I killed someone. He deserved it, but I can't stop picturing his dead eyes staring up at me in shock. And the blood… all the blood."

The way she trembled had me pulling her against my chest. Ari shivered in my hold and gripped my shirt between her fists.

"He was touching me in places I didn't want him to, saying things I never thought I'd hear out of his mouth. I needed it to stop. Had to make it end." Her hands clasped my shirt tighter. "I never want anyone to touch me like that again, not when I don't want it, when I have no control."

I stroked her curly hair, wishing I could take away her pain. I wanted to erase all the hurt she was experiencing. I wanted to smash the cunt's skull in. He would have died worse if I'd got my hands on the sick fuck.

"Where did he touch you?"

"I can't."

"Tell me."

I rubbed her back with my other hand, reassuring Ari she was safe. She could tell me the truth. I'd already covered up her crime. Not like I would expose what she'd done to anyone else.

"He put his mouth against my neck, squeezed my breasts and… and his other hand was between my legs," she whispered. "I didn't give him a chance to put his hands under my clothes. My dad made me carry a knife for protection, so I stabbed Justin in the neck again and again. I… I wanted him to die after he told me he betrayed Dad. I wanted him to burn when he touched me. I'm not sorry he's dead. He deserved worse."

Hearing the fear followed by the vehemence in her voice had me clenching my jaw.

"No one is going to touch you that way again. Not without your consent. I won't allow it."

Ari burrowed her face deeper into my chest. I could feel her breathing me in.

"Are you okay with me touching you?"

She pulled away and blinked. I don't know why I asked. She appeared deeply distressed by what had occurred between her and Justin. I needed to know she wasn't uncomfortable now.

"Yes… I mean, I agreed to this, didn't I?" She made a face before her features cleared. "You might be super intimidating, but I'm not afraid of you."

"No?"

Her eyebrow curled upwards.

"Are you going to touch me inappropriately when I don't want it?"

"It depends on what you mean by inappropriately."

She released my shirt and put her hand on my chest instead. My skin tingled at the contact.

"Sexually," she murmured, her eyes intent on mine.

"No. I already told you I'm not interested in that."

Liar. You fucking liar. She knows you're lying and so do you.

"Then I have nothing to be afraid of."

"And if you do want it, Tink? What then?"

"Isn't that a moot point when you don't?"

"Answer the question."

I needed to know. Had to be sure I wasn't alone in this fucked up attraction. My eyes tracked the way her tongue ran across her bottom lip.

"I'd tell you."

It wasn't the exact answer I wanted, but I'd take it. Stepping away before I did something stupid, I tugged on her leash. She followed me back into my office without saying a word and knelt next to my chair without complaint. I took out a bottle of water and a small bag of sweet and salty popcorn from my desk. Setting them down in front of her, I took my seat.

"For you," I murmured before turning to my screen.

Last night, I'd questioned her at dinner about what she ate and told Arlo to make sure I had adequate snacks for her in my office. He'd done it, but I was pretty sure he wasn't pleased with being tasked with making sure I had everything I needed for Ari.

I watched her pick up the bottle of water from the corner of my eye. She was just reaching for the popcorn when my office door opened. Arlo walked in, looking like he was about to blow a fuse. He paused when he noticed Ari next to me. Turning, he shut the door and let out a frustrated breath before proceeding to talk to me in Italian so Ari wouldn't understand what was being said.

"I swear I'm going to kill your brother."

"What did he do?"

I did him the courtesy of replying in Italian. Whatever he had to say about Enzo wasn't for my little pet's ears.

"He asked me how Lissa is, as if he deserves to know after he left without saying a fucking word to her."

Alissa was Arlo's younger sister. She and Enzo had been friends since childhood, as they were of a similar age. I paid their friendship no mind, but Arlo couldn't stand it, given Enzo's reputation.

"He doesn't give a shit about anyone but himself. I swear, Zayn, if he doesn't stay the fuck away from her… I won't be responsible for my actions."

My attention went to Ari, who was struggling to open her little bag of popcorn. I put my hand down, indicating she should give it to me. She handed it over, looking up at me with a grateful expression on her face. I opened the bag as Arlo continued raging on about Enzo. I patted my leg, keeping a hold of the bag. Ari frowned, so I reached out and took her arm, pulling her towards me. She came willingly, crawling into my lap and settling herself in it. I stroked her arm as confusion flitted across her features.

"She was miserable when he left, crying all the time about how he'd gone and hadn't told her anything about it. I don't want him seeing her. He'll only upset Lissa again," Arlo raged on.

I dug my hand in the popcorn, bringing some out and offering it to Ari. She squirmed in my lap for a moment but opened her mouth to let me feed her. I gave her some more, watching her chew. Her cheeks were bright red. A sense of contentment washed over me. Taking care of her made me… happy.

"What do you want me to do about Enzo?" I said to Arlo, interrupting his diatribe against my brother.

Arlo paused in his pacing and levelled his gaze on me. His eyes narrowed at me feeding Ari, but he didn't make a comment about it.

"He won't listen to you, even if you tell him to stay away from Lissa."

"He's a little shit, but I'll put the fear of God into him if I have to."

Arlo snorted.

"Did you put it in her?"

He indicated Ari with his head, his eyes going to the collar around her neck.

"Perhaps," I mused, giving Ari more popcorn.

He shook his head.

"Do you need me for anything?" he asked a moment later.

"No, just make sure Enzo leaves and doesn't bother any of the girls. If he goes near Remi, inform me immediately."

Arlo gave me a nod and smirked before he left the room. He gave me enough shit about Remi as it was.

I turned back to Ari, who was watching me with a bemused expression on her face.

"Yes?"

"Why are you feeding me when I'm perfectly capable of doing it myself?"

I set the bag down in her lap.

"I want to."

"That's not an explanation."

I smiled and gathered up some more popcorn.

"It's the only one you're getting."

She opened her mouth, allowing me to continue feeding her. I didn't have another explanation. I just wanted to. It was in my nature to take care of my possessions.

Before I could remove my hand from near her mouth, Ari's tongue darted out and brushed over the pad of my forefinger. My breath caught in my throat at the contact. She watched me with a rather deviant look in her eyes as she licked my thumb, cleaning the lingering popcorn taste from my skin. I didn't stop her. How the fuck could I?

I didn't know if she was doing this to wind me up or to prove I'd lied about my interest in her. It was working. My dick had certainly got the message.

"Tinkerbell." Her nickname came out all breathy and hushed from my lips.

She leant back and chewed her mouthful before giving me a smile.

"I didn't want you to have sticky fingers, sir."

Picking up the bag from her lap, she stuffed more in her mouth, daring me to say something.

Fuck. You are a little brat and I like it way more than I should.

I knew she was going to be trouble. Knew it deep in my fucking soul. And I wanted it. Fuck, did I want it… maybe even needed it. My life had been stagnant until Arianna Michaelson had shown up covered in blood. Now I was in hell… and I didn't care. All I cared about was keeping her. And never letting go.

ELEVEN

Arianna

It had been far too quiet for the past few days in Zayn's house. We hadn't returned to the club. Instead, he'd been ensconced in his office ninety per cent of the time. The rest was spent making sure I ate, went to bed when he told me to and obeying his rules to the letter. I swear the man was the strictest person I'd ever met. This was how I imagined what being in the military was like. Made me question what madness possessed me to come to him for help. Then I pictured my father's disappointed face and was reminded of what I had to lose.

I sighed as I walked along the hallway towards the kitchen to get a drink. Zayn hadn't given me a great deal to do, so I was bored as hell. Maybe I should have told him, but disturbing the man was like taking your life into your own hands. I might not be afraid of Zayn, but it didn't make him any less intimidating.

Voices filtered through the slightly open doorway of his office. I paused, having heard Arlo arriving earlier. He didn't come and say hello to me. In fact, if I was in the room, he'd speak Italian to Zayn so I wouldn't understand what was being said. It was mildly frustrating being the only one in the room who wasn't privy to what was going on.

My ears picked up a voice I knew all too well. My father's, but I couldn't make out the words properly. What the hell was my father doing here? He couldn't be. I needed to know what was going on. I stepped closer to the doorway, pressing myself against the wall outside.

"You saying McGovern ain't got her?" came my father's voice.

"That's what he said, fam."

I recognised the second voice as one of my father's men, Jamal.

"Don't trust him."

"Swear down, he ain't got Ari."

"Then who the fuck has, huh? My fucking daughter is gone. And Justin, where the fuck is he? Got to be McGovern. Them Peckham boys got my girl. I ain't standing for it."

"What you going to do?"

I heard the slap of a hand on a table.

"We're going to make them pay for taking Ari. No one fucks with my family, you feel me."

My hand went to my mouth, holding back all the words wanting to spill from it. I'd known running would cause trouble, but I didn't imagine Dad would try to blame my disappearance on McGovern. It was exactly what I had been trying to avoid. If things escalated, people would end up dead. It's what happened in gang wars. The knives would be out. Not to mention the illegal guns they'd get their hands on. My father owned two of them himself. I wasn't meant to know about them, but I'd seen him with them one day, so he'd ended up showing me how to use one without allowing me to hold it. No matter how much he tried to keep me out of his gang life, I was all too aware of what went on. Dad only told me what he thought was important to keep me safe and protected.

"That's all he managed to get," came Arlo's voice.

"Did he say anything else about what Bennett is planning?" Zayn replied, his deep voice sending a shiver down my spine.

"Not yet."

"Find out more for me. We need to monitor it in case it escalates."

"If he goes after McGovern, it will start a war."

"You think I don't know that? Get me more information before it does."

The shuffling of feet made me tense up.

"You going to tell her about it?"

Zayn didn't respond immediately. I held my breath. This involved me. I'd come to Zayn for protection and to prevent a war. My disappearance had only made it worse.

"No."

"Fair enough."

The word no echoed in my ear. What the fuck? Why wouldn't he tell me? I had a right to know. I had a right to be involved. This was my family. My life.

Before I knew what I was doing, I shoved open the door and stormed into Zayn's office. He was standing by the fireplace. Arlo was nearby, holding out his phone as if that was how they'd listened to the recording of my father.

"Not going to tell me my father is planning a fucking war over me?"

Zayn turned his head slightly and met my eyes.

"Arianna."

There was a warning note to his voice, but I ignored it, slapping my chest instead as I spoke.

"I deserve to know what's happening with my father. He's my family. Why wouldn't you tell me about this?"

I watched him straighten and turn to me fully. Arlo tucked the phone into his pocket, but his face remained as stoic as Zayn's.

"This is business. Something I have explicitly told you has nothing to do with you."

I took a step towards Zayn.

"Business? My dad starting a war over me is business?"

"Yes."

I wanted to slap his fucking face if only to provoke some emotion out of him. His voice was utterly calm. Too calm.

"I came to you for help to make sure he didn't go to war. You cannot possibly think I will allow him to go after McGovern over me."

He put a hand in his pocket.

"You're not allowing anything."

"Are you going to stop it?"

He looked me over, blinking slowly as he did it.

"Right now? No. I'm not going to do anything."

I swear I misheard him. He couldn't sit back and do nothing. I knew my father. He would act. I was his everything. His precious daughter, who he fought to keep out of his world. I was in it anyway. I'd killed his brother and run to a man I shouldn't have to hide the truth. Tears sprung behind my eyes. My fists clenched as I blinked them away.

I would not cry. I was not going to cry.

You are strong. You're going to do what's necessary to stop this.

"If my dad goes to war, he may not come back from it. Everything I did would be for nothing. This shit with you, it would be for nothing. I won't let him die for me."

Zayn stepped towards me. He stared down at me with those terrifyingly calm, almost black eyes of his.

"What does that mean, Arianna?"

"It… it…" I faltered, trying to find where the fuck my courage went.

It ran away with his closeness, turning all of my senses against me. Made me want to burrow myself in his stupid chest and cry my eyes out over the thought of my father dead, shot in the fucking street like an animal. It's what McGovern and his gang would do. Execute my father. They would do it in a heartbeat if provoked.

I hated myself for the urge. I hated myself even more because I knew my next words would only end with me being punished for my outburst. Somehow, I couldn't find it in me to care.

"It means I'll go back to him and stop this madness," I whispered because my voice was a traitor against Zayn and his intimidating presence.

Zayn leant closer.

"You know I can't let you do that. It's not part of the deal, Arianna, not when you're mine."

"I don't want to be yours."

Why the hell did you say that?

He reached up and tucked a curl behind my ear. It was as if I was a small child trying to tell off a grown man and failing miserably. That's how he was looking at me. And I absolutely downright hated it.

"Yes, you do, my fiery little fairy. You might not want to admit it, but we both know you need me."

I slapped his hand away from my face and glared at him.

"Don't touch me," I hissed. "I'm not your fucking toy, pet, or possession, as you so like to call me. And I don't care what you do, I'm leaving."

Zayn merely stared at me as if daring me to walk out the door. We both knew I wouldn't. I had no idea where the fuck I was. I had no money, and I was pretty sure Zayn had my phone.

"Are you quite done with this little… tantrum?"

I wanted to stamp on his foot… no, I wanted to knee him in the fucking balls for that. This was not a tantrum. I was scared for my father, the only family I had left in the world after I'd stabbed my fucking uncle in the neck. My mother was a mystery to me, so I didn't consider her family.

"Calling my concern for my father a tantrum? Real fucking nice, Zayn. What's next? You going to call me a bad little girl and send me to my room without dinner?"

Zayn's eyes flicked over to Arlo, who I had all but forgotten was in the room.

"I'll catch up with you later. I need to deal with this little issue… alone."

"Yes, boss," came Arlo's response, followed by his retreating footsteps.

The front door slammed a minute later. I swallowed hard when Zayn met my eyes again.

"You've broken the rules, Tinkerbell."

He didn't move to touch me.

"If you aren't on your knees in the next ten seconds, I'm going to have to increase your punishment tenfold and you're already about to feel the effects of your disobedience quite severely. I doubt you want to add to it."

I don't know why I stayed where I was. Why I didn't drop to the floor like he'd told me to. There were far more important things at stake than his rules and this fucked up game.

"I need to protect my father."

"You need to do what you're told."

He was pissing me off now. I hated his rules. Hated how he wasn't taking my concerns seriously.

"Or what? Huh? What the fuck would you do if I walked out and went to my dad?"

"You wouldn't make it out the front door. I don't allow my possessions to leave without permission. As for what I'm going to do now, well… it's time you learnt a lesson."

The very next thing I knew, I'd been shoved to the ground, landing hard on my knees. Zayn kept his hand on my shoulder, making me stay down.

"You will stay there unless you want me to treat you like a naughty little girl and spank you until you're crying. That's not really my thing, but if it's what you desire, then I will."

My cheeks burnt at the thought of him bending me over his knee and punishing me with his tattooed hand. A hand I preferred wrapped around my throat.

What the fuck? Where did that come from?

I didn't have time to process it because Zayn straightened and walked around me. I turned my head to watch him approach his desk and pick up that fucking collar and leash from it. He hadn't made me wear it since the club. I didn't like how it made me feel about him. Right now, I wanted to hate everything the man represented. I wanted to, but I couldn't... because a part of me wanted him to punish me.

He brought it over and held it out to me.

"Put it on."

I took it from him, our fingers brushing together. The contact made my skin heat. Damn him for making me want this. Making me crave something I didn't even understand.

I buckled the leather collar around my throat and handed him the leash.

"Take your clothes off."

"What?"

"Did I not make myself clear?"

"Why do you—"

"They are a privilege you do not currently deserve."

The very idea of him seeing me naked again had me wanting to hide. Being stared at by a man who claimed to have no sexual interest in you was unnerving. I didn't believe him when he told me that for a second time. Not when I could feel the tension between us. It made the air thicken, and it grew harder to get oxygen into my lungs.

My shaky fingers rose to my top. Zayn released the leash so I could pull the top off my body without it getting tangled. He fisted it again the moment the fabric dropped to the floor. I heaved out a breath, fingers working the clasp of my bra. My skin rose up in goosebumps when it joined my top. I refused to look up at him. I didn't want to see the emotionless expression he often wore staring down at me.

My jeans came next, followed by my socks and underwear. I knelt again and bowed my head, my hands fisted on my thighs to stop myself from doing something stupid.

"Crawl to my chair."

Somehow I managed to raise up on my hands and knees. I let him lead me over to his desk. He sat behind it, leaving me to kneel beside him.

"Give me your hand."

I raised it up, still refusing to meet his eyes. Zayn snapped cold metal around my wrist before he attached the other end to the arm of his chair. He'd threatened to handcuff me to his desk at one point. I shouldn't be surprised he was a man of his word.

"You're going to stay there for the rest of the afternoon. When it is dinner time, you will sit with me and submit to being fed. Then, when it is bedtime, you will crawl upstairs because you aren't permitted to walk. You're going to stay with me since you've threatened to leave. Clearly, you can't be trusted and until you can, you will sleep on the floor where I can see you."

My head whipped up to his. He wasn't even looking at me, but I couldn't stop staring at him. I was going to stay in his bedroom. *His* bedroom… with him… naked.

My thighs squeezed together as I tried to deny how it made me feel.

How the fuck was I going to survive that? I'd never been in his room. And now I would see it, but not under the circumstances I secretly wanted to. No, this would be a punishment on a whole other level. One I was not looking forward to… at all.

TWELVE

Zayn

This fucking girl was driving me crazy. And not in a good way. More like in the 'I wanted to gag her so she couldn't provoke me' type of way. Her mouth with those damn full lips of hers had me thinking things I shouldn't be. Had me wanting things I had no business even considering.

My eyes flicked down to the floor of my bedroom, eyeing the dark shape on the rug. I wasn't completely heartless. She had a blanket and a pillow, but she wasn't allowed clothes. Something I regretted dictating given the constant battle I had seeing her that way. Especially when I'd made her sit in my lap at dinner and fed her by hand. She hadn't appreciated it at all, but she took her punishment. She knew I would make it worse if she kept breaking the rules.

Having her naked in my lap had been a mistake. I had been so close to giving into the urges coursing through my veins. I kept it together. There was no other choice. This was about teaching her a lesson. It did not include touching her inappropriately. I couldn't without her expressed permission, anyway, having given her my word. I didn't want her thinking I'd try to take things she wasn't willing to give like her uncle.

The cunt was lucky he was no longer alive. The more time I spent with Ari, the more possessive I became over her. I couldn't let her leave. She was *mine*, even if she was currently making my life difficult.

You wanted a challenge, didn't you? You wanted a change from all the fucking boredom. You've got it right here. She's it and you can't get away from it now.

Ari thought I would allow her father to provoke McGovern into war over her. No one wanted a war. Not when it would bring problems to my door. Bennett wasn't just a lowlife gang leader, he was in business with both me and my father. It wasn't common knowledge, of course. He wanted more than just to run shit in Hackney. It was about securing a future for him and his family beyond the petty squabbles between boroughs. The one man who could make it happen was my father. Bennett wasn't a stupid man, but his daughter was his everything. He would do anything to protect her.

I didn't know what happened to her mother nor why he was the one to raise her, but I knew Ari was his world. He always talked about how proud he was of his little firecracker. To me, Ari always seemed more like a little fairy with her wings clipped by the environment she'd been born into. Didn't matter if she'd been sent away for school. You could take the girl out of Hackney, but you couldn't erase the fact she was born into the underworld.

It was something I could never escape. Neither could she.

My problem now was Ari wouldn't forgive me if her father got himself killed. I couldn't let that happen. I wanted to keep her, not make her hate me for life.

In order to protect her and him, I needed more information. I needed it all before I could make a move. So much was at stake here beyond just me and her. If I pulled the trigger and intervened, I would get questioned by my father. Something I didn't need under any circumstances. Especially now he'd made it clear he wasn't going to leave me to my own devices any longer. He wanted me to step up. Pity he didn't realise I had no incentive to until now. Until… her.

There was one major thing I didn't understand. Why had her uncle intended to give her to McGovern? It made no sense for Justin to be disloyal to his family. At least, not from what I had heard about him and his relationship with his brother. It had niggled at me since the day she'd showed up in my office. What the hell was Justin's game?

Ari shifted, pulling the blanket higher over her bare shoulders. I hadn't heard her breathing even out since I'd turned the lights off. She wasn't asleep. It seemed both of us were suffering from an overactive mind. At least, I assumed it was why she couldn't sleep other than being uncomfortable on the floor.

"Arianna."

"Yes, sir?" came her soft voice almost immediately.

"Come here."

"Why?"

I almost shook my head. She knew the rules. Obey me without hesitation.

"Now, Arianna."

103

She was slow to move, but she did. Ari kept the blanket wrapped around her as she stood and came over to the bed. I hadn't laid down, merely sat up against the headboard with the covers pulled over my legs.

"Sit."

I waved my hand at the end of the bed. She planted herself right at the edge, as far away from me as she could get. It made me smile. Silly girl. I wasn't going to hurt her. She'd told me not to touch her earlier. I'd made her angry enough to show the fire burning beneath her skin. I would never tell her this, but it gave me a thrill to see her so riled up. It made me angry too. I couldn't help the way I equal parts loved and hated how it turned me on to watch my little fairy stamp her feet and demand things from me. As if she was in charge here. I owned her, not the other way around.

"I need to ask you something."

"Then ask," she responded, looking down at the covers rather than at me.

"What exactly did your uncle say to you about Derek McGovern?"

She flinched, fingers curling around the ends of the blanket to hold it against her tense frame.

"I don't want to talk about that night."

"You need to tell me why he was going to give you to Derek."

"Why?"

"Look at me."

Ari's eyes flicked up to mine. We couldn't fully see each other in the dark, but I needed her attention on me. To know how fucking serious I was.

"I know it's difficult for you, but this is important. Answer the question."

"What difference does it make if I tell you? Not as if you're willing to do anything about my father starting a war."

My hand clenched into a fist by my side. The only sign of the way her defiant attitude affected me.

"There's one very important lesson you clearly haven't learnt about our world, and that is knowledge is power. It may not seem important to you why I need to know what your uncle had to gain from giving you to Derek, but I assure you, it is."

Ari fidgeted for a long moment before she let out a sigh. Her eyes lowered as if she couldn't bear the thought of maintaining eye contact.

"Derek doesn't care about a war with my dad, I don't think… not really. He wants… he wants… me."

"Wants you how?"

She scoffed.

"Like in a creepy 'I want to lock you in my basement and make you fall in love with me' sort of way. I mean, he's never said that, but the way he looks at me…"

She didn't need to fill in the blanks. I was well aware of the type of shit a man like McGovern would do to someone like Arianna. None of it would be good or consensual.

"You've met him often, then?"

"No… not outside of him showing up on the estate to piss my father off."

"Then how do you know he doesn't want a war?"

"Justin told me Derek doesn't care if my father comes after him. I'm what he wants."

The cunt wasn't going to lay a finger on her. I would kill him first.

You can't go around killing gang leaders, Zayn, not without repercussions.

I knew that. I fucking knew and yet I still wanted to wring his goddamn neck for even thinking he could have my little fairy.

"And Justin? What did he have to gain by betraying your father?"

"He didn't say."

So, McGovern wanted her, but I was no closer to understanding why Justin would be complicit in his plans.

"I still don't fully understand why you came to me rather than your father with this."

Ari stood up, clutching the blanket to her chest. This conversation was making her uncomfortable, but I needed her cards out on the table to keep her safe.

"I already told you, I panicked."

"I don't think that's why, Tink."

She paced away.

"It doesn't matter why. All that matters is I did." One of her hands fell to her side and clenched into a fist. "I want to change the terms of our deal."

I almost scoffed. What a way to change the subject.

"To what, exactly?"

I knew what she wanted, but it didn't hurt to ask.

"I want you to stop the war before it happens."

I threw the covers off my legs and stood up.

"That's an awfully big ask, Arianna. What on earth do you think you have to offer me in return?"

Her frame trembled beneath the blanket. She turned and faced me. Her curls framed her face in the low light. I could see her teeth digging into her bottom lip as if she was contemplating something bad.

"What you keep telling me you don't want."

I swallowed when she dropped the blanket, letting it pool at her feet.

"I don't believe you don't want me, sir. And before you deny it again, I've felt evidence to the contrary."

For a moment, I didn't say a single word. No, I just stared at the girl like she'd lost her fucking mind. Then I strode towards her, gripped her by her curly hair and turned her face up towards me.

"You expect me to believe you'd barter your body to stop a war?"

"I'm already yours, so what difference does it make if we take it one step further?"

I leant closer. After everything she'd told me, this didn't seem like her at all. She didn't want anyone touching her without her consent. She wanted to choose who had access to her. Giving herself to me like a fucking payment went against everything I knew about this girl.

"Why?"

"I'd do anything to protect my father."

Her voice shook on her words, leading me to believe she didn't want this, but she was stupid enough to put her father's life above her own. This fucking girl would be the death of me.

"You shouldn't be offering yourself up to anyone like this without a fucking thought for what they might do to you if you did."

"You won't hurt me."

My grip on her hair tightened, making her wince.

"I wouldn't be so sure about that if I were you."

"I'm not scared of you."

"So you keep telling me."

She reached for me, her small hand landing on my chest. I was wearing a t-shirt, but it felt like her touch burnt through it. Like it was on my bare skin. Maybe it was wishful thinking on my part, wanting her naked body pressed to mine. But not like this. I didn't want it like this. Not to mention I couldn't touch her intimately. It would be wrong and so fucking forbidden.

"Why would I put my life and my safety into your hands if I thought you were going to hurt me? I'm not stupid, even if you think I am."

"I never said you were stupid, but this shit right here? This is stupidity at its finest. I don't make deals involving sex. I'm not going to fuck you in exchange for making sure your father doesn't get himself killed."

Tears filled those chestnut eyes. I was angry over her demand, but this didn't require anger or rage. Ari's fragility was punching a fucking hole in my chest. I had to be delicate with her.

"I understand you're scared for him, Tinkerbell, but this… this is not the way to go about asking me for something." My grip on her hair loosened and I placed my other hand on top of hers on my chest. "I don't want a war any more than you do. It's bad for business."

Her lip trembled and tears streaked down her cheeks.

"I'm sorry, sir. I'm so sorry," she whispered, choking out the words.

I tugged her against my chest and held her close, allowing her to purge her emotions.

"Shh, it's okay, my little fairy. It's okay."

She clung to me, sobbing silently into my t-shirt. I don't know how long the two of us stood there. Didn't matter as long as she felt better after crying all over me.

"I'm so scared," she murmured after she'd settled down. "He's all I have. I just want him to be safe, but he can't be… not in this world."

She rubbed her face against my t-shirt. I didn't ask her to stop. It was already damp from her tears. She might as well use it as her tissue at this point. Ari pulled away and stared up at me.

"I don't know how to stop disobeying you."

I almost smiled at her statement. Instead, I reached up and stroked her curls.

"Fear makes funny creatures of us all."

"Even you?"

"I'd be lying if I said there's nothing in this world for me to be afraid of. Everyone fears something."

Images of my mother laying in a bed on a fucking ventilator because she couldn't breathe on her own flitted across my mind. My father had a lot to answer for. Too much. And my inability to go against him was the only thing plaguing me in this world.

Ari nodded before extracting herself from my embrace. I watched her lower herself to her knees in front of me. My breath caught when she planted her hands on the floor and bent her head, exhaling when she kissed the top of my foot.

"I'm sorry for everything, sir. Please forgive me."

When she straightened, I put my hand out to her. She took it, allowing me to pull her to her feet before I swept her up in my arms. She let out a squeak when I carried her over to my bed and set her down on it. I pulled tissues from the box on my bedside table and mopped up her face. Discarding them in the bin, I then pulled my t-shirt off and got into bed next to her, yanking the covers over both of us.

"What are you doing?" she whispered when I tugged her into my arms, tucking her up against my chest.

"Taking care of you."

I think she was stumped because she didn't say another word. I smiled to myself as her breathing evened out over the next few minutes and she fell asleep. If I was a sensible man, I wouldn't have put her in bed with me, but I didn't care. Every part of me wanted her close, where I could keep an eye on the damn girl. She was giving me whiplash with her ever-changing moods and demeanour.

I liked it… even though I shouldn't.

I shouldn't like her at all.

Yet… I did.

Too fucking much.

It was the only way I could explain why I'd let her get away with so much right now. And why I'd forgiven her for it all already. The most fucked up part of it all was… I think I always would.

I'd forgive her.

Every. Single. Time.

Arianna Michaelson had become important to me. I would protect her with my life. And I would stop this fucking war from happening, no matter what it took.

THIRTEEN

Arianna

Waking up in *his* bed had me feeling extremely embarrassed by my behaviour last night. Practically throwing myself at Zayn to save my father was a terrible idea. One I hadn't really thought out beforehand. It just happened. Mostly out of fear for my father's safety. Zayn hadn't denied wanting me this time when I'd offered myself to him. He'd merely said he didn't make deals involving sex.

What if it had nothing to do with a deal? What if I just wanted it because for some fucked up reason I want him?

I had to admit the truth to myself. Everything about Zayn Villetti was attractive to me. His deep voice. The intense look in his eyes when they were on me. The way he took care of me despite my pushing and testing his patience. I even liked the way he punished me for it.

I didn't give a shit if he was twelve years older than me and I'd known him most of my life. My father would have something to say about me being with a man who was only a few years younger than him. A man who was permanently tied to the criminal underworld due to who his father was. One who had a reputation for ruthlessness. Who owned a sex club where the rich and powerful could indulge in their most depraved fantasies away from prying eyes. None of what Dad said would be good or positive. And yet… I wanted Zayn, regardless.

Clearly, I had lost all sense of self-preservation when it came to him. I may have threatened to leave yesterday, but the very idea of walking away now had my heart in knots. Not to mention I needed to uphold my side of our deal. I wasn't the type of person who ignored her responsibilities. Dad had drilled it into my head from a young age. Loyalty. Responsibility. Being true to yourself. Our world wasn't an easy one, but you didn't let down those who relied on you no matter what.

It's what my uncle had done. Let down both Dad and me. I couldn't go to my father with Justin's betrayal. It would destroy him. And me? Well, I was afraid of letting my dad down too. Afraid of what he might do to me for killing his brother. I knew for a fact Dad trusted Justin with his life. Would he believe me over a dead man? I didn't truly know the answer. It's why I ran away to Zayn instead of facing my dad.

Stupid really, but I couldn't take it back. Zayn was right last night. Fear made us do things we wouldn't consider under normal circumstances. Like making deals with mafia princes to become their pets in exchange for safety. Like offering their bodies to save someone they loved.

The thing Zayn didn't know was I actually wanted him to lay his hands all over me. I desired more. If I didn't know myself so well, I would have thought it had to do with him being so forbidden. It had nothing to do with that. I wasn't stupid or blind to my own desires or needs. And it certainly wasn't because of our deal. It was him. All of his dark and dangerous self had me enthralled in a way I'd never been about another person before.

Zayn had shown me a different side to him than the mask he wore as the mafia prince and owner of Desecration. He had cared for me more in the time I'd been here than at anyone else at any other point in my life, even if he was strict with his rules and doled out punishments. He held me when I cried without complaint or hesitation. I never once thought he would be capable of such things. To be caring and patient. To see to all my needs without me having to ask.

I didn't think I'd seen the true Zayn underneath his layers, but maybe one day, if I stuck around long enough, I would.

Opening my eyes, I peered out of the covers. I'd felt him leave earlier. The room was empty of his presence. I didn't know if I felt relief at being alone or not. Maybe it was better. I could feel my embarrassment over his rejection alone without his prying eyes sensing my every thought.

His room was sleek and modern. The bed was fucking massive with black sheets. Unsurprising for a man with midnight black hair and matching eyes. I sat up, clutching the covers around my naked body. My eyes spied a note sitting on the bedside table. I reached out, plucking it from its perch. Zayn's handwriting had me jealous all over again by the beautiful cursive lines.

*Wash, dress, and meet me downstairs when
you wake up.*

At the end of the bed, there was a pile of clothes for me. I set the note down and climbed out of his bed. He had a bathroom off his bedroom. It was all grey slate and dark tiles. I took a shower, careful not to wet my hair, before dressing and making his bed. Everything in his house was neat and orderly. I didn't think leaving his room in a state would be met with anything but another round of discipline.

And why do I like the sound of that?

Cursing myself for wanting a man like Zayn, I wandered out of his room and into the one he'd given me to sort my hair out. I wrestled it into two braids down the sides of my head, tying them off at the ends.

As I walked out of the bedroom, I heard the doorbell go. My feet carried me to the stairs. I ducked down behind the bannisters when I spied Zayn opening the front door. I held back a gasp when I saw his father, Gennaro, and two men on the doorstep. Zayn's back stiffened when he took them in.

"What are you doing here?"

The irritation in Zayn's voice was pronounced. He clearly hadn't been expecting Gennaro.

"That's no way to greet your father, Zayn," came Gennaro's clipped response.

"Hello, Father. Might I inquire why you have graced me with your presence?"

I almost snorted at the sarcasm in his tone, but put a hand over my mouth instead, watching Gennaro's eyes narrow on his son.

TYRANT

"We have things to discuss."

Zayn let out a heavy sigh and pulled the door open wider, stepping back to allow his father and men inside. I'd seen those two before when my father met with him. Gennaro's bodyguards. I didn't know their names. Zayn shut the door behind the three of them. The tension in his shoulders had me wanting to soothe his stress away. A stupid urge, but one I couldn't help all the same. A part of me wanted to care for Zayn the way he did for me.

Zayn leant against the wall next to the stairs. I had a feeling he knew I was there, but he wasn't going to alert his father to the fact. It would end in disaster for us both if he did.

"Well, what is it?"

"Bennett's daughter is missing."

I stiffened, my eyes on Zayn, who didn't react to his statement.

"Is she?"

Gennaro nodded, giving his son the once over. I was used to Zayn's calm in the face of chaos by now, having been on the receiving end of it. His lack of reaction annoyed me all the same. I wanted to see him rattled.

"Did he tell you?" Zayn asked when Gennaro didn't offer up anything else.

"No. My man on the inside did."

It didn't surprise me to learn that was how he found out. After hearing the recording Zayn had, I surmised he had a man on the inside too.

"If you're going to discuss this with me, then they can leave."

Zayn looked at the two bodyguards with a blank expression. They both gave Zayn a dark look, even as Gennaro waved his hand at them.

"Are you sure, boss?" the taller one asked.

"Yes. My son isn't a threat to me."

The way Zayn's eyebrows shot up at his father's statement had me biting down on my lip. Somehow, I didn't think his assessment was accurate.

The two bodyguards gave their boss a nod before leaving the house and shutting the front door behind them. Zayn waved a hand in the direction of his office. Gennaro moved towards it, turning his back to both of us. Zayn looked up at where I was hiding and gave a subtle shake of his head. It was all the confirmation I needed. He knew exactly where I was.

He walked along the hallway after his father, leaving me to creep down the stairs. I didn't care if he'd shaken his head at me, I needed to hear what his father had to say. Zayn disappeared into his office as I reached the bottom. He didn't close the door behind him. I moved silently until I could press myself against the wall by the door.

"Her disappearance isn't a good sign, Zayn," was the first thing Gennaro said. "Things in the city are already at a tipping point. This could be the final straw."

"She's not that important, is she?"

I didn't think Zayn meant it in a bad way, but I couldn't help the sinking feeling in my stomach at his words.

"In the grand scheme of things, no, but when you combine everything that's happened recently together… I fear it will get worse before it gets better."

It made little sense to me why Gennaro would be so concerned about petty gang wars when he was head of the mafia. It wasn't like he ran in the same circles as men like McGovern. My father was a different matter entirely. He wasn't meant to be involved with the Villettis.

"Will it affect your business?"

"Our business, Zayn, *fai parte della famiglia*."

"Yes, yes, I know, I'm family, but you forget I'm not involved in your business the way Gil is."

I assumed *famiglia* meant family since I'd heard Arlo say it too.

"You should be. It's your responsibility as my eldest."

"Did you really come here to discuss my role in our family? I already know what's expected of me. You've made it very clear."

Gennaro made a noise of exasperation. I shifted on my feet, trying not to make a sound.

"What Bennett does outside of our business dealings has nothing to do with us. We should let him fight his own battles."

For a long moment, there was absolute silence. I didn't know how I felt about Zayn's comment or why he'd said it.

"You're right."

"I'm always right."

Gennaro grunted, but I didn't know whether it was in agreement or not. I rolled my eyes. Of course, he thought that about himself.

"Have you thought any further about what we spoke of at your club?"

"What? About you wanting me to find a wife?"

I stifled a squeak of surprise.

"Yes."

"I haven't had time."

"You promised me you would."

I could imagine Zayn's face right now. The thought of his father commanding him to do something had me wanting to laugh. Zayn didn't seem like the type of person who would take orders from anyone, let alone ones involving his personal life. No wonder he was so pissed off by his father's presence at his club. Things were beginning to make a whole lot more sense.

"It's not even been a week. What do you expect? For me to magic a woman out of thin air?"

"Don't be impertinent."

"Then don't make unrealistic demands."

Gennaro said nothing in response. I waited, but it seemed they were having a silent standoff with each other. A part of me felt wrong about eavesdropping on another conversation I shouldn't be, but then again, they had been talking about my father to begin with.

"I told you I would find someone. Let me do it in my own time, Father."

"Fine, but don't take too long."

I heard footsteps coming towards the door. I practically ran from my spot towards the kitchen. When I reached it, I skidded across the floor and hid behind the kitchen island. Their voices carried down the hallway, but I couldn't make out what they were saying. The front door slammed shut a few minutes later.

TYRANT

I uncurled myself from my prone position on the floor and peered over the top of the counter. I was met with two disapproving eyes staring at me from the doorway where the man they belonged to leant against the frame. The man who made my heart race and skin tingle.

"Good morning, Tinkerbell. I trust you slept well."

FOURTEEN

Arianna

*O**h shit,** didn't even cut it. I'd been caught out by him. There was absolutely no way in hell I would escape disciplinary action now. Why was I always so reckless? Maybe if I stopped to think about things, I wouldn't get into so much trouble all the time. Or maybe playing with fire was my thing, especially when it came to Zayn Villetti.

Knowing I had to accept the consequences of my actions regardless of my internal turmoil over him, I straightened to my full height and rested my hands on the counter.

"I did."

"Good."

His expression and response were bland. It scared the shit out of me. I had no way of knowing what he intended to do as he shoved off the doorframe and approached me with even steps. My heart pounded in my ears, my whole body on high alert. I watched him come around the counter and stop behind me. My breath hitched when he leant his hands on the counter next to mine, effectively caging me in.

"I thought you might be a good girl for me today," he murmured in my ear, his breath dusting across my skin. "After all, you were very disobedient yesterday now, weren't you?"

"Y-y-yes, sir."

I could hardly breathe, my knees threatening to buckle. His nearness had an extreme effect on me. I'd been tucked up against his hard body last night. I'd felt the bare skin of his chest against my own. The memory of it flooded my senses.

Damn him.

He lifted his tattooed hand, curled it around my throat and pressed my body back against his. It made it worse. Parts of my body that weren't meant to throb did. They ached with a need I would rather not acknowledge after what he said to me last night.

"Did no one ever teach you it's rude to eavesdrop?"

I knew I should answer him, but my mouth was bone dry.

"What did you hear, Tink?"

His voice was low and demanding. I had no choice but to give him the truth.

"Gennaro knows I'm missing and… and he wants…"

His hand around my throat tightened.

"Wants what?"

"For you to get married," I whispered.

The thought of another woman standing by his side was like a punch to the gut. It shouldn't make a hot wave of jealousy spread down my spine and infect me with a need to claw some imaginary woman's eyes out. I had no claim to the man currently holding onto me. I had no right to feel any type of way towards him.

Did any of it stop me from wanting to spin around and tell him I wanted him to claim me? No, but I had enough self-control not to act on the urge that would only end in absolute disaster for me.

"And what do you think about that?"

I swallowed past the lump in my throat his question caused.

"Your business has nothing to do with me, so I think nothing of it."

The chuckle echoing in my ear had me flinching.

"Maybe you have been listening to the rules despite flouting them at every turn."

"Maybe I like disobeying you."

I'd muttered the words, but I knew he heard them from the way his body tensed against mine.

"You like our little games," he whispered, his voice soft against my earlobe.

"Yes."

There was no point in lying. He knew I couldn't help myself or the sick need inside me. The one desperate for someone to bend me to their will while I pushed and pushed and pushed back against them.

"My little fairy, such a troublemaker." His other hand rose and stroked down one of my braids. "Are you bored, Tink? Is that why you keep acting out?"

I nodded, but then shook my head.

"Me being bored isn't why, and you know it."

If he hadn't cottoned onto the fact I wanted to provoke some kind of emotion out of him, then it was his loss. No way I would admit it out loud.

"Ah, but you are bored."

I nodded.

"And you didn't tell me. Did you forget who takes care of your needs?"

"I didn't want to disturb you."

He expelled a breath as if my comment irritated him.

"It wouldn't be disturbing me, Ari. I want to take care of you. It's my responsibility and I take those very seriously."

"Does that include your responsibilities to your family? You didn't sound like you had any intention of carrying out your father's wishes."

Before I could stop myself, the words were out of my mouth and settling in the air between us. Why the fuck couldn't I stay silent? Why did I have to push this man? I should know better.

"You know nothing of my family and what it means to be a Villetti," he responded a moment later, his tone light despite his words.

He was right. I didn't, but I wanted to know. I wanted to know him, as stupid as that was.

"I didn't mean—"

"If you're asking whether I intend to pursue another woman when I have you with me, the answer is unequivocally, no. I don't want a wife. The institution of marriage is... abhorrent to me."

His admission had me faltering. What did anyone say to that? I was relieved by his reassurance there wouldn't be anyone else but wondered at the same time why he hated marriage. Not that I had any designs on him. Hell, I shouldn't even want him… but I did.

"And you are to keep that piece of information to yourself. Do you understand?"

"Yes, sir."

As if I would tell anyone. I wasn't able to speak to a soul outside of him. My best friend was probably wondering where the fuck I'd got to. Kaylee wasn't from my world. I met her at private school. She came from money and privilege. I didn't begrudge her upbringing or class. She was the only nice person at our school who didn't treat me like shit for being working-class scum, as they called me. Where I came from didn't matter to her.

I couldn't imagine explaining my father being in a gang to her, nor anything about Zayn, the mafia prince. The one I was becoming hopelessly enamoured with. Before all of this, I knew very little about Zayn despite having been around him many times over the years. It was different now. Everything had changed because of my decision to come here instead of my father. To ask Zayn for help.

"Now, go sit at the table. You need breakfast."

"Aren't you going to punish me for eavesdropping?"

His chuckle made me shiver.

"Oh, Tink, of course you're going to be punished, but not before you've eaten."

He released me, stepping back to give me room. I didn't know how my legs were still holding me up. Somehow, I managed to make my way to the table. When I was about to take a seat, I heard him speak.

"Not there, on the other side, where I can see you."

I walked around to the other end of the table and dropped into a seat. I placed my hands on the table and watched him move around the kitchen like he belonged in it. His eyes were on me even as he made breakfast. It unnerved me, not knowing what he would do after I'd eaten. Zayn had been very clear when explaining his punishments to me before he carried them out. Now, I had no idea what would come next.

When he was done, he brought over a plate and set it in front of me, along with a cup of tea and cutlery. I didn't hesitate to start. He would only scold me if I didn't eat everything he gave me. Earning his ire now would be a mistake.

He took a seat next to me with a cup of coffee in his hands and kept an eye on me. I had got used to him doing it. As if I wasn't trustworthy enough to finish my meal. Then again, I'd given him more than enough reason not to trust me.

I set my knife and fork down on the plate when I'd eaten, before cradling my mug to my chest and looking down at the table. My leg bounced on the floor tiles. Zayn's hand shot out, stopping my movements in their tracks. My eyes flicked up to his and found a smirk on his face.

"Nervous, Tinkerbell? You worried about what I'm going to do to you?"

I bit my lip.

"A little."

He leant closer, taking my mug from my hands and placing it on the table. His hand remained banded around my thigh, keeping me pinned to the chair. It prevented me from squeezing them together at his proximity. My fear of what he would do and the pit of desire he caused warred inside of me. It created a cocktail of lust I wasn't sure I could hide from him. Not when he had a knack of picking up on every little cue I gave him.

"Why disobey if you don't seek punishment?"

Zayn was far too close to me now. My eyes darted to his mouth. I had thrown myself at him last night and he'd rejected me. The thought of it happening again was the only thing preventing me from doing something stupid, like crawling into his lap and begging him for something neither of us should want from each other.

"How are you going to punish me?" I whispered, not trusting myself to speak louder.

He cocked his head to the side, his hand sliding higher on my thigh. I choked on my own breath.

"That mouth of yours gets you into a lot of trouble. I think it's time I shut you up."

Something dangled in front of my vision, preventing me from seeing him properly. I pulled back slightly, finding a gag hanging from the fingers of his free hand.

"Zayn—"

"Open wide."

I looked between him and the gag. If he put it on me, I couldn't say a damn thing to him. My mouth formed the word "No," before I even had a chance to think about it. Zayn's expression darkened. Then he was gripping my face with both hands and forcing my mouth open without a second thought. I struggled against him, trying to escape his hold.

"I told you I have no qualms about making you obey, Arianna."

I didn't know why him gagging me was something I couldn't deal with after everything else he'd done.

"I don't want—"

He shoved the gag in my mouth, preventing me from saying another thing before buckling it around my head. I reached up, wanting to rip it off, but he took hold of my hands and pinned them behind my back. I tried to speak, the sounds coming out all muffled. The way he smiled sent a chill running down my spine. I wanted to tell him to go fuck himself, but I couldn't. I couldn't do a single thing. He had me restrained and gagged.

"Don't you want to be good for me?"

I shook my head, continuing to wriggle in his hold, wanting to get free and rip this fucking thing from my mouth. His eyes roamed across my face, taking in the annoyance and frustration he could probably see in it.

"I've been far too lenient with you." He shook his head. "That's going to change today."

He stood up, dragging me with him. Zayn spun me around, keeping my hands pinned behind my back before pushing me towards the door. I tried to stop him, but it was futile. He was stronger than me. He herded me into his office, where he took out the handcuffs from his drawer and secured my hands behind me. His hand on my shoulder pushed me to my knees in front of him. I swayed there, my head tipped back to meet his eyes. He reached out and tugged on one of my braids.

"I'm very disappointed in you, but I think you already know that."

I glared because I could do fuck all else. This man was driving me crazy. Here I was restrained, and yet inside I was a mess of need, wanting him to touch me. To make the ache between my legs disappear. Even though I'd tried to stop him from gagging me, it didn't change how his punishments made me feel. And right now, I really fucking hated him for it.

"Can't spit fire at me now, can you, Tinkerbell?"

I screamed against the gag. It only made him smile wider.

"And to think I was going to take you out today. Such a shame you couldn't behave yourself."

He left me there, walking away to his desk and sitting behind it. There was nothing I could do but kneel there in the middle of his office. When he took this gag off, I would have a few choice words for the man about this shit. I knew I should take my punishment without complaint, but I was far too angry to think straight. Angry and turned on. Pressing my knees together, I tried to ignore the pulsing ache of need inside me.

Get your shit together!

No matter how pissed at him I was, it hadn't stopped me from wanting the stupid man. And he had absolutely no idea.

He wanted to teach me a lesson for all my wilfulness. Well, I was going to give that man a few of my own just as soon as he let me out of these handcuffs. He thought he was so calm and collected. I'd show him. Zayn Villetti was going to be as affected by me as I was by him before I was done.

FIFTEEN

Zayn

Ari silently seethed on the floor of my office for the rest of the morning. Such a provoking little thing she was. Driving me absolutely insane with her mouth. I'd known she wouldn't like the gag, but her behaviour since yesterday had been less than stellar. I didn't entirely blame her for being angry, but she had to learn she wasn't going to get her way with me.

I had planned on taking her out to choose a camera for her photography today. Her being idle in the house wasn't a good thing. Instead, I texted Penn and asked him if he could find something for me. Even if she was being a disobedient little madam right now, it didn't mean I was going to withhold the things she enjoyed. Maybe she'd settle if she had something to occupy her time with.

I almost sighed as I stood from my desk and walked over to her. The rage in those chestnut eyes hadn't dimmed in the past couple of hours, but it was lunchtime and she needed to eat. I wouldn't allow her to disrupt the routine I'd set, even if she didn't appreciate it yet.

Leaning down, I took her by the shoulders and tugged her up to her feet. Ari tried to talk around the gag. I reached out and unbuckled it, pulling it off her.

"I hate you," she ground out as I looked at the gag in my hand.

The ball part was covered in her spit. I tried not to react to the sight of it. It made me want things I shouldn't.

Who says you can't have them, Zayn? Don't you want to see spit running down her face after you've thoroughly abused her mouth with your cock? Or is it that you want to spit in her mouth and make her swallow it? Either way, you can take what you want from her. She's yours.

I swear my mind was trying to kill me alongside Arianna. I couldn't deny I was ridiculously attracted to this fucking woman in a way I'd never felt before. It was more than just wanting to fuck the living daylights out of her. Let's face it, she needed an attitude adjustment, and I'd quite happily give it to her over and over until she begged for it to end. But no, it wasn't about sex. Here I was, doing everything in my power to take care of her. I was even considering intervening in petty gang wars to keep her damn father alive. The only reason I'd told my father to leave it alone was so he didn't come sniffing around and ruining everything. If he found out what I planned to do, there would be no telling what shit would be coming my way. This had to be done under the radar if I was ever going to succeed.

My need to make sure I gave Arianna everything she required was alarming and a complete mind-fuck. I was trying to catch up with my own fucked up desires while keeping her from throwing us both off a cliff. The storm between us had been brewing since the day she showed up at my club. I had a feeling we were both about to capsize, no matter what I did.

"You hate me. How original." I threw the gag on the desk and took hold of her jaw. "Hate me all you want, Tink, doesn't change the fact we have a deal and you're not upholding your side of the bargain."

The glare I got made me smile.

"This is some power trip for you, isn't it? Getting to be in control and making me do everything you tell me."

I shook my head. Silly girl. If she thought I was drunk off power, she was mistaken. All of this was for her own fucking good. Ari could deny she needed someone to take care of her, but I could see it in her eyes. She wanted it.

"Is that what you think of me, huh? That I'm a tyrant?"

"Yes," she practically spat.

She had no fucking idea. I could make her life hell if I wanted to. What she'd experienced so far was nothing.

"Mmm, I don't think you know who I truly am, Arianna."

Before she could say a word, I forced her mouth open with both hands and held her tongue in place with my thumb on the end of it. Her eyes widened when I leant over her, gathered up a ball of spit and let it trail down from my mouth to hers. It pooled on her tongue. Seeing it satisfied me in ways I couldn't begin to explain.

"*Sono tuo padre, bambina.*"

I forced her mouth closed and released it. Arianna blinked as if she was stunned by what I'd just done. To be honest, I hadn't exactly thought about the consequences, merely acted on instinct. She swallowed and swayed on her feet, making me wrap an arm around her back to steady her.

"*Padre,*" she whispered, her eyes flicking down to the tattoo on my neck.

I thought it was a little on the nose to have daddy tattooed on my neck and I wasn't going to have *papà* either. It was too informal for my tastes.

Her brow furrowed for a long moment, then she looked up at me. I could practically see the thoughts running through her brain. She was struggling to understand what I meant.

"You… you…"

I didn't say a word, just kept staring at her beautiful face. She'd get there, eventually.

"You're… you want to be… you want me to call you…"

Something about the look in her eyes had me moving closer until our faces were inches apart and wrapping my free hand around the back of her head, cradling it.

"Call me what, Tink?" I murmured.

She swallowed before licking her bottom lip.

"Daddy."

Her sweet little voice sunk into my bones. It was the best sound I'd heard in my entire life. I didn't know how much I needed it until I heard it out of her mouth. It was something I'd been into for years, but to have my little fairy say the word was something else entirely.

I was about to respond when Ari did something unexpected. She pressed her mouth against mine, stealing all my fucking words and thoughts out of my head. I was frozen on the spot as this maddening girl kissed me. It wasn't shy or tentative. She moved her mouth against my still one, her tongue darting out to lick the seam of my lips.

I shouldn't kiss her back. In fact, I should rip myself away from her and ask her what the fuck she was playing at.

Did I do that?

No.

The moment her tongue met my lip, I groaned, opening my mouth for her to slide inside. It was all I needed to respond. My tongue curled around hers, then I was attacking her mouth and pressing her against my body. She let out a little squeak of surprise, but it didn't stop me. I wanted to feast on her pretty mouth until I was breathless and gasping for air.

Ari rubbed herself against me the best she could with her hands cuffed behind her back. She moaned in my mouth, kissing me back with as much passion and ferocity as I gave her. It was like she wanted to crawl inside me and make herself at home. My hand tightened around the back of her head, angling it so I could kiss her deeper.

It wasn't enough. I wanted more. I needed… more.

Backing her away towards the wall, I pressed kisses to her jaw, tasting her delicate skin.

"Don't stop, please," she gasped, her voice all breathy and wanton.

I pinned her to the wall and captured her face with both hands, pressing my mouth back on hers. If I stopped, reality would come flooding back, and I wasn't ready for it. The only thing I could see and feel right now was her. It was all I wanted. To stop denying myself this insane urge to own every part of this frustrating girl.

"Mine," I growled against her lips. "You're fucking mine."

"Zayn," she whimpered, a sound I swallowed because it drove me crazy to hear her say my name with such desperation.

My pulse pounded in my ears, urging me to slide my hands all over her body. To see if she was wet for me. Judging by the way she was trying to get closer, even though there was already no room between us, she clearly wanted this. Had last night really just been about her wanting me to save her father?

The thought brought me up short. I pulled away abruptly, panting as I stared down at the wide-eyed girl with swollen lips, breathing just as heavily as me. She'd always been beautiful, but right then, Ari was the most stunning person I'd ever laid eyes on. And by fuck did I want to make her mine in every possible way I could.

"Why'd you stop?"

I stepped back, leaving her against the wall. She shifted on her feet but stayed where she was.

"That shouldn't have happened."

The words were like fucking razor blades in my throat, but I had to say them. Kissing her wasn't part of the plan. I couldn't get intimately involved with Arianna. Not in the way I wanted to. The mere thought of what I'd have to do to make it safe for her to be mine was a difficult pill to swallow. Having Arianna by my side would mean going against our families. Both of them. And my father was not a man you wanted to make into an enemy.

It killed me to see the confusion in her eyes. Did she not realise this couldn't happen? I wasn't being cruel or unkind, but in my world, you didn't get to make daughters of petty gang leaders yours. I wasn't going to insult Ari by making her some kind of mistress to me. A girl I fucked and kept hidden in the shadows. She didn't deserve that, and I refused to be the kind of man my father was.

"Why not?"

"Are you really asking me that?"

"Yes, I am."

I ran a hand through my hair, frustrated she was making me spell it out for her.

"This is not a part of our deal, and you're too young for me. I'm almost your father's age, not to mention I'm in business with him and he would likely want to gut me for touching you. Kissing you was wrong."

She let out an indignant squeak.

"I kissed you first! And I'm more than old enough to choose who the fuck I go around kissing, with or without my dad's approval, thank you very much."

"That's beside the point."

She shook her head and glared at me.

"I don't care how old you are. Hell, you could be fifty, wouldn't change a single damn thing. I'd still want you."

I swear my heart just about stopped hearing her say that.

"You what?"

"I want you."

She couldn't possibly mean that after telling me she hated me. What the fuck was happening? I mean, she'd kissed me, but it didn't mean shit, did it? This was a mess. I was a fucking mess after our kiss. I needed to get my shit straight and I couldn't do it when she was staring at me with those chestnut eyes so full of emotions I didn't want to see.

I reached out and grabbed a hold of her arm, tugging her with me towards the door.

"No, you don't," I ground out.

She struggled against my hold, but it's not like she could do much with her hands behind her back.

"You don't get to tell me what I do and don't want, Zayn."

"It's sir to you."

"Oh, is it? I thought you wanted me to call you da—"

I shoved her in front of me and slapped my hand over her mouth. If I heard her say it again, I might not survive it.

"You are going to shut up, Arianna, because so fucking help me, I will show you how fucking tyrannical I can be if you don't."

It was a struggle to get her upstairs because she kept fighting me, but I managed it. I shoved her into the bedroom I'd given her, holding her in place while I unlocked the handcuffs. Then I was retreating to the door as she spun around. Before she could move towards me, I was out of the room and pushing the door shut. I turned the key in the lock. The handcuffs dropped from my fingers as her hand slammed down on the other side of the door.

"What the fuck, Zayn!"

I didn't say a word, merely leant both my hands against the frame and took a deep breath.

"You can't lock me up because you don't like what I had to say. That's not fair."

This entire situation was unfair. I had to be in some kind of nightmare. Arianna didn't know who I really was, so how the fuck could she say she wanted me. She didn't know what she was saying. She'd been angry at me. There was a fine line between hate and lust.

Her tiny fists hammered against the door. I should have walked away, but I couldn't move. I couldn't leave her.

"I don't even understand why the fuck I want you. You're mean, you punish me and don't allow me to do a single thing without your say so." The gasping breath she took had my heart squeezing hard in my chest. "But then you can be kind too… you take care of me. Fuck, you even let me cry on you last night and sleep in your bed when I was supposed to be on the floor. I don't know why you do that, Zayn, but I need it. I need you." Her voice cracked on the last word, absolutely gutting me. "I don't care about our stupid deal. All I want is to stop wanting you and I can't, so you can punish me for it, but it won't make it go away. I just want it to go away."

I want to stop wanting you too, Tinkerbell, but I can't either.

SIXTEEN

Zayn

The thump of her body hitting the floor had my hands squeezing around the wood of the doorframe. Her words made something break inside me. I hadn't told her the entire truth about why this would be impossible between us. Yes, her age and her father were two huge fucking issues, but the worst one was my own family.

My father's presence today reminded me I was expected to marry a woman he approved of. One who would fit into our family. No way in hell would he ever accept Ari, not that I actually planned on marrying anyone, let alone her. Didn't matter if he was in business with her father. Gang leader's daughters were not appropriate wife material for the son of the mafia kingpin.

So you admit you want her as your partner. Not your pet. Not a girl you fuck. But a woman to stand by your side.

How else could I explain why this caused me such a fucking headache? Sure, I could take her to bed and not have it mean anything. The only problem with that was I already cared about her far too much to let her leave me.

If I told her my father wouldn't think she was good enough for me, it would be fucking insulting. I didn't think that about her at all. She was strong, fiery and beautiful in my eyes... so fucking beautiful. I longed to tangle my fingers in her curly hair, kiss every freckle on her skin and worship her curves. To look after her at all times because she was my responsibility. I couldn't give her up now I had her here with me. I just... couldn't.

"I didn't know I needed someone to take care of me until you started doing it," she murmured through the door, her voice shaking with each word as if she was about to cry. "I'm not saying Dad neglected me, but it wasn't easy for him with his gang life and being a single parent. I felt like a-a-a burden to him. You never made me feel that way even though you didn't have to do any of it... but now... now I feel like I'm one to you as well."

The soft sounds of her crying when she finished seized my entire fucking soul. Her words were damning on every single level. No fucking wonder she thrived under my care. I'd been putting her needs first without a second thought. No one else in her life had done that for her.

"I'm sorry," she sobbed. "I'm sorry I came to you for help and made a mess of your life. I didn't want to disappoint Dad. I thought he wouldn't believe me if I told him about Uncle Justin and... I was scared. I killed a man in cold blood. I guess

I thought you would understand and… and you were capable of keeping me safe. I just fucked everything up instead."

She hiccuped on her sobs. I couldn't take it, hearing her misery and knowing I was responsible for it. My hands fell from the doorframe and went to the lock.

"Move away from the door, Tinkerbell," I told her, keeping my voice soft as I turned the key. "I don't want it to hit you."

Her shuffling movements told me she'd heard. I turned the handle and cracked it open, peering in to find her close by. She was hugging her knees with tears spilling down her cheeks unheeded. The sight of it gutted me. Pushing the door open wider, I strode in, got down on my knees, and pulled her into my lap, cradling my little fairy to my chest. She buried her face in my neck and curled her arms around me, breaking down completely in my embrace.

"Shh, I'm here," I whispered, pressing my mouth to the top of her head. "I'm right here."

"I'm sorry."

"Hush now, it's okay. You don't need to apologise." I rocked her gently, wanting to reassure her I wasn't angry. "You're not a burden, my little fairy. Quite the opposite. I want to take care of you as much as you need me to."

My words only made her cry harder. Fuck, I was confusing her. On the one hand, I kept driving it home that I wanted to take care of her, but on the other, I'd told her we couldn't be anything more than what we already were. If only I could kiss away her tears and reassure her things would be okay. I'd find a way to make it work. The realistic part of me knew there was no simple answer. No way out that didn't require both of us going against our families for each other. And somehow I knew it would only end in bloodshed one way or another. The way of our worlds was violent and unforgiving.

"I… I don't want to… to… to need you," she sobbed into my neck. "Not when you… you… you won't give me m-m-more."

I'd never resented the life I'd been born into more than I did right then. And I'd built up a hell of a lot of resentment towards my father over the years.

"I can't change who we are."

"If… if things were different, would you want me?"

I pressed my mouth harder against her hair to stop myself from answering immediately with the truth. If I told her yes, then it would cause more problems, and yet I couldn't exactly say no either. She wouldn't believe me after the way I'd kissed her. Hell, I'd fucking told her she was mine.

"You can't ask me that," I murmured. "It's not fair on either of us."

She pulled her face from my neck and stared up at me with bloodshot eyes.

"I just bared my feelings to you. The least you can do is the same for me."

If I thought her being upset would tame her damn mouth, I was mistaken.

"I think you already know the answer."

She wiped her tear-streaked face with her sleeve before reaching up and stroking her fingers along my jaw. I tensed when she leant into me, only stopping when her mouth was almost dusting over mine.

"If you won't say it, then show me."

"I can't—"

"Kiss me… daddy."

My eyes darted between her eyes and her mouth. That fucking mouth of hers.

"Don't call me that if you don't mean it," I whispered.

Her other hand slid up the back of my neck into my hair. Nails dug into my scalp, making my lips part in a silent grunt.

"And if I do?"

I searched her expression. There was nothing but honesty in it.

"Fuck it."

I said it more for my benefit than hers as I crashed my mouth against hers. My fingers went to one of her braids, gripping it in my fist and pulling her head back slightly. It allowed me to kiss her deeper. I let myself drown in Ari, so tired of denying I wanted her more than I'd ever wanted another person in my entire life. This would only end in fucking disaster, but at that moment, I couldn't bring myself to care.

Ari shifted around in my lap, straddling me and pressing her chest to mine. My free hand went to her hip, gripping it to stop her from moving further. If she ground herself on me, I wasn't sure I could control myself any longer. My self-restraint was hanging by a thread. It was so fucking hard to think straight when she'd made it very clear she desired more from me. Especially when she tore my hand off her braid and pressed it to her neck, wrapping my fist around it.

I released her mouth and stared down at her. My fingers squeezed her airway, testing her limits. There was only need in her eyes. A desperation I couldn't quite put into words.

"Is this what you really want, Tink? To be all mine?"

"Yes." She released the word on a breath, swallowing against my palm the next moment. "I know I can't, but I want it anyway."

I leant my forehead against hers and closed my eyes. There was too much for me to think about. Too many things to consider.

My phone buzzing in my pocket saved me from responding. I released her, taking it from my pocket and noting Arlo had sent me a few messages. Ari didn't say a word as I opened them. There was a video from a news source, along with a note from him.

ARLO: THINGS ARE GOING TO GET OUT OF HAND VERY SOON. WE'LL HAVE TO ACT FAST.

I clicked on the video and the sound blared from my phone along with images from a helicopter of the police surrounding a man lying dead in the street, blood pooling around his body.

"A man was shot dead in Peckham in the early hours of this morning. Police have identified him as twenty-two-year-old Kieran Brown."

I paused the video and looked at Ari, who was staring at the screen. Her face had gone pale. Maybe I shouldn't have played it when she was right here, but at the end of the day, what was happening with her father was her business. I had no intention of telling her what I was planning to do about it, but she could help me in some small way, given who she was.

"Someone you know?"

She nodded slowly.

"One of Dad's men… no one important." She winced at her own words. "I mean, in his organisation, that is." She shook her head. "I can't believe he's dead."

It couldn't be easy for her knowing someone her own age had died. And it meant I needed to do something about Derek McGovern before this got worse. There was no doubt in my mind it was his handiwork. I needed Arlo to find out exactly what happened. Then I could come up with a plan to make this little problem go away.

I clicked out of the video and typed out a quick message to Arlo before tucking my phone back in my pocket. My hand went to Ari's jaw. I stroked my thumb along her cheek.

"I'm sorry, Tink."

She gave me a sad smile.

"Not like I haven't seen it before."

The heartbreak in her voice had me pressing a kiss to her forehead.

"Our world is unforgiving."

"You'll keep me safe, though, won't you?"

"Always."

The lie stuck in my throat. Keeping her safe wouldn't be easy. There were things I had to do she wouldn't like, but in times of war, you had to get your hands dirty.

"Now, come, let me clean you up and then you can help me make us lunch."

She blinked.

"You want me to help you?"

"Mmm, you can cook, yes?"

She nodded even as a little furrow appeared in her brow.

"Then you can help me."

Without letting her respond, I shifted her off my lap and got to my feet. I put out my hand and pulled her up to hers. Then I took her into the bathroom and wet a cloth to wipe her face with. She was quiet as I did it and made her blow her nose in a tissue.

I pressed a kiss to her mouth when I was done without thinking about it. It was my first instinct to show her affection, even though I shouldn't.

"Good girl," I whispered, pulling away and taking her hand.

When I glanced at her after tugging her from the room, her cheeks had darkened with a blush. It made me smile as we made our way downstairs. I set her a few tasks in the kitchen before my phone rang. Moving away into the dining area, I answered it.

"Yes?"

"Our contact tells me Bennett went after McGovern, but he was ambushed by Derek's men," Arlo said without preamble. "That's how the kid ended up dead. They're all laying low, but it won't be for long. If you want to intervene, you need to do it before that happens."

Arlo knew I had to do this for Ari, even if he didn't approve of my relationship with her. I'd spoken to him about it more yesterday after Ari's little interruption. He'd do as I said, even if he didn't agree with my plans.

"Find a way to get info on Derek's activities and then we'll go from there," I said in a low voice so it wouldn't carry.

"Consider it done."

"Is my brother behaving himself?"

"Other than flirting with anything that moves? Yes, but it won't last long. Enzo never stays out of trouble."

"Maybe he should have stayed abroad."

Arlo scoffed.

"I wish the little shit had. He's already been in contact with Lissa. She's refusing to see him, which is suspicious."

"Did she ever tell you what he did before he left?"

"No. I need to make her tell me."

No doubt Enzo had fucked up somehow.

"Interrogating Lissa won't end well, you know."

"Pot. Kettle. Black. Need I remind you of Remi and now, Ari?"

My free hand curled into a fist. I didn't interfere in Remi's life… much. It reminded me I needed to check up on her. I didn't trust Penn within three feet of her and Liza had told me he kept hanging around in Desecration when she was on shift. For someone who had a lot of clients, he spent far too much time in my club watching the girl I thought of as my little sister.

"Maybe I should remind you of who pays you."

Arlo laughed.

"Ah, Zayn, you wouldn't cut me off. You need me too much."

He hung up before I could respond. What was with people today? First, I had my father here, then Ari driving me crazy and now Arlo being a cheeky fuck. I swear it was 'give Zayn shit day'.

My eyes went to Ari as I tucked my phone back into my pocket. She gave me a smile before going back to slicing a cucumber. Seeing her in my kitchen this way made my chest ache. It was so very domesticated. Something I never wanted… but with her, I didn't think it would be so terrible.

Whatever dirt Arlo managed to dig up on Derek McGovern for me, one thing was very clear after what Ari had told me last night. That man would never get his hands on my

149

girl. In fact, no one else would ever touch her again if I had anything to say about it.

Arianna belonged to me. I was going to have to swallow that difficult pill and go against both our families if I was ever going to keep her. And make the girl mine completely.

SEVENTEEN

Arianna

I f I'd thought laying out all my feelings would change everything between me and Zayn, I'd been mistaken. The past two days, he'd kept me at arm's length, making me sleep in the room he'd given me and hadn't kissed me again. To say it upset me was an understatement, but I was trying not to show it. It didn't help that I was unnerved by Kieran being shot dead. First blood had been drawn. The war neither of us wanted was coming.

I couldn't blame Zayn for telling me it was impossible for us to be more. I understood his concerns, even the ones he hadn't voiced out loud. It didn't take a rocket scientist to put together the hints he'd given me about his family. Gennaro expected him to marry and, no doubt, it would have to be someone his father approved of. I wouldn't meet those standards. Zayn telling me he didn't want marriage hadn't made a difference. There was a reason people didn't cross Gennaro Villetti. It was the same reason my father had gone into business with the man. It was smart to gain favour with the man who controlled the mafia in London.

I let out a sigh as I walked into the living room. Zayn had told me to join him there after lunch. He'd had a meeting with one of his associates earlier, but he'd made me stay upstairs, so I had no idea who it was.

I paused when I spied him lounging on the sofa with his arms resting on the back of it. There was a smile playing on his lips. He wasn't looking at me, but at something on the coffee table. A wrapped box with a bow on it.

"What's this?" I asked, narrowing my eyes on it.

"Come here."

I walked over to him and knelt in between his legs. He leant forward and stroked the wild curls I hadn't bothered to tame this morning.

"I bought you a present."

"Why? I haven't exactly been a good girl."

He didn't react to my statement, merely waved at the box.

"Open it, Tink."

I turned around and shuffled closer to the coffee table. Reaching out, I touched the box, then ripped off the wrapping paper. My hand went to my mouth. He'd bought a digital camera I'd had my eye on for ages. It was expensive, hence I'd not been able to buy it myself. There were no words. How he even knew was a mystery to me. I might have told him I was a photographer, but I didn't expect him to do this. Hell, I hadn't expected a single thing I'd learnt about Zayn Villetti. Each small piece I gained, I treasured. It was like fitting together tiny pieces of a puzzle to a man who wore more masks than I could fathom.

I spun on my knees and crawled into his lap. I wrapped my arms around his neck and held onto him, needing desperately to show my appreciation for his gift.

"Thank you, daddy."

It slipped out without me thinking about it. I don't know why I wanted to call him that any more than I understood his need.

"You're welcome."

There was an odd note to his voice like he was bottling up some kind of emotion he couldn't let out. I pulled away to take in his expression. Those black eyes of his were guarded.

"It's the one I wanted." I leant closer, drawn in by everything about this man. "I don't care how you knew, I just appreciate it."

My fingers went to his jaw, stroking across his stubble and adoring the way it grazed my fingertips. He didn't move when my fingers brushed along his bottom lip. All I wanted to do was close the distance and kiss him, but I wasn't sure if he would allow it. Not after the way he'd treated me for the past two days.

"Go play with your new camera, Arianna," he murmured as he pushed my hand from his face. "I got you it so you wouldn't be bored."

His words deflated me, but I chose to ignore the feeling. I didn't want this shit between us to put a damper on things. Not when he'd got me a gift. I hauled myself out of his lap and got the camera out of the box. It took me a while to adjust all the settings for the lighting in the living room. Then I snapped a few photos of things like the plant he had sitting in one corner. It had wide, dark green leaves. I liked the texture of them.

Zayn watched me the whole time, not taking his eyes off me as I moved around the room to take photos of different objects. I came to rest in front of him, holding the camera in one hand. I'd secured it around my neck with the strap.

"Would you let me take some pictures of you?"

He cocked his head to the side, his eyes roaming across me.

"Why do you want to do that?"

"I like taking portraits as much as I do objects. And…" I shrugged. "I like looking at you."

"Is that so?"

"Yeah, Zayn, you know how attractive you are… unless this is you fishing for a compliment from me."

The way he scowled at me had me smiling.

"I'm not fishing for anything, Arianna. I was asking you a question."

"And I answered. Now, are you going to let me photograph you or not?"

He leant back against the sofa and bit his lip.

"If you really want to, I suppose I'd be okay with it… on one condition."

I waved a hand at him, wanting to know what it was.

"They're for you and you alone."

I ran my tongue over my bottom lip. As if I wanted to share this man with anyone else. I couldn't stomach the idea of him having another woman. Touching someone other than me. It didn't matter if he wasn't mine. No one else could have him. I wouldn't allow it.

"Deal."

He smirked before digging his hand into his pocket and drawing out his cigar case. I watched him light a cigarillo and sit back. Raising my camera, I snapped a few photos of him blowing out the smoke. Then continued to take them as he raised it back to his mouth using his tattooed right hand. He clearly knew exactly what he was doing. I was trying not to get turned on by this man and failing miserably.

After I'd taken a few more shots, I moved closer, kneeling on the sofa beside him to take some closeups. I took the cigarillo from him for a moment and placed his tattooed hand on his jaw before shooting that. He didn't object to me adjusting the way he was posing for me. Even when I had to pop his cigarillo into the ashtray on the table.

I looked down at the small screen to check the photos a few minutes later.

"I'd love to edit these, make some of them black and white," I said without thinking.

"Then I'll get you a laptop with the right software."

My eyes flicked to him.

"You will?"

"If it makes you keep smiling like that, then yes."

I put my fingers to my mouth, not realising I was doing it. Zayn ran his teeth over his bottom lip. I was quick to snap a photo of it. A close up of his mouth. Then I sat back, an idea popping into my head. Shifting further onto the sofa, I took a seat next to him and took hold of his tattooed hand, positioning it on my bare thigh. I was wearing a short skirt today. His fingers curled around it as if on instinct. I was already snapping photos of our legs next to each other in an artsy sort of way.

I froze a moment later when his fingers caressed my inner thigh. His breath dusted across my ear before his teeth grazed it.

"Tell me, Tinkerbell, is this strictly for the art, or are you trying to get me to touch you?"

I swallowed. It hadn't occurred to me, but maybe I was subconsciously wanting it as he had barely touched me since the day we kissed.

"Will I be in trouble if it's the latter?"

"Oh yes, you'll be in big trouble," he whispered as his hand moved higher. "Especially if I find out you've made a mess of these."

I squeaked when he brushed his fingers along the edge of my underwear.

"Have you, my bad little fairy?"

Holy. Fuck.

Was I dreaming right now? This was a one-eighty for Zayn. I didn't know what the hell to do with myself. I just didn't want him to stop.

"What are you going to do if I have?"

"Take them off you."

"And then?"

"Put them in your mouth and let you taste your disobedience."

I think I'm going to faint.

And yet I felt like there was something I'd missed. A sign he'd changed his mind about us taking things further.

"What are we doing right now?" I whispered.

He nuzzled his face into my neck, pressing a kiss to my skin.

"Something we shouldn't."

"You've been distant these past two days."

His other hand curled around my waist.

"You're a temptation I shouldn't indulge in."

"Does that mean what I think it does?"

His teeth ran across my skin, making my breath hitch.

"It means if you tell me you've been a bad girl, I'm going to punish you regardless of whether we should cross this line or not, Tink."

He wanted me to give him permission. I'd told him I didn't want anyone to touch me without my consent. Did he not know he had it in spades? I would let him do anything he wanted to me if it meant he touched me. If it meant he kissed me. If it meant he fucked me.

"I've been a very bad girl, daddy."

He ran his finger along my damp underwear. His resulting groan had me shaking. I felt the deep notes of it resonate in my soul.

"Such a messy girl," he murmured before grabbing hold of my underwear and tugging at it. I raised my hips so he could pull it off me. He dangled it in front of my face after dragging it down my legs. "Look at what you did. Is that for me, hmm?"

"Yes."

He tutted in my ear before wrapping his other hand around my jaw and prying it open. Then he shoved the damp fabric in my mouth, forcing me to taste myself and how wet he'd made me.

"If you keep them in your mouth, I'll reward you… but first, you're going to stand up for me."

I did as he asked, trying to keep my legs from turning to jelly. This man was going to kill me. I was sure of it. And I didn't care.

He stood up behind me and pressed his mouth to my ear.

"Put the camera down and come with me."

I slid the camera from my neck and placed it on the coffee table. He took a hold of my arm and pushed me towards the door, keeping himself behind me. I was manoeuvred into his office and made to stand in front of his desk. He came around and shifted some things out of the way before pressing against my back and making me bend over it.

"Hands flat and don't move them unless I tell you to."

I flattened my palms on the desk, trying not to shift around too much. The way I was turned on right then made it difficult. I needed friction between my legs.

He leant over me, stroking my curls back from my face.

"If you'd been a good girl, I might have let you look me in the eye. Bad girls don't get to see what their masters have planned for them."

I didn't know whether to complain about it or not. I wanted to see him, but if this was the only way I'd get him to give me what I'd been craving, then I'd submit. At this point, I would beg him to fuck me if I had to. There was no way in hell we were leaving this room without it happening. Not if I had anything to do with it.

EIGHTEEN

Zayn

I'd tried, really fucking tried my best not to give in. Not to want her so damn much. It was impossible now I knew what her lips felt like. Now I knew what she sounded like when she called me daddy. And fuck, when she smiled so wide over her gift, it was everything.

I knew letting her photograph me was risky, but the intimacy of it and the way she looked at me was the final straw. Now I had her bent over my desk in a rather compromising position. One I wanted to take full advantage of.

I was done playing games. Done tiptoeing around this thing between us. My desire for her had overridden any rational thoughts I had left. This was me giving in.

Ari whimpered behind her makeshift gag when I slid a hand down her side and flipped her skirt up.

"Are you going to make a mess of my fingers, Tink?"

She nodded, making me smile as I stroked them up the back of her thigh.

"How wet are you? Wet enough to take them all? I want to split you open, sweet fairy, make you cry from the pleasure and pain."

The sound of her moaning in agreement was all I needed. My tongue made a path along the shell of her ear, while my fingers delved between her lips, finding exactly how wet her pussy was for me. It had been obvious how turned on she was getting when she was taking pictures of me. The flush of her cheeks. The way she kept biting her lip. And when she put my hand on her thigh, it was the last fucking straw.

I didn't hesitate in sliding two fingers inside her, groaning at the feel of her wet heat. Her back arched into me as I laid my other hand over one of hers on the desk, spreading her fingers out so I could place mine between them. If I could hold on to her hand forever, I would.

"It's not enough, is it?" I asked as I fucked her with my fingers. "You want more. You'll always want more with me."

Whimpers were all I got along with the shift of her hips, rocking back into me. I smiled against her ear. Should I have my fingers buried in her pussy? Fuck no, but I wasn't going to stop now. I wanted her to fall apart underneath me. To lose herself because I'd lost the fucking will to fight my needs any longer. She had to drown with me, capsizing in the sea of desire swirling around us.

I pulled my fingers out before sliding all four in, making her moan louder. Spreading them slightly, I pressed my fingers deeper, stretching her out for me. She was being so good, so willing to take what I was giving her. I intended to sample every part of my fairy. My Tinkerbell. To take what was fucking mine. The moment she'd said yes to our deal while covered in her uncle's blood, it had set this all in motion. Put us on a collision course. I knew it was fucked up and would cost me everything I'd built.

I'll burn it all for you, Tinkerbell, but you'll never know how much I'm sacrificing for you.

"That's it, my dirty little fairy. You can take it. You're going to have to take a whole lot more before I'm done with you."

The wet sounds of me fucking her pussy mixing in with her whines behind her underwear were music to my ears. She kept moving her hips with my rhythm, encouraging me to keep going.

"You're doing so well. Such a good girl for taking them, aren't you? My little Tink, all worked up and needy."

I pulled my face from her ear to stare down at her flushed cheeks. Such perfection. I knew she would be responsive. I'd been stupid to think this was only about making her my pet. I needed to make her my everything. And right now, I was going to claim her in the most primal fucking way possible.

"I want you to put your hand between your legs and touch yourself. Show me how you like it."

She shifted, lifting her free hand from the desk and shoving it underneath her. Her fingers stroked across mine as she reached her pussy. Then she was rubbing her clit in time with me, impaling her pussy on my fingers over and over. She whined and ground against me.

"Good girl," I whispered, pressing a kiss to her cheek.

She tried to say something to me, but it was muffled. Letting go of her hand momentarily, I pulled her underwear out of her mouth.

"Fuck," she gasped as I used more force behind my thrusts.

I gripped her hand again, lacing our fingers together.

"Zayn, please."

"What do you want, Tink?"

"You, I want you."

I nibbled her jaw, making her shudder against me.

"My fingers are in your pussy. What more could you possibly want?"

"It's not enough."

I chuckled, continuing to press kisses to her skin.

"Oh? Is there something else you're craving?"

"Yes," she moaned. "Please. I need… I need you."

"Tell me exactly what you want, little fairy."

I knew what she wanted, but I wasn't going to let her get away with not telling me what it was. I needed to hear her say it.

"You… I need you to… to… to fuck me."

"I thought that's what I was doing."

I thrust my fingers harder inside her, stretching her out to her limits. She kept shifting underneath me, begging me for more with her body and mouth.

"No, I want your… your…"

"Use your big girl words or I won't give you what you're asking for."

Her cheeks were bright red, her eyes wide and full of need.

"I want you to fuck me with your dick, please, Zayn, please give me your dick," she whimpered.

I slid my fingers out of her pussy. It didn't occur to me to tell her off for calling me by my name. It only made me want her more. The sound of it on her lips had my cock throbbing harder than it already was.

"If you clean my fingers with your mouth like a good girl, then I'll fuck you the way you need." I straightened, letting go of her hand. "Open your dirty little mouth."

She did as I asked. I took a hold of her jaw and shoved all four fingers in, groaning when she licked them clean, covering them in her spit. Removing them from her mouth, I stared down at her saliva. I couldn't help sticking them in my own mouth one by one, sampling the lingering taste of her pussy.

Ari watched me as my hands went to my belt, unbuckling it before I unzipped myself. Her lips parted when I freed my cock, stroking a hand down the hard shaft. With my other hand, I dug my fingers into her hair and pulled her head back. I leant over her, rubbing the head of my cock along her wet pussy.

"Is this what you wanted, Tinkerbell? You want me to fuck you?"

"Please."

"Do you think you've earned it, hmm? Have you done everything I told you?"

"Yes, yes, I have. I swear."

"Then take it, my dirty little fairy. Take what you've earned."

I gave her a helping hand by placing my dick at her entrance. Ari pushed back against me, pressing her hands on the desk to give her more leverage. I bit my lip as she took me, sinking my cock into her wet little pussy. Of all the ways I'd imagined doing this to her, it hadn't occurred to me to make her take me. To put my girl in control of the pace. I'd let her have it for a while before I took over. For the moment, I was revelling in the feel of her encasing my cock.

"Oh shit," she cried out, stopping her movements with me halfway inside her.

I stroked my hand over her hip. She didn't sound like she was in pain, but I was concerned all the same.

"You okay, Ari?"

She nodded as best she could with me gripping her hair.

"Yes, it's just…"

"Just what?"

"You're so thick," she whispered, making me grin.

"I think that's the first real compliment you've given me."

The way she spluttered at my statement had me smiling wider. Watching her get flustered over me was so fucking intoxicating. I wanted to wind her up and watch her explode. Leaning closer to her, I gripped her hair tighter in my fist.

"Why do you think I stretched your little pussy so wide with my fingers, Tink? You took them. You can take my cock. All of it. You know it's going to feel good when I fuck you so deep, you won't know your own name any longer."

To prove a point, I inched closer to her, making her take more.

"That's it, there's my good girl, taking my cock just like you were made to. This pussy belongs to me. You're going to give me what I want. Every part of you is *mine* for the taking, you hear me? Say you hear me and understand. Tell me what belongs to me."

I pushed harder, sinking so deep, she whimpered with it.

"Say it, Arianna."

"My pussy belongs to you."

"And what else?"

"Every part of me does. You can have it all. I belong to you."

"That's right. What a good girl you've been. I'm going to reward you now. Show you what it means to be mine."

She squirmed, twisting in my grip as if my praise gave her a high. When I felt her relax, I pulled out slightly and pushed my way back in. Ari moaned as I fucked her with shallow strokes so she could get used to the feel of me. I pressed her face back down on the desk, keeping my fist in her hair. She cried out when my thrusts got harder. She felt like heaven wrapped up in a beautiful package, made just for me.

I'd forgotten how long it had been since I'd been inside a woman. No one had got me worked up the way this girl had. I was already addicted to the feel of her wrapped around my cock. How could something so wrong feel so fucking right?

"*La mia brava bambina.*"

"What does that mean?"

"That you're my good girl."

Her hands curled into fists on the desk.

"I swear you're trying to kill me," she muttered. "He even says good girl in Italian."

Leaning over her, I brushed my lips along her earlobe.

"I could whisper dirty things in Italian in your ear, but I think you'd rather me tell you in English how well you're taking my cock and how good your pussy feels around it, wouldn't you?"

She pushed her hips back against me.

"Yes, daddy."

For that, I only fucked her deeper. She arched her back, moaning and shifting underneath me. The girl knew my weakness now. She knew I would do anything for her if she kept calling me that.

It's lucky for you I already plan to burn the world to the ground to keep you, Tink.

There wasn't any other way. We'd have to fight tooth and nail for this to work and she might end up hating me for the things I had to do, but it would be worth it. She was worth it to me.

Digging my hand between us, I slid my fingers over her clit.

"Does my good girl want to come?"

She let out a little whimper.

"I don't know if I can."

"No?"

She flattened a hand on the desk.

"Sometimes it's hard for me to… I can't let go."

I pressed a kiss to her jaw.

"That's okay. I don't want you to feel pressure to. I know that can make it worse. Just relax and let me make you feel good."

Her soft sigh and the way she instantly melted onto the desk were all I needed to know I'd said the right thing. I wasn't going to pressure her. It had always been in my nature to make sure my partner was satisfied in whatever way they needed. Sex wasn't always about orgasms and climaxes. It was the physical intimacy that mattered the most.

"Thank you," she whispered. "I just want this… this is perfect."

"Your wish is my command, my dirty little fairy."

I didn't slow my movements or rhythm, nor did I stroke her clit with the intention of making her come. All I wanted was for her to enjoy it. To know I wanted to be in her as much as she needed me to give it to her.

When she pushed back against me, I pulled her head back, turning it slightly so I could capture her mouth. She moaned into my mouth, making me swallow her cries when I increased my pace. It was only pushing me closer to the edge.

"You feel too fucking good," I groaned against her lips. "Fuck."

"Give it to me."

I pressed my forehead against hers, looking into those beautiful chestnut eyes. It shoved me over the edge. I slammed into her a few more times before erupting. My breaths were harsh as spots formed in my vision, but I could still see her. My little fairy, taking everything like a good girl.

I slowed my movements before pressing a kiss to her mouth when the sensations faded. Letting go of her hair, I stroked her cheek and kept kissing her. Then I let her go and straightened while I caught my breath. She laid her face on the desk, breathing in and out as if she was trying to regain her equilibrium too.

"Zayn…"

"Yes?"

I pulled out of her, my hands resting on her hips. She didn't look at me. It made my body tense up with concern.

"I'm not on, you know, birth control."

"Oh. You don't need to worry about that."

She abruptly flipped herself over on the desk and sat up, staring up at me with confusion.

"What do you mean? You just came in me without protection."

I reached behind her to pick up the box of tissues I always had on my desk. She was still looking alarmed when I straightened again.

"I had that taken care of years ago, Arianna."

"What?"

"Well, I don't want children and I didn't want any surprises, so I made sure it couldn't happen."

Her eyes went wide.

"You had the snip?"

I nodded, not seeing why it was a big deal. I mean, I suppose it was, considering it wasn't something men were keen on doing, but I didn't give a shit. The odds of an accidental pregnancy might be slim, didn't mean I trusted it not to happen. This way, I knew I was safe and didn't have to worry about it, regardless of whether I used condoms or not.

"Oh. I see."

"Does that bother you?"

She gave me a little shrug as if to say she didn't know what to think.

"Not really."

"Good. Now, I'm going to take you upstairs and get you cleaned up, then we'll order in for dinner. Does that sound okay to you?"

She gave me a shy smile.

"That sounds more than okay."

Taking her chin between my fingers, I kissed her, knowing it would not be the end of our conversation, but not wanting to ruin what just happened with talk of what my choices meant for the future.

"You were such a good girl for me, Tinkerbell," I murmured when I pulled away. "So tonight you get to sleep with me."

I had no intention of merely just sleeping. After all, there were still so many parts of her body I had yet to sample. And I planned to savour each and every piece of my dirty little fairy.

NINETEEN

Arianna

The whirlwind I'd been on with Zayn today almost felt like a dream. The only reason I knew it wasn't had everything to do with the way he'd fucked me on his desk. Holy shit, did he know what he was doing. I thought I enjoyed being at his mercy but being stretched out and pounded into by that man and his thick cock was something else entirely. Something I wanted again and again.

Zayn Villetti made every man I'd been with before seem like amateurs. And the fact he made me feel perfectly normal when I told him I struggled to orgasm was the icing on the cake. Whoever put this man on earth, I thanked them profusely.

He'd been awfully sweet to me after all the dirty things he'd said in my ear during sex. From taking me upstairs and getting me clean to cuddling me on the sofa in front of the TV after we ate dinner. It was the first time I'd seen him wear anything casual. The man lived in shirts and suits. Tonight, he'd been in a zip-up hoodie, a t-shirt and jogging bottoms. It made him less… intimidating. He was just a normal guy and not the sex club-owning mafia prince everyone else saw him as. Although, admittedly, Zayn was far from normal. More like overwhelmingly attractive, stern and unyielding with a secret caring side.

He led me upstairs when we were done with our film, my hand clasped tightly in his larger one. I didn't know what to make of the change in him today, but I wasn't going to complain about it. It was exactly what I wanted… wasn't it? For him to be with me, even if it meant it was only just for now. A thousand obstacles stacked against us were still there. I'd take what I could get with this man.

Don't lie to yourself, Ari, you're obsessed with everything about him. If he makes you leave after your deal is through, it's going to hurt like you've never been hurt before.

I didn't want to think about him letting me go or tossing me aside because I wasn't fit to be his partner. It made my heart ache too much. And right now, I wanted to savour every second of me and him without the outside world looking in.

Zayn tugged me into his bedroom, shutting the door behind us. He released my hand to turn on the bedside lamps. I walked over to the end of the bed, my fingers dusting along the covers. It took everything inside me not to imagine a future where I could call this my room too.

He took a hold of my face with both hands, tipping my chin up towards him.

"Don't think so hard, Tinkerbell," he whispered as he leant closer. "There's nothing but you and me right here."

It was as if he knew exactly what was running through my mind. My tangled thoughts and emotions about what this meant. When he kissed me, I held onto his forearms, desperate to forget about everything but him. His hands slid from my face into my hair. The way his fingers grazed my scalp had me melting on the spot.

He had been in sole control earlier when he'd pinned me to his desk. I wondered if it would be the same now. To test the waters, I released his arms and went to push off his hoodie. He released me to allow it to slip off his shoulders and pool on the floor below us. My hands were on his chest, stroking down his t-shirt and wanting to feel his bare skin. Zayn kept kissing me, his tongue tangling with mine as his hands circled my waist and brought me closer to him.

I trailed my fingers underneath his t-shirt, making him hiss into my mouth before he bit down on my bottom lip. I groaned when his hands pushed at my own shirt, shoving it up my body to expose my skin to the air. Lifting my arms up, I let him pull it off me. He kissed his way down my neck, along my chest, to the top of my breast. His hand was there, tearing down the bralette and pinching my nipple. Covering it with his mouth next, he sucked, licked and nibbled, making me squirm in his hold.

"Zayn," I gasped, breathless all of a sudden.

As he continued to tease my nipple with his tongue, he tore my skirt down my legs along with my underwear, leaving me bare.

"On the bed, little fairy," he demanded against my skin before he pulled back.

I swayed on my feet, momentarily dazed. He gave me a little nudge, setting me into motion. I crawled on the bed, pulling my bralette off as I went. Laying back against his covers, I watched him smirk. Those beautiful hands of his went to his t-shirt, pulling it upwards to expose his chest to me. The last time I'd seen him this way, it'd been too dark for me to make out much. His right arm had ink snaking up it. It curled over his shoulder to meet his neck. I swallowed hard as he continued undressing until he stood at the end of the bed, his hands resting by his sides and his eyes boring holes into mine.

"Spread your legs."

The command sent shivers down my spine. I complied, drawing my legs apart for him. His eyes darkened, pupils dilating further with every passing second he stared at me.

"What an enticing display," he told me as he put one knee on the bed. "Is that all for me?"

"Yes, sir."

He was slow to move towards me, crawling up the bed and making me think of a predator about to devour his prey. Zayn stopped between my legs, placing his hands on both my knees and spreading my legs wider for him. He ran his teeth over his bottom lip as he looked from my pussy to my face. My hands curled around the covers below me, wanting to reach for him. To touch him. My desperation for this man was overwhelming.

Would it ever be enough?

Would my craving for him ever really go away?

Both of his hands slid down my inner thighs as he lowered himself. My lips parted when his face met my stomach and his tongue darted out, circling around my belly button. His tattooed right hand planted on my stomach and he held me down on the bed while he parted my lips with his other one, exposing me entirely.

"Good girl," he breathed over my clit, making me tremble.

All of my attention narrowed to him when his tongue swiped over it. His eyes remained on mine, watching my every reaction to the way he licked me. I don't know why it made the whole thing far more intense. It just did. I was being studied by this man. Documented. He wanted to know what made me tick. It was obvious from the concentration on his face. The darkness lurking underneath was burning me up inside, along with his tongue on my clit. I fisted the covers and let out a shaky breath.

"Zayn," I whined when his tongue moved faster, finding the right spot that had my back arching off the bed.

He released me before leaning towards the bedside table and fishing something out of it. I didn't care what he was getting, only that I had his mouth back on my pussy where I needed it the most. Lowering himself back towards me with something in his hand, I watched him trail his tongue from my clit to my pussy and lower. I squirmed with the sensation. It wasn't the first time anyone had touched me there. He concentrated back on my clit a moment later, his hands moving below him. When his fingers slid inside my pussy, I moaned. This man had no qualms about giving me more than I had ever imagined I could handle. But I had… for him.

I wanted to be his good girl.

Zayn fucked me with his fingers, continuing to suck my clit. It was pushing me closer to the edge. I was so wrapped up in him, nothing else mattered. My brain was empty of everything but him and what he was doing to my body. He slid his fingers from my pussy and shifted. I heard the pop of a cap and knew exactly what he intended.

"Please," I whispered, giving him my explicit consent.

He didn't stop tonguing me. His finger with cool gel applied rubbed around my other entrance, making me shiver with anticipation. When he pressed a single digit inside me, I groaned. He was gentle with his movements, clearly not wanting to hurt me.

"My dirty fairy," he murmured against my clit. "Do you want me to fuck you here?"

I nodded, biting down hard on my bottom lip as he slid his finger in and out of me. The way he smiled was filled with such wicked desire. He went back to sucking my clit while he fucked me, pressing more fingers inside my tight hole to stretch me out for him. To make it possible for me to take his thick dick.

"Harder... please," I cried out when he pressed three fingers inside me. "I think I'm going to come."

My fists were white around the covers. I wanted this man in me, taking what I'd given him. Taking what was his. When he thrust harder, I was gone. My thoughts collided with each other, as did the sensations driving up my spine. The bloom of pleasure sank into my bones. It only lasted seconds, but they had to be some of the best ones of my life.

I panted as my body turned to jelly as my fingers uncurled from the covers. My eyes closed, letting myself settle after my climax. Zayn slowed his movements. His mouth left my clit, and he kissed his way up my inner thigh, letting me know without words what a good girl I'd been.

When I opened my eyes, he was watching me with his head resting against my thigh and his fingers were still buried inside me. His gaze made me feel like I was the only woman he had eyes for.

"Do you want to stop?"

I reached for him, wanting his body against mine, my hands all over him.

"No, please, I want you."

He pulled his fingers from me and sat up, kneeling between my still spread legs. He gripped my hip and tugged me into his lap to give him a better angle. I watched him finish prepping me and himself. Then he was against me, pushing inside me and making it ache in the best possible way.

"Fuck," I ground out through my teeth at the feel of him. The stretch wasn't uncomfortable, but the pressure was intense.

After he used a wipe to clean his fingers off, he placed a hand over my hip and stroked my clit with his thumb to ease me into it. I felt myself relaxing into his touch, into taking him. He was slow as he moved in and out of me. It was so fucking good.

I reached for him again, desperate for more physical contact. Zayn smiled as he adjusted the two of us, pushing my legs up into my chest and leaning over me. He caught my mouth with his, kissing me as he fed me his cock.

"Good girl," he murmured against my lips. "My good little fairy."

"More, please," I gasped.

I couldn't help touching him, running my hands down his chest. The dark hair on it tickled my fingertips, but I liked it. I was enamoured by everything about Zayn.

He took one of my hands, pressing it down on the covers by my head and lacing our fingers together. He watched me as he fucked me, eyes intent on mine as if he didn't want to miss a single moment of this. The sheer intimacy of it had my heart racing out of control.

I pressed my feet into the covers and moved against him, matching his rhythm and encouraging him deeper. He didn't have to tell me I was making him feel good. I could see it in his face. See it in every movement he made. I didn't want this to be all about my pleasure. It had to go both ways.

He took my other hand, pushing it between us and making me touch myself for him. He didn't stop fucking me even as he pressed my own fingers into my pussy, filling me up further. The heel of my palm rubbed against my clit. I felt so full, so much pressure inside me building up to something I wasn't entirely sure I was prepared for. My head might have been too full to even think about coming earlier, but this was different. I was done for when it came to this man and the things he did to me.

"That's it, Tinkerbell, fuck your pussy for me. Show me how much you love taking me and your fingers."

I complied even as he kept his hand on mine, making me touch myself for him. He caught my mouth with his to swallow all my cries until I was shaking under the onslaught.

"Zayn," I cried into his mouth as the world shattered around me. At least, it felt like it. Or maybe it was me succumbing to him. To everything he did to me and made me feel. I was hopelessly addicted to the man inside me.

He groaned, fucking me harder. Letting go of my mouth, he buried his face in my neck, panting as his release washed over him. Almost as if he didn't want me to see him come undone.

The two of us caught our breath for a long minute when we were spent. He pressed kisses to my skin. They were like brands, reminding me of who I belonged to. As if I could forget.

Zayn pulled out of me before plucking me from the bed and taking me into his bathroom to clean me and him up. He put me back in bed, turned out the lights, and joined me. The covers were tucked around us as we lay there facing each other. He took my hand and kissed my fingertips, then laced them together between us.

"What's on your mind?"

I looked away, unsure of how to answer him. Zayn didn't like that because he took a hold of my chin and forced me into meeting his eyes in the dark.

"Arianna."

"You said we couldn't do this, so I'm confused and… and a little scared you're going to be distant again when I wake up tomorrow because our circumstances haven't changed."

"You're right. They haven't."

"Then what—"

He put his fingers over my mouth.

"I'm not finished." He let out a little huff of air. "I didn't mean to be distant, Tink. That has never been my intention. And the rest? Just let it be what it is right now." He moved closer, pressing his forehead against mine and curling his fingers into my hair. "I'm going to take care of you. Do you trust me on that?"

I nodded. I'd trusted him from the start. It hadn't changed because we'd slept together. If anything, it only made me trust him more. He'd looked after me all this time in ways I never knew I needed.

"Say it."

"I trust you."

He pressed a kiss to my mouth and pulled me against his chest, tucking me into his body. I curled an arm around him, wanting to be closer.

"Don't worry, my little fairy," he whispered into my hair. "I protect what's mine."

I settled into him, trying my hardest to shake the weird feeling I got with his words. While Zayn had reassured me things would be okay, he hadn't explained anything. I couldn't forget who he was and why he had a reputation because if I did... I might forget to protect the one thing I knew I couldn't give him when things were so up in the air.

My heart.

TWENTY

Zayn

I sat back as my office door opened, and Remi walked in just as Enzo reached it. She stopped when she saw him, disapproval written all over her features. Unsurprisingly, she wasn't my brother's biggest fan. She was with Arlo when it came to Enzo and his antics. In all honesty, so was I, but he was my brother. Abandoning my family was something I couldn't in all good conscience do. It'd been ingrained in me from a young age, family came first.

"Remi, what a pleasure it is to see you," he said, stepping aside to let her in.

"The feeling isn't mutual," she muttered, brushing past my brother. "And you saw me earlier, so don't try your shit with me."

"One day you'll stop being such a stuck up b—"

"Enzo," I warned, stopping him from saying something to make Remi kick him in the nuts. It wouldn't be the first time. Nor the last.

"Prick," he said under his breath before he stalked out of the room, slamming the door shut behind him.

"Your brother is a dick," Remi said with an eye roll as she walked towards my desk.

"You've noticed."

She grinned and leant her hand on the wood.

"And I've told him to impale himself on a sharp instrument more times than I can count since he started working here."

Enzo was just another problem I had to deal with. If he did as he was told, then I wouldn't have to keep an eye on him. The idiot didn't want to listen, as usual. I swear he was living on borrowed time with all the shit he got up to.

"He deserved it, no doubt."

"I'd prefer Gil and his silence to Enzo constantly talking random shit while I'm trying to work. I swear that boy likes the sound of his own voice far too much."

Remi wasn't going to like what I was about to ask her to do, considering it involved said pain-in-the-arse brother.

"I'm sure Gil would be honoured to hear he's preferable company."

"He'd just grunt and blush if I told him that."

She wasn't wrong. Gil didn't know what to do with female attention. He was too busy trying to be the golden child to notice women staring at him. His quiet, introspective nature was only one of the things that hindered him in our world. Probably why he worked so hard to prove he was more than just the sum of his parts. I loved my brother the way he was, but I wasn't our cunt of a father who wanted to mould us all into his perfect little mafia princes. What a fucking joke. Gil didn't need to prove a single thing to anyone. If only he could see that.

"Anyway, Liza said you wanted to see me."

I stood up, not wanting the desk between us as I walked around it. This required me to be big brother Zayn and not boss Zayn. Resting against the wood, I crossed my arms over my chest and levelled my gaze on her.

"How are things?"

"Fine." She shrugged. "Same old. How's your friend?"

"She's fine." I flicked a hand out. "Actually, she's why I asked for you."

Remi looked instantly suspicious, narrowing her eyes at me and shifting on her feet.

"Did you upset her and want my advice on how to grovel?"

Why the hell would I ever ask her what to do? They were only four years apart in age, sure, but I didn't need advice on how to handle Ari. She was a fierce little thing. It was part of her appeal, to me, anyway. I respected her forthcoming nature, even if it got her in trouble with me on more than one occasion.

"What? No. What makes you think I've done something wrong?"

Remi's brows rose.

"Because you never talk to me about women, and I figured with her being your girlfriend…"

Excuse me?

"She is not my girlfriend, Remi. I already told you she's staying with me for the time being."

She waved a hand around.

"Yeah, yeah, about that. Who is she exactly, Zayn? This whole thing is making me question why you would let some random girl stay with you if she didn't mean anything."

I let out a huff. Remi had a knack for being blunt with me. She had that in common with Ari. I appreciated her honesty, but I didn't need her questioning my life and decisions.

"It's complicated and none of your business."

There was a glimpse of hurt in her expression before it cleared, and she looked away. If there was anyone I wanted to confide in other than Arlo, then it would be Remi. I couldn't when it came to this. There was too much shit on the line right now. I didn't want her getting pulled into this life any more than she already was. Sometimes I wondered if I'd done the right thing when I'd made a deal with her mother. And sometimes I thought about telling Remi the truth. The need not to tarnish her memory of Roberta any further kept me silent on the matter.

"Then why do you want to talk to me about her?" Remi asked, her brow furrowing with the question.

"I'm worried she's getting restless, as she's at home all the time."

"Well, I can hardly blame her if she has to hang out with you all day."

"I'm going to pretend you didn't say that."

She gave me a wink before her expression fell.

"You're treating her okay, right, Zayn? I know you wouldn't hurt a woman, but what I saw when I met her…"

Dropping my arms from my chest, I reached out and took Remi's hand.

"Why are you so concerned about someone you don't know?"

She sighed and rubbed her thumb over the back of my hand.

"It's hard not to be with all the shit the girls here have seen in their pasts. They talk about it to me and it's disheartening how cruel the world can be."

"They're safe now."

"I know they are. You did that for them, giving them this and the power to take their lives back." She waved her free hand around the office, indicating the whole building. "Sometimes I'm sad no one gets to see what you've done for them." She looked up at me. "No one sees how kind you are."

"You know why that is."

"I do."

Remi might not know about the inner workings of my family or my life, but she knew enough about the responsibility and burdens I carried as the son of Gennaro Villetti. The life I led wasn't an easy one by any stretch of the imagination.

I wasn't sure why she seemed so melancholy, but I resolved to find out after I'd told her why I wanted to see her.

"I'm not treating her badly if it makes you feel any better. In fact, you can ask her yourself because I want you to take her out for the afternoon."

Remi's eyes widened.

"You what?"

"Ari needs to spend time with someone other than me. For her own safety, she can't be around her family or friends right now. I trust you to be a friend to her."

She dropped my hand and gave me a disbelieving look.

"You want me to take your girlfriend out on a friend date?"

"Do I have to tell you again she's not my girlfriend? And yes, I do. Go indulge in some retail therapy."

For a moment, she didn't say a word. Then she shook her head.

"You do know I'm not a fan of that right? I'd rather take her to a museum than look at racks of clothes for hours on end."

"Does that mean you will take her out for the afternoon?"

She rolled her eyes.

"You've made it very difficult for me to say no."

"Remi."

"Yes, of course, I'll take your girlfriend out, Zayn."

"She is not—"

"Yeah, yeah, you keep saying. I'm not sure who you're trying to convince, me or yourself."

Ari was categorically not my girlfriend. Our deal was still in place. She was my pet. And the rest of it? Well, it hadn't been a part of the plan.

"Just take her shopping and get a coffee afterwards," I told her, ignoring her comment. I didn't have time to explain shit to Remi about my complicated relationship with Ari. "And I'm sending someone with you to make sure you're both protected."

"Oh great, a babysitter." She gave me a smile to let me know she was joking. "I suppose Arlo isn't so bad."

"I hate to be the bearer of bad news, but Arlo has other things to do."

She narrowed her eyes.

"Then who are you sending with me?"

186

"Enzo."

Remi threw her hands in the air and scowled.

"You cannot be serious? He can't even tie his own shoelaces without supervision."

I reached out and took her hand again.

"My brother isn't completely devoid of competence, Remi, even if he acts like it. And he's been warned about keeping his mouth shut."

"You could send anyone else with me, Zayn. Literally anyone. Hell, I can protect her better than that twat."

I pulled her closer to me.

"Do this for me… please. I want Ari to have a nice afternoon and for you to get to know her. She's not my girlfriend, but she means something to me, okay?"

Remi's expression softened.

"Okay, I'll put up with Enzo, but only because it's you."

"Thank you."

"You owe me for this, though."

I ruffled her hair with my free hand.

"I'll pay up any time, you know that."

She gave me a half-smile and shrugged.

"Yeah, I do."

Squeezing her hand that was entwined with mine, I stroked her shoulder with the other.

"What's wrong, Remi? You seem down."

She bit her lip before looking up at me.

"I'm okay."

"No, you're not. Tell me what's going on."

Remi didn't always confide in me, but I wished she would. If she'd just tell me about Penn's attention, I'd do something about it. She'd told me in no uncertain terms I was not to interfere in any aspect of her life unless she asked for help. I never wanted Remi to feel like I was being overbearing.

"I'm lonely, Zayn," she whispered. "It's like everyone else's lives are moving on without me and I'm stuck here, waiting for something to happen to me when I know it won't unless I go out and do it."

Her fingers tightened around mine as if she needed an anchor to admit these things to me.

"You've been busy the past few weeks with your girl, I mean, Arianna. Not that I'm upset about it, but you're never here and I have no one else to talk to or who even cares about me. You know I have like no friends. I'm awkward, weird and all I do is spend my time here and at home."

The sadness in her voice cut through me. Remi hadn't had it easy.

"Come here."

She let me tug her into my arms and hold her, wrapping her own arms loosely around my back.

"I'm sorry you've felt like I haven't been there for you. That's a failure on my part. If you need me, Remi, I'm here. You just have to tell me."

She let out a little sigh and placed her cheek against my chest. We'd never been particularly affectionate with our pseudo-sibling relationship, but I could sense she needed comforting.

"I know you are. I think I'm feeling a little adrift… and it's making it hard not to feel alone."

I tightened my hold on her.

"Have you thought any more about getting in contact with your dad?"

She shook her head.

"I don't know what I'd even say if I did. Things were pretty shit when they split up, you know? He didn't even fight her for me."

Roberta never told me exactly what happened between her and Remi's father. Remi hated talking about it, so I didn't hassle her, either. I was only mentioning it now because I knew she'd lost most of her family and she felt like she'd missed out on so much of her heritage.

"When you're ready, I'll help you."

"Thank you, Zayn. I don't know what I'd do without you."

She turned her face up and gave me a smile, showing me she was okay. It was at that moment the door to my office opened and Arlo walked in, followed by Ari, who immediately faltered when she saw me and Remi. Her expression darkened a moment later, leaving me with the distinct impression she wasn't happy to find me hugging another woman even if I'd told her Remi and I were just friends.

Oh, little fairy, don't you realise I only have eyes for you?

TWENTY ONE

Zayn

No matter what Arianna thought, my relationship with Remi was purely platonic. I wasn't going to make my little sister feel shit or that we'd done anything wrong, so I turned my attention back to her and smiled, giving her a wink. Then I released her, letting her step back from me. Her head turned, and she spied Arlo and Ari. I'd made him take Ari on a tour of the club to give me time to talk to Enzo and Remi.

"Oh, hey," Remi said, giving Ari a wave.

I could tell Arianna was struggling to keep the jealousy off her face, but she managed it and gave Remi a tight smile.

"Hi."

Remi looked at me again.

"Does she know about today?"

I shook my head. I hadn't informed Ari beforehand, but now I was in for one hell of a conversation with her.

"Go get Enzo to bring the car around and she'll meet you by the back door, okay?"

Remi reached out and squeezed my arm before giving Ari another smile.

"See you in a bit, I guess."

She flounced out of the room with a spring in her step. Arlo looked between me and Ari, whose expression had darkened, and hastily retreated from the room, closing the door behind him.

Coward.

When she didn't speak, I almost sighed. Sometimes Ari let her emotions rule her, but that was fine. I could allow her to have her angry kitten moment and then we could get on with the real reason I needed to speak with her.

"I have a surprise for you."

Ari didn't respond. She gave me daggers and crossed her arms over her chest. I dug my hands into my pockets and took a step towards her.

"You don't want to know what it is?"

"I don't care what it is."

"Tinkerbell."

"Don't you 'Tinkerbell' me when I walked in here and found you touching another woman."

How adorable. Such a jealous little thing you are.

I took my hand out of my pocket and rubbed my chin.

"I see. So when I told you Remi is a friend, you chose to ignore that and jump to the worst possible conclusion when you walked in here and now, you're jealous."

Her expression soured even further.

"I'm not jealous!"

"I would say the look on your face and the fact you're refusing to come over here says otherwise, Ari."

She was about to open her mouth when I put my hand up, stopping her. There was no point in us having a stupid argument like this. Remi was in my life. Ari had to deal with it. She could hash it out with Remi this afternoon if she wanted to.

"Listen, this is very cute and all, but you have nothing to be jealous over. Remi is like a little sister to me." I took another step towards her, cocking my head to the side. "She's certainly not the one I like to collar, bend over my desk and fuck until she's begging for a reprieve now, is she?"

The way Ari's face coloured up at my words had me smiling.

"Come here."

It'd been almost a week since I'd first fucked her over my desk at home. Yesterday, I'd enjoyed having Ari sit on it with her wet little pussy on full display for me while I worked. Hearing her make those pained little noises of frustration behind the gag I placed in her mouth for misbehaving. When I finally did fuck her, she'd been so beautiful, clawing the desk and begging me to stop when I'd made her come too much. Some days, she struggled when she had too much on her mind, which was perfectly okay. I had ways of making it happen if she wanted it, like working her up so much, she could think of nothing else but the pleasure I gave her.

Ari closed the distance between us, staring up at me with confusion in her expression. I reached out and stroked her curls.

"Do you need me to kiss that look off your face so you stop being irrational?"

"I'm not being irrational."

"You are, Tink. It's adorable."

She shoved my hand away from her hair.

"I'm not being adorable, Zayn. This is me being angry at the situation we're in. I don't get to call you mine because of the shit in our lives, so excuse me for hating the idea of someone taking you away from me."

Now I knew the real reason she was upset. Seeing me with Remi reminded her we weren't actually together, nor could we be. At least... not yet.

Reaching up, I gripped her neck with one hand and tugged her closer, forcing her to look at me. I could see the war going on in her mind. She wanted my hand around her neck, but she was irritated with me at the same time.

"The only woman I have any interest in is standing right in front of me, Arianna. This disobedient little brat who can't seem to keep her mouth shut even though she knows she'll get punished for it. I'm convinced she enjoys it when she's in trouble. She likes it when I punish her, and she especially appreciates it when I follow it up with my cock deep inside her. If I didn't have a surprise for her, I'd put her over my desk right now, stretch out those beautiful little holes of hers so I can fuck her until she remembers who she belongs to because she seems to have forgotten. Now open your mouth."

She did as I told her, staring at me with wide eyes as she watched me dribble spit down into it.

"Swallow it like a good girl and I'll consider this little outburst forgiven."

Ari closed her mouth and swallowed.

"I'm sorry, daddy," she whispered before biting her lip.

I leant closer so I could use my teeth to detach hers from her lip and bit it myself. Then I kissed her until she was melting against me with her hand dug into my hair. When I released her, Ari was flushed and looked like she desperately wanted me to bury any part of me inside her body. I didn't have time for that, however.

Taking her hand, I brought her around my desk and made her sit on it as I took a seat in my chair. I slid my hand into my pocket and brushed my fingers over the small box in it.

"Firstly, I've asked Remi to take you out for the afternoon so you two can get to know each other. And you can see exactly why you have nothing to be worried about."

"But it's not safe for me to go out."

"My younger brother is going with you and will keep you safe, Ari. He's under strict instructions about where to take you so it's safe and no one will know, okay?"

She looked worried for a moment more before nodding.

"Okay. It would be nice to get out for a bit... and I guess I'd like to get to know Remi if she's important to you."

I fought against the urge to smile. Instead, I took a hold of her hand and placed the box from my pocket in it.

"And this is because I thought you would like it."

I let go of her hand and sat back, watching her stare down at the box with a raised eyebrow. She opened it with her other hand and gave a little squeak. I'd seen her wear these before when my father took business meetings with hers and she'd been there. It was a little golden ear cuff with a chain attached to a stud.

She took it out and set the box on the desk. I knew she liked it from the joy written on her features. Ari wasn't used to getting gifts. She'd told me so last week in bed, but she appreciated it when I bought her things.

"It's so pretty."

I took it from her fingers. She hopped off the desk and sat in my lap, turning her head so I could put it on her.

"Thank you, daddy."

"You're welcome."

The way she'd taken to calling me that had my heart in knots every time it happened.

"Now, come on. Remi and Enzo will be waiting."

She slipped out of my lap so I could stand up. I took her hand and pulled her over to the office door, stopping just short of it. Cupping her face with my free hand, I stroked my thumb over her cheek.

"Are you going to be a good girl for me?"

"Yes, sir."

I pressed a kiss to her lips, then took her out of the office and along to the back door, where Remi and my brother were waiting. He raised an eyebrow when he saw Ari. I'd warned him not to fuck up and say something inappropriate. After introducing her to my brother, I left Ari with Remi, who I knew would take care of her.

I walked back into my office. I was just taking a seat when the door was thrown open and in strolled Penn.

"Have you heard of knocking?"

"Why would I knock when you asked me to come here?"

I almost rolled my eyes. There was no telling with Penn what kind of shit he would decide to pull. I might trust him to do his job but dealing with him was another matter.

"Where's Remi going, and was that Bennett's daughter I saw with her?"

I levelled my gaze on him, wondering where the fuck he got the audacity to ask me about Remi from.

"Take a seat."

Penn shrugged and sat down in front of my desk with his legs wide open and his tattooed hand resting on his thigh. I was surprised he had any space left on his body that wasn't covered in ink.

"You in a mood today, Z?"

"No, I'm not, but Remi and Arianna have nothing to do with you."

He rolled his eyes.

"You sure about that?"

"I'm very sure. Now, I don't have time for your shit today, so sit and listen, because I have a job for you."

He sat forward and rubbed his hands together.

"Must be important if you called me in here."

I swear to fuck if Penn wasn't so useful, he would be in the fucking grave already many times over. Not by my hand, but by someone else he'd managed to piss off. He had more enemies than clients, but the sneaky fuck was good at what he did. He would never let anyone get the better of him.

"I need you to go view some properties for me."

Penn's eyebrows shot up.

"Me... look at houses... for you?"

"Not houses, Penn. Office spaces. I need you to make sure they're suitable."

I swear Penn was looking at me like I'd grown two heads. This couldn't be done through my usual contacts. It had to be under the radar.

"Suitable how?"

"Well, I need somewhere that's got lots of natural lighting, so big windows are a must. It needs to be a large, open-plan space, a bit like a studio. That would be best. And it needs to be secure. It'll need to have the highest security installed, anyway, but I don't want to take any chances."

I almost smiled at the thought of it, imagining Ari making the space her own. Seeing her setting up shots, adjusting her backdrop depending on what was required, with little minions running around helping her.

"You want me to find you a studio space?"

"Yes."

Penn leant back in his chair and blinked before tapping his black painted nails on his thigh.

"What the fuck do you need a studio for, Zayn?"

"If I needed you to know why, I would have told you. I pay you to do what I ask and not question why. I'm not getting you to kill anyone today. I would have thought you'd been grateful for the change of scenery."

The fucker laughed and stood up.

"I take it you'll send me the listings."

I gave him a nod. He leant forward and tapped his fingers on my desk.

"You've been acting differently since that Michaelson girl showed up. I'm going to find out why."

Before I could say a word, he strolled out of the room with his hands in his pockets, whistling away like he had no cares in the world. I would have to nip that shit in the bud. Penn did not need to meet Ari, and he certainly didn't need to get involved in my personal business.

Ari was personal to me. She was *mine*. It was why I was getting him to find a studio space in the first place. When this was all over, I wanted to give her a future and a space to take her photographs in. Even if that future she had didn't end up including me in it.

TWENTY TWO

Arianna

My fingers absentmindedly played with the chain of the ear cuff Zayn had given me while I stared out the car window. To say this was an awkward journey was an understatement. Enzo kept eyeing me in the rearview mirror, and Remi was fidgeting next to me as if she had no idea what to say. Clearly, Zayn had made them agree to take me out today.

I turned my head and stared at Zayn's brother. It was the first time I'd ever met him. My dad told me Gennaro had three sons. Zayn, Gilberto and Enzo. I had the distinct impression the two younger brothers had no idea Gennaro was in business with my father. Zayn had only told Enzo my name was Ari, not Arianna. He was keeping my identity a secret. It made me question how much he trusted his younger brother.

Maybe Enzo was suspicious about who I was and that's why he kept staring at me. He looked like a younger version of Zayn but with a short beard and dyed blonde hair, with his dark roots showing. I wasn't sure what to make of his brother, but Zayn had assured me Enzo would keep me safe.

My trust in Zayn was probably stupid on my part. I couldn't help myself with that man. I'd never been so enamoured with another person in my life. Probably explained why seeing him with anyone else brought out all of my possessive instincts. I wanted to own him in the way he owned me. Again, a stupid urge. Who could really own a man like Zayn Villetti? He wouldn't bow to anyone, let alone me. Didn't stop me from wanting it. From desiring a future with a man I couldn't have.

"So, Ari, where are you from?" Remi asked. "I mean, what part of the city?"

I glanced at her. She seemed genuine, but I had no real clue what to make of the girl Zayn called his little sister.

"Hackney."

Remi's eyebrow quirked up.

"No offence, but you don't sound like it."

I gave her a sad smile.

"I used to until Dad shipped me off to private school. Kids can be cruel, you know. Was easier to fit in if I sounded more like them."

Not that it helped. I was still seen as common working-class scum to them.

Remi reached over and gave my arm a squeeze. I could tell from her expression she understood. I didn't want to make assumptions about her, but it was hard not to notice she came from a mixed background like me.

"People suck."

I snorted.

"Yeah, they do."

She leant closer to me and lowered her voice.

"If Enzo says anything fucked up to you, just tell me and I'll kick him in the nuts."

"Why would he?"

She rolled her eyes.

"He's a dick who doesn't know when to keep his mouth shut."

I glanced at Enzo, who was giving Remi a dirty look through the rearview mirror.

"I see."

I didn't, but I wasn't going to ask Remi what her beef with Zayn's brother was. After all, I didn't want to be at odds with any of his family if I was ever going to be with Zayn. The thought of it made my heart hurt. My hand went to my chest, rubbing at the sore spot. I was definitely living in fantasyland. I knew very well that Zayn and I couldn't be together. Not when everything was stacked against us.

Enzo pulled up in a car park a few minutes later and got out. Remi unbuckled her seatbelt, prompting me to do the same. We both slid out of the car. Enzo was waiting for us by the front of it, looking bored already.

"Where are we?" I asked as he led us out onto the street.

"Chelsea," Enzo grunted. "Zayn gave me instructions to take you here and I'm supposed to tell you to get whatever you want. I have his card."

I may have lived in London all my life but venturing far from my home turf wasn't something I often did. Shopping in Chelsea would be a whole new experience for me.

"Only the best for Zayn's girl," Remi whispered to me.

"I'm not his girl."

"He said the same thing, but I don't believe him or you."

Remi gave me a wink, leaving me slightly speechless. I didn't think she would be this friendly with me from the outset. Made me feel stupid for getting jealous earlier. I knew there was nothing between her and Zayn except friendship.

Enzo took us into a boutique clothing shop. He waited by the door as Remi and I browsed through the racks. When I looked at the prices, I almost baulked and wondered what the hell Zayn had been thinking, telling Enzo to take us here. Then I remembered he was Gennaro Villetti's son and had likely also amassed a fortune on his own. He was rather generous when it came to me, something I wasn't used to. I still hadn't got over the fact he'd bought me an expensive camera and a few days ago, a laptop was dropped off. I'd started to edit the photos I'd taken of him. I wanted to get framed prints done to hang on his walls. The urge to stamp myself all over his life was all-consuming, but I couldn't do that.

He's not mine. I hate that he's not mine so fucking much.

"So, anything you like?" Remi asked with a slightly bored look on her face.

"You don't like clothes shopping?"

"Not particularly, but Zayn told me to take you out, so here we go." She grabbed a beautiful deep purple dress from the rack and held it up to me. "I bet he'd like you in that."

My cheeks warmed at the thought of Zayn's eyes on me, followed by him bending me over, pushing it up my hips before he fucked me from behind with his hand wrapped around my throat. Shaking my head, I looked away.

"I'm not going to buy something just to suit his tastes."

Remi laughed.

TYRANT

"You shouldn't, but you'd look like a knockout in this, regardless. Try it on."

I gave her a small smile and a nod. We picked out a few more things together before heading to the back, where the dressing room cubicles were. I slipped inside, hanging up the clothes and stripped out of my own.

"So, you and Zayn?" Remi asked through the curtain.

"We're not… it's not… we're not in a relationship."

"So, he's just banging you, then?"

I almost choked on my own breath at her words.

"Are you always this blunt?"

"Not really, but Zayn's no-nonsense, and if you're with him, I figure you can handle it."

I put the purple dress on and looked at myself in the mirror. It perfectly accentuated my figure, hiding the bits I wasn't so keen on and highlighting my curves. Remi had been right. I opened the curtain and stepped out so she could see. Her eyes roamed over me for a moment before she smiled.

"Well, damn. Be glad Enzo's over there or he'd be saying something inappropriate."

"You have good taste."

She shrugged and gave me a smile. I slipped back into the dressing room and tried something else on, coming out to show her. After I'd chosen a few outfits, Remi called Enzo over, who dutifully paid for them and held the bags. If Zayn was going to treat me to new things, I might as well be grateful and actually get clothes I liked. I doubted my coming back empty-handed would please him. It might earn me a punishment. I didn't want any more of those today. What I did want was for him to hold me, care for me and reassure me everything would be okay.

"Why are you being so quiet?" Remi asked Enzo when we were walking to the next shop.

"Other than my brother threatening me if you told him I'd been a dick?"

"Did he tell you he'd take your toys away?"

Enzo opened his mouth, then closed it, settling for shooting Remi daggers instead. I hid a smile behind my hand. Remi clearly had no qualms about telling it like it was, and I respected that. In fact, she was more like me than I realised. I was beginning to see why Zayn wanted me to get to know her.

It made me miss Kaylee all the more. I wanted to talk to her just once to make sure she was okay. To make sure she wasn't worried about me. I had to think of Dad too. He'd hate me being gone. It made my stomach sink. Here I was getting treated to an afternoon out and they had no idea where I was. Dad thought I'd been taken by another gang.

Berating myself over the situation wouldn't help matters, so I shoved the thoughts away.

Just enjoy getting to know Remi. She's important to Zayn. And he's important to you.

I stuck to my resolve as we visited a few more shops, adding to the bags Enzo was holding for me. And when we got coffee afterwards. Remi turned out to be a lot of fun. She'd been awkward at first, but as the two of us relaxed into being around each other, she opened up to me and I did her. She was twenty-six, four years older than me and had known Zayn most of her life, just like me. I discovered she lived alone in a small flat and didn't get out too much, so this was as much of a treat for her as it was for me. I decided I liked her and hoped we could be friends, that I'd get the chance to spend more time with her.

I was glad she didn't ask me more questions about Zayn because I didn't know how to answer them. Telling her the truth, that I'd made a deal with him in exchange for him covering up the fact I'd murdered my uncle wasn't something I could do. And nothing else could explain why my situation with him was all kinds of fucked up.

We were walking back to the car, joking with each other about Enzo's arms being completely full of shopping bags. He was scowling at the two of us and looking like he'd rather be anywhere else. I'd just nudged Remi's arm when a black van pulled up beside us, wheels screeching to a halt. The next thing I knew, several men in balaclavas piled out. One of them grabbed a hold of me, shoving Remi out of his way in the process. She let out a yelp, falling onto the ground as the man pulled my arms behind my back. I struggled in his grasp, wanting to know what the fuck was going on.

"Let go of me!"

He shoved a gag in my mouth and a hood over my head, making everything go black. I was picked up and held against a chest, so my arms were restrained. I kicked out instead, trying to scream behind the gag.

"Keep back, fuckin' keep back," a man shouted from nearby.

"Get away from her!" Remi screamed.

"Get in the fuckin' van."

I was thrown down stomach first onto a metal floor. A body pinned me down on it. The van door slammed shut. We were jolted forward as it took off. I tried to kick out at the person holding me. He got off me, grabbing a hold of my arms and tying my wrists behind my back. I kept kicking, but my legs were tied too. My heart pounded so hard, I could hear it ringing in my ears. My fight-or-flight response was in full force. I breathed in and out, trying to calm my nerves. I couldn't scream or move properly, so I stopped struggling to conserve my energy. Yes, I was terrified and rightly so, but making things worse for myself wouldn't do me any favours.

I had to take stock of my situation. Had to work out what was going on.

What the fuck just happened?

Had I just been kidnapped in broad daylight?

If so… by whom and why?

Zayn assured me I'd be safe with his brother and Remi. So what the hell was I going to do now I'd been taken by fuck knows who to fuck knows where?

You stay calm and you wait. All you can do now is wait.

My heart sunk right down to my feet. This was bad. Really fucking bad, but I couldn't afford to lose my shit. The only way out of this was to keep my head on straight until I could find out how to escape. Until I could find out who wanted me and why.

You can do this, Ari. Be strong. Make Zayn proud of you for not falling apart.

And it was the only thought that carried me through the journey in the van to whoever had the audacity to take me away from the man I was pretty sure I was falling in love with.

TWENTY THREE

Arianna

The van came to a stop. I didn't know how long we'd been driving. It felt like forever, but who really knew. The door opened. I was dragged along the floor and hauled over someone's shoulder. No one spoke. I could hear gravel crunching under their feet and the sound of a metal door being opened. Whoever was carrying me grunted at someone. Then I was placed down in a chair a few minutes later.

I breathed in and out through my nose, fearing what would come next, but knowing I had to keep myself together. There were low voices near me, but my heart was hammering so hard, I couldn't make out what they were saying above the noise.

Keep your shit straight, Ari.

How did anyone stay calm when they'd been kidnapped by unknown people?

I didn't have a knife or anything to defend myself with. Not like I had done with Uncle Justin. Reminding myself of that night wouldn't help matters. I should have told Zayn I needed one, but I'd put all my trust in him to keep me safe. To protect me from outside threats. I didn't think I'd need it. Turns out, I really fucking did.

"Did you hurt her?" came a voice from my left. One that sent a chill running down my spine.

"No, we fuckin' didn't, boss man."

The hood on my head was pulled off. I blinked as the light filled my eyes, almost blinding me with its intensity. The room came into focus a moment later. I was surrounded by men, but it was the one in the middle that had me wanting to throw up.

"Hello, Ari," Derek McGovern said with a sinister smile on his face. "Nice to see you again."

He wasn't a tall man. His men towered over him, but he was intimidating all the same. A deep scar was etched into his left cheek. It gave him a crooked smile. His brown hair was slicked back, and he wore a suit with an overcoat. The surrounding men were in less formal attire. Tracksuits and Reeboks. One of them had a cap on backwards, rubbing his hands together before he cracked his knuckles.

My eyes darted around the room. We were in some sort of warehouse. It was cold and my skin had broken out in goosebumps, but I figured it might also have something to do with the fear seeping into my veins.

The one person I wanted to stay as far away from as possible had a hold of me.

"Take that shit out her mouth."

Derek waved at me. Someone stepped up behind me and tore the gag from my mouth. I hadn't realised they were there.

I coughed, spitting out the cloth fibres stuck to my tongue and the roof of my mouth.

"That's better. Now we can have a little chat, can't we?"

I might be scared shitless, but his words pissed me off. This whole situation made me angry. Angry at the fact the moment I'd been away from Zayn, this had happened. Angry that I'd been taken against my will. I was just plain fucking angry the person who'd done it was Derek McGovern. Anyone who knew me was well aware of my temper and how I didn't take shit lying down. I let the rage fill me, allowing it to overtake my fear. I was not weak. I was Bennett Jerome Michaelson's daughter, raised to be strong as fuck, and no one, not even McGovern, was going to take that away from me.

"What the fuck? Are you fucking crazy?" I ground out a moment later, not caring to heed my language. "Kidnapping me in broad daylight? Real fucking smart."

Derek's smile fell. I might have only met him a few times, but I'd never mouthed off to the man before. Perhaps it wasn't real smart of me either, but I was too pissed off to care. Too worked up to stay calm any longer.

He took a step towards me, his brown eyes narrowing on my face.

"Watch your tone with me."

I snorted and shook my head.

"Oh, I'm sorry. Did you think I was a meek little girl or something? Is that why you want me?"

His eyes widened.

"Yeah, I fucking know, Dezza. Justin told me what you wanted."

I watched his hand flex at his side. He definitely didn't like me calling him that, but who gave a fuck? He was the one who had his men hustle me into a van, tie me up, and bring me here.

"Did he, huh? And where the fuck is your uncle, Ari, hmm? He's been missing just like you. Makes me think you had something to do with that."

I shrugged and arched an eyebrow at him. He didn't deserve to know what I'd done to Justin, nor would I admit it to a room full of people.

Derek looked around at his men, a dark expression settling across his face. Then he waved a hand at them.

"All of you, out."

The man nearest to him spluttered.

"What, why?"

Derek turned on him.

"I fuckin' said so. Get out."

The men scattered like the wind with the irritation in Derek's voice, leaving me all alone with a man I was beginning to despise more and more by the minute. He took a step closer to me. I didn't shrink back in my chair, instead, I met his eyes head-on.

"Where have you been?"

"As if I'm going to tell you that."

He shrugged out of his overcoat and threw it on a table. Then he took off his suit jacket, letting it join his coat, leaving him in a shirt and a waistcoat. Unbuttoning his cuffs, he rolled up his sleeves. He tucked his thumb into the pocket of his waistcoat before approaching me. I flinched when he reached out with his free hand and brushed a finger along my jaw.

"Quite the mouth on you, girl. It would be a pity to mar such a pretty face now, wouldn't it?"

He dropped his hand, shoving it in his pocket and drawing out a small pocketknife. He flicked open the blade and ran his finger down it.

"You wouldn't dare."

He smiled at me.

"Wouldn't I?" He let the hand with the blade in it fall to his side. "It would serve your father right. Out here trying to muscle in on my fuckin' turf."

"He wants nothing to do with you or Peckham."

Derek eyed me, running his yellowing teeth over his bottom lip. He kept a hold of his knife while drawing out a cigarette packet. He extracted one and lit it. Taking a drag from it, he blew out the smoke in my face. I coughed, hating the smell of it. I didn't mind Zayn's cigarillos, but this made me queasy.

My heart ached at the thought of Zayn. What I wouldn't do to sit in his lap while he smoked and breathe in the scent of him right now.

"Oh, I know. That's just what I'm telling my boys, but then you had to go make a fuckin' mess of it all. Now he's out here, threatening my boys, demanding to know where his whore of a daughter is." He waved his cigarette at me. "As if I fuckin' knew after Justin disappeared. He was supposed to bring you to me. That was the fuckin' deal."

I wanted to spit in his face. Calling me a whore. How original.

"If I'm such a whore, why do you even want me? You going to tell me my pussy is used and you're doing me a favour by wanting to fuck me?" I did spit at him then. "As if I would ever want your weak dick anywhere near me. I'd be doing you a favour, not the other way around."

Probably wasn't sensible of me to antagonise Derek. In fact, it would only get me in trouble. My reckless streak was out in force. I couldn't shove her back in her box, nor did I want to.

Derek reacted fast, his hand whipping out and pressing the tip of his knife at the corner of my mouth. He shoved his cigarette in his mouth and glared at me.

"No one is going to want you after I deface this mouth of yours. I'll cut you up, you little bitch, then the only man who will pay you any attention is me. Don't need you looking pretty, and everyone will know who you belong to. Me. I'll fuck you up so bad, you won't know your own name any longer. All you'll be is a whore who takes my dick."

The sinister look on his face almost made me keep my mouth shut, but I'd been intimidated enough in my life by men like him wanting things I wasn't willing to give.

"I wouldn't do that if I were you."

"No? And why the fuck not? I'm not scared of Bennett."

"He's not the one you need to be afraid of."

Derek's eyes narrowed.

"Who then, bitch? I don't see anyone coming to your fuckin' rescue."

There was no way for anyone to find me as far as I knew, but I wasn't going to let Derek think he would get away with this. Surely Remi and Enzo would have told Zayn I'd been taken by now. Would he stop at nothing to find me? He kept telling me I belonged to him, and he'd protect me. I had to trust in that. I had to… if I didn't, I would have no hope at all.

When I said nothing, Derek laughed at me, pulling his blade away from my face.

"You're full of shit, Ari, thinking you can pull a fast one on me."

The longer I kept him talking, the better my chances. I had to find a way out of here. Not that I could go anywhere with my hands and feet tied.

"Why was Justin taking me to you?"

Derek snorted at my change of subject and paced away, twirling the blade with his movements.

"Didn't he tell you?"

"No."

"We had a deal. You, in exchange for your father's head, making way for Justin to take over… and he'd answer to me." He slapped a hand on his chest. "My fuckin' puppet. No one would question a Michaelson in charge, but they'd never accept me."

My hands shook at his words. Derek was going to kill my father for my uncle. Justin's betrayal was much worse than I first suspected. So much worse.

"Justin wanted Dad dead?"

"Of course. Jealous fuck wanted to run things. Bennett was in the way. I was going to enjoy torturing that cunt and now everything's gone to shit." Derek spun around and advanced on me, shoving the blade in my face. "Now, where the fuck is Justin, Arianna? I need the little shit, don't matter if he didn't uphold his fuckin' side of the deal. He is the key to my fuckin' takeover."

My hate for my uncle stuck to my veins like tar. Not only had he tried to rape me and deliver me to McGovern, but he was also going to have my father killed. His own brother. How could he? How could he do such a thing?

"Where is he?" I let out a nasty laugh, pure rage sinking into every pore. "He's fucking dead."

Derek's eyes went wide.

"Dead?"

"I killed him."

My mouth formed a smile. The guilt I'd felt at taking a life disappeared with the knowledge of what my uncle had planned. He deserved it. And I'd do it again in a heartbeat, even if it had left a permanent stain on my hands. I didn't want to wash it away. I wanted to wear it like a badge of honour.

"I stabbed him in the neck and made him bleed out all over himself. And if you think I'm ever going to bow down to you, you're fucking mistaken. I'll kill you too."

Before Derek had a chance to say a word to me, there was a loud shout from somewhere in the building, then a shot fired, followed by a thump as if a body had dropped to the floor.

Derek's head whipped around to the door as it opened and in walked the man who made my heart lurch in my chest and left me breathless every time I was in his presence.

The sex club owning mafia prince with a gun hanging by his side and a calm expression on his face.

The man every inch of my being belonged to.

Zayn Villetti.

TWENTY FOUR

Arianna

I t didn't occur to me to question Zayn having a gun. Strict gun laws here didn't mean criminals couldn't get access to illegal weapons. My dad had two. Zayn belonged to the mafia, so it went without saying he would have the means and contacts to own one himself. All I felt was relief that he was here.

"Hello, McGovern," Zayn said, his deep voice displaying no emotion as he stopped just inside the room, taking both Derek and me in.

I knew that tone, and it scared the crap out of me. It was usually followed up by punishments for me. Derek was in huge fucking trouble right now. Especially given the fact he had a blade in my face.

"I suggest you step away from my property. I'm not a forgiving man, nor do I tolerate anyone touching things that belong to me."

Why the hell was my heart flipping over in my chest at his words? The first time Zayn had referred to me as his property, I hadn't been very impressed. Now, I was practically swooning and wanting to lay myself at his feet to say thank you for coming for me. I wanted to kiss his shoes, let him collar me and spit in my mouth. The first time he'd done it, I'd been too stunned to process the whole thing. He'd done it again earlier without giving me any warning. I didn't know why it made my legs shake and my body hot, but it did. Questioning the desires Zayn brought out in me was futile.

Just like I called him daddy, I wanted him to spit on me.

Did it matter what the reason was?

No.

It just mattered that I liked it, and so did he.

However, I shouldn't be thinking about that when I was tied up with a knife in my face.

Priorities, Ari, get them straight!

"Not so full of shit now, am I?" I hissed at Derek, who was staring at Zayn with confusion in his eyes.

"Who the fuck are you?"

Zayn cracked his neck and stepped closer.

"Someone you should really think twice about disrespecting, Derek."

Derek's eyes went to the gun in Zayn's hand. I watched him swallow, then straighten, dropping the knife from me as he turned to face Zayn.

"Oh yeah?"

Zayn didn't even flinch as Derek stepped towards him with his knife clutched tightly in his fist in front of him.

"Mmm. Arianna Michaelson is property of the Villetti family."

Derek's steps faltered.

"Villetti? Fuck, you're—"

Zayn raised his gun and shot. Derek screamed. The knife clattered on the floor and his hands went to his crotch. His knees fell out from underneath him as he dropped to the floor.

"What the fuck? You fuckin' shot me in the dick!"

Zayn closed the distance and stared down at the crying man in front of him. His eyes flicked up to me and there I saw the concern in them as he took in my appearance. Then he shut it down, his face going blank as he looked at Derek again. He squatted down, leaning his gun on his knee and met Derek's eyes, cocking his head to the side.

"Just so we're clear, that was for your little deal with Justin. You wanted to fuck her, didn't you? Only it wouldn't be fucking, would it, Derek? It would have been rape. Spineless men like you don't deserve to own a cock."

Derek whimpered, staring at Zayn with fear in his glassy brown eyes. I could see the blood seeping into his clothes at his crotch.

Zayn put his gun right next to one of Derek's knees and shot him at point-blank range. The gun going off rang in my ears. Derek screamed again as the bullet shattered his knee.

"That's for your men shoving her in the back of a van."

He put his gun to Derek's other knee and fired again.

"That's for tying her up."

Zayn put the gun down next to him and reached over, picking up the discarded knife. He looked at the blade, then he shoved Derek down on the floor. He put his hand on Derek's shoulder to pin him there. There was a deadly gleam in his eyes as he smiled at the man below him.

"And this?" He put the knife to Derek's neck. "This is for touching what's mine."

I watched in horrified fascination as Zayn dragged the blade across Derek's neck, digging into his flesh and making sure Derek wouldn't survive the wounds he inflicted. He wiped the knife off on Derek's clothes. I noticed he had a pair of gloves on as he tucked the knife into Derek's trouser pocket, meaning his fingerprints wouldn't be on it.

Zayn rose to his feet and watched Derek gurgle and bleed out on the floor with a blank expression on his face. He killed a man in cold blood for kidnapping me. And I didn't know what the fuck to say or think. His eyes went to me as he stepped around the pooling blood on the floor and walked towards me.

"Tinkerbell."

All I could feel was gratitude he was here for me. I should be feeling other things about what he'd done, but my only thought was for him.

"Daddy."

His lip twitched as he approached me and squatted by my feet. I watched him untie the rope around my ankles. He moved around me to untie my hands and pulled me up.

"Come, we have to leave right now."

I had questions. So many questions, but Zayn was too busy pulling me away. He picked up the gun on the way to the door. He burst through it a moment later. A man was lying in a pool of blood on the other side of it. I stared at him as Zayn tugged me down the corridor.

"How… how did you know where I was?"

"We'll talk about it in the car, Arianna. Just keep quiet and come with me."

His hold on my hand tightened and his strides grew longer, making it difficult for me to keep up. I didn't try to talk to him again as he led me outside. There were warehouses everywhere around us. He dragged me away from the one we'd been in. I could hear the sound of cars. I looked behind us just before he ducked around the side of the building, spying a bunch pulling up outside of it.

"Zayn, what's happening?"

"Quiet," he hissed at me.

I was dragged between the two buildings and then out the other side. He hustled me to an idling car, opening the door and shoving me inside it. He got in behind me, forcing me to move across to the other seat. The car set off the moment Zayn slammed the door shut behind us.

"Take this," Zayn said, shoving the gun at someone in the front seat.

My eyes darted to it, finding Arlo driving and Enzo with the gun. Zayn peeled the gloves off his hands before he turned to me.

"Are you hurt?" he asked, feeling my body with his hands to check me over.

I shoved them away because I didn't need him touching me up in front of his brother and Arlo.

"I'm fine, Zayn. What I want to know is what the fuck just happened. Who was in those cars?"

He ignored my question and cupped my cheek, his eyes darting over my face. The worry in his features had my heart lurching.

"Did he touch you?"

I frowned, then realised what he meant.

"Other than to shove his knife in my face, no."

Zayn leant closer, apparently heedless to the fact his brother was staring at us from the front of the car.

"Good. No one touches what's mine."

I swallowed at the intensity in his voice and the way he was looking at me. I couldn't let it stop me from getting answers. Something about this wasn't adding up right. How did he know where I was? How did he know who took me? He hadn't seemed the slightest bit fazed by the fact it was Derek when he walked into the room. Like he already knew.

I shifted back away from him, forcing him to drop his hand from my face.

"Zayn... how did you know where I was?"

He sat back, his features closing themselves off from me. His eyes went to my ear and the cuff he'd given me earlier.

"I put a tracker on you."

The fact he'd answered so readily made me incredibly suspicious. My fingers went to my ear. He'd given me the ear cuff right before I'd left his club. It couldn't be a coincidence. The warning bells sounded in my head.

"This? You put a tracker in this?"

"Yes."

The way he was so calm about it frustrated me. How could he think it was okay? I might have wanted him to keep me safe, but him putting a tracker on me was a step too far.

"What the fuck, Zayn? You tagged me like a dog! Why the fuck would you do that?"

I wanted to rip it out of my ear, but I didn't. My hand shook as I dropped it into my lap and curled it into a fist.

"I needed to know where they were taking you."

It was then I realised why this situation was so off.

"You… you knew they were going to take me? You knew Derek was going to kidnap me!"

He inclined his head once.

"Why? Why the fuck would you let that happen to me? You're supposed to keep me safe. That was the deal. That was our fucking deal."

"He was a threat to you and your father that needed eliminating. You asked me to save Bennett and stop the war. That's what I did." He cocked his head to the side. "I had no other way of getting to Derek. You were my way in because he wanted you. I would've never let him have you, Ari. You were perfectly safe. I was always coming for you. And besides, I had to get to you before your father arrived. We tipped him off to Derek's location, but I couldn't let him find you there. You're mine."

I wanted to shove him. I wanted to fucking scream. And most of all, I wanted to cry because this felt like a horrific breach of trust between us. He'd allowed me to get kidnapped. He'd planned this whole thing and left me in the dark. I didn't even have time to process the fact he'd tipped my father off. That he wasn't letting me go back to my dad. I was too angry about everything else.

"Safe? I was safe? I wasn't fucking safe, Zayn. He was going to cut my face up!"

Zayn looked out of the window behind me. I was going to shout at him again to get his attention when I realised the car had stopped. Turning away from him, I fumbled with the door and shoved it open, scrambling out of the car. Zayn got out the other side and before I knew it, he'd grabbed a hold of my arm and was hustling me down the back alley to the club. Glancing behind me, I noticed Enzo and Arlo following. Zayn's brother was looking between us with a strange expression on his face. I didn't have time to examine why as Zayn shoved me through the back door.

The next thing I knew, we were in his office, and he'd slammed the door shut behind us. I wrenched myself out of his grasp and backed away, curling my hands into fists.

"Arianna, if you'd let me explain…"

"You let me get kidnapped when you promised to keep me safe. How the hell did you think that would make me feel?" I all but screamed at him.

There was nothing but hurt and anger fuelling me right then. My heart burned in my chest, crippling me with its intensity.

"Nothing happened to you."

"That isn't the fucking point! You allowed this to happen, and you didn't tell me. You didn't fucking include me in your plans. Do I even mean anything to you, Zayn? Or am I really just a fucking pet to you, huh? Just the girl you made a deal with."

I let out a shuddering breath.

"Well, guess what? That fucking deal is over. Consider yourself free of me because there's no war anymore. No fucking threat to me. Derek's dead. Justin's dead. All the people who wanted my father to die are fucking gone."

Zayn stared at me like he was unable to comprehend what I was saying.

"What do you mean?"

"Derek was going to kill my father," I choked out. "He was going to kill my father and put Justin in charge as his puppet. That's why my uncle took me. It's why all of this happened! My uncle betrayed me and my father in the worst fucking way."

Tears slipped down my cheeks. I hated the fact I was crying when I was so angry, I could barely control it.

"And now you? You've fucking betrayed me too. You betrayed my trust in you. I thought I meant something to you because why else would you have slept with me when it wasn't part of our deal. But this? This proves I don't mean shit to you."

The fact his expression didn't change, and he didn't flinch at my words, had my heart tearing into shreds. I'd been stupid enough to fall for this man. To let him make me believe we had something real that went beyond the deal I'd made with him. It was all a lie. One big fucking lie.

"You do mean something to me, Ari." His voice was quiet and soft. "I didn't do this to hurt you. I did it to protect you."

The fact he was so fucking emotionless over it killed me further.

"Why should I believe anything you tell me? You didn't trust me with this, so why should I trust you? Why should I listen? You're not even sorry, are you?"

"I'm not sorry I let you get kidnapped. Derek is dead. That's what I needed to happen. But I didn't want this." He waved at me. "I didn't want to upset you."

I swiped at my face. It was too late for that. It was too late for all of it.

"Then you should have thought about that before you set all of this in motion."

I shoved my way past him and ripped the door open, unable to look at his face any longer.

"Where are you going?"

I turned back, finding him staring at me with a dark expression etched on his features.

"Away from you."

"Arianna, you're not going anywhere. Did you forget you belong to me?"

This man was so fucking infuriating. How dare he say that to me after everything he'd done today?

"Oh, you're worried I'm going to walk out of here, are you? Well, you've made that fucking impossible. I can't go back to my father, anyway. I'd have to tell him what Justin did and right now, I can't handle any more pain."

My heart cracked in my chest. It broke right open, and I felt like I was bleeding out. I'd been happy to see his face when he'd turned up. Now I hated the very sight of him. Hated he'd put me through this and didn't trust me or let me in on his plans.

"Don't follow me, Zayn. I don't want to talk to or see you right now. Not when all you've done is hurt me."

And with that, I walked out of the room, slamming the door shut behind me.

TWENTY FIVE

Zayn

I stared at the closed door Ari had just stormed out of moments ago, too stunned to do a single thing. There was a whole part of me screaming inside my head to go after her, but I couldn't. Not after the accusations she'd thrown at me. After seeing so much pain in her eyes. Pain I'd caused her.

I'd known she would be angry with me for lying to her about today. I had planned to mitigate the damage by sitting her down and explaining it to her afterwards. However, I was not at all prepared for her to tell me I'd betrayed her. For her to think I didn't care. That I didn't trust her.

I do care. Fuck, seeing you tied up by that cunt, his knife in your face, Tink… it was torture.

I wanted to make it safe for her to go back out into the world again. By killing Derek, I'd stopped the war in its tracks. I protected her father even though I didn't have to. I did it for her. And I wasn't going to say I regretted it. It would be a lie.

What I did regret was not realising Ari's feelings for me ran far deeper than I ever suspected. And because of that, I'd managed to fuck everything up between us.

I'm sorry. Fuck. I just want to tell you I'm sorry.

The door swung open and my brother stormed in, followed by Arlo, who looked incredibly concerned.

"What the fuck was all that shit about, Zayn?" Enzo demanded, his dark eyes fixed on my face and irritation etched all over his features.

"What shit?"

He waved at the open doorway.

"That's Bennett Michaelson's daughter, isn't it? Why the hell is she here and what the fuck did she mean about you two having a deal?"

I didn't have time to placate my brother right now. No, I needed to think about how I was going to deal with the mess I'd got myself into with Ari. How to apologise to her. How not to lose the only person I'd ever wanted to keep by my side.

"It has nothing to do with you."

"Nothing to do with me? You fucking involved me." He stabbed a finger in my direction. "You demanded I take her and Remi out and to let those guys take her. You failed to tell me you were planning on shooting up a gang in the process of getting her back. What the fuck, Zayn!"

Arlo closed my office door and stood by it. At least he had the sense to make sure this conversation was kept private. The rest of the club did not need to be aware of what went down this afternoon. I was still going to have to deal with Remi at some point. I'd left my driver with her when we'd picked up

Enzo so he could bring the other car and her back here. It could wait. My situation with Ari could not.

"Still doesn't make it your business. I told you to do a job, and you did it. What more do you want me to say?"

"I want you to tell me the truth. Why the hell are you involving yourself with those gangs? They aren't your business either. Does *Papà* know about this?"

Did my brother not know when to shut the hell up? Clearly not because right now, he was asking me shit I had no answers for. Not ones I could tell him, anyway.

My heart hurt and my head throbbed from my conversation with Ari. Well, it wasn't really a conversation, more her shouting at me and me having no clue what to say to her in return. I still didn't know, and Enzo wasn't helping matters. The tight hold I usually had on my emotions snapped. He had some fucking nerve questioning me when he was a waste of space who didn't give a shit about our family reputation, unlike me.

"Do you ever wonder why no one tells you a single fucking thing, Enzo? Do you? If you stopped for one fucking moment, you'd realise we all treat like a child because you behave like one."

"I'm not a child."

The way he spat it at me only fuelled my ire.

"You are fucking clueless when it comes to this family. All you do is cause trouble for everyone and leave us to clean up your messes. I asked you to do one fucking thing for me." I slapped a hand on my chest. "One fucking thing to help me after everything you've put this family through and you dare stand there and question me about my life like you have any right to it."

My feet carried me over to my brother and I got right up in his face.

"Let me make something crystal clear to you. The things I've done and sacrificed for this family? You wouldn't be able to handle it. You don't understand what it means to be the eldest and have every-fucking-thing weighing on your shoulders. Not even Gil truly fucking understands what the man we call father has done. What he has forced me to be complicit in. And you, of all people, don't get to question me until you grow the fuck up and start acting like a Villetti instead of a petulant little brat."

Enzo blinked. Never in my life had I lost my temper with my brother, but he had to keep pushing me.

The thought of my father made me sick. How he'd chased after my mother when she'd worked up the courage to leave him because of all his affairs and the emotional abuse he subjected her to. The way he'd beaten the living daylights out of her for it. And now… now she was on life support at home because he put her there. My father refused to let her go, even though she required a ventilator to breathe because she couldn't do it on her own. He'd paid off his doctors to make sure no one else knew about the condition he'd left her in. He was still punishing her almost ten years after he put her in a fucking coma.

Enzo and Gil didn't know about that. They thought she'd been in an accident. If you counted my father's fists as "an accident." Gennaro Villetti was a liar and a sadistic piece of shit. There was no fucking way I was ever letting him get near

Arianna. He could never know I had her and how I felt about her. Never. He might rip away the only good thing in my life if he did. That is, if I hadn't already destroyed things between us all by myself.

"If you go to our father and breathe a word of this, make no mistake, I will make you sorry you dared cross me, you hear me, Enzo? I will make you pay because this shit with Ari and her father, it's my business. Not yours, not our father's, but mine. Because she's fucking mine. And I will not allow you to jeopardise any of it by involving Gennaro."

Enzo took a step back from me. My breathing was heavy and my fists clenched at my sides. The pent up rage coursing through my veins was going to burst if he didn't get the fuck out of my sight.

"What did *Papà* do to you?" he whispered with wide eyes and a confused expression on his face.

"You think you've had it bad with him, Enzo, but you aren't privy to the real Gennaro Villetti. Despite what you think of me, I hope for your sake you never become acquainted with him."

Enzo might be a massive pain in my arse, but he was my baby brother. I cared about the idiot regardless of his attitude to everything and everyone around him.

"Zayn…"

I shook my head.

"Promise me you won't breathe a word of this to him."

"I won't. I promise."

My fists unclenched.

"Good. Now get the fuck out before I do something we both regret."

Enzo's eyes were full of sadness, anger and confusion as he left the room, slamming the door shut behind him. I didn't have the energy to give a shit about it. As long as he kept his word, he could do whatever the fuck he wanted.

I didn't look at Arlo as I walked over to the sofa and threw myself down into it, putting my head in my hands.

What a fucking mess.

"You okay, Zayn?"

"No, I'm not fucking okay," I ground out through my teeth.

"Need to hit something?"

I dragged my fingers through my hair.

"No. I need… I don't know what I need."

I did know. I needed *her*. The thought of Ari walking away from me… I couldn't cope with how it made me feel. How my insides were tearing apart like someone had gutted me.

"She's still here, in case you were worried she'd left."

I deflated, slumping back against the sofa as my fingers went to the bridge of my nose.

"I fucked up."

"I told you she'd be trouble."

I hadn't wanted to listen to Arlo when it came to Arianna. Apparently, I'd been too busy being enamoured with the girl, consumed with the need to take care of her, to become her everything because she made me feel alive for the first time since my mother had been put in a coma.

"You failed to warn me she'd cause trouble here." I laid my other hand on my chest. "She's going to put me in an early grave."

I heard Arlo snort. Dropping my hand from my face, I looked at him. The fuck was smirking.

"I'd question how a twenty-two-year-old managed to get you all twisted up like this if I hadn't met her or watched the two of you together."

"What's that supposed to mean?"

"I know I was against you helping her, but now, I genuinely think she's good for you, Zayn. So how about you stop moping around and go fix what you broke."

I sighed and looked away.

"I would if I knew how."

"An 'I'm sorry' might be a start."

Normally, I wouldn't make apologies to anyone. She was different.

"She thinks I betrayed her because I didn't trust her with the plan. That I don't care about her."

"Do you trust her?"

Dragging my teeth across my bottom lip, I pondered his question. She had given me no reason not to trust her other than when she threatened to go back to her father. Ari hadn't done anything since then. Fuck, she'd stayed in the club even though she was angry, hurt, and upset with me. I didn't know if it was because of her feelings for me or because she dreaded telling her father the truth about Justin. Or... was it both?

"Yes."

Arlo didn't look remotely surprised I'd answered that way when I turned my gaze back to him.

"Then prove it to her."

"How?"

He shrugged.

"You know her best, not me, but my suggestion would be to tell her the truth about your family and give her the option to walk away from all of this."

I hadn't explicitly told Arlo why I was so hell-bent on protecting Ari. On keeping her away from my father. He knew who Gennaro was behind his mask, and he knew me, so no doubt he'd guessed.

"I can't do that. I can't let her leave me."

"Then work it out yourself. I think you know what she wants to hear. Give it to her or be prepared to have an uphill battle on your hands."

Did I know what Ari wanted to hear? I thought I had until today, but I was wrong. It wasn't about what she wanted to hear, but what she needed. Her words from earlier, when she'd got jealous over Remi, rang in my ears.

"I don't get to call you mine."

What my girl truly wanted... what she needed... was to know I was hers. The fucked up thing about it was I had been since the day she walked into this very office, covered in her uncle's blood and had begged me to save her.

Arlo was right. I knew how to fix Arianna and me. How to keep her next to me even though we still had so much stacked against the two of us. I may have eliminated the immediate threat of Derek McGovern and made it possible for her to go back to her father if she wanted to. However, all of it paled in comparison to Gennaro Villetti and his need to make me his perfect heir to take over his kingdom. He would never accept what I wanted. And I didn't know how to deal with the threat my father posed without spilling more blood than I'd ever willingly commit to.

"I need you to find out what happened when Bennett turned up at McGovern's hideout for me. I need to know he's not going to cause more trouble and get himself killed now I've destroyed his enemy for him. He has to be safe for her sake."

"You got it."

I nodded at him before he left my office. Then I sat there trying to work up the strength to go in search of Arianna and make up for every single thing I'd done to hurt her.

TWENTY SIX

Arianna

I could throw something at that stupid man's head right now. In fact, I could do with hurtling all the abuse in the world at his face. I didn't do either of those things. Instead, I stormed down the hallway of his club and shoved open the doors separating the private rooms from the back offices. I stopped a few feet away from them and let out a scream of frustration, not caring about where I was nor who could hear me.

"God, I fucking hate you," I ground out, slamming my hand against the wall next to the door that read number ten. "Why do you have to be so fucking infuriating? And why the fuck do I even care about you after all the shit you just put me through? God-fucking-damn you, Zayn Villetti! Damn you for making me feel a single fucking thing about you!"

I couldn't help screaming again. The anger and hurt I felt inside needed to come out. It was eating me up inside. My heart had shattered in my chest when I realised he didn't trust me enough to let me in. He'd used me for his own fucking gratification without ever giving me pieces of himself like I'd given him. I'd been brutally honest with my feelings. Well, okay, so I hadn't told him I was falling for him, but it was far too soon to broach the subject. Now I was glad I hadn't said a word about the feelings in my heart.

"Who the fuck does he think he is, huh? Letting me get kidnapped like that's fucking normal." I threw my hands up and paced away from the wall. "You don't put someone you care about in danger like that."

My hands curled into fists, wanting to hammer themselves into something. How could I have ever trusted Zayn? Why was I so stupid? Here I thought he felt something for me, but how could he when he involved me in this kidnapping plot? When he didn't tell me a single fucking thing about it. Then he'd gone and killed a man in front of me without displaying any emotion or remorse. I mean, sure, Derek had got what was coming to him. I wasn't upset he'd died. And the fact Zayn had hurt him for the things he'd done to me? Well, it shouldn't have made me grateful to him. It shouldn't have made me want him all the more. It had, though. It really fucking had made me want to get on my knees and worship the man to show my appreciation.

You're so fucked up when it comes to Zayn.

"I hate you," I screamed again, even though it was a lie. "You can go to fucking hell for all I care, Zayn. In fact, I wish I'd never fucking met you because then I wouldn't have to feel a single thing for you. I wouldn't have a broken fucking heart."

I didn't hate Zayn at all. I hated how he'd kept things from me and had never let me in.

"You know, I'm not sure you want to be screaming bloody murder about the boss in his own club unless you're planning on taking your own life into your hands."

I jumped out of my fucking skin at the sound of a voice from behind me. Spinning around, I discovered a heavily tattooed man leaning up against the wall, his foot propped up behind him as he tapped his fingers on his thigh. He had a scar on the side of his face, grey eyes and brown hair with tattoos in his hairline.

"Who the fuck are you?"

He gave me a smile as he shoved off the wall and came closer. I held my ground even though I probably should have been running for the hills. Zayn had told me not to talk to anyone else without his permission. Well, fuck him and his stupid rules. The deal was off. He didn't get to dictate shit to me any longer.

"Me?" The man put a hand on his chest. "Someone who's about to save you from getting a tongue lashing from the king himself."

Before I could say a word, the man reached me, wrapped an arm around my shoulder and directed me towards the door with a number seven on it he'd been standing next to moments ago.

"What are you doing?"

For some reason, I didn't struggle or try to push him off me when he opened the door and pulled me inside. He shut the door behind us and walked away over to what I realised was a leather bed with leather cuffs attached to all four ends of it.

"If you're going to scream about the boss, it's safer to do it in here. Zayn doesn't allow anyone to disrespect him." He knocked on one of the walls. "Best soundproofing money can buy in this place."

I didn't know what to make of this person in front of me, nor why he'd bothered to bring me in here. Who gave a fuck if I pissed Zayn off by screaming about what a dickhead he'd been to me? He deserved it.

"Who are you?"

The man sat on the edge of the bed and leant back on his hands with his legs spread in a rather obscene manner. I swallowed, realising maybe I shouldn't have let him bring me into this room. Arlo explained to me earlier they all had different functions depending on a client's particular tastes. I hadn't asked much more after that, too embarrassed to question him about the inner workings of Zayn's sex club.

"Penn Harlow. Fixer, tattoo artist and all-around criminal mastermind, at your service." He gave me a little nod. "No need to tell me who you are, Arianna. I already know."

"It's Ari."

"My apologies, Ari."

I fidgeted next to the door, feeling embarrassed knowing he'd heard me raving about Zayn.

"You fix things for Zayn?"

He nodded and gave me a smile.

"In a manner of speaking."

"Like getting rid of dead bodies?"

It only made his smile grow wider.

"Yes, and you're welcome, by the way. Messy job you left me with, but that's okay. I like those."

I flinched and looked away, hating the reminder of what I'd done to Justin even if he deserved it. It was the pain of knowing how deep his betrayal ran that had my stomach in knots. And how I was going to have to tell my father at some point.

"Thank you."

My fingers went to the cuff on my ear, tugging at the chain a little because it irked me, knowing Zayn had tagged me this way. I couldn't bring myself to take it off. It was still a gift from him. A token of something more between us, even if I didn't want to believe it. My heart knew better. He'd picked it because he knew I'd like it. He knew... fuck... he knew too much about me. I'd already cried enough, but another tear slid down my cheek. My hand automatically swiped it away, ashamed of myself for allowing it to fall. It proved Zayn had a deep, all-encompassing hold on me.

"Do you want me to take your mind off what happened?"

My eyes darted back to Penn.

"Why would you want to? You don't know me."

He shrugged.

"You're the boss's girl."

"I'm not *his*," I hissed, even though I knew it wasn't true. I rubbed my chest and scolded myself internally for my own stupidity. "How would you help me, anyway?"

Penn cocked his head to the side.

"Well, if you were anyone else, I'd do one of three things." He held three fingers up. "Tattoo you. Find someone for you to beat the shit out of, torture and kill. Or I'd fuck the living daylights out of you. I mean, you're hot as fuck, so I wouldn't mind taking you for a ride." He let out a dramatic sigh, allowing

241

his hand to fall back on the leather bed. "But I can't do any of those things because you're Zayn's and he would murder me for touching you. He'd torture me first, then he'd kill me slow to prove a point. He's pretty fucking terrifying when he kills. I swear it's like he's dead inside."

The way he said those things in such a matter-of-fact tone had me staring at the tattooed Fixer like he had two heads. And he was right. Zayn was terrifying when he killed. I'd seen it first-hand, and I didn't think I'd ever scrub the image from my mind no matter what I did.

"Then what are you going to do?"

He patted the bed next to him.

"I'm going to teach you something that might save your life one day."

I don't know why I moved over to the bed and sat next to him. He put his hand in his pocket and drew out a small rolled-up leather holder of some kind. When he unravelled it, there were a series of metal pin-like sticks tucked into it.

"What are those?"

"Lock picks."

He snagged one of the cuffs from the end of the bed. I realised they were attached to adjustable chains as he set it in his lap. There was a small padlock on it. Penn selected a couple of his picks and used them to open the padlock without the key. He did it so fast, I had no time to ask him anything about it.

"That doesn't look simple," I said with a frown.

"Oh, it is. You just have to know what you're doing. That's why I'm going to do it slowly this time. Let you see how it works."

He snapped the padlock closed again. I shifted closer to him so I could see better as Penn explained how the picks worked. Then he told me about the lock mechanism and what a key did to allow it to open. He showed me how he picked the lock by setting each pin inside the lock in place, so it clicked. The way he spoke was calm and meticulous, stopping every so often to make sure I understood what he was telling me. And, by some miracle, his demonstration helped clear my mind of the shit I'd gone through today.

"Now, it's your turn. Don't worry, I'll help you."

Penn handed me the picks and the lock. I set to work, failing my first time around until he took my hands and physically helped me do it until I could pick the specific lock on my own. He got up and went over to the drawers nearby, pulling out various types of locks from them. He laid them out on the bed for me with a smile.

"Now, let's see how long it takes you to do these and maybe I'll take you to pick a door lock next."

I grinned up at him, strangely excited about the challenge he'd set me. I didn't know this man at all, but he'd been kind to me and had taken my mind off Zayn even if he'd hit on me in the process. Somehow, I didn't think revealing that piece of information to Zayn would *ever* be a good idea.

Over the next hour, Penn let me pick as many locks as I wanted to in the club. We snuck into the staff room, where he gave me a short lesson on how to deal with combination locks. We didn't try to break into the lockers. I told him it would be an invasion of privacy. I didn't think he cared much about that, but I did, so he hadn't pushed it with me.

By the time we reached Zayn's office door, I'd calmed down completely, knowing I needed to bite the bullet and talk to the damn man like an adult. I hadn't allowed him to explain things to me, not that he'd even tried, but I was going to give him a chance to. I didn't owe Zayn anything. However, my heart wouldn't let me walk out of here without knowing the truth.

"Thank you for distracting me."

Penn reached out and took my hand. He pressed his little leather lock pick case into it.

"You're welcome. Take this. You never know when you might need it."

"But it's yours."

He shrugged and backed away from me.

"I have a ton at home."

I watched him stroll away towards the private rooms again. Then I turned and took a breath before raising my hand and knocking at Zayn's office door. It was time to be brave. No matter my anger, my heart wanted what it wanted. And it was the man on the other side of the door from me.

Whether it made me foolish or not, I didn't care. I couldn't give him up.

Not yet.

Not… ever.

TWENTY SEVEN

Zayn

It had been my intention to go in search of Ari after Arlo left. Instead, I'd had Remi in here demanding answers from me. The whole fucked up situation I'd got myself into came spilling out. Normally, I kept my private affairs to myself. I didn't have it in me to hide it from her. My walls were down because a girl had ripped my chest open and forced me to take a good look at myself and my choices.

Of course, Remi had been less than impressed with my decision-making skills when it came to Ari. The words "you're a fucking idiot" had left her mouth… twice. Along with "fix this with her" and my favourite one of all, "if you don't make it right, I'll punch you in the dick for being a cunt to her."

Remi was known for being more bark than bite, so I wasn't expecting her to carry out that threat. There was no need. I would make things right with Ari.

I need her.

The thought of losing her crippled me. I couldn't let her leave. I just wanted to take care of her. It hadn't changed because I'd let her get kidnapped. If anything, it intensified. Made it all the more imperative to show her she meant something to me.

Remi had noticed there was blood on my shirt cuff before she left the room. I was just beginning to button up a clean one when the knock at my door came. Leaving my shirt unbuttoned, I strode over to the door and ripped it open, utterly sick at the thought of having to handle more problems today.

Ari stood on the threshold, her chestnut eyes full of caution. My hands flexed at my sides, wanting to grab a hold of her and never let go. Her gaze flicked down to my open shirt. She swallowed at the sight of it. I didn't bother covering up. She'd seen it all before, anyway. I'd had her in my bed every night for a week and bare-chested was how I always slept.

"We should talk," she said in a determined voice that was rather at odds with her wary expression. "And by talk, I mean you have some explaining to do."

"Okay."

She blinked, her eyes meeting mine again. It was clear she wasn't expecting me to acquiesce so readily without a fight. I stepped back to allow her entry. She didn't immediately move, clearly caught off guard by my behaviour. Did she think I would be unreasonable? Maybe I had been in the past, but she'd made me stop and think about the way I treated her.

Ari steeled her shoulders and walked in. I closed the door behind her, subtly flipping the lock, as I didn't need any further disturbances today. When I turned around, she'd seated herself on my sofa with her hands tucked under her knees.

I stepped over to her, coming to a halt just shy of her feet. Ari stared up at me, her cheeks flushing slightly.

"Are you going to sort your shirt out?"

I fought the urge to smile.

"Why would I when it's just you and me?"

"It's distracting. How am I meant to pay attention to what you have to say when that's on display?"

There my blunt girl was. The one who never did anything other than give it to me straight apart from in the bedroom. I put it down to her being too turned on to form coherent sentences.

Instead of giving her a hard time over it, I did what I'd intended to do the moment I was in her presence again. Prove to her I cared. That she had me if she still wanted me.

I lowered myself to my knees by her feet. Ari's eyes widened.

"What are you doing?"

I reached out and took one of her hands from under her knees, enfolding it in both of my own.

"I'm sorry."

Her bottom lip trembled.

"You're sorry?"

"Yes, I'm sorry I didn't trust you with my plans. I'm sorry I hurt you. And I'm especially sorry I failed you as the person who takes care of you."

Lifting her hand, I pressed a kiss to her fingertips.

"I've been alone for a very long time. I don't answer to anyone but myself, but I want to answer to you... and not because of a deal we made between us. I want you as my partner."

She choked out a breath, understanding the significance of my words. We could talk more about that later once I'd told her why I'd had her kidnapped. I felt it was important to apologise to her first about everything. She needed to know I cared about her.

"As for what happened today, it was business. But... for you, I will explain just this once why I did it."

I set her hand on her lap.

"I like to keep an eye on anything involving my business. I have informants, people who feed Arlo information for me. However, the one person I needed information on the most, I had nothing to go on and no time to turn one of his men. Instead, I used what I already knew... what you'd told me to get what I wanted. Derek had to be eliminated. I wasn't going to let a man walk around the place thinking he had any right to you. I used you as bait to get to him because he was a slippery piece of shit who covered his tracks well."

I set my hands down on my thighs. She was quiet and her expression pensive.

"You asked me to stop a war, Ari. You asked me to save Bennett. The only way to make sure it didn't escalate further was by cutting the head off the snake. That's how I handle most things in this world. Destroying them at the source so they can't come back to bite me. Men like Derek McGovern are parasites. They'll cling on if you give them an inch. He had to die. And I only had one chance to find out where the fuck he was before it was too late."

I let out a breath. I'd never explained myself this way to anyone before. Everyone who knew about my underhanded dealings came from this world. They already understood why you had to be ruthless and uncompromising. Anything else could be exploited or seen as weakness.

"I realise now I should have told you what I intended to do, so you'd have known I was coming for you no matter what. So you knew I cared because I do care, Ari. I care about you far too fucking much."

She sat there, watching me with no real discernible emotion on her face. Ari wore her heart on her sleeve, but right now, she was as closed off as I'd always been. I couldn't stand it. It made me aware of how I must come across to her. Before I knew what I was truly doing, I leant closer and laid my head in her lap, my hands banding around her thighs to have something of her to hold on to. Arlo told me to allow her to leave if she wanted to, but there was no fucking way I was losing my little fairy. No way I was letting her walk out on me. I didn't give a shit what type of a person it made me. She was mine. This smart, brave, and incredibly strong girl was mine.

"If I was a better man, I'd tell you I could let you go if you couldn't forgive me. But I can't do that, Tink. I can't let you leave me. I won't do that. You're *mine*." I let out a breath. "Please stay with me. Stay with me and let me be yours too."

For a moment, everything was utterly still and all I could hear was my own heart beating in my ears. Then Ari's hand was on my head, stroking my hair before she leant over me, pressing her temple to mine.

"I can't leave," she whispered. "Nothing else in my life makes sense except you."

Relief flooded my veins, making my body slump against hers. If she'd been anyone else, I wouldn't have knelt at her feet, given her an explanation and told her not to leave me. I wouldn't have allowed myself to show any sort of vulnerability. For her, I'd do anything. Show her the man behind the mask if it proved I trusted her. If it proved I cared.

"Being with me won't be easy. Not with my family and not with the life I lead. Are you sure you want that?"

"If it means I have you, I don't care about the rest. Don't you understand what I've been trying to tell you this whole time? The only thing I want is you."

I shifted, forcing her to lift her head away from mine. I sat up again before shoving myself between her legs and taking a hold of her face in both my hands. She blinked as if startled by my sudden movement.

"You have me."

The way her eyes filled with tears made me press my forehead against hers.

"Please believe me." I took her hand and pressed it to my bare chest beneath my shirt. "I need you, my sweet little fairy. Let me take care of you. Let me be—"

"Daddy," she choked out.

My mouth was on hers a second later, stealing her breath as I kissed her. Ari clutched my arm with her free hand, her nails digging into my shirt. I could feel the desperation radiating off her like she needed me closer.

I chose her. I picked Ari over my family. She didn't fully comprehend what I'd done. Despite what Arlo had told me to do, I wasn't ready to give her the whole sordid truth about my father and my family. In time, I would be. Right now, I needed things to be okay between us. I needed her to understand she was the only person I'd ever wanted with me, always.

"Stay," I whispered against her mouth. "Stay with me, Tinkerbell. No more deals. Just you and me, okay? You and me."

"I'll stay."

I tugged her against me, pressing her soft body into mine with one hand on her back. The other snaked around her neck, gripping her throat because it was where my hand fucking belonged. I tipped her head back slightly, staring into her chestnut eyes.

"I'm going to collar you, make you get on your knees, and punish you when you disobey me. You understand that, right? Even if I consider you my equal, you're still going to submit to me. You're still my little pet."

"Yes, daddy."

"Good girl."

Her hands slid under my unbuttoned shirt, dancing across my skin like she needed to touch me more than anything else. I allowed it. Giving her what she needed fuelled me. I'd spend a lifetime taking care of her.

"Do you forgive me?"

She nodded, biting her lip as she continued to explore my body. I extracted her teeth from her lip with my thumb.

"Words, Tink. Use them."

"I forgive you."

I smiled, dragging my thumb over her bottom lip.

"You seem a little distracted. Does my little fairy need daddy to make her feel good?"

Her eyes fixed on mine, need and lust swelling in those brown depths.

"Please."

I pressed my thumb between her lips.

"You understand why I'm going to punish you for shouting at me first, don't you?"

She licked the pad of my thumb and nodded. That little tongue was going to be put to very good use in a minute.

"Good." I pulled my thumb from her mouth and leant back. "Now come, I have plans for you."

I got to my feet and put my hand out. Ari slid her fingers between mine, allowing me to tug her upright. She followed me over to my desk, waiting next to me while I cleared a space in the middle of it, setting my computer to the side. I turned to her, giving her a smile.

"On your knees, my bad little fairy. It's time you showed daddy you can be a good girl. If you are, I'll reward you, but make no fucking mistake… I'm going to take everything. You better be ready to have all your little holes stretched and used because you won't be leaving this room until I've reminded you of exactly who you belong to."

TWENTY EIGHT

Zayn

Ari moved in between me and the desk, lowering herself to her knees by my feet. Her head tipped back so she could meet my eyes and await further instruction. I didn't know what I'd have done if she'd wanted to walk away from me. I was fucking glad she'd stayed. And now I was going to make sure she understood how things would be between us going forward. What it meant to be my little pet while also being my woman. I wanted to push my girl to her limits until she broke apart from the pleasure I would give her.

I slid my shirt from my shoulders, throwing it on the desk behind her. Then I pointed at my belt and raised my brow. Ari reached up, unbuckling it for me and unzipping my trousers. Her eyes remained on mine even as she tugged the sides apart and stroked her fingers across my boxers.

"Take it out and put your hands behind your back."

She did exactly as I asked, tugging at my clothes enough to free my cock from its confines. Her hands went behind her back, her lips parting as she stared at what was about to get shoved down her throat. She knew it was coming. I didn't have to warn her.

Raising my hand, I spat into it a few times, making it nice and slick before I ran it along my shaft, coating my cock with it.

"You want this? You want my spit?"

"Please, daddy."

"You're going to have to clean it from my cock then, aren't you?"

Her eyes flashed with need.

"Open your mouth, show me that little tongue you're going to worship me with."

Her mouth dropped open immediately. She stuck her tongue out, ready for me to give her what she desired. I dug my fingers into her hair, tugging her closer before taking a hold of my cock. Running the head over her tongue, I bit my lip, watching her take over and twirl it around the tip.

"Does that taste good?"

She nodded, her eyes never leaving mine. I pressed my cock into her mouth, watching her close her full lips around it.

"That's it. Take as much as you can."

Using her hair as an anchor, I pressed deeper until I hit the back of her mouth. Pulling back, I thrust in again, setting a steady pace. Ari opened her mouth wider, encouraging me deeper.

"Does my dirty little fairy want her face fucked, hmm? Should I make a mess of your pretty mouth?"

Her little moan around my dick was my answer. I held still for a long moment, watching this beautiful girl who was all mine patiently wait for me to ravage her. Make her gag and choke on me. Then I'd clean the spit running down her chin as a result with my tongue.

I gripped her hair tighter and wrapped my other hand around her jaw. Shunting my hips forward, I felt her gag around me as my cock slid deeper. Pulling back, I shoved my dick in her mouth again, my pace increasing until she was choking on it. Her eyes got watery, but she kept her hands behind her back. My good little fairy took my cock down her throat so well.

I pulled out entirely to give her a moment to catch her breath. She gagged, spit dribbling out of her mouth. Fuck, I couldn't take it. Seeing her with all that mess on her face. It was too much. My dirty girl looked utterly stunning.

I tugged Ari to her feet by her hair, shoved her back against the desk, then my mouth was on hers, trading spit between us. I licked and sucked on her tongue before nibbling her bottom lip. My tongue slid over her chin, cleaning up her spit and making it my own.

"Pull your fucking jeans down," I growled into her mouth. "I want what's owed to me."

Ari's hands fumbled between us. I pulled back, only to spin her around and push her into the desk. My body was against hers, grinding into her even as she struggled with the buttons on her jeans.

"Now."

The demand had her pulling them down off her hips, exposing her pale green underwear.

"Those too. Show me that pretty pussy, Tink. Show me how wet you are for my cock."

Her hands pulled them down, giving me a perfect view of her behind. The way her body curved had me grinding my teeth in desperation to touch, to run my hands all over her skin. To brand each and every inch of this woman into my memory. I needed her to know how much I adored her. To prove I wanted her more than anything.

"Bend over and spread your legs."

She did as I asked. I groaned at the sight of those beautiful holes on full display for me.

"Mmm, do you want my cock inside you, Tink?" I slid it between her legs, revelling in the wetness that coated it, her arousal making me harder than ever. "Want me to fuck you so hard, you scream?"

"Please, Zayn, please fuck me."

She spread her legs as wide as she could with her jeans around her thighs.

With one hand planted on her back and the other wrapped around her hip, I slid home, making her moan.

"Good girl, taking this dick so well, aren't you? Mmm, my perfect little fairy."

"Yes, fuck, please, give it to me."

I leant over her, planting my mouth by her ear.

"Listen to you begging like a needy little slut desperate for daddy's dick."

I pulled back and thrust in again, harder. The hand that had been on her back dug into her hair instead.

"Is this what you want, huh? To be my good little fairy slut who takes my cock in all her holes and asks for more?"

"Yes," she whimpered as I kept hammering into her pussy, making her feel every inch of me.

"Beg for it."

"Please, daddy, please give me more. I want to be good for you."

So perfect. So sweet. So inviting.

"Tell me what you are."

"Daddy's dirty little fairy."

My hand left her hip and dug between us. My fingers stroked her entrance, where my dick was sliding in and out.

"Can you take more, Tink? Do you want to know what it feels like to be stretched so wide it fucking hurts, but it's like heaven too?"

She let out a harsh pant when I pressed one finger inside her next to my dick.

"Zayn," she whined.

"Good girl. You get one today, but soon I'll make you take more. I'll make you take them all while you sit on my cock and ride me."

I didn't move my finger in time with my thrusts. I just held it there for her to get used to. My girl would take it all one day.

"Oh fuck."

She shuddered beneath me as if the thought of what I was going to do scared and excited her at the same time.

I straightened and pulled my finger from her. Reaching over, I tugged open my desk and extracted a small tube. The cap was flipped open with my thumb and cool gel squeezed over my fingers after I released her hair.

"As good as your pretty pussy feels, I told you I'm going to fuck all your holes." I ran a lube covered finger over her entrance, making circles around it. "Such a beautiful sight you are, so ready for me."

She arched her back as I penetrated her with one finger.

"Good girl," I murmured. "My little fairy slut wants her tiny little hole filled with daddy's dick."

The moan ripping from her throat had me giving it to her harder as I stretched her out for me. By the time I had three fingers buried in her arse, she was gripping the edge of the desk and pressing herself back against me.

"Please, fuck, please, I want it so bad."

"Tell me what you need."

"Your cock, please, fuck me."

"Who does this hole belong to?"

"You. It belongs to you. I belong to you. All of me."

I pulled out of her pussy, grabbing the tube and thoroughly coating my cock in lube. Placing it against her entrance, I stared down at Ari.

"Who does this cock belong to, Tinkerbell?"

"Me," she whispered.

I smiled and pressed against her.

"Are you going to take it? Every inch? Show him where he belongs?"

"Yes, fuck, yes."

She moved against me, relaxing into it as my cock slid into her. I wasn't in a rush, wanting her to be comfortable. She was far more eager for it than I expected. Ari backed into me, taking more and more until my body was flush with hers. It was the most exquisite fucking pleasure.

"Fuck," she moaned. "So. Full."

"You didn't want to take it slow."

She looked back at me, her face all flushed and her pupils blown.

"I need it too much. You feel so good inside me… please, fuck me, daddy. Show me who I belong to."

I pulled back to apply more lube before pressing into her again. She watched me, her eyes urging me to be rough with her. To show her how fucking desperate I was for every part of her.

First, I cleaned my hand, making sure to be thorough so I could fuck her pussy with my fingers. Then I leant over her, pressing my lips to hers while I dug my hand under her.

"You are mine," I whispered against her lips as I fucked her harder and shoved three fingers into her pussy.

She let out a cry into my mouth.

"You like this, huh? Feeling me everywhere?"

All I got were gasping breaths in response.

"My little slut needs more than just my cock, doesn't she? Mmm, I'm going to get you a little gift. Another cock. I don't share, so it'll be a toy, but I'll fuck your pussy with it while I'm up in this tight little arse. You can get a taste of what it feels like to be double penetrated."

I pushed my fingers deeper as I fucked her.

"Put your fingers inside you with mine. Show me how much you want that."

She let go of the edge of the desk and shoved her hand beneath her. Her delicate little fingers pressed inside her pussy next to mine, making her cry louder.

"Zayn!"

"Fuck yourself, Tink. Rub your palm against your clit. Make it feel good."

She squirmed beneath me but did as I told her, letting out these almost keening cries of pleasure.

"Fuck, I'm so close," she gasped.

I pressed my mouth to her ear again.

"I want to fuck this little pussy with my cock and a fake dick at the same time. I want to stretch you wide, so you can take both. You'll look beautiful taking it. So fucking stunning. And all mine. Then you'll truly be my little fairy slut."

Ari clamped down so hard around me, I grunted. A muted scream left her lips with her release, my words sending her over the edge. It was the most incredible sight, watching her fall apart. Seeing her drown in me this way.

Then it hit me too, making me spill inside her as she continued to pulse around me.

"Shit, Tink."

I was in complete ecstasy from this experience with her. In pushing her to new heights of pleasure, she didn't know she could reach. I hoped I'd proved with my actions how much I wanted her. How much she meant to me. I'd tried to do it with words before this and I hoped she understood. She'd stayed, so I figured she had. This was me cementing our connection. Deepening it.

I pulled my fingers from her before shifting back. She let out a breath as she slumped on my desk, clearly spent from the intense sex we'd shared. I gave her a minute while I cleaned myself up before doing the same for her. Then I picked her up from the desk, carried her over to the sofa and sat down with my girl in my lap.

Ari curled herself around me. I held her tight against my chest and pressed kisses to her hair.

"You're okay, sweet fairy. I've got you."

She nuzzled her face into my neck.

"You're mine," she murmured against my skin.

"That's right. All yours."

No one else could have me. Not when this girl in my arms was burying herself inside me so deep, I didn't think I could extract her without destroying who I was. And I didn't want to because I was hers as much as she was mine.

TWENTY NINE

Arianna

The deliciously sore feeling between my legs after the most intense sex I'd ever experienced in my life had me trying not to wriggle in Zayn's lap. I held onto him tighter, needing his embrace to ground me. The things he'd said to me were unexpected but hot as fuck. I wanted him to carry out the threats he'd made to stretch me wide open and make it hurt so good, I cried with it.

I never imagined Zayn would be the type of man who apologised and admitted he was wrong. Ruthless mafia princes didn't show mercy, nor did they apologise for who they were. Zayn showed me the man behind the mask. The one who couldn't stand to lose me under any circumstances. Who wanted me as his partner. His equal.

How could I not forgive him and accept his apology after that?

How could I not let myself fall so fucking deeply in love with this man, I couldn't breathe without him?

I'd never taken the time to consider what I wanted from a partner. Then I'd made a deal with a man who showed me more love, care and affection than I'd ever received before in my entire life. His punishments and discipline weren't to hurt me, they were to show me he cared. He gave me exactly what I needed from him.

And now he'd given me the one thing I'd desperately craved with every inch of my being.

Him.

I could call him mine.

It was probably stupid, but it meant the world to me.

"Daddy," I whispered.

"Yes?"

"What... what you called me... when you said I'm your slut, you're not going to say that outside of sex, right?"

He kissed my hair.

"Of course not. Did it bother you? I won't call you it if it does."

I shook my head.

"It didn't. It kind of turned me on."

"Then you'll strictly be my little slut when I'm fucking you."

I shivered, even though I didn't think I could take any more sex after the way he'd used my body. Maybe later when he took me to bed. I'd have to ask him to be gentle with me. Let's face it, I couldn't get enough of Zayn. I craved the connection between our bodies. The insatiable need to have him inside me, owning me with each thrust and dirty word in my ear, wasn't something I wanted to control. It could rage through me like a wildfire. I'd let it drown me if it meant I experienced the highs he gave me over and over again.

"Did you get anything nice when you were with Remi?" he asked a moment later. "I really did want you to get to know her, Ari. It wasn't all because of my other plans."

I'd known that because he wouldn't have involved Remi otherwise. He was protective of those he loved. I could see that now. Even if he'd put me at risk, it was a calculated one. And if Derek had hurt me, Zayn's vengeance would have been worse. What he did was fucked up but seeing the efficient way Zayn had dispatched the man had me realising he may have gone easy on Derek. As if shooting a man three times and slitting his throat was "going easy." It was violent and bloody. Yet, he could have tortured Derek until he was a sobbing mess begging for death... of that, I was sure.

"Yeah, didn't think you'd be happy if I came back empty-handed. And I like her a lot, by the way, despite how blunt she is."

"Reminds me of someone else I know."

I pulled my face away from his neck so I could look at him. Those dark eyes of his were twinkling with amusement.

"Oh yeah? And who might that be?"

He moved closer, running his nose along the side of mine.

"A rather adorable little fairy who isn't afraid to tell me when I've been a dick to her."

"I'm not adorable!"

The way he smirked at me had my blood pounding in my ears.

"You are the most adorable little thing I've ever seen and if you continue to tell me otherwise, I'll be forced to punish this mouth of yours again for daring to question me on a statement of fact."

Jesus Christ, I think this man may kill me.

I had no idea where playful Zayn had come from, but I liked him a hell of a lot.

"Did you forget I like your punishments?"

"How could I? You take them so willingly."

My cheeks heated, but I didn't hide it from him. He pressed a kiss to my mouth, making me melt against him as his hand stroked along my back.

"I should take you home," he murmured as he pulled away. "I'll make you dinner and run you a bath."

I stroked my fingers down his bare chest, staring at them so I didn't have to meet his eyes.

"In the one in your bathroom that's big enough for two?"

"Is this your way of asking if I'll join you?"

"No."

He caught my chin between his fingers, forcing my face up. "Don't lie to me."

I bit my lip. Fuck, the stern voice he used did things to my insides.

"Will you get in the bath with me please, daddy? I don't want to be away from you."

He was fighting a smile. I could see it in the way his face twitched.

"If that's what you need, then yes."

"Thank you."

Zayn stroked my cheek and gave me a smile before kissing me again. When he released me, I climbed out of his lap and let him straighten my clothes. He sorted himself out, putting a shirt on before he took my hand and led me from the club. The car and his driver were waiting outside for us.

Zayn let me curl up against his side with his arm around me for the entire journey home. His driver brought the bags from the boot with him and placed them in the hallway after Zayn opened the front door when we arrived. He spoke to the man for a moment, then shut the door.

"Go put those away in my room while I make dinner."

He pointed at the bags of clothes I'd bought with Remi. I picked them up, a little surprised he'd explicitly told me to put them in his room. I didn't question it, taking them upstairs with me. I found he'd moved things around in his cupboards when I got there and wondered when he'd done it. The man was constantly doing things for me without being asked. I didn't know how I got so lucky.

Zayn and I shared a quiet dinner together. It was nice to just be with him, knowing there was no deal hanging over our heads. I was no longer indebted to him or forced to stay. We were together because we wanted to be.

After we cleaned up and put the dishes away, he took me upstairs. I stood by the sink counter as he turned on the taps for the deep bath and poured bubble bath liquid into the running water. He came over to me, making me raise my arms up so he could undress me. When I was bare, he spun me around and took a band from the counter I'd left there. With such gentle care, he gathered up my curls, piling them on the top of my head and tying them up so they wouldn't get wet. He leant down and placed a kiss on my shoulder, brushing his hands down my arms.

"You're perfect," he murmured. "Every inch of you."

I could see in his eyes as he stared at me through the mirror, his appreciation of my body. The way his hands stroked my curves. No one had ever made me feel more at ease with myself. At least now we knew each other intimately. There was no need to cover up. No need to hide away the thickness of my thighs or any other part of me. Zayn looked at me as if I was precious. As if I was a goddess he wanted to worship.

I didn't need him to make me feel beautiful or to fuel my self-worth. It merely made me happy knowing he wanted me the way I was. There was no expectation to change a single thing.

I spun on my heel, wanting to look at his face for real. The softness of his expression as I gripped his shirt and tugged him closer had my heart twisting in my chest. Words formed on the tip of my tongue. Ones I knew I couldn't say. Not when he'd warned me things wouldn't be easy for us. Not when I knew he meant his father and the demands placed on him by the man he was beholden to. He didn't need to tell me. I already understood.

I shoved those thoughts away and kissed him instead. I didn't want to ruin our evening with the future. No, we needed the here and now.

I think I'm in love with you, Zayn. And I'm scared that even though you're mine, I might not get forever with you.

Did I want that? Wasn't it too soon to imagine sharing a life with him?

I didn't care if he didn't want marriage or children. Those things didn't seem important when he was all I desired. If I could just have Zayn, I would be happy, content and fulfilled.

He stroked my cheek when I released him before turning away to check the bath. He flipped off the taps and undressed, leaving our clothes in a pile on the floor. Taking my hand, he helped me into the warm water. I sank into the bubbles, watching him get in the other end and sit up against the tub. It was a freestanding bath with the taps in the middle so we could comfortably sit at each end.

He laid his arms across the back of the bath, watching me sink under the water until only my head was visible. The way he smiled gave me butterflies. There was such contentment in his expression as if giving into his wants when it came to me had settled something inside him.

"Do you want to see your father?"

I stiffened at the mention of Dad.

"Yes… and no."

"Because of Justin?"

I nodded, raising slightly out of the water and wrapping my arms around my body.

"I don't think Derek lied when he told me Justin wanted Dad dead. It will hurt him, knowing his own brother betrayed him."

"He betrayed you too."

I nodded, looking down at the bubbles settled on top of the water.

"I'm not sorry I killed him, but I'm not particularly keen on doing it again. Taking someone's life, I mean."

Zayn dipped his hands into the water and took hold of one of my feet. I let out a little groan when he massaged the instep with his thumbs.

"You don't need to kill. You have me."

I looked at him then, dropping my arms from my chest and leaning back against the tub.

"Do you often get your hands dirty like that?"

"No, generally I have people to do it for me." His dark eyes turned serious. "I take threats against you personally, Tink, and when it's personal, I deal with it myself."

I swallowed. He didn't need to elaborate. I understood all too well. If someone hurt or threatened me, Zayn would deliver justice first-hand. It probably shouldn't make me find him more attractive. He might be a stone-cold killer with no remorse for taking lives, but it didn't matter. When he was with me, caring for me, fucking me until I couldn't take it any longer, Zayn was full of emotion. I wanted to bask in it. In him.

"If I wanted to see Dad, would you let me go?"

The deal was off, so there wasn't anything keeping me from seeing my father. Well, apart from me not wanting to tell him the truth. I didn't need Zayn's permission, but I wasn't stupid enough to think I could go without asking him.

He placed my foot back down and picked up the other one, proceeding to massage it.

"I want to because I shouldn't keep you from him any longer."

"But you can't."

"It's complicated, Ari. If your father didn't know mine…"

"I get it."

He eyed me with wariness in his expression. I don't know what changed, but it felt like he was making an effort not to hide behind his mask with me.

"Do you?"

I nodded, pulling my foot from his hands and shifting in the water. I crawled towards him, mounting his lap and setting my hands on his chest.

"My dad will probably tell yours. There is no way in hell Dad will approve of me being with you, not that he has a say, but it will be an issue. My point is, I get it."

Zayn reached up and stroked my cheek with his wet thumb.

"Don't you want to get married and have a family of your own?"

Well, that was a loaded fucking question. And one I had an instant answer to.

"No," I whispered. *I want you.*

"I can't give you those things."

I leant closer until my mouth brushed against his. Didn't he realise when he asked me to stay, I was agreeing to be with the man who'd already told me he found marriage abhorrent and had made sure he couldn't have children? I hadn't gone into a relationship with him blind.

"I grew up without a mother in a world where life is fleeting. I never dreamed of pretty white dresses, flowers and the end of an aisle. I spent my wishes on Dad coming home to me safe each night. All I've ever wanted was to take photographs and for those I love to survive. If that's simple and unambitious, I don't care. I don't want the world and everything in it."

I pressed my mouth against his briefly.

"If having you means it's just you and me, that's all I need, Zayn. You're more than enough."

He wrapped his tattooed hand around my throat. The way his eyes darkened, glittering with violent desire, had me trembling.

"My sweet little fairy," he murmured. "You're enough for me too."

I reached between us in the water, gripping hold of his cock between my fingers and stroking down the length of it. I'd felt him harden against my stomach when I straddled his lap, clearly aroused by my proximity.

"I need gentle," I whispered, pressing my mouth to his as I shifted, rubbing his cock against my pussy with my hand.

His grip on my throat tightened as his other hand wrapped around my back, steadying me.

"For you? Always."

And with his words, I sunk down on his thick length, choking out a moan with the delicious ache. I needed to cement our words with the physical expression of our feelings. I wanted him to know I wouldn't leave, no matter the cost to both of us. Because there was going to be a cost. I just wasn't sure which one of us would end up paying the steepest price for wanting someone we should have never sought to have.

THIRTY

Arianna

When the doorbell rang, I'd been in the blue bedroom, taking my clothes out of the wardrobe to transfer them into Zayn's bedroom. He was downstairs in his office with Arlo. They were talking business, so I was keeping out of Zayn's way. It had been a few days since the kidnapping incident. Blissful days of being with Zayn with nothing weighing on us. I'd pushed everything else to the back of my mind, like going back to my life before this and my future career prospects. They didn't matter when I was finding my feet in a relationship with a man twelve years my senior who could afford to give me the space to work out what I was going to do next.

Even though I knew I shouldn't, I crept out of the bedroom and hid behind the bannister as I spied Zayn going to open the front door. He was wearing his glasses today. For the most part, Zayn lived in contact lenses, but there were days when he didn't bother with them if he wasn't planning on leaving the house. I always appreciated those days because he was hot in those frames. He was hot at all times, but there was something about him in glasses that made my stomach get all fluttery.

Zayn pulled the door open. My butterflies turned to sickness when I saw who was standing on the threshold. Gennaro's bodyguards didn't wait for Zayn to let them in. They forced him back into the house, with Gennaro following them.

"What are you doing?" Zayn ground out, his expression souring.

"Find her," Gennaro said to his men.

I backed away from the bannister, knowing immediately he was referring to me. Where the fuck did I go to hide? I moved faster, running towards Zayn's bedroom on silent steps. I ripped open the cupboard door, shutting it before burying myself behind his suits. My hand went over my mouth to keep myself silent. Fear coated my veins, making my heart race out of control.

Fuck. Fuck. Fuck.

I knew hiding was futile. If Gennaro Villetti wanted to find me, he would. The mafia kingpin wasn't a man you messed with. Dad had told me as much. It was safer to be in business with him than make the Villettis your enemies.

I could hear a commotion outside of my hiding place. The door to the bedroom burst open, followed by Arlo's voice telling them they couldn't go in there. My hand curled into a fist at my side, ready to swing at the first person who opened the cupboard and tried to take me. I dropped my left hand from my mouth and curled that one into a fist too. I wasn't going down without a fight.

I held my breath as the door opened and hands dug through the suits. Instead of waiting, I burst through and swung at the man, my fist connecting with his jaw. He stumbled slightly, grunting at the impact. Dad had taught me how to throw a punch.

"What the fuck?" came the other bodyguard's voice.

I ignored him, stabbing my other fist in the first bodyguard's gut. He was the taller of the two.

"Jesus fucking Christ," he grunted, trying to grab me.

I darted around him and ran straight into Arlo. He pushed me behind him and glared at the two bodyguards.

"If you put your hands on her, I will cut them off," he told them. "No one touches the boss's woman without his permission."

Arlo's threat had me clutching the back of his shirt. The two bodyguards looked at each other, clearly sharing a silent conversation. The one I'd punched rubbed his jaw and scowled at me while the other one met Arlo's gaze.

"Fine, but she's coming with us. Gennaro wants to see her."

I was worried about what I would find downstairs.

"I'll bring her, not you."

The first bodyguard nodded. Arlo turned to me, his expression dark.

"You okay?" he asked quietly.

I nodded even though inside I was shaking like a leaf. There was no way I was going to show my fear. Not to anyone but

Zayn. He needed me to be strong right now, anyway. Strong in the face of his father.

Arlo let me lead the way downstairs, keeping himself between me and the bodyguards. I held my head up, not caring if the bodyguards were giving me daggers. I would have kept hitting them if I thought it would have saved me.

We found Gennaro and Zayn in the office. Zayn was standing by his desk with a blank expression on his face, but I could almost feel the undercurrent of rage and violence radiating off him. Gennaro was leaning against the fireplace, looking every inch the mafia king he was in a three-piece suit with his thumb tucked into his waistcoat. His dark hair was greying and his eyes matched Zayn's.

I didn't run to Zayn, knowing I couldn't go to him for comfort right now. Instead, I stayed close to Arlo near the door after the bodyguards walked in and stood near Gennaro.

"There she is," Gennaro said with a smile. It sent a chill running down my spine.

"Hello, Mr Villetti," I said, keeping my voice even and steady.

Arlo angled himself between me and Zayn's father, his eyes darting between him and the bodyguards. For a man who didn't seem to like me very much, he was certainly loyal to his boss. He wasn't going to let anything happen to me.

"Your father will be happy to know you're safe. He's been very worried about you."

The fake concern in his voice had me shoving my hands behind my back so he didn't see my clenched fists.

"I'm sure he has."

No way in hell I was telling this man how much I hated distressing my father. Nor that I missed him terribly and wished everything had been different.

Gennaro's attention went to his son, effectively dismissing me from the conversation.

"You're probably wondering why I'm here."

Zayn didn't react other than to rest his gaze on his father. My eyes were fixed on him, needing to soak up every inch of Zayn. I was scared of what would come out of Gennaro's mouth. Of what would happen next.

"Gilberto had some rather interesting things to share with me about your activities."

I saw Zayn's fingers twitch at the mention of his brother.

"Gil told you."

Gennaro tapped his fingers on his chin.

"Your brother understands loyalty, unlike you, it seems."

Zayn's jaw clenched and I could almost feel him grinding his teeth.

"You going to tell me how Gil found out?"

That made Gennaro smile.

"Enzo was upset with you after your little talk with him."

For the briefest of moments, pain flashed in Zayn's eyes. I don't think Gennaro caught it, but I did. It made me take a step towards him. Arlo put a subtle hand on my arm, holding me back. My heart squeezed, knowing underneath his cold exterior, Gennaro's words had hurt Zayn.

If he'd spoken to Enzo, did it mean his brother had put two and two together about me and who I was to Zayn? If that was the case, then I could see how this would be an act of betrayal. Him telling Gil and Gil going to Gennaro.

"It doesn't matter how I found out, son, it matters that I did," Gennaro continued, his voice growing harder. "It matters because you have been lying to me."

Zayn's jaw ticked, but otherwise, he kept his mask in place. Arlo's hand curled around my bicep. He knew I was so close to running to Zayn, holding onto his hand and making sure he knew I would stand by him through thick and thin. I couldn't do that. He needed me to remain where I was, no matter how much I hated it.

"I know what you did for her." Gennaro stabbed a finger in my direction. "And I know why."

"Do you?" Zayn asked, his tone almost bored.

"*Attento a come parli, figliolo.*"

"I'll watch my mouth when you explain to me why you barged into my house and into *my* business."

"Your business? That girl is not your business. This is not how we do things, Zayn, making deals for protection. She is not *famiglia*. And *she* is not worthy of you."

My insides twisted, making me sick to my stomach. He knew we were intimately involved. He knew and now he was confirming what I'd known deep down. Daughters of gang leaders weren't fit to be a part of his family. I wasn't fit to be Zayn's partner in Gennaro's eyes. I wasn't some mafia princess who would make a good, obedient wife. Who would stand behind her husband no matter what he did. No matter the violence and chaos he committed in the mafia's name. I wasn't that girl… but I was Zayn's regardless. I belonged to the man Gennaro thought I wasn't worthy of.

Zayn didn't say a word in response to Gennaro. He didn't do a single thing. My eyes darted to Arlo, who was frowning at the men in front of us.

"You cannot have her and you know why. You know where she comes from." His gaze swung to me. "Clearly, you didn't tell her." He scoffed. "Here you are, making her believe this is real. Poor thing has no idea… well, you were always a good liar. You learnt from me, after all."

The way he smiled chilled me to my bones.

"You cannot have my son, Arianna. He does not belong to you. He belongs to *me*. And what I say goes. It's time I reminded him of that."

I flinched and stepped closer to Arlo, feeling small at that moment. Feeling like I was nothing. He didn't need to tell me why he disapproved of me. I already knew. I'd known it my whole life. I wasn't the right class. My father was a gangster. I would never be anything other than where I'd come from in Gennaro's eyes.

Zayn didn't feel that way. He never looked at me like I was below him. He looked at me like I was precious. He'd told me I was perfect. There were things he hadn't told me, but Zayn didn't lie about his feelings towards me.

Gennaro looked at his son again, leaving me to process my feelings alone.

"You are going to send her back to where she came from. Back to Bennett. And you are going to leave her alone. She is going to stay away from you too. If you disobey me in this, you will face the consequences and you will not like them. I don't want to hurt you, son, but this is not a debate or a negotiation. You will obey me."

For a long moment, nobody spoke. Then Zayn turned to Arlo, his eyes skipping over me.

"Take her home... take her home to her father."

I tried not to let my emotions overwhelm me. Tried not to allow myself to drown in the hurt caused by his words.

"Yes, boss," Arlo replied.

"No," I whispered. "No."

He started to pull me away, but I didn't move. I refused to move.

"No, I won't leave you, Zayn. I won't."

"Arlo, take her."

For some reason, Arlo released his grasp on me rather than taking me from the room. I took it as a sign. My feet moved, practically running towards Zayn. I threw myself at him, wrapping my arms around his neck and breathing him in.

"Please, don't make me go home."

He didn't speak. I knew he couldn't. Going against his father was not an option right now. And I'd only said those words for the benefit of the people in the room.

Lowering my voice to a whisper as I pressed my mouth to his ear, I told him exactly what he needed to hear from me before Arlo took me away.

"It's okay. I know you can't go against him and it's okay. I know you'll find a way because I trust you. I. Trust. You."

I swallowed hard. This wasn't how I wanted to say these words. It wasn't how I wanted any of this to be, but he'd told me it wouldn't be easy. This was the part where I had to put my faith in the man I didn't think I could live without.

"I need you to know before I walk out of here that I love you. I love you, Zayn. I'm yours and you're still mine, no matter what he says."

He let out a silent breath. I knew it was the only answer he could give me. I knew he'd understood what I was saying. What I was admitting and the magnitude of it.

I let him go as Arlo placed a hand on my shoulder, pulling me away. To keep up the act, I struggled against him as he pulled me back.

"No, no, don't make me go. Please."

My eyes told a different story. They met Zayn's as Arlo dragged me from the room. I saw the flicker in them. I saw it clear as day. He was going to fix this. And it was the only reason I allowed his right-hand man to take me away from him.

THIRTY ONE

Arianna

Even though I trusted Zayn, the abject misery I felt sitting in this silent car with Arlo driving me home to Hackney permeated the air surrounding us. I watched the city with my head leaning against the window, seeing the places I'd grown up around the closer we got to home. Dread laced my veins. I was going back to my father and away from the man I'd fallen in love with. I should be happy to see my family again, but I wasn't. Not when there was so much to explain. Not when I had to do it all by myself without support and someone to hold my hand.

When we pulled up outside my father's house on the estate I grew up in, I bit down hard on my lip to stop myself from crying. My hands were clenched in my lap. I didn't want to do this. I didn't want to walk into that house and tell my father the truth about his brother. About what I'd done to him. How I'd run away and covered it up instead of coming home to him. And how I'd fallen in love with the wrong person. At least, it would be the wrong person in his eyes. In my own, Zayn was everything I'd ever needed. He was my lifeline. My safety. My hope.

Be strong, Ari. Do it because you believe in yourself. You can. He wouldn't have sent you back home if he didn't think you could.

I unclenched my hand and rubbed my chest, staring at the house I grew up in. Staring at the place that no longer felt like home. My home was no longer a place in this world. It was a person.

I didn't look at Arlo as I opened the car door and climbed out, slamming it shut behind me. My feet remained on the pavement as I kept staring at the house. I barely heard the other car door opening and the footsteps coming to a halt next to me. My eyes darted to the side, finding Arlo looking at the house too.

"If you're going to convince your father that you're okay, I'm going to suggest you don't go in there looking like a puppy got kicked."

For some reason, his words made me smile.

"That's your advice?"

"If you wanted to know how to torture someone without leaving marks, I could help you with that. Talking isn't really my strong point."

"That why you refused to say a word to me all this time?"

He looked down at me, his eyes crinkling at the corners as he smiled.

"I don't get paid to talk. I get paid to keep him safe, and by extension, you."

"Me?"

"The moment he took you in, you became his. He claimed you. I would give my life for his. And now I would give my life for yours too. That's what he expects of me." He waved at the house. "You'll be safe here... for now, but don't think he's not watching over you. He will always watch over you, Ari. That's who he is."

I didn't know what to say other than it meant a lot that he'd reassured me about Zayn's feelings towards me.

"Thank you."

He patted my arm. I felt his fingers press against my coat as he slid his hand down the fabric before he stepped back.

"Go see your father."

He handed me my handbag. The one Zayn had taken from the crime scene when I killed my uncle. I took it and opened it, finding my house key inside, along with my phone and purse. Arlo moved away, stepping back out onto the road to get in the car again.

I walked up to the front door, clutching the key between my fingers. Who knew if my father was even home right now. All I knew was I had to do this. Had to make sure I wasn't going to throw the fuck up.

Unlocking the door, I stepped inside and looked back. Arlo was in the car. He gave me a nod and pulled away as I shut the door.

"Dad? You home?"

There was a noise behind me. I turned around and came face to face with the man who raised me. He stood in the doorway of the living room, his dark eyes wide. It felt strange seeing him after all this time. To witness what my disappearance had done to him. There were dark circles under his eyes, which were glassy. His brown skin had an almost sallow appearance to it as if he'd been sick with worry for me. And it wasn't just about me. His brother had disappeared too.

"Arianna."

I ran, and he caught me up in his arms, holding me tight against his chest. He didn't ask me where I'd been or questioned why I was home now.

"You're here."

"I'm here, Dad, I'm home."

But it's not where I want to be. I want to be with my… I couldn't bring myself to think it in the presence of my father. I'd called this man daddy when I was a child. Now I called another man that for an entirely different reason. He took care of me, made me feel special, wanted and needed. I was safe. And fuck did it hurt knowing I had to be away from him. The man I wanted for the rest of my life.

Dad pulled back, holding me at arm's length as his eyes roamed over me, taking in the expensive clothing Zayn had bought me.

"You're okay? No one hurt you?"

"Yeah, I'm okay."

"Okay. Okay… Ari, where the fuck you been?"

I sighed, looking away. Nothing about this would be simple. Telling my dad about Justin and Zayn was going to bring down a world of trouble on my head, but I'd run away once. I couldn't do it again.

"It's a long story."

Dad nodded before directing me into the living room. I sat down on the sofa in the familiar surroundings. The faded blue wallpaper and dark brown leather sofas Dad had got when I was five. Being here made me feel out of place. I didn't belong in this life any longer.

"Tea?"

"Please."

Dad left to make it, giving me time to collect myself. To work out how the hell I was going to explain everything. It didn't seem real, me being back here.

He came back far too soon, handing me a cup of tea and taking a seat on the sofa on the other wall. I curled my fingers around the mug, staring down at the beige liquid.

"I ran away, Dad. I ran away because I did something I couldn't take back."

He didn't respond. I could feel his eyes on me, but I couldn't look at him. Not when I had to tell him I'd murdered his brother.

"I killed… I killed a man." I swallowed. "I killed Justin."

"You what?"

"I killed Uncle Justin. He was going to hand me over to Derek McGovern… and he tried to r-r-r-ape me."

There was no point beating around the bush. That was never me, anyway. I was honest to the point of blunt.

Dad jumped up from the sofa and paced the room.

"Oh my days. You killed Justin. *You* killed him."

I put my mug down on the coffee table and watched him, hating myself for being the bearer of this news.

"Yes."

"Where is he now? Where's his body?"

"I don't know."

"What you mean, you don't know?"

I fidgeted, curling my hands around my knees.

"A Fixer cleaned up the scene and disposed of his body."

I genuinely didn't know what Penn had done to Justin, nor did I care at this point.

Dad stopped his pacing and stared at me in disbelief.

"A Fixer? You shouldn't know they exist, Ari."

"I didn't! I didn't go to a Fixer. I went… I went to…"

He took a step towards me.

"Where the fuck did you go? You should've come to me, innit." He slapped a hand on his chest. "Me."

I dug my nails into my knees.

"I went to Desecration and made a deal with Zayn Villetti because I was scared you wouldn't believe me if I told you Justin betrayed us. I didn't know if you would trust me when I told you why I killed him to save myself."

He took a step back like I'd slapped him. And in a way, I had by telling my father I didn't trust him, but how could I lie about why I'd done it?

"You ran to the mafia? What the fuck were you thinking, Ari?"

"I was thinking I didn't want to go down for murder, Dad."

Dad let out a tsking sound and turned away from me, dragging his fingers along his forehead.

"You should've come home."

"Would you have believed me? Would you have covered up Justin's death? Because Zayn did and he made it go away. He kept me safe."

His hands twitched as he dropped them to his sides. Like the mention of Zayn's name bothered him.

"If you made a deal with him, why you back now?"

I didn't want to answer his question. Didn't want to tell him Gennaro had found out about my relationship with his son and made it very clear I couldn't be with him.

"You didn't answer my question. Would you have believed me? Justin betrayed us. He betrayed you. And it goes beyond taking me. He was going to have you killed. Derek was going to kill you and let Justin run Hackney for him."

"You what? Nah, nah, nah, man wouldn't do me like that."

"See? You wouldn't have believed me."

He turned on me, a mixture of annoyance and contrition on his face.

"You're my daughter, course I'm going to believe you."

I shook my head, hating how untrue it was when it came to my uncle. He'd said himself, Justin wouldn't have done him like that. But he had.

"Justin wanted the gang, Dad. I know because Derek told me himself."

"When the fuck was you with Derek?"

I let out a sigh. Zayn hadn't told me I couldn't tell Dad what happened.

"The day he died, right before you turned up. Derek kidnapped me and… and Zayn killed him for it."

Dad took a step back, his eyes widening.

"You telling me Zayn Villetti killed Derek? Why would man do that? Man owes me nothing."

"Me. He did it for me."

Dad's brow furrowed.

"You?"

I nodded, biting down hard on my lip.

"I told you, I made a deal with him. He killed Derek to make sure you didn't go to war. I asked him to keep you safe."

"What did you give him in return?"

I looked down at the floor.

"Me. I gave him me. And before you ask, he didn't ask me to sleep with him. It wasn't about that. I just did what he told me to. Kept him company. It's hard to explain, but it wasn't... sexual."

The ground needed to swallow me right up. Telling my dad I'd become Zayn's pet was embarrassing as hell.

"You telling me he didn't make you his side ting?"

"He doesn't have a girlfriend, Dad, so no. I'm not his bit on the side."

Zayn wouldn't treat me that way. He'd assured me there would be no one else when I was with him. And now we were together... or, at least, I assumed we were still together even though his father made Zayn send me away. It was different. All of it was.

"What does that even mean, Ari? I don't get it. If he didn't want to bang you, what did man want?"

I stood up, nervous energy flowing through me. I couldn't keep still any longer.

"It means I made a deal with the mafia prince to be his little pet, so he could have complete control over me."

"Like that dom and sub shit?"

"Yeah, like that."

Dad looked at me as if he didn't know who the fuck I was any longer. And to be honest, I didn't know. Being with Zayn had changed me.

"Fuck, Ari. I ain't judging the man, but what was you thinking agreeing to that shit?"

"I told you, I didn't want to go down for murder. I was scared. And it wasn't so bad, okay? He took care of me... he takes care of me."

My heart hurt. I wanted Zayn so much right now. I needed the courage to be honest about what happened.

"It started out as just that... it started like that, but then..."

Dad stepped closer.

"Then what?"

"Then I wanted more, then... then I fell in love with him."

"You what? He's almost twice your fucking age, Ari. I'm in business with him. And you said he didn't want to—"

I put a hand up.

"I know what I said, but things changed. And no, it wasn't anything to do with our deal. In fact, the deal is off now. I could have come home after he killed Derek, but I didn't. I stayed because I want to be with him. I want Zayn, Dad. I want him so much it hurts."

Tears filled my eyes, blurring my vision. I didn't want to cry over what happened earlier, but it broke my fucking heart to leave him.

"I had to come home because his dad found out about us. Gennaro doesn't think I'm good enough for Zayn."

For a moment, Dad did nothing, just stared at me as tears slid down my cheeks. Then he walked over and bundled me up in his arms.

"Shh, shh."

"I love him. I know you probably don't approve, but he's everything to me," I sobbed into his chest, hating myself for

291

crying over the whole situation. It made me feel weak. I wasn't fucking weak. "Zayn had to send me back to you. He couldn't go against his father."

Dad stroked my back.

"Gennaro is a fucking piece of work. No one messes with him."

At least he wasn't railing at Zayn for letting me go. In fact, he'd not said a word about my confession of love for the mafia prince. He just held me while I cried on his chest until my sobbing abated.

"Got to be honest, Ari. I ain't happy about you being with him."

I stiffened in his hold.

"I ain't happy, but I ain't going to stop you either. If anyone's going to keep you safe and give you a better life, it's him."

"You mean that?" I whispered.

"Gennaro's full of shit if he thinks you ain't worthy, but man can't have beef with him. If you do this, you do it by yourself, innit?"

I nodded. Dad couldn't afford to jeopardise his position with Gennaro. It would be suicidal.

"Glad you're home, Ari. Missed you."

"Missed you too, Dad."

He held me closer.

"We got to talk more about what you did."

"I know."

I knew we still had to talk about Justin, but at the very least, he hadn't gone ballistic at me over Zayn. He'd sort of given me his blessing. If telling me he wasn't going to stop me from being with Zayn was his blessing.

He pulled away and wiped under my eyes with his thumb before checking his phone.

"Not now. I got to meet Jamal. You going to be okay here?"

"Yeah. I'll be okay."

He nodded.

"Talk at dinner, okay?"

"I'll make us something."

He gave me a smile and left me standing there. When I heard the front door slam, I picked up my handbag from the sofa and trudged upstairs. I sat down on the bed of my childhood bedroom and wiped my face with my coat sleeve. Then I dug my hands in the pockets. Frowning, I felt a piece of paper. I pulled it out and looked down at the yellow post-it note that hadn't been there before.

He promises he'll come for you soon.

There was no signature. I knew immediately it was Arlo who'd put it in my pocket before he'd left earlier. It gave me so much fucking hope seeing it there in writing. Zayn wasn't going to abandon me. My trust wasn't unfounded. I could survive this time away from him, knowing he cared and wanted me still. I laid back against the sheets, staring up at the ceiling, and knew I had to hold on tight to that hope. It would see me through the further difficult conversations I'd have with my dad. The difficult conversation I would have to have with Kaylee because I'd disappeared. It would allow me to endure.

I'll wait for you, Zayn. I'll wait forever if I have to. I promise.

THIRTY TWO

Arianna

My eyes were fixed on the ceiling in the living room. Dad had just left. Talking about my uncle with him over the past three days was tough. He'd wanted to know everything. What Justin said. What Derek had told me. How I'd killed his brother. He didn't, however, ask me any questions about Zayn. Didn't want to know about my forbidden relationship with the mafia prince. I couldn't blame him. What father would want their twenty-two-year-old daughter with a man who was almost their own age? Who was the son of the most powerful mafia kingpin in London. I didn't know if he would ever approve, even if he'd said he wouldn't stop me.

My soul hurt when I thought about how much I missed Zayn. How much I needed him. Three days wasn't even that long. It felt like an eternity when I'd been by Zayn's side for weeks. When every waking moment had been consumed by his presence.

Kaylee had come over yesterday. I hadn't wanted to leave the house in case Zayn got in contact with me. She hadn't minded dropping in after work. Kaylee had just landed herself a modelling contract. I'd taken the photographs for her portfolio as a favour. Legs for miles and willowy, Kaylee Grant was beautiful and loved the attention. I was a behind the camera girl, but I had no interest in being a fashion photographer no matter how much Kaylee bugged me about it.

It'd been nice to catch up and bring back some normality into my life. Only it didn't make me feel normal. It made it all the more obvious this wasn't me any longer. I had changed. I wanted to be the woman who stood beside Zayn. To be in his world. To be his.

I miss you. I hate not waking up next to you. I hate not hearing your voice. I hate everything.

I put my hand over my eyes and groaned. It was ridiculous, me sitting here pining for him, but I hadn't heard a single thing. Arlo's post-it note was stuck on the mirror in my room, reminding me not to fret and worry. To have faith.

The doorbell rang. I dropped my hand from my face. Who the fuck could that be? I didn't think we'd have any visitors since Dad was out with his men.

Hauling myself up off the sofa, I trudged into the hallway and opened the front door. My hand shook when I saw Arlo standing there. I knew it was him, even if he had a hoodie on. He was dressed like he belonged on the estate.

"Arlo? Is… is everything okay? Is he okay?"

Arlo gave me a slight nod.

"Can I come in?"

I wasn't sure if I should let him. The neighbours would notice. They were nosey as fuck around here. However, if I left him outside and they overheard what we were saying, it would be worse for me. Hopefully, they'd think Arlo was one of Dad's men. They were often in and out of here.

"Yeah, okay, probably a good idea."

I stepped back, opening the door wider. Arlo shoved his hands in his pockets and walked in. Before I even had a chance to start shutting the door, another hand belonging to someone else slammed down on it. They walked in after Arlo, tugged the door from my grasp, forcing me to back up before they closed it behind them.

"What's going on? Who are—"

I couldn't speak, my voice shutting off the moment Arlo's companion flipped his own hood down.

"Tinkerbell."

My knees almost buckled at the sound of his deep voice saying my nickname. The one *he'd* given me.

"Daddy," I whispered, completely forgetting Arlo was there now all I could see was Zayn. He was right here in my dad's house staring at me with so many emotions on his face, I could barely count, let alone process them.

He moved, gathering me to him with his hands on my face before he was kissing me. My arms hung at my sides, still in too much shock to process the fact he was here. My lips were overtaken by the sensation of his pressing against them. Owning them. Reminding them of who they belonged to. Who *I* belonged to.

"Arianna," he murmured, pressing a kiss to the side of my mouth. "Take me to your bedroom. Now."

"What about Arlo?"

"He's here to protect me while I speak to you. Now take me upstairs. I'm not asking, I'm telling."

I knew better than to disobey Zayn, especially when I could feel his demand vibrating through my skin. Taking one of his hands from my face, I backed away towards the stairs. Zayn followed me, a dark glint in his eyes that had my body trembling in anticipation of what he would do to it.

"Help yourself to tea in the kitchen," I called over my shoulder to Arlo as Zayn hurried me up the stairs like he was on a deadline. I wasn't sure what the rush was all about.

The moment I opened my bedroom door, he shoved me inside, slammed it shut and backed me up against a wall.

"My little fairy," he practically growled, gripping my throat before he kissed me again.

I was pinned to the wall by his bulk. My hands gripped his clothes, trying to process his urgency. His free hand was on my body, grabbing a hold of my thigh and hooking it around him.

"Zayn, what—"

"I need you."

Those three little words had me abandoning my questions. Had me abandoning all thoughts. Zayn was here. He was here. And I needed him too.

His lips hovered over mine, those dark eyes on me, intent and waiting. He ground into me, making his intentions very clear. I could feel how hard he was.

"Daddy," I whimpered.

"That's my good girl."

My arms circled his neck when he kissed me again. I moaned when he shifted. He smiled against my lips like he knew the exact effect he had on me. I would melt for him. Always.

His hands went to my clothes, pulling my loose jogging bottoms down my legs. My underwear followed next. I arched into him when his fingers stroked between my legs. He gathered my wetness before massaging my clit, sending jolts of pleasure up my spine.

Zayn was clearly in a hurry to have me because he stopped too soon. He tugged at his own clothes, freeing his cock. He lifted me, bracing me against the wall with his body caging mine in. Then he sank inside me, groaning with the sensation. I let out a choked sound with his thick length impaling me, making me take every inch with no respite.

When he'd fully seated himself, leaving me panting and my pussy clenching around his cock, he gripped my chin.

"I know, little fairy, I'm sorry it's too much." His eyes were pits of black with a fire raging inside them. "I can't sleep knowing you aren't by my side where you belong. I can't breathe. I'm not okay without you. I. Need. You."

My words died in my throat, too choked by the emotion he stirred up in my chest. He pulled back and thrust in again, forcing an almost pained sound of need through my constricted throat.

"You. Are. Mine." He thrust again. "Mine." And again. "No one gets to have you but me." Another. "No one gets to breathe you in." Again. "No one gets to see you, touch you, or fuck you." He pushed deeper this time. "I. Own. You."

I was utterly consumed by Zayn and the hard thrust of his body into mine. The ache it caused inside me. The ownership he had over me.

"I missed you," I whispered as a tear leaked from my eye as the heavy weight of loving Zayn Villetti settled in my soul.

He wiped the tear away with the pad of his thumb before licking it from his skin.

"My precious little fairy. I'm here. I'm right here."

Taking a step back, he held onto me as he walked to the bed, sitting down on the end with me in his lap. I looped my arms around his shoulders, bringing our chests flush with each other. Dipping my head, I ran my tongue along the graffiti tattoo he had on his neck, tracing the lines of the text. He tipped his head back, giving me full access.

"*Padre*," I murmured against his skin.

"You worked it out."

I nodded. It became obvious the first time he told me he was my daddy. And it suited him. It fit the man so fucking well.

My body rocked into his, sending delicious sensations rushing through me when his cock hit the right spot. I pulled back, my hands going to his clothes. He let me tug off his hoodie, followed by his t-shirt. Zayn and Arlo had come here incognito.

My hands ran over his bare chest, stroking his skin, branding it on mine. I leant forward again, licking it with my tongue. He didn't stop me. Instead, he leant back against his hands, allowing me to explore him. Letting me worship his body in the confines of my childhood bedroom. It felt illicit. My father would not be happy if he knew I was fucking Zayn here. That only made it hotter.

"Is this your way of demonstrating how much you missed me?"

My eyes flicked up, noting the wicked look in his.

"Yes, and no."

His eyebrow raised.

"I grew up in this room, Zayn. It feels almost forbidden having you here. And I like it."

My words only made his gaze grow ever more wicked and deviant. He lay back completely, tucking both his arms under his head.

"Then be my dirty little fairy and fuck the king forbidden to you by our fathers."

My insides clenched, making him buck up into me.

"King?"

"I rule over you, Tinkerbell. That makes me king."

Jesus fucking Christ.

I pressed a kiss to his breastbone, right by his heart.

"Do I get to be your fairy queen?"

"If you're a good girl and make daddy come."

My mouth went dry. Then I sat up, pulling my t-shirt off, leaving me naked above him. I hadn't bothered putting a bra on today. My hands went to his stomach, my hips rocking faster. The way he ran his teeth over his bottom lip as those dark eyes roamed across the expanse of my body made my cheeks heat.

"That's it, ride my cock like the little slut for daddy you are."

Watching him lay there, allowing me to do all the work, to pleasure him the way he always did me, was empowering. It made me feel stronger. Like I had the control, even though we both knew if he wanted to take it back, he could in an instant. He would always own me in the bedroom. I'd bend to his will, allow him to push my body to the extreme in the name of pleasure.

"Daddy?"

"Mmm?"

"Can I have your fingers please?"

He looked me over once more.

"Where do you want them, hmm?"

He always did this. Made me use my words. Forced me to give him the truth of my desires. I liked the way he insisted on it, pushing me past the embarrassment of my needs.

"Inside me. I want you to put them inside me."

He untucked his tattooed hand from behind his head, reaching up to draw them over my mouth. I parted my lips, letting him slide inside.

"Here?"

I shook my head even as I sucked on them. He made me take all four inside my mouth, coating them in my spit.

"No? My fairy slut wants them somewhere else?"

He withdrew his fingers.

"Tell me where."

Ever since he'd said it in his office at Desecration, I'd wanted it. There was a dark part of me craving the way he stretched me wide open for him.

"In my pussy," I whispered. "You said you'd make me ride you and take them at the same time. I want it... please."

If I thought Zayn's intense expression couldn't undo me further, I was mistaken. The sheer need and desire in it had me trembling.

"I need you to be sure. It will hurt. I can't avoid that." He ran his spit covered finger over my lip. "Do you have lube? I'm not doing it without that."

I was prepared for it to hurt as I got used to it. As my body stretched to allow his fingers and cock inside me at the same time.

"In my drawer. And I am sure. I wouldn't have asked if I wasn't."

I'd had our fingers inside me together while he fucked me in the arse. I was pretty sure I could take this too. I *would* take this. I wanted it.

THIRTY THREE

Arianna

ayn pulled me off him so he could strip off the rest of his clothes and sit up against my headboard. I watched him grab the lube from my drawer and set it on the bed next to him.

"Come here."

I crawled up his body and straddled his lap, sitting back down on his cock. He circled my hips with both his big hands, making me rock on him. The tips of my nipples brushed against his chest with each movement.

"We're going to take it slow and if you need to stop, we stop. There is no shame in it hurting too much or if you don't enjoy it, okay?"

"I know. I promise I'll tell you if it's too much."

The fact he worried about me this much only made me want it more. I might be his little pet, but he wanted to make sure I was comfortable. Damn this man and his considerate nature. At least with me.

He pressed a kiss to my lips, then he stuck his finger in my mouth, making me coat it with my spit.

"Stroke your clit for me, Tink. Focus on the pleasure."

I shifted back slightly, putting some room between our chests. One of my hands rested on his shoulder while the other dipped between us. He watched me stroke myself as I fucked him. Then he popped the cap of the lube, coating his fingers in it. He slid them between us, stroking the first one along my entrance, where his cock slipped in and out of me. I kept breathing as he pressed it inside me. The stretch made me bite my lip.

"That's it, what a good girl you are, taking my cock and my finger."

His encouragement fuelled me. It made me want to be good for him. To take what he was giving me. I kept my pace steady to get used to the feeling, the sensations. Being filled by him every way I could be was my goal.

"More, daddy, please."

He withdrew his finger only to press two next to his cock. I couldn't prevent a cry from leaving my lips, even as I kept fucking him. The need to feel him this way overrode my body's reaction to the stretch and pinch of pain.

"Such a good little fairy. You're doing so well. That's it, keep fucking daddy. Keep riding my cock."

Zayn's mouth was going to kill me one day. It was a turn on, especially with his deep voice telling me such dirty things.

"Oh fuck," I moaned.

"Do you like that, Tink? Do you want me to fuck you with them?"

I nodded, my nails digging into his shoulder.

"Please."

With each stroke of his cock inside me, his fingers moved too. It was such a new feeling, but a good one. I liked the pressure, the intense way he filled me. Zayn had introduced me to something I couldn't get enough of. It's not as if we never had tame sex where he fucked me into the mattress and made me cry out his name without any extras. I loved that too. I loved everything he did to me.

"Yes, fuck, it feels so good."

He licked his lip, keeping a tight hold of my hip to guide me.

"Mmm, I bet it does. Your little pussy is getting all stretched out. Such a beautiful sight."

I moaned at his words. This was enough. I didn't think I could take more right now. He didn't let up, kept pushing his fingers into me as I rode his cock. Leaning closer, I caught his mouth with mine, kissing him for all I was worth.

Having him with me now made the past three days feel worth the agony of being without him. Even so, a part of me knew I'd have to wait longer before he could bring me back home with him.

My hand left his shoulder, sliding over his jaw and stroking across the stubble there. I released his lips and instead leant my forehead against his.

"How long can you stay?"

"Long enough for us to talk after this."

I nodded before rubbing my face against his. He let go of my hip to cup my face, cradling it with his palm.

"What's wrong, little fairy?"

"Nothing."

"Don't lie to me."

I closed my eyes for a moment. I'd wanted to stay in the moment with him, but there was something I needed to say first. Opening my eyes, I looked right into his.

"I hate that I wasn't looking at you when I… when I told you how I feel. And I hate that he was there."

He didn't blink.

"You're looking at me now."

"But it's not the first time—"

His hand tightened on my face.

"I don't care. First times or first moments or what-the-fuck-ever moments are what we make of them. If you want to tell me something, you say it. You're my fearless, blunt little fairy. You want me to remember this as the first time, then make it your fucking moment. Make it count."

I chewed on my bottom lip, letting his words sink in. He was right. I'd said those words in the moment because I needed to. Now, I could make it mean something more.

"Give me another finger, daddy."

The way his eyes searched mine had my heart pounding louder in my ears. Whatever he saw there had him slipping his fingers from my pussy. He let go of my face to apply more lube to them. Then he was carefully sliding three into me alongside his cock. The stretch was almost too much, but I took it even as my body started to sweat with the strain. It hurt, but I wanted the pain.

"More, give me them all."

A flash of concern flitted across his features, but he didn't say a word. No, he did as I asked, sliding the three out to replace them with all four. A loud yelp followed by a groan left my lips. I went still, unable to keep fucking him.

"Fuck. Fuck."

"Do you want to stop?"

"No. No. I need a moment... just a moment."

Closing my eyes, I breathed through it. My fingers on my clit helped. I focused on them rather than the stretch. I wrapped my other hand around his shoulder, digging my nails into his flesh. Then I moved again, rocking on his cock and his fingers.

"Good girl," he murmured, his breath fanning across my face. "You're such a good girl for taking them. So fucking brave and strong."

I felt it in those moments. So I kissed him, pushing my tongue into his mouth to own him the way he was owning me. Rocking back and forth on him for the much needed friction. Taking my pleasure and pain from the deadly mafia prince who had become my world. He was king in my heart and soul.

He tugged his fingers from me without warning, wrapping his hand around my hip instead as he thrust up inside me. His other hand cupped the back of my neck, anchoring me to him as he kept fucking me. I let him take control. Allowed him to set the pace. I would always crave his control over me.

"That's it, going to fuck you until you make me come, Tink. Do you want that? Want me to take my pleasure from you? Use you like my little slut after you took all my fingers?"

"Yes," I panted.

"Such a needy little fairy, desperate to be daddy's slut."

I moaned, holding onto the man for dear life as I kept stroking myself.

"Oh god, fuck, Zayn!"

He took my bottom lip between his teeth, biting down hard. I was thrown off the cliff's edge without warning. Apparently, all I needed was for him to push me beyond my limits and I was putty in his hands. I cried out, shaking with the sensations rushing up my spine and making me boneless. Zayn kissed his way down my jaw before nuzzling my neck. His cock kept punishing my pussy with harsh strokes. His grip on my hip kept me in place. Allowed him to ravage my body without resistance. As if I even wanted to say no or stop.

"Good girl, coming so sweetly for daddy after he stretched your little pussy so wide."

I swear if anyone else heard the things this man said to me, they would be blushing as hard as I am.

"Zayn," I whimpered, pulling my hand from my clit and pressing it to his chest instead. There were too many feelings inside me, desperate to come out. The intense orgasm had burst through the door and now I couldn't control them.

"What is it, Tinkerbell?" he whispered, slowing his thrusts down but not stopping.

"Are you still mine?"

His brow furrowed slightly.

"Of course I am."

"Good... because... because I love you and I don't think I can live without you."

He brought his hand from the back of my neck to the front, gripping my jaw as he stared at me.

"I'm not going anywhere. We may have to be apart right now, but I'm here, Ari. I'm *here*. I'm yours. I can't live without you either. This isn't one-sided. I. Am. Yours."

I nodded, hating how I needed the reassurance from him. And when he kissed me, I melted against him, pushing away the need to berate myself. Zayn understood why I was scared. I had every reason to be, no matter how much I trusted him. The fear of his father keeping us apart was very real.

We didn't talk anymore. I dug my fingers into his hair, kissing him back as he started to fuck me again. I moved with him, driving him closer to the edge. I could feel his body tense up with his need to come. And I was right there, clenching around him, encouraging him to claim me all over again.

"Ari," he groaned into my mouth. "Fuck."

I only kissed him harder, my fingers pressing into his scalp. His hand around my neck tightened until I could hardly breathe. Then he erupted, pulling his head back and closing his eyes. His muscles in his neck strained as he gritted his teeth. I watched him fall apart in front of me. The vulnerability he exhibited in those moments. Almost as if this was his way of showing me what I meant to him. Allowing me to have access to him in the way he always did me.

As his breathing evened out, I rested my head on his shoulder, staring up at his jaw as I stroked it with my fingers. He let go of my neck to wrap his arms around me, circling them loosely around my waist. Contentment and a feeling of being home washed over me.

"Am I your fairy queen now I've made you come?" I whispered.

He chuckled.

"You have always been my fairy, Ari, but you became queen the moment you walked into my office, covered in your uncle's blood. That's when I saw you as a grown woman who wasn't afraid to make a deal with a man she shouldn't have ever trusted to save her own skin. The one woman I couldn't have, even though I wanted her."

"You told me you didn't want to have sex with me."

His chest rumbled as he laughed harder.

"I lied."

I prodded his rib.

"You better not be lying to me now."

"Does Queen Tinkerbell need me to get on my knees and pledge allegiance to the pussy I'm currently in, promising to pet and worship it every day until its owner is a trembling mess, begging for more?"

"Zayn!"

"Just say the word, Ari. I'm more than willing. Or did you also want me to pledge allegiance to the rest of your holes? I very much want to pet those too."

I shook my head before burying it in his neck.

"You are terrible."

"Are you sure you don't want me—"

"Don't you dare."

The way he laughed had me smiling through my embarrassment over what he was suggesting. It didn't matter if he'd not told me the truth about wanting me the day we made our deal. It's not like either of us expected to end up needing each other this way. All that mattered was we were together now. We had each other, even if outside forces were trying to keep us apart. I just wondered what Zayn was going to do about it and how he'd make it possible for me to come home where I belonged.

THIRTY FOUR

Zayn

The past three days without Ari by my side had tested me. I'd never needed anyone before, but I needed her. There was a desperate ache inside me, knowing she was back with her father. Even as I tried to plot a way out of this mess, I found myself pacing my office in agitation and snapping at Arlo every five minutes. It was a miracle he was still speaking to me at this point. And why he'd all but insisted I come and see her today, not that I'd objected. I needed her presence like I needed air.

It had been a mistake to think I could keep my relationship with her from my father for long. The fact it had been my brother who had told him was something I didn't wish to think about. Whatever the fuck Gil's motives were, I didn't have time to deal with it or him. I should have known by refusing to bow to my father's pressure regarding my role in the family would cause problems. I'd wanted Gil to take over the mafia from our father. He would be a better fit than me. What I hadn't wanted was for him to become so blinded by loyalty, he would betray his own brother. And it was partially my fault. I hadn't allowed him to see the monster hiding in plain sight.

Gennaro showed me his true colours. I was his heir, who refused to do what he was told. I saw his darkest parts. Ones that made me hate him more than I'd hated anyone in my life. The monster had deprived us of our mother. And here he was, trying to deprive me of the only slice of happiness I'd had since I found out what he did.

I wouldn't allow that to happen. He couldn't take Arianna away from me. She belonged next to me. She was my queen. My little fairy. My Tinkerbell. My fucking everything. And these past three days had only confirmed that for me.

Ari pulled away and got off me when I stopped laughing. She tugged on her dressing gown and disappeared into the bathroom across the hallway to clean up. I took that as my cue to get dressed. As I did it, my eyes darted around her bedroom. The place she'd grown up in. The walls had framed photographs and there was a board with a collage of pictures of her family and friends. There was one of her from what looked like a Halloween party. I rubbed my bottom lip as I realised she'd gone as Tinkerbell in a green dress, golden wings and her hair up in a bun. On the shelf next to those photos was a little model of Tinkerbell sitting on a log with her arms crossed. And stuck to the wall by her headboard, a little silhouette of Tinkerbell sat.

"Tell me, Ari… is this a coincidence or did the nickname I gave you when you were four mean more than you've let on?"

I turned and found her staring at me from the doorway. Her cheeks were tinged red and her hands twisted in front of her.

"I don't know what you want me to say."

"The truth."

She walked into the room, closing the door behind her and leant against it.

"It doesn't mean I had a crush on you if that's what you're thinking. It wasn't like that. I just related to her and her plight. She just wanted to be number one in Peter's life, you know."

I grinned and closed the distance between us. She looked up at me as I stroked her cheek.

"She's a jealous little brat with a heart of gold. I can see why you relate to her."

"Shut up."

I leant closer, brushing my lips against hers.

"I happen to like bratty little fairies who demand all my attention and want to be taken care of. One, in particular, has me so crazy about her, I'm defying my own father to be with her. She's fiery, passionate and likes to call me daddy… maybe the two of you have met."

"Maybe we have," she whispered. "She sounds fun."

I kissed her, pulling her against me because I couldn't get enough of this woman and her mouth. Ari was my air. She made it possible for me to keep breathing.

When I released her mouth, she pressed herself against my chest, leaning her cheek on it. I rocked the two of us from side to side as I held her, never wanting to let go.

"My father isn't happy with me. He's been monitoring my activities so I couldn't come any sooner. I'm sorry I had to make you come back here, Ari. It's not what I wanted."

"It's okay. I understand. I'm not good enough for him."

My arms tightened around her. The fact my father had told her that pissed me off. It didn't matter where she came from. It mattered who she was. Ari was the only person I wanted by my side. She was my match. The equal I'd never aspired to find. I didn't want to bind myself to another person the way I did her. My stance on marriage hadn't changed, but I'd give Arianna something more. I'd pledge my entire life to her, protect her and give her anything she wanted because she'd given me something so fucking precious. Her heart.

"I hope you know I don't feel that way."

"I do. And I don't care what he says either. You're mine."

My heart squeezed in my chest. It happened every time she said it. Told me I was hers. I'd never wanted to belong to anyone before her.

She looked up at me a moment later.

"Are you going to fix this?"

There was the woman I was utterly enamoured with. She wasn't afraid to demand answers from me.

"Yes. I'm working on it."

I pulled away and led her over to the bed, forcing her to sit down. There were a lot of things I needed to explain to Ari. I set about picking up her clothes before kneeling at her feet so I could dress her.

"My father is a powerful man. No one says no to him… well, that's not strictly true. I've said no to a lot of things. If he had his way, I wouldn't have Desecration, and I'd be his perfect obedient heir, standing by his side, learning the ropes from him and ready to take over the mafia at a moment's notice."

Ari snorted and rolled her eyes as she put her arms up so I could put her t-shirt over her head.

"I can't imagine you being obedient to anyone."

"I maintain the illusion I am to him. I had no real reason to go against his word until you. He doesn't get to take you away from me."

She reached out and cupped my face.

"I'm not going anywhere."

I sighed and took her hand away from my face, pressing a kiss to it.

"I wish that was true, but if I don't do something, he will take you away from me… permanently."

Her eyes clouded over and her face paled slightly.

"You mean he'd… he'd…"

"Yes."

My father would have Ari killed if I didn't give her up.

"I'm not telling you this to scare you, Tink. I'm telling you so you understand the consequences of me going against my father's wishes. So you understand the danger you're in by choosing to be with me."

Her hand shook.

"I don't want to die, Zayn."

Dropping her hand, I cupped her face with both of mine. The misery on her face cut me.

"You aren't going to, I promise. You're safe with me. I will protect you from him with my life if I have to."

She shook her head, her hands curling around my forearms.

"You can't die either. How am I supposed to live without you?"

I tugged her closer, pressing my forehead to hers.

"Shh, that's not happening, Tink. No one is dying, okay?"

"I'm terrified of losing you."

I let go of her so I could tug her down on the floor with me and cradle her against my chest.

"You have me," I whispered, pressing my face into her hair, "I need you to be strong for me and remember, I'm yours. Can you do that? There's more I have to tell you, but I won't if you can't handle it."

She nodded, clutching me to her like her life depended on it.

"I can. I promise I can take it."

"Good girl."

I knew telling her the truth about what Gennaro might do wouldn't be easy for her to hear, but there was no other way. She trusted me with everything. It was time I did the same thing for her.

"My father has all the power right now. What I have to do… what I need to do is become more powerful than he is, so he can't threaten us any longer. And in order to do that, I have to make everyone else bow to me. Everyone, Ari, including your father, who I'm not sure you realise how deeply embedded with mine he is."

She said nothing for a long moment. Then she pulled her face from my chest and met my eyes.

"Dad told me if I wanted to be with you, he couldn't be a part of it. I don't know what his deal is with Gennaro, but I know he won't go against him for me."

"My father is his investor. Your father and his gang grow. They make a hefty profit doing so. My father is in bed with the Met Police Commissioner, so it keeps them off your father's back. It's the perfect scheme. Its only flaw is that I know everything. I've been there every step of the way. They use my land to grow on. My properties. And that's what I'm going to use to bring your father to heel. Do you understand what I'm saying?"

She nodded.

Ari knew her father dealt in drugs, but until now, she had no idea how deeply involved he was with my father. She didn't realise the power he held over Bennett.

"That's why you're here, right? Not just to see me... but for him too?"

I shook my head.

"No, I came because I had to see you. I needed to talk to you first before I do anything. You didn't appreciate me keeping you in the dark last time. I'm not making the same mistake. I'm trusting you with the truth here, Ari. I'm giving you the facts and letting you decide whether or not this is worth it to you. And before you say anything, you are worth it to me. I would burn everything to the ground, kill everyone in my fucking way just to keep you by my side if you want to stay there."

I took a breath before I laid out the rest of my cards on the table.

"If I do this, I will have a lot of blood on my hands before we are done. The criminal underworld used to have a king. I'm going to replace him, but I'll be different. I won't rule with fear. I'll rule with respect. I'll do all of that to force my father to accept I'm no longer his heir, but the man who has amassed more power than he can ever fucking dream of. I'll do it so I can have you."

Ari blinked as if she wasn't expecting this to be my plan. There wasn't any other way. Gennaro needed to be put in his fucking place. If I was going to make it safe for Ari and me, then I had to do what was necessary and make him bow to me.

"If you don't want this, you have to tell me now."

"There's no other way?" she whispered.

"Unless you want me to take out my own father."

She shook her head.

"I don't want that."

Ari looked away. I gave her time to process my words. She hadn't pulled away or run. I knew she needed a minute to get her thoughts straight.

When she met my eyes again, there was a softness in her chestnut ones. Reaching up, she cupped my cheek.

"If you have to burn the world for us, daddy, then burn the world."

I turned my face into her hand and kissed her palm.

"I'll burn it for you, Tinkerbell, as long as you'll be my fairy queen."

"I'll strike the match, you carry the flame and we'll burn it together."

I took her hand and laced our fingers together, leaning closer until our noses brushed against each other.

"Deal."

She smiled, but before I could kiss her, a loud noise from downstairs followed by an angry voice startled the both of us.

TYRANT

"What the fuck do you think you're doing in my fucking house?"

THIRTY FIVE

Zayn

A ri scrambled off me at the sound of her father's
voice, her eyes wide and her body tense. She got to
her feet and stared down at me with concern.

"I didn't think he'd be home early."

I stood up, took her hand and pulled her out of her room
with me. Arlo shouldn't have to deal with a pissed off Bennett.
This was my responsibility. I'd come here to see his daughter.
If he was going to be angry at anyone, it should be me.

"We did get carried away," I murmured as we made our
way downstairs, knowing more time had gone by than either
of us had expected.

"So worth it."

I couldn't deny it. Having Ari take all my fingers and my
cock at the same time had been magnificent to watch. She was
such a good girl for me. I didn't have time to be thinking about
it when we had a situation to deal with. Didn't matter if I
wanted to replay the ecstasy on her face over and over. And

when she told me she loved me again. Fuck, it brought on a whole other set of emotions I couldn't process.

We found Bennett and Arlo in the kitchen. Arlo didn't look fazed at the knife in his face. Wasn't the first time someone had threatened him. Wouldn't be the last. It was part and parcel of being my right-hand man.

"Dad! What are you doing? Put the knife down," Ari all but yelled, letting go of my hand and storming over to her father. "He is not a threat to you."

Bennett turned to her.

"You let him in my house?"

Then he saw me and he visibly stiffened. He lowered his knife and stepped back. Bennett wouldn't fuck with me or my men. He knew better. I wasn't someone you played games with.

"You."

I waved a hand.

"Mmm, yes, me. I'm here to see her, not cause trouble."

He turned his attention to his daughter.

"You didn't tell me."

She crossed her arms over her chest.

"I didn't know he was coming, Dad, or I would have. You going to stand there and tell me I'm not allowed to see my boyfriend in my own home?"

Bennett stepped closer to her while keeping an eye on me. I tried not to smile at her calling me that to his face like she was proud I was hers.

"I can't have him here. My crew don't know I'm in business with the mafia, you feel me?"

Ari let out a huff.

"Does it look like they walked in here announcing who they are to the world? No, so don't use your crew as an excuse."

Bennett let out a sound of frustration. I knew exactly where Ari got her blunt nature from. Her father. He might not have displayed it now, but he'd made no bones about telling me how it was when we did business together.

"Ari—"

"No, Dad. This is how it is. I'm with him. Deal with it."

Bennett pursed his lips in annoyance at her cutting him off. Ari's eyes, which matched her father's, dared him to say another word. The two of them had a standoff, neither speaking, just glaring at each other, waiting to see who would break first.

Arlo moved around them and came over to me. I didn't blame him for not wanting to get in between father and daughter. I wasn't going to fight Ari's battles for her. She was perfectly capable of doing that herself. It was one of the things I admired about her. She certainly fought me enough. It made it so much sweeter when she finally submitted.

"You do realise loud noises carry in this house," Arlo hissed.

I gave him a smile.

"You insisted on me seeing her. Did you think I wasn't going to play with my little pet after three days apart?"

He shook his head, giving me side-eyes. I didn't give a shit if he heard me fucking Ari. I'd missed her. The moment I saw her face earlier, I had to have her against me. It was like I could finally breathe again and the only way I could feel alive was if I was inside her, reminding Ari of who she belonged to. Of what I was fighting for. Her. I would always fight for her because that fucking girl had gone and made me care about her. Made me want a life with her. I wanted to be her future. She was the most precious thing in the world to me. So no, I wasn't going to apologise for it.

"Shame is not a word in your vocabulary."

"Why would it be? Knowing how to satisfy a woman is my pleasure." I raised an eyebrow. "Why isn't it yours?"

"I'd tell you to shut up if I thought it would make a difference."

"And I'd tell you to go find some female company instead of pining for someone you think you can't have if I thought you'd listen."

Arlo glared at me. I merely shrugged. I knew about his little lovesick puppy shit. As if he could ever hide it from me. As quiet and deadly as he may be, didn't mean he could stop me from seeing right through him. We'd known each other since we were children. There were no secrets between us.

"He can stay," Bennett finally said to Ari, even though he did not look happy about giving in to his daughter.

You and me both, Bennett. She's a force to be reckoned with.

"Thank you," Ari replied, looking relieved things hadn't escalated further.

She looked over at me. I gave her a nod. She didn't need my approval, but I had a feeling Ari needed reassurance from me. I would have her back. She didn't need to worry about that.

"As I'm here, Bennett, we should talk," I said, walking over to his dining table and taking a seat in a chair like I wasn't an interloper in his house.

Turning my head, I watched Bennett's expression sour and Ari give him a sharp look. He schooled his features and came around to sit across from me. Their house wasn't big. He'd inherited it from his aunt when she died. Bennett had got into the drug trade at twenty-one when she got sick so he could keep a roof over their heads. His aunt had custody of him and Justin because of their parent's neglect. I was aware of his circumstances because my father had checked into his background before agreeing to be his investor.

I looked back at Ari before patting my leg. Her eyes widened slightly and her cheeks went pink. She walked over and took a seat next to me, but not before leaning down and whispering in my ear, "I'm not sitting on your lap in front of my father. I would never hear the end of it."

I kept a straight face, even though I wanted to smile. Bennett wouldn't be impressed to discover his daughter called me daddy nor that I treated her like my little pet.

"Ari ain't involved in man's business," Bennett said, giving his daughter a pointed stare.

I took a hold of Ari's hand under the table, tugging it into my lap and lacing our fingers together.

"Let's get one thing straight. Your daughter is *my* partner and if I want her here for this conversation, she's going to be here."

Ari's hand tightened in mine. I didn't look at her, instead stared down her father who sat back and waved at me to continue.

"Give it to me then."

I stroked my thumb down the back of Ari's.

"Your deal with my father ends today."

327

Bennett sat up straighter.

"You what?"

"From now on, you will answer to me. I will keep you in business. Let's not forget who owns the land you use for your little drug trade. You can maintain the illusion with Gennaro, but everything goes through me. I will make sure you are very well compensated for your trouble, protect your assets and guarantee his wrath does not fall on your head." I leant forward in my seat, maintaining eye contact with him. "My father thinks I'm loyal because I let Arianna come home to you, but that's far from the case. He has no idea of the lengths I'll go to keep her by my side."

Bennett's brows knitted together.

"I'm sure you disapprove of my relationship with her, but I know you want your daughter to be happy. I intend to do everything in my power to give her the life she deserves. She will want for nothing and will be free to do whatever she pleases. I'm not going to keep her in a gilded cage like the rest of my family do to their women. That's not who I am."

Ari's hand shook in mine. I glanced at her face, finding those beautiful eyes full of emotions. I would give her the world if she asked it of me. She deserved it all.

My attention went back to her father because I needed to finish this.

"Don't make the same mistake as my father by underestimating me. There are two options in front of you, Bennett. You continue to ally yourself with a man who will stab you in the back if it suits him or you stand with me and your daughter. I assure you, I'm not a man you want to fuck with."

For a long moment, Bennett said nothing. I sat back, letting go of Ari's hand, only to wrap my arm around her shoulder, pulling her closer. She didn't resist, allowing me to show her affection in front of her father.

Bennett stood up and paced away. He stopped by the kitchen sink and stared out into the back garden.

"Ari's the only fam I have left. She deserves better than what I can give her." He shook his head, placing his hands on the counter. "Justin betrayed me. Betrayed her. I put my trust in him and that pussy'ole didn't fucking deserve it." He paused, his fingers gripping the counter harder. "I didn't protect her, but you did. I owe man big fucking time for that, you feel me? I owe man for keeping my girl safe."

"Is that a yes, then?"

"We got shit to work out, but yeah, it's a deal."

Bennett came back over to the table and sat down. Ari got up to make tea while I spoke to her father about how shit would be going forward. My queen deserved to know how I would treat her father. So she'd know I wouldn't fuck him over. It wasn't about the money for me. It was about making sure her father survived this battle between me and Gennaro.

Arlo looked at me when we were done and I knew it was time we left. As much as I hated having to walk away from Ari right now, I needed to be at the club soon. I'd come for her when I could. Bring her home. She belonged with me in *our* home. I didn't see it solely as mine any longer.

Ari saw us to the door. Arlo hung back so I could have a moment with her. Ari wrapped her arms around my neck and buried her face in it.

"I hate being away from you."

"I know, Tink. It's not for long. I promise."

If I brought her home now, Gennaro would know. I could only spend time with her when I could slip by his fucking watchers. Arlo had made it possible today, but we had to be careful.

I dug my hand into her hair, pulling her head back so I could kiss her. She trembled in my hold, clearly trying to keep her emotions in check. It didn't make me feel good about having to walk out of here, but Ari knew what was at stake. She knew what we were fighting for.

When I let her go, she stared up at me with sadness in her eyes. She took hold of my hand and pressed it against her cheek.

"I love you."

Leaning closer, I kissed her forehead. My chest ached with her words. It made leaving her that much harder.

"I'll see you soon, my sweet little fairy. Stay strong for me, okay?"

"Yes, daddy," she whispered. "I promise I will."

"Good girl."

Arlo and I left her on the doorstep, watching us walk away down the street.

"I take it she said yes to your plans."

I looked over at him.

"Did you think she wouldn't?"

He snorted.

"I was fifty-fifty on her response. She went ballistic at you last time."

"She didn't know what I was planning. Now, she's involved. She knows I trust her."

"You sure this'll be worth it?"

We reached the car. Arlo unlocked it and opened the door, but didn't get in.

"She's worth everything. One day, you'll understand if you stop acting like a little bitch and go get your girl."

I got in the car, leaving him to stew over what I'd said. Arlo needed to get over himself. And I needed to get to the club to start putting my plan in motion. Bennett was only the first step. It was time to take over London and put an end to Gennaro Villetti's reign of terror over me for good.

THIRTY SIX

Zayn

Colm Moran rubbed his face as he sat in the chair in front of my desk. He'd taken over the Irish mob after he'd killed the previous leader, Mac McCarthy. He was less troublesome than Mac, but it didn't stop him from being a pain in the neck. All of these gangsters were. It was high time they got their shit together. Too much petty squabbling as they vied for top dog. Shame they were all too stupid to see the bigger picture. A shame for them. It was a blessing for me.

"You're fuckin' kiddin' me, right?"

I leant back in my chair, folding my hands together on my chest.

"Do you think I make idle threats, Mr Moran? I know what you did to Mac."

He stood up and paced away.

"He was a fuckin' traitor working with Russo, lyin' to us like we were mugs. He was a fuckin' cunt. So what if I offed him? It's been long enough. No one's sniffin' around his death."

I smiled. These gangsters always thought they were so secure in their leadership. Shame they had no idea that secrets always have a way of coming out. I liked to collect information about their dirty dealings. It was the best way to keep people under control. Blackmail was a powerful incentive.

"Is that what you think? Pity you forgot about Mac's younger brother."

"Ach, Robbie left this life behind."

"Did he now? I suppose that explains why he's looking for answers then, doesn't it?"

Colm turned and stared at me.

"Robbie's in Ireland. My men have fuckin' eyes on him. Can't be too careful."

I spread my hands.

"He might be there, but his associates? Well, they're here and they're getting awfully close to the truth. Men like Robbie never truly walk away from this life, you know that as well as I do."

Colm bared his teeth at me. There was a gap in them where he'd lost one in a fight. I wasn't scared of him. We might be alone in this office, but I never took meetings with gangsters unarmed and ready to execute them if necessary. Of course, it would create a mess, but Penn wouldn't mind cleaning up after me. He enjoyed that part, the sick fucker.

"What the fuck do you want with me?"

"Me? Why do you think I'd want something?"

He shook his head.

"Spit it out. Haven't got all day, Mr Villetti."

I leant forward, placing one hand on my desk.

"I'll make sure your little Robbie problem goes away."

"I'm supposin' you want a favour for that."

I cocked my head to the side.

"No favours. Just know I own you and your gang now. You can continue to run things your way but know I rule this city. You'll answer to me if I deem it necessary."

Rising from my seat, I met Colm's eyes as I tugged at my sleeves to straighten them.

"You see, Russo thought he was smart when he ran this city, but fear only breeds dissent. I'm a fair man, Mr Moran. The only thing I demand is respect. You respect me. I'll make sure your little problems go away without causing a scene. Keep you in the position you've become accustomed to. And if you betray me, I'll repay the favour in kind. Am I making myself clear?"

He stared at me for a long moment.

"In case you're struggling with your decision, I know you've been angling for membership here for quite some time. Consider it a welcome gift. You can stay for my special club night, see if it lives up to its reputation."

I flicked a piece of lint off the sleeve of my suit.

"Just know, if you refuse my very generous offer, you might not live to see next week. I won't kill you, but Robbie… I can't make any promises there. Choose wisely, Mr Moran."

Colm's face went a rather unattractive shade of purple. I knew he would probably mouth off at me if he thought it would do him any good. Watching him try to compose himself amused me. He'd played right into my hand, and it was obvious he hated it.

"Ach, you've made yourself very clear, Mr Villetti," he ground out through his teeth.

I came around the desk and put my hand out to him.

"Do we have a deal?"

For a moment, I thought he would refuse, but Colm stepped forward and shook my hand.

"Pleasure doin' business with you," he said with as much fake enthusiasm as he could muster.

"I assure you, the pleasure is all mine."

I led him away to the door and opened it. Standing outside with a rather bored look on her face was Remi. She plastered a smile on it the moment she saw us.

"Now, Remi here will show you around." I pushed him towards her. "Just a word of warning though, she is not on the menu. If you touch her, I will remove the offending body part with my own hands. Have a nice evening, Mr Moran. I'll be in touch soon."

I shut the door behind him, but not before I caught him paling at my words. Remi was used to me threatening men to keep their limbs to themselves on her behalf. She might not like me interfering in her life, but her safety was a different matter. No one in the club was touched without their explicit consent. Even the clients with the most fucked up depraved fantasies weren't allowed to stray outside of the boundaries they'd set with my staff. There were no debates or second chances. Fuck up once, you're out.

I let out a long sigh and rubbed my face. The past couple of weeks had been rough. Making backroom deals and forcing gangsters and criminals into obeying me wasn't my idea of fun, but it was necessary. You don't become king without putting the work in. There was still more to be done, but I'd brought the major players into the fold by manipulation and force. My father had no fucking idea what he'd unleashed the moment he told me to send Arianna back to Bennett. Told her she wasn't worthy. My *queen* was more than worthy of her crown.

There was a light knock at my door. I smiled when it opened, revealing my Tinkerbell. She walked in and stood before me. Neither of us spoke for a long minute. We took each other in after two long fucking weeks apart.

"Do you like it?" she asked, running her hands over her very short, blood-red dress.

"I think whoever picked it has excellent taste."

The way her chestnut eyes twinkled had me licking my lip.

"Then I should thank him."

"You should."

She reached out, taking my hand in hers and pressed her lips to the centre of my palm before releasing it. Her way of thanking me for the dress I'd sent with Arlo. He'd left two hours ago to give her ample time to get ready to be my date for the special club night. I couldn't go another minute without her. My father was still watching me, but I didn't give a shit. He wasn't going to keep me from her any longer.

"You changed your hair."

It was braided, and those small braids had been piled on top of her head in a sleek bun.

The shy smile on her face made me want to tug her against me and devour that pretty mouth until she was a panting mess.

"I did."

I stepped closer so our bodies were brushing against each other. I leant down and ran my nose up her cheek.

"Beautiful. You always are, but tonight my pretty little fairy is exquisite."

She let out a little whimper that had me wrapping my arm around her waist and pulling her body flush with mine.

"I've missed you, Tinkerbell," I whispered, staring into her eyes. "I need you."

"Kiss me, daddy, I've missed you too."

So I did. I kissed her sweet mouth, letting myself get lost in her. It wasn't enough. It would never be enough. The ache in my fucking soul burnt with the need to be in her. I pulled away because the temptation to shove her down over my desk and fuck her until she cried was making me a little crazy. While I liked seeing her messy, I could indulge after the club night was over. I planned on it.

"Come, the king needs to be seen by his subjects."

Ari snorted. I'd been careful when kissing her so as not to ruin her lipstick. She reached up and wiped it off my mouth before letting me take her hand.

"Arlo said you do these regularly. Do you go to all of them?" she asked as I led her down the hallway to the main floor of the club.

"Most of them."

"And do you usually take a date?"

"No. Never."

I caught her smiling at that little detail. She should know by now she was special to me.

Tonight would send a very clear message. Arianna Michaelson belonged to me.

I opened the doors to the main club and swept in with her on my arm. A few people stared as we crossed the club floor towards the velvet upholstered seating at the back. I unbuttoned my suit jacket before taking a seat, my legs spread and my hand resting on my thigh. Arianna sat next to me, crossing one leg over the other. She placed her hand over mine in an act of possession that had me fighting a smile.

The first show had already begun on one of the raised platforms where the poles were. A woman was cuffed to a St Andrews cross with her back exposed. Her Domme had a whip in her hand and kept cracking it before striking out against the sub's skin. Ari's hand tightened over mine as her eyes landed on the scene in front of her.

"Curious, Tink?" I murmured, watching a few women take their seats next to us.

It made my fairy stiffen, her body growing tense beside me. Such a jealous little thing she was.

"Arlo didn't tell me what to expect," she replied in a quiet voice so no one could overhear our conversation.

I chuckled.

"No, he wouldn't have."

Arlo preferred to watch the patrons on event nights in case things got out of hand. Not to mention he was here to protect me and Arianna should something go wrong. He didn't talk about what went on here. None of the staff did. Privacy was important to our clients.

"I don't think I'd like that."

"Being whipped?"

"No."

She shifted closer to me. I angled my head towards her while watching the room.

"I know what you like, Tinkerbell. Getting that little pussy stretched so wide, it hurts."

Her cheeks went bright red.

"Zayn! Someone could hear us."

I ran my teeth over my bottom lip.

"Let them listen. It's no worse than the requests my clients make of my staff. Haven't you missed daddy's cock inside you? Don't you want me to stretch you out so you cry when you come?"

Ari didn't respond. She stared out over the club floor, her eyes betraying the desire coursing through her veins at my words. I slid my hand from under hers so I could place it on her bare thigh, my fingers brushing her delicate skin. She let out a harsh breath, her red cheeks darkening.

"No? Mmm, that's disappointing. I had planned on rewarding you for being so patient. Unless you want me to punish you instead? Is that it? Do you want me to gag you so you can't beg me to stop?"

She bit down on her lip before turning her face into mine and pressing her lips against my ear.

"I've been a good girl, daddy, please don't punish me."

"I have plans for you later, little fairy. If you want to continue being a good girl, you'll behave for daddy by watching the show and making it very clear to everyone here you belong to me. Do you understand?"

For a moment she didn't speak, then she tightened her hold on my thigh.

"Where's my collar, daddy?"

"In my pocket."

"Put it on me."

"As you wish."

She sat back as I let her go so I could slip it out of my pocket. Ari allowed me to place the leather collar around her neck. The leash hung down from the metal ring. She picked it up and handed it to me. After I took it from her, she slipped off the padded seat and settled herself on her knees between my spread legs. She wrapped her hand around my calf and rested her cheek on my thigh.

Arianna made it crystal clear to everyone here tonight she was my little obedient pet. My queen made me fucking proud of her. And I was going to make sure she was thoroughly rewarded before the night was over.

THIRTY SEVEN

Zayn

Ari remained obedient the whole evening. She sat at my feet, watching the various dancers and shows. I had one of the girls get us refreshments to keep her from getting dehydrated and hungry. Like the good little pet she was, Ari allowed me to feed her and make sure she sipped her drinks. She stayed quiet when a few clients approached me to talk business. My girl proved she was my queen by behaving and not letting her inner brat out. Of course, I knew she would eventually do something to push my buttons. Ari couldn't help it. She liked being punished as much as I enjoyed making her submit.

The club cleared out around midnight, the staff going about their cleaning tasks around the room. I pulled Ari into my lap and stroked her back as she rested her head on my shoulder.

"You've been a good girl for me," I murmured as I rested my cheek on the top of her head.

"Thank you, daddy. I wanted to make you proud of me."

"I'm very proud of you, my little fairy queen."

She snuggled closer, wrapping her hand around my neck and stroking her fingers along one of my tattoos.

"Are you going to take me back to my dad's?"

I shook my head.

"No, I need you home… as long as you want to be there with me."

"You're my home, Zayn. Wherever you are is where I want to be."

Her words made my chest tighten. I felt the same way about her. My house was empty without her presence.

I watched the staff disappear from the room, knowing they would give us privacy. I'd asked Liza to relay the message to them earlier.

"We're not going quite yet."

She raised her head from my shoulder and met my eyes.

"No?"

"Stand up."

She shifted out of my lap, standing in front of me with a tentative expression on her face. The music was still playing, with the volume down low.

"I want you to dance for me."

Her eyebrows shot up.

"What?"

"If you want me to fuck any of those tight little holes of yours tonight, you'll continue being a good girl and dance for me. Otherwise, I'll take you home and put you to bed. It won't be with me, Tink. It'll be by yourself."

Her mouth dropped open and her hands clenched into little fists at her sides.

"You wouldn't dare."

"Try me."

She pouted. I laid my hand on my thigh and flexed my fingers. Her acting out was unsurprising. The routine I'd set out for her had been disrupted by my father's interference.

"I suggest you don't test my patience. I might have missed your bratty little mouth, but that doesn't mean I'll tolerate your disobedience. So dance, Arianna. Show me you're still daddy's desperate little slut."

Ari gave me a disparaging look before she schooled her features and shook her hands out. Then she closed her eyes and took a breath. I let it slide. I knew she'd missed me and didn't like the prospect of spending another night without me by her side if she misbehaved.

"What kind of dance would you like, sir? Should I try twirling around one of those poles… or did you want a lap dance?"

"Both."

Her eyes snapped open. She gave me a little nod before moving towards the nearest pole. Stepping up onto the platform, she kicked off her heels and grabbed a hold of the pole. Then she swayed in time to the music, rocking her hips as she moved around the pole, seemingly working out what she should do. She'd seen enough tonight to get an idea of the type of thing the girls did here. It wouldn't matter to me what she did. Ari herself was enticing to me. It didn't take much to make me want to impale her on my cock any way I could.

She shifted around, putting the pole to her back with one hand placed above her. Then she was moving to the beat and slowly lowering herself down. I couldn't keep my eyes off her luscious body clad in that very skimpy red dress I'd made her wear. It clung to her curves and rode up her thighs as she bent her knees until I could see the black lace she wore beneath.

I had to adjust my dick because it was straining so hard against my zipper, it fucking hurt. Her eyes narrowed in on the movement, and a small smile played at her lips as she rose up again. Then she was twirling around the pole, continuing to move her body to the beat.

"Come here," I all but growled, unable to take the distance between us any longer.

Arianna was quick to obey, stepping off the platform. I held my hand up before she could come any closer.

"Crawl to me."

She lowered herself to her hands and knees. The leash hung down, the handle dragging along the floor as she moved closer, her eyes fixed on mine. She took her time, making me wait for it. Each movement she made only had my need to have her increasing tenfold. This woman was going to kill me and I didn't give a fuck.

When she reached me, she crawled between my legs and sat up on her knees. Her hands went to my thighs and ran up them until she met my belt.

"Take your underwear off and give it to me. Now."

She let go of me to carry out my demand. After she'd shimmied out of them, she put them in my hand. I set the wet lace down on the seat beside me, keeping my gaze on her.

"Stand up and show me you deserve my cock in your pussy."

Ari got to her feet and leant over me as she moved her body. She dragged her hands down my chest before turning around and all but planting herself in my lap. She moved against me, grinding her behind on my painfully hard cock. Her little pussy was on display as her dress had ridden high on her hips. I slid my hand over her thigh and brushed my fingers through her folds, making her let out a little gasp.

"Mmm, so wet for daddy, aren't you?"

"Yes," she panted, continuing to grind on me to the beat.

My other hand went to my belt, unbuckling it so I could get my cock out.

"You're being such a good little slut."

I let go of her to free myself, almost groaning in relief as the cool air met my hot skin. My hand curled around her hip, tugging her back against me again.

"I want this pussy, Tink. I want you to fuck yourself on my dick."

She pulled away from my embrace, spinning on her heels between my legs to face me. Her chestnut eyes were full of heat and need. Ari straddled my lap, holding onto my shoulders before sinking down on me. Her mouth parted with a barely audible whimper.

I wrapped my hand around the leash, tugging her body flush with mine. My other hand slid behind her neck.

"My little fairy," I murmured, brushing my lips over hers. "I don't want to spend another day without you."

"Is it safe for me to come back home… like permanently, not just for tonight?"

Gennaro was still a problem, but I was tired of his interference in my life. Done with playing the good son.

"The honest answer is no, but I have a family dinner tomorrow night and I want to take you."

She stopped moving and stared at me, her brow furrowing slightly.

"Are you trying to make him angry?"

"Yes, and no. He won't make a scene in front of my aunt and cousins, but he won't be happy either."

Her hands tightened on my shoulders.

"Zayn, I trust you, but this feels reckless."

"Isn't that right up your street?"

Ari bit her lip, clearly trying not to smile.

"Being reckless by pushing your buttons is less dangerous than turning up at a family dinner to deliberately piss your father off."

I let go of the leash, gripping her hip and forcing her lower on my cock.

"Mmm, say that again."

Ari's eyebrows shot up.

"What? That we're going to make your father angry?"

I pulled her up and shoved her body back down on my cock.

"Yes."

The smile lighting up her face had me biting my lip. I moved then, picking her up and pressing her down on the seat before I towered over her body. My hand went to her throat, curling around the collar.

"He's never keeping us apart again, Tinkerbell. You belong to me. He's just going to have to get used to the fact his son does not bow to him. I'm the king now, not him."

"My king," she whispered as I pressed inside her again.

"All yours."

348

Neither of us said another word. We kissed, our bodies moving in sync with one another. It wasn't frantic or needy. It was slow and sensuous. I never wanted it to end. Never wanted to come up for air. She was all I needed to survive. I was half alive before she walked into my office that fateful night. Just existing in this fucked up world. And now I couldn't go another day without a glance at the girl below me.

I'd defied my father many times in the past, but this was different. I was taking a stand against him, no longer affiliating myself with the family business. It was all for her. She was the reason for my courage. It wasn't so much I didn't have the balls to tell Gennaro to go fuck himself in the past. I just had no incentive to. He let me go about my life in the way I wanted because he thought I would eventually return to the fold. Pity for him it was a foolish notion. The moment he deprived me of my mother, he became my nemesis. And now I would show him why he should have never alienated his eldest son.

Right before I came, I pulled out of her, straddled her chest, and pulled open her jaw. Ari stared up at me with wide eyes as I shoved my cock between her lips and let her taste herself on me. My other hand cradled her head as I came, spurting in her mouth. I sat back, panting when I was spent, my hands resting on my thighs. She swallowed and ran her tongue over her lips to catch the stray drops.

"My good girl," I whispered, stroking her flushed cheek.

She rubbed her face against my palm, giving me a smile.

"I'm tired."

"Then let's get you home."

I shifted off her and adjusted my clothes before doing the same for her. I collected her heels from the platform before sweeping her up into my arms and carrying her from the club. My driver was patiently waiting for us outside. I set Ari down in the car and slid in next to her. Before she had a chance to get settled, I was on her, pressing her dress up and burying my face in her pussy.

"What are you doing?" she hissed, tugging at my hair to stop me.

I ignored her protests, sliding all four of my fingers inside her pussy. Lewis would turn a blind eye to what was going on in the back of the car, so she needn't worry about him watching.

"Fuck," she whimpered, "Zayn!"

It wouldn't matter if she tried to stop me. I needed to taste her. To reward her for being so good for me this evening. My other hand banded around her thigh. Her nails dug into my scalp, but it wasn't to push me away any longer. It was to keep me there. I thrust my fingers inside her harder, making her let out a loud moan.

That's it, Tink, let go. Let me make you feel good.

I looked up to find her eyes closed and her mouth parted. It made me smile. Ari knew better than to disobey me. When we got home, I wanted to put her straight to bed. This was the only time I had to feast on my little fairy.

"Harder," she panted. "Please, fuck."

I gave her what she asked for, thrusting my fingers inside her and tonguing her clit. She was clenching around me minutes later, letting out a little cry of pleasure with her climax. I watched her body tremble with it, her hand fisting tighter in my hair. She was stunning when she let go. My beautiful little Tinkerbell.

TYRANT

I let her curl up in my lap when she came down from her high. She buried her face in my shoulder, closed her eyes and fell asleep. When we reached the house, I carried her inside to my bedroom. I stripped her out of her clothes and tugged one of my t-shirts over her head. I don't think she even noticed when I wiped her face to remove her makeup before tucking her up under the covers.

I stood at the end of the bed, watching her. She looked so small and peaceful in my bed... our bed. This was her home as much as it was mine. Walking around to her side, I leant over Ari and pressed a kiss to her forehead. There were a few things I needed to do before I got in with her.

"I'm happy you're home, little fairy," I whispered, stroking her cheek with one finger. "I've missed you more than you know, *mio amore*."

I'd tried to be more open with Ari about my feelings towards her. There was one thing I was holding back. It wasn't because I didn't think she deserved to know. I'd just never said it before... never felt it for anyone. Instead, I'd tried to show her without words how much she meant to me. Actions always spoke louder than words. Although, I could admit hearing those three little words from her would never get old.

I've never loved anyone before, Arianna, but I think I'm in love with you. And I want to tell you... I'm just not ready yet. Please wait a little longer for me, my precious little fairy, and I promise I'll give you what you want most in this world... my heart.

THIRTY EIGHT

Arianna

3 ayn stepped into his father's house, pulling me with him as Arlo followed along behind us. One of Gennaro's bodyguards opened the door and had thrown me a rather disapproving look. No doubt this was only the first of many, given I hadn't exactly been invited to Zayn's family dinner. Gennaro wouldn't be happy with my presence at all. Not to mention what he was going to think about his son blatantly disregarding his order to stay away from me.

I was pretty sure my grip on Zayn's hand was hurting him, but he didn't say a word about it. He knew I was nervous about coming here tonight. I'd told him as much before we left the house. It was going to be a disaster in the making. Zayn kept telling me Gennaro wouldn't make a scene, but I wasn't so sure about that.

"Breathe, Tink," Zayn murmured as he let go of my hand and helped me out of my coat, handing it off to the bodyguard.

"I'm trying," I whispered back, taking a hold of his hand again. I needed him to ground me.

I might be strong and confident in myself, but I was out of my element here. I didn't know how my presence would be received by the rest of his family.

Zayn leant down and pressed his lips to my forehead as he led me into a room just off the hallway. It was his way of reassuring me, but it didn't do any good. I was still feeling like we were walking into the lion's den.

The moment we entered, the conversation drew to a dramatic halt. All eyes were on me and Zayn. It made my skin itch all over.

My gaze was drawn to Gennaro first, who was standing with a woman who looked to be in her late forties. She had pale skin, auburn hair and grey eyes. Sat on a sofa next to her were three women. The eldest had dark blonde hair, pale skin and brown eyes. Next to her was a woman with dark brown hair, tanned skin and brown eyes, like her sister. Last was a girl who looked to be not much older than me. She had tanned skin, dark brown hair, grey eyes behind her glasses and her nose buried in a book. She looked up, her eyes searching past me and Zayn to land on Arlo. Her cheeks went red almost immediately. I didn't have to question why that was as my eyes took in the other two occupants in the room who were standing near the bay windows, Zayn's brothers, Gil and Enzo. Clearly, she had a crush on Arlo. Why else would she be going red?

"Good evening, I hope you don't mind me bringing a guest, Father," Zayn said with no emotion in his voice.

The way Gennaro's eyes darkened at Zayn's words had me trembling. I shouldn't be afraid. I knew Zayn would protect me, but the fact he'd told me Gennaro wouldn't hesitate to have me killed if I got in the way weighed heavily on my mind.

"Not at all. What a pleasant surprise to see you again, Arianna," Gennaro replied, his voice laced with fake enthusiasm.

"Good evening, Mr Villetti," I said, unable to hide the way my voice shook on the words.

Zayn squeezed my hand. I stood a little taller, trying desperately to compose myself. I'd dealt with worse. Hell, I was the daughter of a gangster.

Get your shit together, Ari.

The auburn-haired woman came forward, her eyes on me even as she stood before Zayn.

"Martina," he said with a warm smile before they gave each other air kisses. "This is Arianna, my partner. Ari, this is my aunt."

"Your partner, you say?" Martina's eyebrow quirked up. "Well, aren't you beautiful?" She gave me a bright smile before enfolding me in her arms.

"Um, thank you," I said. "It's nice to meet you."

"Come, meet my daughters."

Martina released me and linked my arm with hers, forcing me away from Zayn. I looked back at him. He gave me a nod before he stepped over to his father with Arlo on his tail.

"These are my daughters, Verona, Sofia and Rina," Martina told me, indicating each of them when we reached the sofa containing the three women. "Say hello to Arianna, your cousin's girlfriend, girls."

Martina left me with them, moving away towards Zayn, Arlo and Gennaro. I didn't know what to make of her dumping me with her daughters.

Verona was the dark blonde girl who gave me the once over with an almost sneer on her face. Sofia jumped up immediately and shook my hand. Rina, on the other hand, was still blushing and barely put her book down to glance up at me.

"Zayn has a girlfriend, eh? Did hell freeze over when I wasn't paying attention?" Verona said with a smirk. "No offence, but you don't even look old enough to drink. I'm seriously questioning what our cousin thinks is age-appropriate."

I almost choked on my own breath, not expecting her to lay into me or Zayn straight away without warning.

What the fuck? Who does this woman think she is?

"Verona! Don't be so rude," Sofia said, giving her sister a withering stare before turning to me with an embarrassed smile. "Sorry about her, Arianna."

I plastered a smile on my face. I'd dealt with girls like Verona at school, and I wasn't going to take her shit.

"Oh well, thank you. Nice to know I'm retaining my youthful looks. No offence, but I can't quite say the same about you. What are you? Thirty?"

Verona's face coloured up. Sofia hid a smile behind her hand and Rina looked at me like I was crazy for giving it right back to her sister.

"Excuse me?" Verona spluttered.

"Oh… did you expect me to be nice after you all but accused your cousin of sleeping with a teenager? Not that it's any of your business, but I'm more than old enough to drink,

356

which makes me old enough to fuck whoever the hell I want. I suggest next time a member of your family brings their new partner around, you might want to try being a little more tactful. Maybe then they won't make false assumptions about you."

I didn't bother to look at her again as I turned on my heel and stalked away towards the window where Zayn's brothers were standing.

"I don't think I've ever seen Verona speechless before," Enzo said, looking at me with newfound respect. "Do you talk to Zayn like that?"

I crossed my arms over my chest and glared at him. He was partially responsible for this mess we were in with Gennaro, as was Gil. I might not have seen him before, but it was obvious he was Zayn's brother. They all looked so alike.

"Sometimes."

"I'm surprised he lets you."

I shrugged. He didn't exactly let me. I usually earned a punishment for using my smart mouth on him. And I couldn't say I didn't do it on purpose either. I wasn't about to divulge that information to his brothers.

For a long moment, the three of us were silent. Gil was scrutinising me with unnerving intensity. I didn't know what to say to him or if I should introduce myself. In all honesty, I wanted to go back to Zayn, but he was in deep conversation with his father and aunt. I didn't want to go near Gennaro if I could help it.

"Have you two met before?" Enzo asked as he looked between us.

I shook my head.

"I know who she is," Gil said, his voice rather soft and unassuming. I didn't know what I was expecting, but it wasn't for him to be so soft-spoken.

"Then you also know why your brother is less than pleased with the both of you," I replied, my tone clipped.

"Seriously? What the fuck is Zayn's problem this time? I swear I did everything he's asked of me," Enzo replied with a frown. "I'm so sick of him."

Before I could respond, a lady walked into the room to let us know dinner was ready to be served. I didn't realise Gennaro had staff, but it shouldn't really surprise me. Zayn immediately left his father's side and collected me, giving both of his brothers a death glare. He whisked me away into the dining room through the open double doors on the other side of the living room. Pulling out a chair, he made me sit down. He took his place next to me and slid his hand over my thigh. I'd opted for a demure navy dress this evening in an attempt to make a good impression on his family.

"Your cousin, Verona, is a bit of a bitch," I whispered to him.

His hand on my thigh tightened.

"What did she say?" he murmured back.

Everyone else was taking their places at the table.

"Made out like you were robbing the cradle, but don't worry, I put her in her place."

He lifted his other hand and stroked my cheek. I shivered under his touch. I'd never cared about our age difference. It was barely something I even considered when I found myself attracted to him. Needing him. Twelve years was nothing when you loved someone the way I loved Zayn Villetti. He was it for me.

"Good girl."

Knowing Zayn trusted me to handle the situation on my own made my heart swell. After I'd given him such a hard time over his decision not to let me in, he'd been more open and honest with his feelings. He showed me with his actions, he had faith in me. It meant the whole fucking world to me.

He dropped his hand from my face as Arlo took a seat next to him. Zayn told me Arlo was treated almost like family in his household. He didn't go many places without his right-hand man. Especially not right now when he'd been making waves in the criminal underworld. He hadn't told me how he'd gone about it, but I knew the past two weeks had been a busy time for him.

Dinner was livelier than I'd expected. Zayn's aunt was sitting on my other side and engaged me in conversation. Her husband, Gennaro's younger brother, Orsino, had died a year ago. She'd been left widowed with the three girls who were now twenty-eight, twenty-five and twenty-three. It didn't surprise me that Rina was around my age. She was sitting across from me but spoke to no one throughout the meal. In fact, she was too busy gazing at Arlo every so often. When Zayn nudged him and nodded at Rina halfway through dinner, Arlo scowled at him and I could have sworn the words "shut the fuck up" were uttered. I might have to ask Zayn what was going on between Arlo and Rina later because, clearly, something was up.

When dinner was over, the rest of the family retired back into the living room while the staff cleared the table. Zayn lingered at the table with me, seemingly lost in thought.

"You okay, daddy?" I whispered, leaning my head against his shoulder.

"Mmm."

"Did Gennaro say anything to you when you were talking to him?"

"About you? No. He probably would have if Martina wasn't here."

"Why? Because she's a woman and it's a man's business?"

"Yes."

I rolled my eyes and took his hand, linking our fingers together.

"Wow, so he's sexist as well as a bad father. What's next? You going to tell me he's a serial abuser?"

Zayn let out a sigh and rubbed his chin with his free hand.

"I would laugh if it wasn't so close to the truth," he muttered.

My heart sank at his words.

"What do you mean?"

He looked over at the other room where everyone else, including Arlo, seemed to be in deep conversation.

"It's better if I show you."

He got up, pulling me with him. I let Zayn lead me out of the dining room into the hallway and towards the stairs. He seemed to deflate with each step he took up the stairs. It made my skin prickle with nerves and I couldn't find my voice to ask him where we were going.

Right at the back of the house, Zayn opened a door and walked inside, pulling me along behind him. It took me a moment to register what I was seeing when we came to a standstill by what looked like a hospital bed. There was a woman with dark hair lying in it, hooked up to various machines. The whooshing noise coming from one of them had my eyes darting to the tube attached to her throat. She was on a ventilator. There were other tubes attached to her body, presumably for feeding and draining fluid. I had never seen anyone on life support before. It was unnerving, especially considering Zayn's words before we came upstairs. It left me with the distinct impression Gennaro was responsible for whatever had befallen her.

"Zayn," I whispered, my hand trembling in his. "Is that who I think it is?"

THIRTY NINE

Zayn

It hadn't been my intention to bring Ari upstairs to see my mother this evening, but what she'd said about my father had hit a nerve. She didn't know the true extent of my father's cruelty. The man behind the mask. My mother's current vegetative state was a literal representation of how far he would go to punish someone for their crimes against him. Not that I thought the so-called crime fit the punishment, but it was neither here nor there.

"*Mamá, questo è il mio amore*, Arianna."

Ari let out a little noise of distress. She might not know I'd just introduced her to my mother as my love, but she knew what *mamá* meant.

"Did he do this to her?"

I couldn't look at Ari. Her words cracked open the harsh wounds inflicted on me by my father when he told me what he'd done to my mother. What disobeying his orders would be met with if I ever tried to seriously go against him.

Noemi Villetti had once been full of life, laughter, and love. Now she was a shell, barely alive, and I hated him for leaving her like this.

With my free hand, I reached out and stroked my mother's hand, feeling desolate. I didn't come up here often. It broke my soul to see her like this. I brought Ari here because I wanted my mother to know I had found happiness with a girl I shouldn't have ever wanted but somehow ended up needing.

"Yes."

Ari let go of my hand and curled herself into my side, wrapping both arms around me. The fact she was comforting me had me swallowing hard. I was the one who took care of her. It being the other way around was foreign to me, but I'd noticed her checking in with me more and more often to make sure I was okay. Maybe it should go both ways. I could let Ari take care of me in her own way. It wouldn't be a bad thing to allow myself to lean on her. She was my partner. That was how it should be. Partners supported each other.

Curling my arm around her, I pressed my lips to the braids on top of her head and breathed her in. She smelt like home and it helped keep my sadness at bay.

"You have to promise me something, Tink."

"What is it?"

"If I tell you the truth about what happened to her, you cannot tell another soul. Enzo and Gil don't know everything and right now, it has to stay that way."

Ari trembled, her hold around me tightening.

"I promise."

Perhaps it would be cathartic to tell someone else what happened. Arlo knew, but it wasn't the same. He'd been there with me when my father explained what he'd done. He vowed to remain by my side when I'd broken away from the family over it. Arlo was the only person in my life who had never betrayed me... until Arianna. She had my trust.

"She left him because he has always been incapable of remaining faithful and the emotional abuse got too much for her. She endured it for me and my brothers, but there comes a time when everyone breaks. She couldn't take it any longer." I sucked in a breath. "When he tracked her down, he beat her to within an inch of her life and then he paid off his doctors to keep her alive. She's been this way ever since."

"When was this?"

No one spoke about my mother. Most people had no idea she remained under my father's roof, trapped in purgatory. They assumed she disappeared and none of us had disputed the assumption.

"Almost ten years ago."

Ari stiffened.

"T-t-ten years?"

I nodded. I'd just turned twenty-five. It was a day I could never forget. Seeing her battered and bruised body in a hospital bed with tubes coming out of her, keeping her alive. It destroyed my faith in my father. It was why I did everything in my power to help those who had been dealt a similar hand by the world. Why most of the women who worked at Desecration were survivors who I'd given choice back to. My mother had no choice, but they had one now.

I'd allowed Ari a choice when she came to me. Be mine or walk out the door. She kept choosing to stay even when everything got tough. Even when I pushed her away. She never gave up on me. On us when there wasn't an us to speak of. I didn't want to coerce her into a relationship with me. It wasn't the type of man I was.

"Yes."

"She's not coming back, is she?"

"No."

The next thing I knew, Ari ripped herself away from me. I turned my head to find her staring at me with disbelief. She shook her head. Horror flitted across her features.

"This... this is barbaric, Zayn." She waved at my mother. "How can he keep her this way? It isn't a life. It's cruel!"

For a long time, I'd been filled with rage over the situation. It had eventually given way to apathy and resignation when I realised my father would never let her go.

"He's punishing her for leaving him. No one leaves Gennaro Villetti without consequences."

"That makes it so much worse." Her eyes turned sad. "Can't you do something about it? It's not fair. How is this fair?"

I stepped towards her.

"It's not. Nothing about this family is fair. I've wanted to unplug this shit from her body a thousand times over, but you know what he'll do to me if I disobey him. The same thing he'll do to you for getting in the way." I pointed at my mother's bed. "This is who Gennaro Villetti really is. A monster. He rules with an iron fucking fist with no one standing in his way. Fuck, Ari, he has the police commissioner under his thumb. He's dangerous. Make no mistake, he will end us both if I don't play this right. If I don't have enough power behind me to make him back down. I'm doing that for you. So I can have you. So you can be safe with me."

Tears welled in her eyes. This wasn't me trying to scare her. She needed to understand how precarious our position really was. How much of a risk I was taking, all because I wanted her.

I'll burn it all for you, Tinkerbell, that's what I've been trying to tell you. I'll do anything to keep you.

"I can't save my mother, Ari. Not while he still lives."

She was quiet for a minute, contemplating what I'd said. Then she stepped into me, reaching up to place a hand on my cheek.

"I'm sorry."

"What do you have to apologise for?"

"I'm sorry I can't take your pain away."

I sighed, pressing my face into her hand. Allowing her warmth to consume me. Having Ari here made this bearable. Gave me something to hold on to. My life had been dark and unforgiving for so long. She was the life force I needed to breathe again.

"I don't need you to do that, Tink. All you have to do is be here with me. That's what I need. I need you just the way you are."

She stared up at me for a long moment before her hand slid from my face. I watched her lower herself to her knees in front of me. She bent over and pressed her lips against the soft leather of my shoe. Then she leant her cheek against it, wrapping her hand around my other foot.

"I'm not going anywhere, sir. I'm yours. I'll walk through fire for you. I'll burn if it means we're together. I'll do it because I love you."

I didn't stop her from staying there for as long as she needed. It reassured me she'd be with me no matter the risks. She understood why I couldn't do anything about my mother at this moment in time. One day, I'd be able to let my mother go peacefully. Ari would be there with me to help me say goodbye.

"Tinkerbell."

She didn't raise her head.

"Yes, daddy?"

"If my *mamá* wasn't in this state, she could see how happy you make me. I hate that she'll never know you."

She let go of me, raising up back to her knees. Ari's eyes were full of understanding.

"I might not have a mother to introduce you to, but I hate that too."

I put my hand out to her. She took it, allowing me to pull her to her feet and wrap my arms around her.

"What matters most is we have each other. You and me against the world."

She nodded. Even if everything fell apart after tonight because I'd outwardly defied my father, I'd still have her. I hung onto that fact as I pulled away and stroked her face with my thumb.

"We should get back downstairs."

I moved back towards my mother and leant down, pressing a kiss to her forehead.

"Ti voglio bene, Mamá."

She might not be able to hear me, but I needed her to know I would always care for her. That none of this was her fault. If only my father hadn't found her when she'd left him. If only

I'd known what he'd do. Wishful thinking on my part, really. Life had dealt us with a shitty hand. One day, I'd find a way to set her free from my father.

Ari took my hand, and we walked back out into the hallway together. When we reached the bottom of the stairs, Enzo was standing in the lobby watching us.

"Can I do something for you?"

Enzo squared his shoulders.

"Yeah, you can tell me why the fuck you're pissed off at me this time."

I frowned.

"Where did you get that idea from?"

"She said you weren't happy with me."

I looked down at Ari. She gave me a sheepish smile. My eyes went back to my brother, who gave me a dirty look. I didn't need his shit right now, but apparently, I wasn't going to get away without a confrontation with him tonight.

"I see." I let go of Ari's hand and took a step towards him. "You promised me you wouldn't say a word about her to our father."

"And I didn't!"

"No, but you told Gil."

Enzo's face paled slightly, but he kept glaring as he shoved his hands in his pockets.

"Gil isn't *Papá*. And so what? I couldn't talk to you about this shit you've got yourself into without you biting my head off again. I kept it in the family, didn't I?"

"Keeping it in the family, huh? Some fucking family we have. You can imagine my surprise when I discovered Gil told the one person I didn't need interfering in my life about

Arianna. This is what I mean about actions having consequences, Enzo, something you still fail to comprehend. You should have kept your mouth shut."

His face fell slightly.

"Gil told him?" He shook his head. "I can't believe that. He would never. I trust him. He promised."

Something about Enzo's tone made me pause. Gil didn't break his promises when he made them. We'd grown up in a family where your word was law. If you made a promise, you stuck to it under the pain of death.

Before I had a chance to follow that train of thought, my father came out into the hallway and looked at the three of us with disdain written all over his features. He closed the door to the living room, shutting out the noise coming from there.

"Well, if it isn't both of my wayward sons." His eyes went to Ari before he waved at me. "And this one's whore."

I flinched and clenched my fists. Arianna was not a whore. She was a fucking queen. The fact he called her that made my blood boil.

"What did you just say?"

Gennaro gave me an evil smile.

"What else would she be, Zayn? Not like you would ever make her your wife. You think I don't know that you were choosing to placate me by insisting you would find your own woman? I'm not a fool. You have no intention of getting married. You never have."

He stepped closer.

"Whatever it is you're planning, you should know I won't standby idly and let you bring this whore into our family. She will never be a Villetti. She will never be *famiglia*."

FORTY

Zayn

I wasn't planning on having it out with my father this evening, but apparently, he had other ideas. No part of me cared that we had an audience. It was high fucking time he learnt I wasn't going to bow down to him any longer.

It was time he bowed to me.

"Is that the best you can do? Tell me she's a whore and she'll never be family?" I scoffed. "I thought petty insults were below you, but apparently, I was mistaken. It's a shame you can't see past your own bullshit because if you did, you'd know why I've chosen her. I don't need her to be *famiglia*. Who the fuck wants to be a part of this family, anyway? I certainly don't after the shit you've put me through, after the shit you've put my brothers through, and let's not mention what you did to our mother."

Gennaro's expression turned dark at my words. I no longer cared if Enzo found out the real reason our mother was in a vegetative state. I didn't care about anything other than sticking it to my father.

"Watch your mouth."

"You don't get to tell me what to do any longer. If anything, you should be taking orders from me. After all, I'm the fucking king of this city."

My father took another step towards me, his face going an ugly shade of puce.

"What did you just say?"

"Oh, hadn't you heard? All those petty criminals you didn't have any time for, the ones who were below you? They belong to me now. All of them do. And your little drug trade? Well, it's mine too. Bennett didn't want to anger the man who will take care of his daughter for the rest of her life. Nor did he want to be turfed off the land he uses. I'd introduce myself as the new king of the underworld if I thought you'd recognise it."

I spread my hands.

"It's about time someone took away your toys, Father. I just didn't think it would be me who rose above the great Gennaro fucking Villetti to take the crown."

I swear I'd never seen my father look so angry in his entire life. While I knew he was still a formidable threat to me and Ari, it felt fucking good to put him in his place.

"You think this changes anything?" he spat.

"Oh, don't worry, I'm not an idiot. I know it'll take some getting used to… knowing your son bested you. I don't expect you to bow to me or anything, just accept what I've been trying to make clear to you for years."

He gritted his teeth.

"And what's that?"

"You have more than enough loyal servants willing to take over from you. I'm not your fucking heir. I'm not going to get married to some mafia princess you deem worthy of me. I don't answer to you."

I watched his hands curl into fists at his sides and smiled at him.

"And you were right earlier. I have no intention of getting married to Arianna or anyone else. The idea of marriage makes me sick. And the person I have to blame for that? Well, it's you. Seeing the way you treated *Mamá* like she was less than fucking human cemented my thoughts on the matter. I have no interest in an institution that has a history of forcing ownership of women by men. People like you perpetuate that fucking misery. And before you ask, yes, Arianna is perfectly aware of my feelings on the matter and, unlike you, doesn't seek to force me into a life I don't want to lead. That's what a partnership is, Father. Something you clearly don't understand."

Gennaro didn't immediately respond, clearly weighing what I'd said in his mind. I didn't care what he thought nor what he said. If it burned my bridges with my family, so fucking be it. I didn't want to be a part of it if he was going to remain in charge. I had Arianna. She was enough for me. We were enough for each other.

"You think by bringing all of that scum under your thumb you were going to force me into letting you go?" He laughed, the sound ugly and demeaning. "Such a foolish, foolish boy." He glared at me. "It doesn't matter if you insist on shacking up with that girl. You'll get bored soon enough. You always do."

He rubbed a hand over his mouth.

"The thing you fail to understand, Zayn, is you're always going to belong to me. You, Gilberto and Enzo, you're all mine. And you will fall in line once you've worn yourself out with these little games you love to play."

I wanted to laugh in his fucking face. Instead, I shook my head. This time was different. This time I had a reason to spit at his feet and tell him to go to hell.

"Your arrogance will be your downfall, Father."

Turning on my heel, I took hold of Arianna's hand and tugged her towards the front door. I didn't want to hear another word out of his fucking mouth. It would only be poison. It's all he did. Spread toxicity.

I stopped by Enzo, who was staring at my father like he was seeing an entirely new person.

"If you knew what was good for you, you'd move out of this place and away from him," I told him, looking back at our father with disgust. "He's only going to continue to make your life hell, just like he's always done to me."

Enzo turned to me, his eyes widening.

"I'll help you, Enzo. All you have to do is ask."

I didn't wait to hear a response from him, striding to the front door and pulling it wide open.

"That's it, run away, boy. You'll be back soon enough," came my father's voice.

Not bothering to look at him again, I pulled Arianna out into the cool night air and slammed the door shut behind me. I tugged my phone out of my pocket and fired off a quick text to Arlo. Ari didn't speak as I led her over to the car. I was absolutely fucking fuming over Gennaro. He had far too much audacity.

I let go of her hand and paced the pavement by the car.

"Fuck!"

It didn't take long for Arlo to emerge from my father's house and make his way over to us. Ari stood silently, watching me with a worried expression on her face.

"Let's get you home, boss," Arlo said as he unlocked the car and opened the back door for me.

"Get in," I almost barked at Ari, who didn't hesitate to move. She knew I wasn't angry at her.

I slid in beside her. Arlo handed me Ari's coat before he shut the door. I set it down in the middle and reached over Ari, tugging her seatbelt across her chest to strap her in before I sat back and did my own. Arlo got in the front and set off a minute later.

Ari reached out and took my hand. She pulled it to her lips and pressed a kiss on the back of it. I wanted to tell her it would be okay, but I knew it wouldn't. Gennaro would never accept her. He'd never accept I wanted to be my own man. He would always be a thorn in our sides, no matter what I did. The futility of it all slammed into my chest, making me want to throw shit.

"Daddy," came her soft voice.

I looked over at Ari. The expression of understanding she wore almost cleaved me in two.

"He's never going to stop, is he?"

I shook my head, not trusting my voice. She squeezed my hand tighter in hers.

Normally, I wouldn't have such a difficult time controlling my emotions, but right now, I felt untethered. I couldn't keep it locked inside. It wasn't like me. I didn't lose my temper, nor did I let my father rattle me, but he had. Was it my fault for underestimating him? I didn't expect him to be happy about current developments, but did he have to make me feel so fucking small? I think that was what bothered me the most. Even after all these years, he still had the ability to affect me.

It didn't help that I was already feeling raw from telling Ari the truth about my mother and her reaction to what my father had done. She was right. It was barbaric. Keeping someone alive who wasn't ever going to wake up. I'd resigned myself to her fate for far too long. It couldn't go on like this. She deserved to be at peace.

The journey home was silent. Tomorrow I could work out what the fuck to do next. When I wasn't feeling worn down. When everything didn't seem so fucking bleak.

Arlo dropped us off, telling me he'd be back in the morning. I took Ari inside, hanging up her coat before I walked upstairs to our bedroom. Undoing the buttons on my suit jacket, I tugged it off and hung it up before undoing my cufflinks and setting them down on the chest of drawers near the window. I could feel Ari watching me from the doorway, but I didn't look at her as I toed off my shoes.

Walking over to the bed, I sat down on the end of it and buried my face in my hands. It was all I could do to not want to tear the room apart. Ari moved about the bedroom, but I didn't look up. I stayed where I was, trying to focus on my breathing. Trying to calm the war waging inside me.

The bed dipped behind me. Ari curled herself around my back, wrapping her arms around my front as she sat behind me.

"It's okay, daddy, you can let it out," she whispered as she rested her cheek between my shoulder blades. "I'm right here. I'll keep you together."

My tense shoulders drooped at her words. I let out a shaky breath, dropping my hands from my face as I leant my elbows on my thighs. I stared across at the bedroom wall and wondered when the last time I allowed myself to feel the anger and resentment I had towards my father was. Being calm and collected was just who I was. I'd always kept a level head in difficult situations. And yet right now, I wasn't that man. I was twenty-five again and hating my father for stealing my mother from me. I didn't have anyone to help me deal with my feelings back then. Now I had someone special who would hold me when the darkness sunk into my bones. She would keep it at bay.

"I hate him," I gritted out, "I fucking hate him."

My hands curled into fists.

"I've imagined killing him so many times. Wringing his fucking neck and burying him in an unmarked grave. He doesn't deserve to be mourned over or immortalised. He deserves to fade into fucking obscurity."

I wanted him to die so fucking badly, it burnt in my veins. He would never stop haunting me unless he was dead.

"But I can't do it."

There was the fucking kicker. I could kill without feeling a single goddamn thing. I didn't kill in anger. I did it out of necessity. When it came to my own father, I wasn't calm about it. I was fucking raging.

"I don't kill in anger, Ari. It's not who I am."

We both knew what would have to happen next. It would never be safe for the two of us if he was still alive, but I couldn't bring myself to say it. To admit out loud, my own father had to die so I could be free. So I could have Ari by my side without fearing for her life.

"We'll always have to live in fear if I don't do it… and I can't deal with that right now. It's too much. I'm too angry with him. Too filled with rage and I can't do it."

She tightened her hold on me. I needed it. I was breaking apart and the only thing holding me together was her.

"You shouldn't have to carry that burden," she murmured against my back. "You should never have to make that choice, Zayn."

"We both know there is no other choice I can make."

"I hate it."

I bowed my head.

"I do too."

For a long while, we sat in silence. Her embrace kept me afloat as my anger and frustration bled out of me. She only let go when I let out a sigh. Climbing off the bed, Ari came to stand in front of me. She'd changed for bed and was only wearing one of my t-shirts. Her braids were loose around her shoulders. There was no doubt my Tinkerbell was a stunning woman.

"Will you let me undress you?"

I nodded and sat up straighter. Ari was gentle as she undid the buttons of my shirt and slid it off my shoulders. She encouraged me to stand as she continued to undress me until I was just in boxers. My sweet little fairy led me into the bathroom, readying my toothbrush and her own. We stood by the sink, finishing our nightly routine together. Something about the simplicity of it helped me stay sane.

Ari pulled back the covers when we moved back into the bedroom and made me get in. Then she left to make sure the house was locked up. When she returned, she turned out the lights and got in bed with me, wrapping herself around my body as I pulled the covers over the two of us.

"It'll be okay, daddy," she whispered as I closed my eyes. "I know it doesn't feel like that right now, but it's like you said... all that matters is we have each other."

Those words helped me fall asleep with my girl holding me close. If I had her, I could do anything... I hoped.

FORTY ONE

Arianna

3ayn had been subdued for the past week after the disaster that was his family dinner at Gennaro's house. He didn't let me go anywhere without him or Arlo. I wasn't expecting anything else when the threat of his father was very real. It was us or him at this point. It made me sick knowing Zayn carried so many burdens on his shoulders. He had to make the worst sort of choice and execute his own father. I understood why he felt like he couldn't. Killing his father in anger would go against his principles. I didn't want Zayn to suffer with that decision.

Zayn helped me out of the car, his hand tightly clasped around mine. It was the first time we'd been anywhere other than Desecration since the dinner. He hadn't told me where we were going nor why, but he seemed less troubled today. Something I could only be glad of. I worried about him and his state of mind. He might be more open with me now, but it didn't mean Zayn had changed completely. He was still the calm, collected mafia prince I'd always known him to be. Gennaro may have rattled him, but Zayn wasn't the type of man to let anyone keep him down for long.

He led me into a building that had huge windows. In the lobby, a man was waiting with a bright smile on his face. He came forward and shook Zayn's hand.

"Mr Villetti, it's nice to see you again. Shall we?"

Zayn didn't introduce the man to me, merely gave him a nod. The man took us over to the two lifts at the other end and we walked into the open one. He pressed the button for the second floor. I tried to keep my mouth shut and not ask questions despite my curiosity.

We stepped out into a huge open-plan space with exposed brick walls on either end. The bank of windows let a ton of natural light in. My head swivelled around, taking it all in as the man waved at us to look around. It would make a great location for photos. A place you could change the space to suit your needs depending on the project.

I let go of Zayn's hand to wander over to the windows. Staring out at the street below, I felt more than a little confused about what this place was and why we were here. I turned back, finding Zayn watching me with an expectant look in his eyes.

"What is this for?" I asked, stepping closer to him.

He cocked his head to the side.

"Do you like it?"

I frowned.

"Why?"

"Answer the question, Ari."

I knew better than to push him.

"It's a great space… a blank canvas. You could do a lot with it, but I guess it depends on what you have planned."

A slow smile spread across his face. I don't know why it made me nervous. He dug his hands into his pockets and stepped towards me.

"I'm glad you like it."

My fingers tugged at the hem of my jumper. It was nice out so I hadn't worn a coat today.

"Why does it matter if I like it?"

"Well, you'll have to sign some paperwork, but once we've closed on it, the building will be yours."

I stood there for a long moment, trying to comprehend what he'd just said to me. My eyes darted around the room again, the realisation dawning on me. Zayn was buying me a building. A fucking building.

"Hold on a sec… did you just say you're buying this building for me?"

"Yes."

"Why the hell would you do that? You've done a lot of things for me, but this is…"

Zayn's smile remained as he closed the distance between us and placed both his hands on my shoulders.

"This is your photography studio, Ari, or, at least, it will be."

I tilted my head back to meet his eyes. Zayn kept telling me he wanted to take care of me and I allowed him to do so. However, I don't think I realised just how far the care he so desperately wanted to bestow on me went until now.

"You're buying me a studio."

"Yes."

"You're crazy."

He leant down until our faces were inches from each other.

"I hope by that you mean crazy for you."

"You can't buy me a building. It's too much."

He lifted his hand from my shoulder to cup my cheek and run his thumb over my bottom lip. I trembled under his touch. Why did this man have to be so fucking perfect? He was everything I never knew I wanted in a partner.

"I'm not allowed to provide you with a future in the career that makes you happy?"

"Buying me a camera and laptop to edit photos with is not the same as buying me a studio space! I dread to think how much this place costs. You can't spend that much money on me."

The amusement in his dark eyes made me scowl.

"If you think me buying you a building in Central London is beyond my means, then you're seriously underestimating the extent of my wealth, Arianna." He brushed his thumb over my mouth again. "I planned to buy you a studio, no matter what happened between us. Let me give you the means to carve out the career you've always wanted. Let me make your future bright… please."

How on earth could I say no to that? Besides, I'm not sure he would listen if I told him I didn't want it. He'd know I was lying. My brain was already in overdrive thinking of all the things I could do to this place.

"You have all the office space you could need on the other floors, but if you don't like it, I'll find you somewhere else."

I shook my head.

"It's perfect. You know it is or you wouldn't have brought me here."

He pulled back slightly.

"Then you'll let me get it for you?"

I bit my lip, reaching out to stroke a hand down his chest.

"Yeah, daddy, I will," I whispered, conscious of the fact we weren't alone.

He pressed a kiss to my mouth, stealing my words away. At this point, I didn't think there was anything this man wouldn't do for me.

Zayn pulled away and tucked an arm around me, encouraging me to walk the room with him.

"This will be your business, Ari. You'll make all the decisions. I'll just be here to support you."

"So you're not going to tell me how to run it?"

"No."

"And how to decorate it?"

"No."

"What if I want to hire an assistant?"

"A decision I would highly encourage you to make."

He was so calm about the whole thing, like him giving me the space to do my own thing was no big deal. It only made me want to push his buttons.

"Look at you, giving up control for once. I never thought I'd see the day."

He gave me a look that spoke volumes. He wasn't amused by my joke at all.

"You and I both know who's in charge," he murmured, tugging me back towards the lifts. "But perhaps you need reminding."

I noticed the man who I now realised was the agent didn't follow us. Zayn pushed me into the lift. As the doors closed after he hit the button for the first floor, he pressed me against the back wall, pinning my hands on the metal.

"I see how it is. Daddy tells you he's going to buy you an expensive gift and you get mouthy. That's no way to say thank you, little fairy."

I let out a harsh breath, knowing I was about to be punished.

"Got nothing to say now? Mmm, seems you do know how to keep quiet when it suits you. I'll just have to give you something to scream about."

My heart rate accelerated with his threat. Knowing he had a lot on his plate, I'd behaved all week, but perhaps Zayn needed this outlet as much as I did.

The moment the lift arrived on the first floor and the doors opened, he dragged me out of it. I was hustled through an office space into a kitchen area. Zayn's hand was around the back of my neck, forcing me to bend over the counter as he pressed my cheek to the granite top.

"Hands by your face," he told me, his voice low and stern.

I placed them on the countertop. My skin prickled with excitement and nerves. It felt rather illicit to be punished in a building he didn't even own yet. Zayn didn't play by anyone else's rules but his own. I'd learnt that lesson many times over.

"Stay right there."

I didn't move as he removed his hand. The sound of his retreating footsteps had me wondering where on earth he was going and what he was planning to do. I wasn't sure how much time had passed, but when he came back, I heard the door close behind him.

"If you think your obedience now will make me go easy on you, allow me to dissuade you of that notion."

I couldn't help the tremors running through my body as he stepped up behind me and placed something down on the counter in my eyeline.

"I was going to give you this after we left, but now I'm going to use this little gift to make you wish you'd behaved."

I raised my face from the counter to better see him unwrapping the box. He drew out a sex toy. My eyes went wide at the level of detail the fake cock had. The memory of what he told me he wanted to do with one of those made me shift on my feet.

"You remember our little conversation about this, don't you?"

"Yes, daddy."

"I thought about getting you one off the shelf, but the idea of you enjoying a replica of another man's dick only pissed me off. I'm the only one who takes care of you and gives you pleasure, Tink. That means the only cock you get to fuck is mine."

I swear I didn't know what to think of his statement until I realised the implication of it.

"Are you saying that's a replica of yours?"

He brought it closer to my face.

"Mmm, don't you recognise it?"

I swallowed. He wasn't kidding. His dick had been up in my face enough times now for me to have memorised every inch. And this was almost like looking at the real thing.

Well… fuck.

The lengths this man had to have gone to get it made for me didn't bear thinking about. I didn't even know what to say. What could anyone say? He'd taken a cast of his own dick to make a sex toy for me. It was the only way he could have possibly gone about it.

Who the fuck does that? I can't even with him over it.

"I can see you do." He set it on the counter and placed a tube of lube next to it. "I'm sure you have some idea of what I'm going to do to you now."

I nodded, biting down on the inside of my cheek. He moved behind me, his hands going to my jeans. He unbuttoned them, tugging them down my legs along with my underwear until they were around my ankles. I shivered when he ran his hands over my behind, spreading me slightly for his view. A gasp erupted from my mouth when he ran his thumb through my folds.

"Mmm, wet at the thought of it, aren't you, my dirty little fairy? Such a bad girl."

Letting go of me, he picked up the dildo and coated it in lube. I'd had his cock and his fingers inside me, but this was something else. The stretch would be intense. Could I even take it? He wouldn't try unless he thought I could.

"Daddy," I whispered, my voice trembling on the word.

"Yes, Tink?"

"I'm nervous."

He shifted on his feet behind me before stroking my back with his free hand.

"We'll stop if it's too much, okay? I promise."

With that statement, he pressed the dildo inside me, making me let out a breath. There was no going back now. Zayn would make me take everything he had to give me unless I'd told him to stop. Every part of me wanted to be a good girl who did exactly as her daddy told her because he would reward me for it. And Zayn's rewards? Well, they were the best part of my day.

FORTY TWO

Arianna

The sex toy filled me the same way Zayn did, but it wasn't warm like real flesh. He thrust it in and out of me a few times before he pressed a finger in beside it. My hands curled into fists next to my face. It wasn't as difficult as last time when he inserted a second one after letting me get used to it. This time I was prepared for the way it would feel, how it would affect my body, the intense pressure and pinch of pain as I adjusted to the stretch.

"Touch your clit, Tink. I want you to ease into it," he murmured.

I immediately obeyed him, sliding one hand underneath me to rub myself. A little moan erupted from my lips as he inserted a third. He kept fucking me with the dildo, making me squirm under the onslaught of pleasure and slight pain from the stretch.

"That's it. Look at you getting ready to take both. Mmm, you're going to look so good all stretched out for me."

His words were making me more eager to give in. To allow myself to relax into accepting everything he had to give me.

"More, daddy, please," I whimpered, pressing back against him.

"Beg all you want, dirty little fairy, we're going at my pace, not yours. Remember why you're bent over this fucking counter, hmm?"

I nodded, my body shaking with need. I hadn't forgotten I was in this position because I'd pushed his buttons. He was in control of this, telling me what to do and when. Giving me what he thought I could take. Zayn knew my body like the back of his hand. He'd explored every inch. Watched every reaction I made. Documented it all so he could give me exactly what I needed. It all spoke of his desire to take care of me in every way he possibly could.

When he slipped a fourth finger inside me alongside the dildo, I cried out from the intensity. The low rumble of approval from his chest let me know I was being good for him. He'd told me he wanted to give me something to scream about.

Zayn let me adjust to the stretch before he moved his fingers. My breathing became erratic with each thrust, my body vibrating with the pleasurable pain. Not all pain was made equal or bad. I'd come to discover I craved the kind Zayn gave me. It made me feel good.

"Do you want me to fuck you? Do you want daddy's cock?" he almost growled from behind me.

"Please."

He pulled everything from me, leaving my pussy empty and clenching around nothing. He set the dildo on the counter. I heard the distinct sound of his zip being undone. It only made me tremble in anticipation. He gripped my hip and pressed inside me a minute later. I let out a sigh. There was nothing better than this, than his body inside mine. Nothing could ever replace this man for me, nor the intimacy we shared between us.

"Your eager little pussy knows who she belongs to. Me. I own you."

I bit my lip. No one else could get away with saying those things to me. I wanted to be owned by Zayn. To be his little pet. His partner. I owned him right back. He was mine too.

He fucked me with deep, long strokes for a few minutes, letting me feel every inch of him. Then he picked up the dildo and pressed it to my entrance next to his cock. I didn't tense, knowing staying relaxed was key. My fingers were still working on my clit to help me take it.

"Ready?"

"Yes, daddy."

I didn't know if I was, but there was nothing more I could do to prepare myself. The moment he pressed the dildo into me, forcing it inside my pussy alongside his dick, I let out a pained moan. It was so fucking intense. The pressure. The stretch. Everything. It took me a few seconds to catch my breath. He held himself and the dildo still, allowing me time to tell him to stop.

"Tink, you need to tell me if you're okay," he said after a moment, his voice coming out all gruff like this was also making him as crazy as me. "I need to know you're good."

I let out a long breath. It wasn't half as bad as I thought it was going to be. His careful preparation made it easier.

"I'm okay. It's not too much. I can take it."

He exhaled deeply. Then he pressed the dildo deeper. I shifted with the sensation, but it didn't make me tell him I'd had enough. With him, I wasn't sure it would ever be enough. I wanted all of him and more.

"Fuck," he ground out through his teeth, moving inside me again.

I whimpered as he fucked me. The intensity morphed into something else after a few minutes. I hadn't fought against it, so my mind and body were at one with each other, melting into a painful sort of euphoria. It was everything and nothing like I anticipated. And I loved every second of it.

"Daddy, fuck… fuck me," I cried out, my nails of my free hand digging into my palm. "Fuck me harder."

It built deep inside me, the need for a release, to come apart under his brutal pounding. He wasn't being gentle any longer. He held the dildo inside me while he fucked me without restraint. I was so blissed out, I didn't care. I wanted him to use me for his pleasure. It only fed mine.

My fingers worked faster on my clit. I was so close. The edge of the cliff approached, and I was ready to dive off.

"Can I come, daddy… please?"

My voice was high-pitched and needy, so wanton. I'd never asked for permission before today. I needed it because I'd been a bad girl.

"Do it, come on daddy's cock."

The freefall into oblivion was all-encompassing. It was a sense of freedom I'd never experienced before. Of giving into something I didn't know I needed until now. I climaxed so hard, I nearly lost consciousness. The physical exertion was almost too much. I had to grip the counter with both hands to keep upright, my legs threatening to turn into jelly when I came down.

Zayn ripped the dildo from my body, chucking it on the counter. Then he fucked me like a man possessed, his fingers digging into my hips with an almost vicious grip. The low rumble of pleasure erupting from his mouth with his own climax had me melting on the counter, utterly helpless against him. He fell forward, planting both hands on the counter as his front pressed against my back. I could feel his laboured breathing with each breath I took. We were both completely undone.

It was a long while before either of us regained our equilibrium. Zayn stroked my fingers with his own, soothing my ravaged body.

"My good girl, you took it so well," he murmured in my ear before pressing a kiss to my cheek. "Such a good little fairy. My queen."

I preened under his praise. It was my reward for doing everything he asked of me.

When our breathing evened out, he pulled out of me. We spent the next few minutes cleaning up and setting ourselves back to rights. He tucked a hand around my neck and pressed my face to his chest as he wrapped his other arm around me. Zayn kissed the top of my head, giving me the affection I needed.

"Daddy."

"Mmm?"

"Can I explore the building now? I want to see everything."

He chuckled, his hold on me tightening.

"Of course. I need to talk to Willis about the next steps, anyway."

I assumed Willis was the agent. Pulling back, I smiled up at the man who had my whole being in the palm of his hand.

"Thank you."

He let me go, but not before stroking my cheek and smiling back at me. Taking my hand, he gathered up the bag he'd stuffed the dildo and lube into and we left the kitchen together. Zayn found Willis waiting for us in the lift lobby. He pressed a kiss to my mouth and released me.

"Go, explore. You can tell me all of your plans for the place on the way home."

I grinned before skipping away to go look at the rooms I hadn't seen on the first floor. There was plenty of office space, more than I needed, but that was okay. I could start small and grow into the building rather than having to find something new if things went well. It excited me, the prospect of having my own photography business. All I'd ever wanted was to take pictures for a living. To capture special moments in time. It reminded me I needed to get the photos I'd edited of Zayn made into prints for the house. I could talk to him about it on our way home.

Zayn was still in the lobby with Willis when I finished with the first floor. I let him know I was going down to the ground floor. He gave me a nod but was fully immersed in his conversation with the agent, so I didn't want to disturb him further. I took the lift downstairs and walked out into the main lobby area. I could have a reception here. The rooms off the lobby would be perfect for client meeting rooms and other such things. I wandered through them, my mind a riot of plans and ideas.

I was so engrossed in looking around, I didn't hear someone behind me until it was far too late. A hand landed on my mouth as a solid body gripped me in its embrace. It immediately felt wrong. This wasn't Zayn. I knew exactly how his body moulded to mine. I struggled as I tried to turn and look at them, letting out a scream. It was muffled by the hand on my mouth.

"Quiet, girl," came a gruff voice.

I didn't do as he'd said, continuing to struggle and scream, trying to fight him off.

"Tut, tut, such a wild thing. I'm going to make you pay for hitting me."

His words confused me as he dragged me backwards through the building. I hadn't hit him, so what the fuck was he talking about? I kicked and struggled, but he picked me up off the floor with one arm pressed around my middle. The man carried me out into the lobby and towards the stairwell. He shoved the door open with his foot. In the stairwell, there was an emergency exit. The door had been propped open.

I kicked out harder, my hands clawing at his hold as I tried to scream again. He didn't budge as he took me out of the building into the alley. He walked me to a side street where a limo was idling on the curb with the back door open. The man shoved me up against the window before pulling my hands behind my back and cuffing them. I was then thrown into the limo, my body sprawling across the backseat before the door slammed shut.

I lay there for a moment, almost unable to comprehend what had just happened. Someone had taken me. They'd fucking grabbed me and stuffed me into the back of a car.

What the fuck?

It wasn't the first time I'd been kidnapped, but that made it even worse. Who the hell had the audacity to take me from right under Zayn's nose? There was no way in hell he would have let me walk around the building unattended if he hadn't thought I was safe. He'd kept me safe under his watchful eye whenever we were out. This was wrong. All kinds of fucking wrong.

When the car moved off, I struggled to sit up, twisting around to right myself. My eyes darted around the limo as I sat up in the middle of the seat. The first thing they landed on was someone sitting directly opposite. I let out a choking sound when I realised who it was. All of my worst fears came true. My worst fucking nightmares. The same ones that plagued Zayn.

"Hello, Arianna," Gennaro Villetti said with a deadly smile on his face. "It's nice to see you again."

And I knew in that moment I was screwed. Completely and utterly screwed.

Fuck.

FORTY THREE

Zayn

When I looked down at my watch, I found I'd been talking to Willis for longer than I realised. There was a lot to think about when buying property. I needed to get in touch with my solicitor to get proceedings underway now Ari had told me she liked the place. I planned to make sure it was purchased in her name. If anything went wrong, she'd still have this place as her own. She wouldn't have to worry. That's all I wanted. To provide Arianna with a secure future regardless of what happened between us. I had no intentions of letting her go. As far as I was concerned, she was it for me.

I didn't believe in soulmates or having a love of your life, but there was no doubt in my mind I loved Arianna to the ends of the earth. I would follow her wherever she wanted to go. Provide her with everything she desired if she'd remain by my side. I needed her as much as she needed me. We were a partnership. We worked in our own way together. So I'd spend the rest of our lives making sure I gave her everything.

"We should find your partner if that's all you need for now," Willis said with a smile.

"Mmm, yes. She's probably still downstairs."

It did make me wonder where on earth Ari had got to. The place wasn't that big, but maybe she'd got lost in planning things.

The two of us went over to the lifts. We rode down in the first one to arrive on the floor. Ari wasn't in the lobby. It struck me as a little off. I didn't want to ignore the warning in my gut as I called out her name. No answer came.

"Will you look on that side?" I said to Willis before I entered one of the rooms on the left.

As I searched the ground floor, she was nowhere to be found. The warning inside me blared louder. When I got back to the lobby, Willis was there, shaking his head. I dropped the bag I was holding and strode towards the stairwell, shoving the door open. There I found the backdoor propped open. My body went still as waves of dread rushed down my spine. I stepped outside and saw the alley was clear. I jogged along to the end, finding the side street it opened out onto relatively empty.

"Fuck."

I ran back to the building, pulling the door shut behind me. My feet carried me up the two flights of stairs to the second floor. It was empty too. I ran back down the stairs and into the lobby, feeling rage building inside me. There was only one explanation. It didn't take a fucking genius to work out what had happened.

Gennaro.

He took Ari. He had to have taken Ari. The mother-fucking bastard had found a way to get to her when I was distracted. I wanted to scream, but I didn't. Instead, I reached Willis, grabbing the bag from next to him.

"I have to go."

I didn't give him a chance to say a word, striding across the lobby out onto the street. Lewis was still parked up nearby. I jumped into the back of the car, threw the bag into the seat and leant forward.

"Take me to my father's house. Now."

"You got it, boss." He looked at me through the rearview mirror. "Um, where's Ari?"

I let out a jagged breath.

"My father took her, so you better fucking step on it."

I sat back, clenching my fists in my lap. Rage built inside me, mixing with my worries and concerns about my girl. This was fucking bad. I'd been so careful about watching her at all times. Making sure she was safe. The building should have been secure.

Lewis set off. It wasn't fast enough for me, but I wouldn't shout at him over it. He wasn't who I should be directing my anger at. Ripping my phone from my pocket, I hit dial.

"Zayn," came Arlo's voice when he answered.

"Are you still with your father?"

"Yes, why? What happened?"

He must have heard the anger in my voice.

"Gennaro took Arianna. He took her from under my fucking nose. I thought it was safe for her to look around by herself, but no, he took her. It had to be him."

I slammed a fist down next to me, unable to contain the emotions inside me any longer. It was my fucking mistake for letting my guard down, but the building should have been safe. Penn fucking told me it was secure.

"How?"

"They got in through the back somehow. The door was propped open."

"I'll get my things together and come straight over. We can go after her."

I shook my head.

"I'm already on my way. I need to get to her. Gennaro won't hesitate. He'll fucking kill her, Arlo. He will. I'm sure of it. I can't have that. I can't lose her. I just can't."

The thought of being without her cut right through me. The woman who had given me my life back. Who had awoken me from the dark and dragged me out of my monotony. I wasn't going to give her up without a fight. I wouldn't let her perish without me. She was my lifeline. Fuck, I loved her and I hadn't even told her. I hadn't said those words or let her know the depth of my feelings. It wasn't fucking fair. None of it was, but I was determined to make it right.

"Just wait and I'll be there soon. We'll handle it together. I'll round up the men. You can't go after him alone, Zayn, that's fucking suicide."

"Watch me."

I hung up the phone. Arlo was too far away. There was no time to wait for him. His father had asked me for help with his investigation into my uncle's death. He was onto something, so I'd sent Arlo because I didn't have time to do it myself. It was the only reason Arlo hadn't come with us to look at the property. I didn't go anywhere except Desecration without Arlo. Not with the threat of my father hanging over my head. Now I was regretting the decision not to bring any other protection with me.

Arlo tried to call me back, but I ignored it. He would only tell me to wait for him again. I couldn't. Ari was in danger right now. Nothing would stop me from going after her.

I opted to phone the other person I was pissed off at instead of dealing with my right-hand man.

"Ah, Z, I was wondering when you'd call. Do you like the studio?" Penn said when he answered. "Not my usual gig, mind, but I did good, didn't I?"

"Did I like it? What the fuck, Penn! You told me the building was secure. You fucking told me it was safe," I all but shouted at him, unable to hold it in.

"Whoa, okay, hold on a minute. I told you it could be secured. I mean, it's not yours, so it's not like I could outfit it with the right stuff yet."

I slammed my hand into the back of the passenger seat. He had to be kidding me.

"I specifically told you to find me a secure building, not one that had the fucking potential to be secure. Jesus fucking Christ, do you realise what you just cost me?"

"Well, I would if you told me why you're losing it right now."

I sucked in a breath. He didn't know who I was buying the building for. I hadn't told him.

"The studio is for Ari. For my fucking woman. I took her with me and you know the fuck what? She got fucking taken. You failed to tell me someone could quite easily get in the back with no issues and someone fucking took her. So excuse me if I'm trying to find a reason I shouldn't hunt you the fuck down and put a bullet in your brain. She's in fucking danger because of you."

For a moment Penn said nothing, clearly processing my words. I wanted to drown the fucker. If Ari got hurt or died because of him, I would kill him. No fucking hesitation.

"Hey now, you can't put that shit on me, Zayn. I didn't know you were going to take her with you. I didn't realise—"

I hung up without letting him finish as Lewis pulled up outside my father's house.

"Give me my gun," I barked at him, stuffing my phone back in my pocket.

Lewis fumbled with the glove compartment, ripping it open and pulling out the weapon I kept in there. He handed it to me.

"Stay here."

I got out of the car without shutting the door and strode off. Lewis would be useless at defending me. He was my driver and had never been in a life or death situation. This was personal, anyway. I was going to deal with my fucking father once and for all. Him taking Arianna was the final straw. I had no choice now. None at all.

As soon as I reached the front door, I slammed my hand down on it repeatedly.

"Open the fuck up."

I kept hammering my fist on the door until it was wrenched open by a rather irate looking Fiore. Before he had a chance to say a word, I shoved him backwards into the house with me and kicked the door shut behind us.

"Where the fuck is she?"

Fiore blinked, looked down at the gun in my hand, then he launched himself at me, pressing me back against the door. He gripped my wrist and slammed my hand against the wood, trying to dislodge the gun from my fingers. In response, I kneed the fuck in the groin and pushed him off me. Raising my hand, I shot him in the head at point-blank range as his hands went to his dick. He died instantly, dropping to the floor in a heap.

The noise brought Stefano out of the living room. He stared at the crumpled heap that was his friend. Then he was fumbling to grab the weapon he kept on him. I aimed my gun at his head.

"Where is she?"

Stefano froze, his eyes going to my gun.

"As if I'm going to tell you."

I smiled at him despite the anger simmering in my veins, consuming every part of me.

"Wrong answer."

Aiming lower, I shot him in the knee. He cried out, dropping the gun he'd pulled from its holster. Blood seeped into his trousers. I stepped over Fiore's body, aiming my gun at Stefano's hand that was inching towards his leg.

"Where. Is. She?"

"Fuck you," he spat, his voice strained.

I shot again, the bullet going right through his hand. He screamed this time. The satisfaction I felt at seeing him in pain momentarily allayed my anger.

"Tell me where the fuck she is."

"Never!"

The noise had to have carried to wherever my father was, likely in his office. I didn't care. He was fucking next.

"Your fucking funeral, Stefano."

The gun went off again. The bullet left the chamber and lodged itself between his eyes. The lights went out. He remained upright for a moment before his body collapsed, just like his fucking friend. My hand fell to my side, and I stepped over Stefano, making my way down the hallway to my father's office.

Fiore and Stefano had got in my way. Their deaths were necessary and done with ease. What came next? Well, it would test me to my limits. I wasn't calm. I was fucking angry.

I kicked open the office door, striding into the room to find my father leaning against his desk with his arms crossed over his chest. He had a fucking smug smile on his face as if he hadn't heard me shoot both of his bodyguards.

"Where the fuck is Arianna?"

"Is that any way to greet your father?"

I ground my teeth, raising my gun and aiming it at his chest.

"Tell me where the fuck she is. You took her. I know you fucking took her."

Gennaro lowered his arms and spread his hands. She could be anywhere right now. Who knew if he'd brought her here or was keeping her in one of his fucking safe houses. He knew I'd come for him. The man wasn't fucking stupid.

"I did take her, but don't you worry. She's safe… for now."

I took a step towards him.

"You're going to tell me where she is or so fucking help me, I will kill you."

He had the audacity to laugh at me. Shoving off his desk, he straightened and dug his hands into his pockets. He bent his head and looked at me through his lashes.

"You won't kill me, boy. You don't have the guts."

I hated myself for hesitating at his words. For having this fucking moral dilemma about killing my own father, even though he was a threat. I needed to pull the trigger. He needed to be put down, but all I could feel was hatred and rage. I didn't kill with those emotions. It went against my principles. My fucking morals. But I needed to get past those. I had to kill him. I *had* to.

My feet carried me closer even as my hand shook around the weapon. Gennaro moved with me, the two of us circling each other until he faced the door and my back was to it.

"See? Can't do it, can you? I had such high hopes for you. My eldest boy… so much wasted potential." He shrugged as he opened his suit jacket and drew out his own gun from its holster. "You could have been a leader, Zayn, but you threw it all away on that club and now, you're throwing it away over a woman. Pathetic and weak. That's what you are."

"I'm not fucking pathetic or weak. You're just a monster."

He laughed, making my anger burn hotter. That was the fucking problem. I was already having enough trouble trying to push it away so I could pull the damn trigger. End this nightmare for all of us. For my mother. For my brothers. For Arianna. And for me.

"A monster I may be, boy, but that's why I rule this family. Why I'm in charge. You can't even kill your own father because of what? Your morality? Such a weak little fool. If you were strong, you would have shot me the moment you walked in here. I've given you ample opportunity to end my life and you haven't taken it."

I watched him raise the gun. It made me freeze, my finger twitching on the trigger of my own.

"Such a shame it has to end here. No matter. Gil will take your place. Goodbye, son."

The sound of a shot going off rang in my ears. And all I saw... was red.

FORTY FOUR

Arianna

I'd refused to say a word to Gennaro the whole ride to his house, nor did he attempt to engage me in conversation. He just stared at me with unnerving intensity, making me wonder what he had planned. The fact he'd taken me was absolute bullshit. I didn't know how to get out of this situation or if I would even be alive by the end.

Gennaro's bodyguards pulled me out of the car when we reached the house. I fought them, but they picked me up between them and carried me inside.

"Get off me!"

"Careful she doesn't hit you again, Fiore," the one who was carrying me by the arms said.

Fiore had me by my legs, so I couldn't kick him. Now I realised he'd grabbed me in my new building. And it was him I hit when they'd come to force me back to my father. He deserved much worse.

"Shut up," he grunted.

They took me upstairs and dumped me on the floor of a room. Neither of them said a word as they left. I heard the lock click when they shut the door behind them after they left.

I lay there on top of my arms for a long moment, wondering what they planned to do with me. Then I used my legs to shift backwards until I hit a wall. Turning on my side, I used the wall to help me sit up against it. Only then did I truly take in the room. It was small and contained very little. The walls were bare and there were no windows. They had left a light on, so I wasn't in the dark, thankfully. Wouldn't be any point in screaming. No one would be coming to my rescue at this point. I had to be practical and save myself.

Think, Ari, think!

The journey here had allowed me to calm the whirlwind of emotions threatening to suffocate me. This time, I knew who had me. It gave me more to work with than the last time I'd been taken.

Gennaro didn't want me with Zayn. He would end both of us for disobeying him. So why had he left me alive? Was I the bait? Would he kill his son? The moment the thought crossed my mind, a choking sound left my throat.

Zayn couldn't die. I would break entirely. He was intrinsic to my life force at this point. It sounded dramatic. Hell, it fucking felt it. I didn't want to live without him. He'd given me a new lease of life. Saved me from the darkness threatening to consume me after I'd murdered my uncle. He protected me and would do everything in his power to keep my father from harm. He gave me hope, something I'd had little of. I couldn't face the prospect of a world without him.

"Don't die on me, Zayn, please," I whispered, knowing he would have trouble killing his own father even if it was the only way we'd both survive.

If Zayn can't kill Gennaro…

I couldn't finish that thought. It wasn't in my nature to kill, but in the face of life or death, people did things they never expected they could.

What the fuck could I do when I was stuck in here with my hands cuffed behind my back?

Nothing.

I had to get out of here. Getting these handcuffs off me would be the first step. But how?

I stilled when I remembered something. Before we left the house earlier, I'd been toying with the lock pick case Penn had given me. Zayn called me downstairs and, on instinct, I'd stuffed it in the back pocket of my jeans. I carried it around with me at all times outside of the house, usually in my bag, knowing one day it might be useful. It was luck this time. Pure fucking luck it was in my pocket.

You have a way out… if you can get to it.

Determination settled into my bones. I had to do this for Zayn. He needed me.

Sliding back down the wall, I rolled on my side again and fumbled behind me, trying to reach into my back pocket. I bent back as far as I could, bringing my legs up behind me to give me a better angle.

After a few tries, I got my fingers in my pocket and wrapped them around the leather case. Carefully, I extracted it, setting it on the floor. I looked behind me, untying the string to access the picks.

Penn had taught me how to unlock handcuffs. I sent a thank you up to him for showing me before extracting the right pick. Bending my hands at an awkward angle, I hooked the pick into the lock and twisted it to disengage the first lock. When I heard the sound, I let out a little sigh of relief. Twisting it around the other way took two tries to get the second lock holding the ratcheted end in place. I pushed at the cuff, releasing my hand from it.

"Fuck," I exhaled as I sat up and shook out my arms.

I hurriedly undid the other lock and chucked the cuffs on the floor. Grabbing the case, I stuffed the pick back in it before approaching the door. I got down on my knees and inspected the lock. It was an older house, so I could peer through the keyhole. There was nothing but a blank wall beyond.

I heard a loud noise from downstairs and the sounds of a struggle before a gun went off. It set me into motion. Grabbing the right picks, I set them into the lock and started to move them. Loud voices floated up the stairs, along with three more gunshots. I worked faster, knowing I didn't have much time left. If that was Zayn, I had to get to him.

I let out a breath when the lock disengaged and I could push the door open. Stuffing the picks in their pouch, I shoved it in my pocket and was out of the door, creeping along the hallway. When I got to the stairs, I peered over to find two bodies slumped in the lobby, both bleeding from wounds. I swallowed and hurried down the stairs on silent feet.

I reached the men, recognising them as the bodyguards. Both of them had been shot in the head and one had a bullet wound to his hand and knee. Next to him lay a gun. I crept over to it, mindful of not stepping in the blood. Reaching down, I picked up the gun. Dad had once shown me how to work a handgun, but he never let me hold it myself.

I moved along the hallway, holding the gun up to my chest. Voices could be heard from ahead of me. I walked in the direction of the sound and they became clearer as I reached the doorway.

"Such a weak little fool. If you were strong, you would have shot me the moment you walked in here. I've given you ample opportunity to end my life and you haven't taken it."

Stepping in, I found Gennaro raising a gun at Zayn, whose back was to me.

"Such a shame it has to end here."

His words made me aim the gun in my hands at his chest. I clicked off the safety, knowing Zayn couldn't shoot his own father. I would have to. Gennaro would kill him otherwise.

"No matter. Gil will take your place. Goodbye, son."

My finger squeezed the trigger. The noise erupting from the barrel was deafening. The kickback forced me to take a step. My eyes narrowed in on Gennaro's chest, watching blood seep from the wound. He looked down at it, his eyes going wide. Without thinking about it, I shot again and again, emptying more bullets into his chest. I wanted him to burn for what he'd done to his wife. Burn for the way he'd treated his sons. Burn for trying to keep Zayn and me apart. But most of all, I wanted him dead so we never had to live in fear of the man again.

Gennaro staggered back with the impact of the bullets. The blood drained from his face. The very next thing I knew, he'd dropped the gun, his hand going to his chest and coming away with blood. He looked up again, his eyes darting between me and Zayn. A moment later, he dropped to his knees as the light faded from his eyes. He swayed in place, then face planted on the floor, his fingers twitching for a moment. His body went utterly still, his chest no longer rising and falling. And I knew he was dead.

I lowered the weapon, the shakes taking over my body. I'd shot a man repeatedly. This wasn't like when I'd murdered my uncle. That was done on pure instinct. This time, I'd killed to protect someone I loved. I'd wanted it to hurt. I needed Gennaro to suffer before he died.

My eyes went to the man I would sacrifice everything for. Zayn stared at his dead father on the floor. He barely moved, making me nervous as hell.

"Zayn."

His head turned slowly. I knew the only person who'd fired was me, but I needed to see for myself he wasn't hurt. Needed to know Gennaro hadn't harmed his son.

"Tinkerbell."

I dropped the gun and ran to him. He caught me up in his arms, holding me against his chest as my feet dangled below me, not quite touching the floor.

"You're okay! Please tell me you're okay, daddy. I need you to be okay," I choked out, tears threatening to fall down my cheeks as I buried my fists in his hair.

He pressed his face to my braids, breathing me in like he couldn't believe I was there.

"I'm okay." His hold on me tightened. "Are you? Did they hurt you?"

"No, they didn't," I whispered into his neck. "I'm fine."

Zayn's body deflated as he set me back on my feet. He leant back, slid his gun into his pocket and cupped my face with both hands. His eyes were dark and sombre.

"You killed him."

I nodded. There was no other choice. Gennaro would have shot him otherwise. I was not going to lose Zayn under any circumstances.

"I did it for you. I had to. He was going to kill you." My voice got hoarse as I tried to hold back my emotions. "I couldn't breathe at the thought of being without you. I can't lose you. Fuck, I would die. I love you so much, so you can't die on me, okay? You cannot die! I won't let you."

His face morphed into an affectionate smile as he nodded before leaning closer and kissing me. I clung to him, desperate for the reminder we were still here. That we'd survived. We were together.

"I love you," I told him repeatedly between kisses, reaffirming to him over and over again he was my everything. That I couldn't let him go. He'd come for me and I'd saved the both of us. I'd made it safe. We didn't have to worry anyone would try to keep us apart again.

Zayn finally released me, leaning his forehead against mine. He looked tired and worn down. This had been taxing for him on an emotional level. I could see it in his eyes.

"Thank you," he whispered. "Thank you for doing what I couldn't."

"Always."

He tucked me up against his chest, holding me close as if he still needed reassurance I was right there with him. I wrapped my arms around his waist, giving him what he needed.

"Tell me what happened."

I nodded against his chest and gave him the rundown of the events leading up to me shooting Gennaro. Zayn stayed silent until I mentioned the lock picks. Then he looked down at me with a frown.

"What do you mean you had lock picks?"

I bit my lip and looked away, remembering I hadn't told him about meeting Penn. Now I was going to have to fess up to it.

"Um… Penn gave me them."

Zayn blinked.

"Excuse me, Penn gave you them? Are you talking about my Fixer, Penn?"

I nodded, realising maybe I should have mentioned this to him before.

"He showed me how to use them."

Zayn looked incensed at my confession.

"When the fuck did you meet him?"

I tightened my hold around Zayn's waist.

"Well, when I was mad at you after the whole Derek kidnapping thing, he found me in the hallway cursing your name. He didn't think it was a good idea for me to be shouting about it where anyone could hear me, so he took me into one of the private rooms. Then, to calm me down, he showed me how to pick a bunch of locks. If he hadn't, then I wouldn't have got out of that room nor come down here and saved you. We wouldn't be free of your father. Fuck, Zayn, you'd be dead.

He would have killed you. So, I'm not sure why you're mad at him, but I'm pretty fucking glad I met him."

He didn't immediately reply. After a minute, his tense body relaxed and he let out a long sigh.

"You have a point. That fuck still has a lot to answer for, but this? Well, I suppose I have to be grateful no matter how much I'm loath to admit he's done a good thing."

I didn't know why Zayn was so mad at Penn or what had gone on between them. As far as I was concerned, Penn had made sure we got out of this alive.

"He did."

"Okay, so you got out of the cuffs and the room, then you came down here, yes?"

Zayn clearly wanted to move on and not talk about Penn any further. I would have words with him about it at a later date. Now wasn't really the time.

"I picked up one of the bodyguard's guns from the floor, then I walked in here, saw him threatening you and, well, you know the rest."

He looked over to where his father's body lay. The blood from his wounds had seeped out into the rug below him.

"I would spit on his corpse, but I'd rather do that in your mouth."

I raised an eyebrow.

"Is that my reward for killing your father?"

His eyes darted back to me. I opened my mouth for him, sticking out my tongue. Zayn smiled before he leant over me and dribbled his spit onto my tongue. I let it pool there for a moment. Then I slid my tongue back into my mouth and swallowed.

"Good girl," he murmured. "I'm so proud of you."

I licked my lip, giving him a shy smile. A noise from outside the room made both of us look around. There was the sound of a door opening followed by footsteps, then a loud voice exclaiming, "What the fuck?"

Zayn and I looked at each other, both recognising who it was. And I wondered how we were going to explain why the two bodyguards and their father were dead.

FORTY FIVE

Zayn

The moment I heard Enzo's voice, I knew I had to take control of the situation. Letting go of Ari, I moved towards the door. Bending down, I picked up what I assumed was Stefano's gun. I had a decision to make about how we explained what happened. Only one of my potential choices kept Arianna from any repercussions resulting from her killing Gennaro for me.

I looked back at my queen. I was so fucking proud of her for what she'd done, but this was on me. All of it. The eldest became head of the family when his father died. It was the way of things. I couldn't afford to look weak in the eyes of the criminal underworld. Perception was everything. If they thought I'd killed my own father, they wouldn't have a fucking word to say about my rule. We would need that in the coming months. When the power structure changed, it always brought about problems. A show of strength was necessary.

"I need you to stay quiet and let me handle this. I have to take responsibility for his death. No one can know you pulled the trigger. It has to be this way to protect both of us. Do you understand why I'm asking this of you?"

Ari walked over, took my free hand, and gave me a smile.

"Yes, daddy," she whispered. "I trust you."

She got it without me having to explain further, just like I knew she would. She understood how things worked.

My sweet fairy. Could she be any more perfect for me?

I pulled her out into the hallway. Standing in the lobby staring down at the bodies were Enzo, Gil and Arlo. Gil was the first to look up. His eyes narrowed, but his expression didn't change otherwise.

"Zayn."

Enzo and Arlo glanced up. My youngest brother stepped over Fiore and waved at the bodies.

"Was this you?"

"Yes," I replied, keeping my tone neutral.

Arlo walked around the bodies and came over to me. His eyes scanned me and Ari, making an assessment about what happened.

"What do you need me to do, boss?"

"Hang on, you need to explain why the fuck Fiore and Stefano are dead first," Enzo interjected.

"I had to kill them. They got in my way."

Gil stepped over both the bodies, ignoring our little brother and kept his gaze on me.

"*Papá* is dead."

I nodded.

"Might I ask why?"

420

My brother was nothing if not perceptive. We hadn't talked for weeks. It was time we had a conversation, but it could wait until after I'd given Arlo instructions.

"I'll explain in a minute." I turned to Arlo. "Get a clean-up team and the doctor here. Dispose of those two by whatever means necessary and have the doctor declare Gennaro had a heart attack. If we have to pay people off to make it happen, do so. Then I want it known to the families it was me who killed him. You know who I'm talking about. We do this fast before anything else goes fucking wrong today. You got it?"

Arlo's dark eyes flickered.

"Yes, boss. Consider it done."

He walked into Gennaro's office, pulling out his phone on the way. I waved Stefano's gun at the office door, my gaze going back to Gil.

"Do you want to see him, or should the four of us talk elsewhere?"

By the four of us, I meant me, Gil, Enzo and Ari. She wasn't leaving my side. I needed her there with me when I explained to my brothers exactly why our father had to die.

"Living room?"

"Lead the way."

Gil turned and backtracked towards the living room. I followed him, nodding at Enzo, who was staring at us in disbelief.

"Come, Enzo, this is family business, and it includes you."

Gil, Ari, and I entered the living room. I set the gun down on the coffee table before standing near the fireplace. Ari stood next to me, keeping a tight hold of my hand. Enzo walked in and threw himself down on the sofa. Gil remained standing, his eyes on me.

It wasn't surprising he hadn't gone off the deep end. He rarely got rattled. Death was a part of our lives. It always had been.

"I need to ask you something before I explain what happened, Gil."

He slid his hands into his pockets.

"Go ahead."

"Father said you were the one who told him about my relationship with Ari after Enzo spoke to you about it. Is that true?"

Gil frowned and looked over at our brother.

"No. I didn't say a word to *Papá*. Why would I? Who you date is none of my business."

"Then how did he find out?"

My brother looked up at the corner of the room.

"The cameras."

Enzo's face fell, and he jumped up, stabbing a finger in Gil's direction.

"What the fuck? *Papá* has the place covered? Why didn't you tell me?"

"Didn't seem relevant."

Enzo rolled his eyes and paced away.

"Oh well, it might not be a big deal to you since you don't live here, but you failed to tell me my privacy was being invaded."

Gil shrugged.

"You never asked."

I put a hand up to stop Enzo from giving Gil any further shit. We didn't have time for it.

"You two can discuss that later. Where is the footage kept, Gil?"

"On his computer," my brother said, levelling his gaze back on me.

Leaving Ari by the fireplace, I made my way over to the door and poked my head out.

"Arlo!"

He walked out of the office, placing his hand over the speaker of his phone.

"Yes, boss?"

"Gennaro has cameras around the house. I need you to wipe the footage of what I did and keep the rest. We may need to see what he's been up to. And get the men to take all the cameras down. I don't want anyone else knowing about them."

"No problem."

He strolled back into the office, allowing me to retreat back to the fireplace. Ari took hold of my hand again, grounding me in the moment. Her quiet support was all I needed to get through this.

"Now that's sorted, we can talk about why our father is dead."

"You better fucking tell us why you did it," Enzo put in, looking increasingly pissed off.

I almost shook my head but decided I was better off just giving it to them straight.

"Would you rather I let him shoot me? That's what would have happened. He wanted me dead for choosing to be with Arianna. I was not about to let him take my life nor hers."

Enzo's mouth opened and closed, his face paling slightly.

"I didn't think he'd kill you for it."

"I've told you so many times, you don't know the real Gennaro. He was a monster." I raised a hand, pointing upstairs. "What he did to *Mamá* only confirms that."

It was Gil who took a step forward at the mention of our mother.

"What do you mean? She was in an accident."

"No, she wasn't. He did that to her. She was trying to leave him, Gil, because of the way he treated her." Ari's hand tightened in mine. "He hunted her down and beat her half to death, then he lied to everyone about how it happened. He paid those doctors to keep her alive to punish her for daring to leave him. She's been in that fucking bed for almost ten years because of him. She's never going to wake up and keeping her that way is cruel."

I ran my free hand over my chin.

"Why do you think I broke away from him? He told me what he did to her and I couldn't take it. He never loved *Mamá*. She was just a means to an end for him."

Neither of my brothers spoke. Enzo looked stricken and even Gil's brow furrowed, distress painted across his features.

"I'm sorry I kept it from you. Maybe if you knew the truth, none of this would've happened, but what's done is done. I wanted to protect you. All this time, I've just wanted to protect both of you from him, even though I couldn't. Not really." I let out a breath. "Now he's dead and I'm not sorry for it. He deserved it."

Enzo dropped onto the sofa, putting his head in his hands as his shoulders shook. Ari looked up at me, then at my brother. I let go of her hand, giving her a nod. She went over to the sofa, sat down, and put an arm around Enzo's shoulders. He deflated further, making my girl curl her other arm around him and rub his shoulder.

"Shh, it's okay," she murmured. "The truth can hurt, but now you can make it right. You can give your mother the peace he never let her have. It's going to be okay, Enzo, I promise."

Gil walked over to me, eyeing Ari and Enzo with a raised eyebrow.

"She's quite something."

I couldn't prevent my lips from curling upwards.

"Isn't she?"

He stroked a hand across his chin.

"I understand why you didn't tell us… and why you killed him, but this leaves us in a precarious position."

Ever the practical one, Gil was more like me than Enzo had ever been. We didn't allow emotions to cloud our judgement. At least, I tried not to. My father was the only person capable of inciting the worst kind of rage inside me. Now he was dead, I no longer had to live in fear of losing the girl I was in love with. Now I could put aside my emotions and deal with the situation with a clear head.

"He didn't tell you what I've been up to, clearly. We have much to discuss but now isn't the time. We'll talk about it when this is handled."

"Agreed."

I looked over at him.

"And we have to let *Mamá* go. I can't watch her like that any longer."

Gil looked at his feet.

"I know you're right."

"But?"

"The thought of saying goodbye is… difficult."

"And our father dying didn't bring out the same emotions?"

He shrugged.

"He was a monster. I've seen him kill, Zayn. He got this look in his eyes like he enjoyed it. Like it fuelled him to cause other people pain. So knowing he did that to *Mamá* doesn't surprise me. In fact, I'm more annoyed at myself for not noticing how things didn't add up. Maybe I just didn't want to see it."

I put a hand on his shoulder and gave it a squeeze.

"Don't beat yourself up over it. No one wants to think their father is capable of all but killing their mother. Besides, I think we're going to have a harder time convincing Enzo it's time to let go."

Our brother was still being comforted by Ari. We'd never been particularly affectionate as a family, so I was glad she could give him support in a way I couldn't. My girl would help me lead my family forward. She was a force to be reckoned with and one I couldn't do this without.

"Mmm. Maybe we give it a little time, let the storm blow over with *Papá's* death first. Then we can broach the subject with Enzo."

"You're right. He needs time."

I'd had all the time in the world to come to terms with the fact my mother was never coming back. It wouldn't be easy to say goodbye to her, but it was necessary. Ari was right. What my father had done to her was barbaric. We needed to set her free.

"I'm going to see her if you don't need me to help with this."

He waved towards the door.

"No. Arlo and I have it covered."

He nodded and walked out, glancing at Enzo on the way, who appeared to have calmed down somewhat. I made my way over to them, putting my hand on Ari's shoulder.

"Are you going to be okay staying with him while I deal with everything else?"

She turned her head towards me, giving me a sad smile.

"Yes, of course, I am. Go fix everything. I'll be here."

I stroked her cheek, then left the room. Arlo was still in my father's office, sat behind the desk. His eyes flicked to mine over the monitor. The look in them told me he knew Ari had killed Gennaro and not me. I walked over to him, stopping in front of the desk and running my fingers along the wood.

"You understand this stays between the three of us, yes?"

He sat back and shrugged.

"What stays between us, Zayn? *You* were the one who executed Gennaro. I saw nothing that said otherwise."

This was why I needed him to go over the footage. He would keep our secret. He wouldn't tell a soul it was Arianna who had littered my father's chest with bullets rather than me.

"Mmm, that's right."

Arlo winked and glanced over at my dead father.

"About time someone gunned him down. He deserved worse."

"All that matters is he's dead. Have you got everything else sorted?"

"Of course. Did you doubt me?"

I smiled.

"Never."

Arlo had always come through for me. There was no one in this world I trusted above him… except, perhaps, Ari, but that was different. She was my partner. My love. I trusted her with my heart, even if I hadn't explicitly told her yet. I would when this shit was dealt with.

The next few hours were spent cleaning up the scene and putting the house back to order without a trace of what really happened. Our doctor had been paid handsomely for his services, turning a blind eye to the truth and noting down the cause of death as a heart attack. He said nothing of the bodyguards. He was as loyal as they came.

Gil remained upstairs with our mother. Enzo had gone to his room, and I was left alone with Ari in the living room. I wrapped my arms around her and buried my face in her braids.

"Thank you," I whispered.

"For what?"

"Letting the world believe it was me."

She stroked my back with her fingers.

"You have to know by now I'd do anything for you, daddy. And honestly, it's better this way. You're the king. People need to see you as a leader. I might be your queen, but I would rather stand behind you than be in the spotlight." She pulled away slightly to look up at me. "Who's going to challenge you if they think you killed your own father for power?"

I smiled.

428

"There's always someone stupid enough to think they can overthrow a king, Tinkerbell. That's the world we live in."

"You'll make sure that doesn't happen."

I leant closer, brushing my nose over hers.

"I have a kingdom and a precious queen to protect. I'll never let them destroy us."

"I know."

With that, I kissed her, knowing the world had almost been set to rights. We were together. And it was all I ever needed in this life.

FORTY SIX

Zayn

Five of us stood beside the grave, staring down at the coffin that had been placed in it. Ari was tucked into my right side, while my brothers stood to my left. Arlo was at the end, his head bowed as the sombre mood descended over us.

A week ago, we'd taken our mother off life support. Enzo and Gil refused to be in the room when it happened, but I'd been there with Ari. We stayed with my mother until she passed. I'd sat by her bedside, holding her hand and reminding her that we all loved her dearly. I was sorry this had happened to her. And the monster who'd done it was gone. I'd like to think she heard me and it helped her in her passing.

Having Ari there with me was a blessing. She gave me the strength to say goodbye. To let my mother go. Even though I hadn't shed any tears, I had found the process difficult. My girl had held me through it. The worst part had been falling asleep that night knowing she was gone. Even though it gave me relief knowing she was finally at peace, it didn't stop it from hurting. Ari had given me an outlet for the pain, allowing me to use her body the way we both craved. Perhaps it was a slightly unorthodox way of dealing with grief, but I didn't care. We all had different ways of coping. Mine was to lose myself in the woman I loved and fall asleep in her arms.

The wind ruffled Ari's hair, drawing my attention back to the present. She'd had her braids taken out. I'd learnt she liked to change her hair often. I loved running my fingers through her wild curls and gripping them when I fucked her, so for now, she'd left it natural. It mattered not to me how she wanted to style her hair or what clothes she wore. To me, Ari was stunning no matter what. During this time of mourning, she'd wanted to make me happy and for that, I was grateful.

The service we'd had earlier in the church was family only. My aunt and cousins had been there along with several members from my deceased great uncle Nevio's side of the family. They were at the wake while we'd opted to be here as my mother was lowered into the ground.

"Do you think she's happy wherever she is?" Enzo asked.

"I'd like to think so," Gil replied.

The three of us had a lot to deal with in the coming months. There was the matter of who took over the mafia side of our father's business. I'd made it clear I was head of the family, regardless. I might not have wanted to take over from my father, but we needed to show a united front or the wolves would circle. We didn't need more trouble right now.

"She's at peace now, Enzo. It's what she would have asked for if she could, to be set free," I said. "*Mamá* only ever wanted to be free of our father."

432

Enzo was still struggling to come to terms with what happened to her, especially knowing she was trying to leave our father and hadn't taken him with her. He might understand why she did it, but I could tell there was some resentment there, considering he'd only been fifteen at the time.

"I wish she'd told me."

Gil put his hand on Enzo's shoulder.

"You wouldn't have been safe from him if she had. She was protecting you."

Enzo went silent, his fist tightening around the white rose he held. Then he stepped forward and tossed it into the grave.

"*Addio, Mamá, ti voglio bene.*"

He turned away and walked towards where the car was parked.

"Do you think he'll forgive her?" Gil asked.

"One day, but we need to give him time. We all need that," I said with a shrug.

Gil nodded and stepped towards our mother's grave. He squatted down and stared at the coffin.

"*Sii in pace, Mamá.* You were always good to us. I'll miss you."

He threw the white rose into her grave and straightened. I watched him swallow back his emotions. This wasn't easy on any of us, but I knew Gil was struggling more than Enzo. Our little brother wore his heart on his sleeve, but Gil kept everything locked up. I hoped he'd find a way to let it out or it would eat him up inside the way shit had done to me.

"I'll make sure Enzo isn't doing anything stupid like trashing the car. We should talk soon. It's time we dealt with the future."

I nodded, and he walked off, leaving me with Ari and Arlo, who took a step closer and looked at me. I gave him a shrug, my arm around Ari tightening.

"Do you think he's going to accept your plans?" Arlo asked, looking over his shoulder at Gil's retreating back.

Things between me and Gil were a little strained because of the uncertainty we faced. He knew I didn't want to run the mafia. He'd been groomed to take over the role from my father, but I wasn't sure if it was what he actually wanted to do. It was a conversation for another time when we weren't mourning our mother.

"Maybe, maybe not. We'll see."

"We should get to the wake."

"Give me a minute to say goodbye and we'll be right over."

Arlo nodded before stepping up to my mother's grave.

"I'm sure you're at peace now, Noemi, and happy your son has finally met his match."

He tossed his white rose into her grave, smirked at me, and walked off. I shook my head and rolled my eyes.

"I didn't realise you let him get away with speaking about you like that," Ari said, looking up at me with a grin and a twinkle in her chestnut eyes.

"He's my best friend. If he can't give me shit, then who can."

She snorted.

"You let me do it."

I raised an eyebrow.

"Do I?"

She stroked a hand over my stomach.

434

"Well, you punish me over it, but you know I like it when you do."

"So the truth comes out. My little fairy admits she wants to be punished. I never thought I'd see the day."

I got a light slap on the chest for my statement, but she was still smiling.

"Hush."

Leaning down, I pressed a kiss to the top of her head.

"Come, let us say goodbye and go deal with the family. It might be a wake, but they're a riot when they're together."

"Really?"

"Mmm, really."

Ari didn't have a big family. She didn't understand how loud it could get around mine. It was lucky we didn't have too many occasions to get together with our extended family. Gil, Enzo and I hadn't gone to Gennaro's funeral a few weeks ago. We refused to mourn the man who did this to our mother. I'd been surprised at Gil not wanting to be there but didn't question him on it. Out of all of us, he seemed most loyal to our father, but looks could be deceiving. It was a lesson I'd learnt a long time ago.

Ari and I stepped forward.

"I didn't know you, Noemi, but I'm going to try to make your son happy for as long as I have him in my life. I'm sure you'll agree he deserves every hard-earned piece of it."

She threw her rose into the grave and let go of me, stepping back and allowing me a moment alone. I was silent for a long time, staring down at the box containing my mother. I didn't know what to tell her. It all felt like it'd been said before.

"You were the best part of our family, *Mamá*. I'll miss you every day." I tipped my head up to the sky. "Wherever you are, I want you to know we'll be okay. I'll keep my brothers safe and our family together. I know that's what you would have wanted."

I pressed my lips to the petals of the white rose in my hand before throwing it down onto the coffin. Taking a breath, I bowed my head, silently saying goodbye one final time.

Turning away, I took Ari's hand and led her towards the car. A weight lifted from my shoulders, knowing my mother was no longer a prisoner of my father. None of us were. We still had a thousand struggles ahead of us, but I could do it with my love by my side, helping me keep my family together. She was my everything. And it was high fucking time I told her that along with a promise I would stick by her forever.

You are the best thing that ever happened to me, Arianna Michaelson. And when this wake is over, I'll show you every day just how much I adore your beautiful soul.

FORTY SEVEN

Zayn

M y eyes went to the door of the living room. I shouldn't be nervous about doing this. The thought of it all going wrong kept playing over and over in my mind. I knew Ari loved me. I knew she wanted to stay with me. This wasn't something I'd ever had to do before. I'd never felt this way about anyone, so of course, I was going to be fucking nervous.

Taking a breath, I walked in and found her watching TV with her legs curled up on the sofa. It'd been over a week since my mother's funeral, and I was ready to move on with our lives. Ari looked up, giving me a smile when she saw it was me. She put her hand out, but I didn't move from my spot. Her hand dropped, and she bit her lip.

"Are you okay, daddy?"

I nodded, stuffing my hands in my pockets and paced towards the TV and back.

"Turn that off, Arianna."

She did as I asked. I could feel her eyes on me as I paced again.

Get it together!

I came to a standstill a few feet away from her and met her confused eyes. Gathering my fucking wits, I slipped my hand from my pocket and rubbed my face.

"I need you to sit there and listen without interrupting. Can you do that for me?"

"If that's what you need."

"Yes, it is."

She sat up, placing her feet down on the rug below the sofa, and gave me her full attention. Her hands went to her thighs, curling around them. I wanted my hands on them, but I didn't move towards her. I needed to get this shit out of my system without being distracted by my fingers on her body.

"The thing is... Ari, the thing is... there are things in this life I can't give you and I know you've told me it's okay that I don't want to get married or have children. That you don't want those things either, but it doesn't stop me from wanting to give you everything you deserve. To care for you every day for the rest of our lives. Because that's what I want with you. A lifetime."

My hand shook, so I clenched it into a fist to stop myself from getting too worked up.

"I can't give you a traditional relationship, but I can give you everything I have and everything that I am. I can promise you'll never want for anything. No matter what happens to me, you'll always be protected and safe. You know my world is dangerous and unpredictable. If this was a marriage, then you'd be afforded all the legal protections possible as my wife, but things can't work that way for us."

I took a breath and shook out my hand. Ari looked up at me, her expression neutral, so I had no idea what she thought about me saying all of this. It didn't matter. I had to push on and make sure she knew what she meant to me.

"So, I've done everything in my power to make sure you'll be okay if anything happens to me. I've had my solicitor draw up all the paperwork necessary, so you'll be named on the deeds of the house and the club. I've had my will changed so you inherit everything as well as giving you lasting power of attorney. There's stuff you'll need to sign for all of this, but I'll arrange for us to visit her offices to do that. Simply put, Arianna, I want to share everything I have with you because I trust you and I need you… and you're everything to me."

The fact her expression hadn't changed bothered me somewhat, but I wasn't finished yet. Moving closer, I dropped down to my knees in front of her.

"I'm not very good at expressing my feelings, which you probably know, but you are the bravest, strongest, and most feisty woman I know. I can't live in a world where you aren't next to me. I promise I'll care for you and be your daddy for the rest of our lives if you'll stay by my side."

I swallowed and stared into her eyes. She still hadn't reacted, so I turned towards the coffee table, pulled open the drawer and extracted a small box from it. Twisting back to face her, I held the box out for her to see.

"I hope this will demonstrate my devotion to you."

I opened the box. It contained a discreet gold chain with a little Tinkerbell charm on it.

"This, if you accept it, will be my permanent collar for you. It doesn't mean you can't wear your leather ones when you want to, but this necklace is my promise that I'll never leave you. I'll always be yours and you'll always be mine. It... it means more than me giving you a ring... because you're my Tinkerbell and I can't be without you. I can't... fuck."

I couldn't contain my emotions any longer. Setting the box down, I took one of her hands and pressed it to my cheek, needing her touch, her warmth, her everything.

"I love you, Tinkerbell. I don't think I have the words to tell you how much, but I'll have to settle for I'm in love with you, my precious little fairy."

Falling silent, I pressed a kiss to her palm and waited for her to say something. I'd managed to get it all out. To tell her I loved her and hope to fuck she liked her gift.

Ari stared at me for a long time, then she pulled her hand from her face and settled both of them back in her lap. My heart was in my mouth at that point. She was making me wait, and it was absolute fucking torture, but I wouldn't rush her.

"Zayn, you had me at 'a lifetime' because I want a lifetime with you too. The rest doesn't matter, but I appreciate it all the same."

I frowned.

"Is that it?"

She leant forward and took my face in her hands.

"Did you need to hear me tell you how much I love you again? Or that I will do anything for you? Or that I'm always going to be your Tinkerbell and remain by your side for as long as we both live?"

I nodded.

"I love you, daddy. You are the best thing that ever happened to me and I'm going to spend the rest of my life making you as happy as you make me."

Before I could respond, she kissed me, making all my stupid worries and fears about telling her I loved her melt away. This beautiful, tenacious woman was mine, and I was hers.

When she pulled away, she picked up the box and took out the necklace. Her fingers brushed over the Tinkerbell charm and her eyes misted up.

"This is perfect," she whispered as she looked at me. "Put it on me, daddy. I want you to claim me with it."

I took the necklace from her. She moved her hair out of the way so I could secure it around her neck. I pulled the chain around so the clasp sat at the back of her neck and the charm lay on her chest. Seeing it there settled me. Made me feel secure about our relationship, not that I wasn't before. It just felt more meaningful now I'd made it clear this was my promise to love her for the rest of our lives.

My fingers went to her hair, digging through the curls to cup the back of her head. I pressed myself between her legs and captured her mouth. She kissed me back with as much passion as I gave her. Ari's fingers curled around my back, making me want her that much closer. I kept kissing her as I shoved her back onto the sofa, forcing her to lie on it. I covered her body with my own, making her aware of who was in charge. Who she belonged to. Who owned her.

"Mine," I growled against her mouth. "Mine forever."

I pinned both her hands down on the fabric, keeping her in place. Her legs parted, allowing me to settle between them.

It didn't take her long to start grinding against me, making it very clear she wanted me to show her exactly how much I loved her with my body.

I kissed my way down her jaw, reaching her neck. I licked a line down to the Tinkerbell charm before I met her eyes. Pressing a kiss to it, I smiled at her.

"Is my dirty little fairy wet for daddy?"

She nodded and bit her lip.

"Is she going to be good and take everything he has to give her?"

She nodded again. I shifted back up and brushed my mouth against hers.

"Are you going to let me love you forever, Tinkerbell?"

Arianna smiled at me, her eyes betraying all her feelings. She loved me as much as I loved her. And we were going to spend eternity showing each other just how much.

"Yes, daddy."

ACKNOWLEDGEMENTS

A huge thank you goes to my bestie and alpha reader, Ashley. You have enriched my life in more ways than I thought possible over the past year. And you know very well Daddy Zayn would not exist without you. You gave me an education in CGL and what it really means to be "daddy". I don't think I could have written this book without you. Never forget how much of an incredible human you are. I love you so much! The Aquarius and the Sagittarius – best partners in crime!

My second huge thank you goes to my PA and alpha reader, Amber. We came into each other's lives at the right time and turns out we both needed each other. I'm so grateful for everything you've done for me, especially helping me with Daddy Zayn's book. The afternoon we spent plotting out half of this book will always stick out to me. It's when I knew asking you to join my little team was the best thing I'd ever done. You're amazing and I love you!

To the Society of Sarah Bailey Stalkers and all my readers – thank you for all your support! You really do make me smile every day and I'm grateful you all love my words so much.

To my mother – thank you for all your help and the support you give me with my writing career.

To my wonderful husband – thank you for giving me the time and space to grow my author business. I couldn't have done it without you.

ABOUT THE AUTHOR

Sarah writes dark, contemporary, erotic and paranormal romances. They adore all forms of steamy romance and can always be found with a book or ten on their Kindle. They love anti-heroes, alpha males and flawed characters with a little bit of darkness lurking within. Their writing buddies nicknamed Sarah: 'The Queen of Steam' for their pulse racing sex scenes which will leave you a little hot under the collar.

Born and raised in Sussex, UK near the Ashdown Forest, they grew up climbing trees and building Lego towns with their younger brother. Sarah fell in love with novels as teenager reading their aunt's historical regency romances. They have always loved the supernatural and exploring the darker side of romance and fantasy novels.

Sarah currently resides in the Scottish Highlands with their husband. Music is one of their biggest inspirations and they always have something on in the background whilst writing. They are an avid gamer and are often found hogging their husband's Xbox.

Made in the USA
Monee, IL
11 August 2023